This one is for Caroline Ridding, my brilliant editor and wonderful friend, who never fails to encourage, inspire and support my work, while smashing records for patience, understanding, and resolving every crisis I unwittingly send her way.

None of this would exist without you and I'll never stop being grateful. Or suggesting we solve all problems with gin.

And to my menfolk, John, Callan and Brad, who continue to make me laugh, supply endless cups of tea, top up the biscuit tin, and pretend to believe me when I start a sentence with, 'When this book is finished, I'm going to...'

Thirty novels in, they know there will always be another story that will have me banging the laptop keyboard within hours of typing The End on the last one.

Gents, thank you for being the best blokes a frazzled, underhydrated, chocaholic writer could have. I love you with everything, always...

A NOTE FROM SHARI...

Dearest Readers,

Thank you so much to everyone who read One Day In Summer last year, and huge gratitude for picking up the latest instalment in my One Day series, One Summer Sunrise.

This book is set on the 3rd July, 2021, but you'll notice a significant omission. I had a long think about whether or not to include the reality of Covid, but after a long chat with my editor, we ultimately decided against it. I've always written escapist fiction, and in this story, we wanted to take readers' minds off the havoc the pandemic has wreaked in our lives.

That said, as with One Day In Summer, I want to dedicate this book to every single person who has worked and sacrificed to help others over the last year – everyone in the NHS, teachers and school staff, the carers for our children, elderly and vulnerable, the armed forces, the shop workers, the delivery drivers, the post office, the bin collectors, council employees, the scientists who developed the vaccines, the police and fire services, public transport workers, the volunteers and the neighbours who have lent a hand and everyone else who has played a part in getting us through this. We've seen the worst in circumstances, but also the very best in people.

And to everyone who has suffered loss and heartache, my heart is with you. No words can make it better, but I hope that you find a reason to smile again in the weeks, months and years ahead.

Hopefully, by the time I write the final instalment in this trilogy, life will be back to some kind of normal. Better times are coming...

Much love,

Shari x

WAKING UP THAT MORNING TO A DAY FULL OF SURPRISES WERE...

Maisie McTeer, 25 – actress, singer, performer, works in catering when she's skint between jobs. Off men for life after being jilted at the altar.

Nathan Jackson, 27 – the (please insert your own sweary word here) groom who stood Maisie up on their wedding day.

Hope McTeer, 23 – Maisie's sister and flatmate, currently doing her rotation as a junior doctor in A&E at Glasgow Central Hospital.

Sissy Bane, 26 – Maisie's pregnant best friend, owner of catering company The Carrot Schtick. Married to the ever-patient Cole.

Scott Bassett, 38 – married to his childhood sweetheart, Kelly, his mid-life crisis has reignited the musical ambitions that he gave up when Kelly got pregnant at 16 with their daughter, Carny.

Kelly Bassett, 38 – Scott's wife and Carny's mum, an estate agent who is struggling with the prospect of an empty nest.

Carny Bassett, 22 – an aspiring set designer, recently graduated with a degree in Theatre Studies and now leaving Glasgow to take up an apprenticeship in London.

Sonya Bassett, 58 – Scott's wonderful, but occasionally scary, mum, brought him up single-handedly, always comes through in a crisis.

Carson Cook, 38 – an engineer in the RAF, he's Scott's kind, big hearted, very eligible but resolutely single, best mate.

Sabrina Smith, 33 – Kelly's younger sister, has found happiness in her second marriage to celebrity restaurant owner, Rick Smith.

Rick Smith, 40 – Kelly's lifelong friend, and teenage ex-boyfriend, who put his wild ways behind him when he married her sister, Sabrina.

Harriet Bassett, 80 – A widow since her husband Dennis died in March 2020, she has outlived her family and friends, leaving her contemplating the loneliness of the life ahead of her.

Yvie Danton, 32 – Caring angel and nurse on the geriatric ward at Glasgow Central Hospital, has a particularly soft spot for Harriet.

SATURDAY, 3 JULY 2021

8–10 A.M.

1

MAISIE MCTEER

Somewhere in that hazy place between being asleep and awake, Maisie decided that as dreams went, this one was pretty rubbish. There were no golden sands or deep blue seas. Not even a half-naked Chris Hemsworth, in indecently small swim shorts, holding up a cocktail while waiting for her on a sunlounger for two. Just a foggy image of her ex, Nathan, running away from her, while she stood, dressed in white, watching him go.

And the noise. Ouch, the noise. The violent thudding sound was so loud, so persistent, it felt like it was making her ears bleed. At first she thought it was the panicked, distraught beat of her heart, but the more she came round, the louder and clearer it got... Bugger, someone was banging on the front door.

She paused to pray that her sister would answer it, then remembered Hope was on an overnight shift at the hospital and wouldn't be home yet.

More banging. Whoever it was, they weren't giving up.

Groaning, Maisie climbed out of bed, immediately regretting it when she had to hang onto the ironing board that was leaning against the wall until a sudden bout of dizziness left her. Damn.

She'd forgotten to factor in her inevitable hangover. That last margarita before bed had been a really bad idea. As had the six she'd had before it. The downside of drinking alone on the couch, with only the Sex And The City reruns on Netflix for company, was that there was no-one there to question the wisdom of an impromptu cocktail party for one.

Palms against the walls for support all the way to the front door, Maisie winced as the decibels shattered her eyeballs. Was it possible for a brain to actually explode? If so, the cream walls were about to be decorated with a natty combination of grey matter, Cointreau, tequila and lime juice.

She wrenched the door open, yelling, 'Okay, okay, I hear you...' As her eyes adapted to the blinding sunlight, there was a horrified pause, then a strangled yelp of, 'Oh Jesus, Sissy!' Suddenly very awake and alert, Maisie gasped as she saw her best mate standing on the front step, face pink, leaning over her nine-months-pregnant-space-hopper-stomach, both hands on her knees.

'How long...' Sissy panted, 'does it take you...' another pant, 'to answer a fricking door?'

'Sorry! Come in! What can I do? Is the baby coming now? Towels! I need towels!' she bellowed to no-one.

Sissy's breath was coming in short bursts, blowing away the tendrils of her long, fiery red hair that were falling from the pleat that curled around her shoulder. 'Nope, we're just rehearsing.'

'Seriously?'

Sissy glanced up at her with absolute incredulity. 'No, of course I'm not serious! Shit, I hope this baby isn't listening. It'll be terrified that you're one of its responsible adults.' Her eyes rose upwards, then narrowed pointedly as she took in Maisie's dishevelled appearance. 'Did you sleep in a bush last night?'

Maisie went for deflective indignation. 'Are we really doing this right now? Let me grab my bag and we'll be at the hospital in ten minutes.'

Sissy shook her head, hands still on knees. 'Nope, it's okay. Cole's here.' She gestured behind her and, for the first time, Maisie noticed the Volvo at the end of her path, with Sissy's husband in the driver's seat, anxiety knitting his eyebrows together. He threw up his arms in a questioning movement. 'I've told him to stay in the car and keep it running,' Sissy explained.

'Okay, I'll come without my bag then,' Maisie offered, taking a step out the door, caring not a jot that birthing partners didn't usually show up in pyjamas and bare feet, sporting hair like a pillow that had been shredded by a Flymo.

'No, wait!' Sissy put her hand up. 'There's been a change of plan. I need you to do something else for me today,' she went on, wincing mid-sentence. Maisie felt a surge of dread. Sissy had this day planned with military precision. There was even a flow chart, laminated and stuck to Maisie's fridge so she could memorise every detail of her role in the step-by-step process between Sissy going into labour and the arrival of her child.

According to Mrs Control Freak, the minute Sissy's waters broke or she had her first contraction, Cole would grab the hospital bag that had been packed and sitting by the front door since halfway through her pregnancy. He'd then whisk his wife to Glasgow Central hospital, coming via Maisie's house to collect her. Maisie and Cole would alternate as birthing partners and general helpers during the early hours of labour ('I don't want him at the business end,' Sissy had categorically stated. 'So you're in for all things below the waist'). Then, when the baby was close to arriving, Maisie would honour the hospital's 'one partner in the delivery theatre' rule by retreating to the waiting room and letting Sissy and Cole bring their firstborn into the world together.

None of the flow chart scenarios covered Sissy arriving at the door at 8 a.m. on a Saturday morning, telling an exceptionally hung-over Maisie, suffering the effects of a bloodstream that was probably still 90 per cent margarita, that there had been a change of plan. The only thing that terrified her more than one of Sissy's agendas was the thought of one of them being altered at the last minute. This couldn't be good.

'Anything! What do you need?' *Please make it something simple. A skinny latte. The return of her beloved chunky cherry Chubby Stick. Paper pants for the below-the-waist stuff.*

'I need you to work on the job I was supposed to be on today. A garden party. I've got Janice and Jane on set-up and food prep, and a dozen temp staff on their way for replenishment and table clearing, but the whole thing needs someone to oversee and co-ordinate everything and liaise with the organisers.' Sissy's catering company, The Carrot Schtick, had been her friend's Plan B when they'd graduated together from RADA five years ago. A year after leaving the Academy, Maisie had still been in love with her career choice, despite only having landed a part as a psycho elf in panto. However, Sissy had realised that she hated being skint and that her dreams of being the next stand-up sensation probably weren't going to materialise any time soon, so she'd taken over the slightly stale family business that she'd worked in part-time for years, renamed it and applied her ferocious drive into making it the success it had become. Sissy had also given Maisie enough part-time, ad-hoc shifts over the years to keep her going between acting gigs and help pay the rent for the garden flat in Glasgow's west end that Maisie shared with Hope.

'But you need me at the hospital for the business end,' Maisie reminded Sissy gently, nodding pointedly towards Sissy's nether region when she vocalised the words 'business end'. It was impossible to hide her disappointment. For months now, she'd been looking forward to the arrival of this new baby for many reasons. It was all those poetic things about a new dawn, a new life. But most of all it would hopefully put an end to Sissy's frankly terrifying hormonal mood swings. Maisie had been forced to disarm her when she threatened a snarky delivery guy with a French baguette last week.

'I do need you but our actual business end needs you more. And you'll mostly love it, I promise. It's all our kind of people.'

Despite the anxiety of the moment, Maisie chuckled.

'Our kind of people?'

Sissy nodded. 'Luvvies. It's the end-of-term fundraiser for the drama department at Glasgow College of Performing Arts. A few of the students who are graduating have organised it. Actually, the one I've dealt with most said she knew you...'

'What's her name?'

'Erm, Carny Bassett.'

'Yes! Carny's lovely. I've met her a few times when I've been in giving a hand with their productions. She's a really talented set designer,' Maisie said, thinking this might not be too bad. Between jobs, she occasionally helped out at the college, doing workshops for the students who were focused on musical theatre or drama. She'd also helped coach the cast of their last couple of productions. For Maisie it was just a fun way to hold jaded cynicism at bay, by tapping into the enthusiasm and bright talent that was coming into the industry. Carny definitely qualified in that category.

Maisie could feel a glimmer of enthusiasm, but it was tempered by the feeling that there was a catch coming. 'Hang on, you said I'd 'mostly' love. What's not to like?'

'It's... well...' Sissy was stuttering again. Another contraction on the way? Anxiety kicking in? Gut-wrenching pain? Maisie soon realised it was none of the above. Instead, it was the absolute dread of a pal asking another pal to do the unimaginable. 'It's in the grounds of The Lomond House Estate.'

Maisie's soul curled up and died. *Not there. Anywhere but there.* She hadn't been back since... 'Noooooo...' Knife. Heart.

Sissy immediately cut off her objection with a frankly unconvincing scream of 'Aaaaargh' as she clutched her belly again.

Maisie's head tilted questioningly. 'Did you just fake a contraction to manipulate me into doing this?' Sissy had been a good actress in college, but not that bloody good.

The pregnant one gave a weak shrug of confession. 'Low blow, I know, but I'm desperate. I can't let them down. Janice and Jane can handle the actual buffet, but it needs to be organised and you're my only hope.' She buckled as she got the last word out, then uttered another pain-laden 'Aaaargh.' Maisie knew she was beat as she put her hands out and let Sissy hang onto them while she endured another contraction. A genuine one this time.

'Okay, okay, breathe, just breathe, I've got you,' Maisie winced through the agonising pain of Sissy crushing her knuckles with newfound superhuman strength.

Unable to contain himself any longer, the gorgeous Cole jumped out of the car and raced up the path, face aghast. 'Sissy, babe, come on. Let's go,' he begged, with all the urgency of a man who didn't want his first child to be born on the front step of a Victorian terrace garden flat, in between two plastic topiary balls and a door mat that said, 'Come on in, bring wine'.

'Please, Maisie,' Sissy pleaded, coming out of the contraction with more deep breaths. 'I'll give you anything. You can even have this kid if I don't like the look of it.'

Maisie laughed, in spite of the turn of events, the horror of what was being asked of her and the crushed knuckles. 'I'll do it. But you can keep the kid. Pay me in gin and therapy.'

'Oh, thank god. Thank you. Thank you. Thank you. I've

already emailed you all the details,' Sissy admitted, a little shame-faced about the presumption.

The two women hugged, before Cole eventually prised his wife from Maisie's arms. Having lost the power of her hands, she gave a weak wave. 'Okay, go, I'll take care of everything, don't worry. And I'll come to the hospital when it's over. If you're any kind of pal, you'll keep your legs crossed until I get there. I love you guys.'

'We love you,' Sissy shouted over her shoulder as she waddled back towards the Volvo. 'And there's a cake for the fundraiser. It's to be cut up and served with the coffees. It's the one-tier sponge in the fridge at the warehouse next to the cake with the penis on it for the hen night that's booked for Thursday night. I made it early in case this happened.'

'One-tier sponge. Next to penis cake. Got it,' Maisie yelled back, wondering if Mrs McPherson next door was clutching her rosary beads and praying for her soul yet.

She watched as Cole helped Sissy into the car, then accelerated off from the kerb with a screech that would make Vin Diesel anxious.

Maisie took a step backwards, closed the door, then thudded her forehead against it. It crossed her mind that maybe that was the answer. She couldn't possibly oversee a catering operation for two hundred guests if she was in hospital with concussion. The pain of knocking herself out wouldn't be any worse than the one that was piercing her heart right now.

How ironic. Only last week she'd auditioned for the lead role in a new Netflix Original series called *The Clyde*, a Glasgow crime show that had the potential to be huge. Not that she had any chance of landing it, but still, it was ironic that her own life was rivalling the kind of storylines that belonged in a soap opera. Any minute now her long-lost evil twin would knock at the door and attempt to steal her life. Well, she could have it. Especially if the evil twin had experience in part-time catering and could take over the function this afternoon.

What were the chances of the stars aligning this way? Why had Sissy gone into labour this morning? Why was she short-staffed? And why, oh why, did this party have to be in the grounds of Lomond House, the place that, more than any other, kept Maisie's nightmares alive and made her heart ache.

Maisie didn't know the answers to any of those questions. All she knew for sure was that, new baby aside, this had the potential to be the second worst day of her life. Because today was now the day she'd be revisiting the place where the love of her life had once proposed to her. The place where they'd planned to marry. And where, only two months ago, he had jilted her at the altar.

2

SCOTT BASSETT

Scott's heart was beating out of his chest and sweat was dripping from every pore in his body. Jesus, it hurt.

'Come on, is that all you've got? Seriously? You're losing your touch, mate,' the six foot three guy who'd just knocked him on his arse ribbed him. For the last hour, they'd been playing a game of one-on-one basketball, using the net that had been attached to the back of the garage as a Christmas surprise for a teenage Scott in 1998. Back then he'd wanted to be Michael Jordan. Now he'd settle for putting the ball in the hoop without pulling a muscle.

The thunder in his ears blocked out the noise of the sliding doors from the kitchen being pulled open, but not the sound of the menacing shout that came next. Thankfully, his mum's house was a three-bedroom bungalow at the end of a quiet road in the village of Frewtown, on the outskirts of Glasgow, and the nearest neighbours were off visiting their family in Fort William this weekend, so there would be no objections to the sound of the thudding ball or the raised voice of warning.

'Carson Cook, you big eejit. If you injure my son on the day of my granddaughter's party, there'll be carnage and you won't come out of it well.' The threat came from Scott's mother, the indomitable Sonya Bassett, who'd slid open the glass doors from the kitchen and now stood in the doorway, clutching a spatula, looking dangerously threatening despite her pink fluffy dressing gown and head full of rollers. 'You two are thirty-eight-year-old men! You've got no business getting up to all that nonsense out there. You'll do yourself an injury.'

Scott took advantage of the distraction to spring to his feet, grab the basketball and dunk it, winning the game.

Carson, meanwhile, regressed from a capable, super-fit, six-pack-sporting engineer in the Royal Air Force, to a blushing, slightly podgy, red-haired teenager who was mortified because he'd just been chided by his best pal's mum. 'Sorry, Mrs B. – but he started it.'

The age-old protest reduced the lot of them to laughter. 'Right, well, your breakfast is about to go on the table, so stop all that messing around and come get it. Hose yourselves down first, because not even my Cotton Fresh Yankee Candles can handle all that sweat.'

Carson picked the ball out of the leylandiis where it had landed after the dunk and whistled. 'I swear to God, if the Russians ever get your mother on their side, the West doesn't stand a chance.'

Scott threw his arm around the guy who'd been his best mate since they were using their jumpers as goalposts in primary school. 'You're not wrong. We try to use her powers for good, but it's not always possible. She threatened to punch a skinhead who skipped her at the handmade pizza counter in the supermarket last week. He's probably still cowering somewhere between the veg aisle and frozen foods.'

Carson's low throaty laugh was infectious, and Scott felt his cheeks begin to ache with smiling. As summer mornings went, this was pretty much perfect so far. He'd only stayed over at his old childhood home a handful of times since he'd married Kelly when they were just kids, straight out of school. Felt like yesterday, yet now the daughter they'd had when they were both sixteen had just turned twenty-two and graduated with a degree in Theatre Studies.

He'd been beyond proud when Carny had landed a job as an apprentice set designer, working for a theatre company in London. Today's party was more than just a fundraiser for the drama department she'd adored for the last four years – it was also a celebration of her graduation and a last hurrah before Carny left tomorrow, so most of the family were coming along to celebrate.

His own house was overcrowded because Kelly's sister and brother-in-law had arrived yesterday and were staying over, so Kelly had suggested that Scott and Carson take his mum up on the offer of her two spare rooms. The alternative would have been for all six foot three inches of Carson to crash in his usual spot on the couch in Scott and Kelly's three-bedroom semi. Kelly had transformed the smallest bedroom into a dressing room with a sofa bed, but it was way too small for a man of Carson's size, so he inevitably slept in the living room. When he was full of beer, the couch was perfectly comfortable, but maybe not the best idea when there were other houseguests who would have to trip over him to watch TV.

Besides, staying with his mum gave Scott and Carson the opportunity to relive countless nights of their youth, when Carson would be parked in Sonya's spare room and they'd spend all day hanging out, playing basketball (Carson's game) and football (Scott's game), their rivalry as fierce as Sonya's wrath when they were late coming in for their tea, or when a window or one of her prize garden gnomes was accidentally smashed with an errant ball.

Scott nipped into his mum's pink-tiled en suite to use her shower, while Carson used the spray over the bath in the main bathroom. Scott avoided that one, as it required a death-defying climb into a tiny bath, careful manoeuvring so as not to knock over several candles, a couple of bowls of potpourri and dozens of hotel shampoo bottles his mum had acquired on her travels over the years, followed by a thigh-burning crouch in order to fit under the shower head. Carson had once said getting into the cockpit of a Typhoon fighter jet was easier.

Ten minutes after they were summoned, they were at the table with enough bacon, eggs, sausage and potato scones to feed a platoon, accompanied by the distant sound of his mum singing Patsy Cline's 'Crazy' in another room. Without conscious thought, Scott realised he was humming along. Sonya's country music had been the soundtrack to his life, the reason he'd first picked up a guitar. It was also why, in the nineties era of Oasis and Blur, of indie rebels, rock 'n' roll excess and Robbie Williams' lion pants, Scott had formed The Hollering Stetsons, the most uncool band in their school's history. They covered Tim McGraw songs, Garth Brooks, plenty of Conway Twitty, and on more than a few occasions the only people in the audience had been Carson, Kelly, Sonya and the band members' families – except for the drummer, whose dad had disowned him after he heard them singing 'Islands In The Stream'. Scott had even been saving the money from his weekend job in the local petrol station to go on his dream trip to Nashville. Looking back, he was pretty sure that every penny of his savings had eventually gone on baby stuff when they found out that Kelly was pregnant. He'd quit the band, the other Hollering Stetsons had gone their separate ways and Scott had never made it further than two weeks in the Costa Del

Package Tour, but they'd had Carny, and she was, without a single doubt, the best thing that had ever happened to him.

Scott used a fork to load up his plate. 'I'm grateful you made it today, bud. Carny would have been gutted if her godfather wasn't here.'

Carson knocked back a slug of his black coffee. 'Wouldn't have missed it. I've no idea how someone like you managed to raise such a cool, talented kid.' He immediately yelped as he felt the sting of a flicked finger on the back of his head, courtesy of Sonya, who had returned to the kitchen and passed behind him just as he'd insulted her beloved son. Carson had military training and yet he'd just let a Glaswegian mother launch a surprise attack.

Sonya gave him the pursed lips of terror, then leaned over, took a slice of toast from the pile and bustled back out again, with a, 'Watch yourself, Carson Cook.'

Despite the threat, the words came with an unmistakable hint of affection. They all knew that, deep down, Sonya Bassett had loved Carson almost as much as her own son, since Scott had sat next to him on their first day of school. The two boys had been inseparable from then until Scott married Kelly and Carson left to join the RAF.

Scott's cheeks were aching again as he gave a self-deprecating shrug and addressed Carson's earlier point. 'I've no idea either. Just one of those freak miracles. I put it down to Kelly's genes and luck. Anyway, come on, dish the details. Did Carny's tutorial on that dating app pay off? Are women lining up round the block to take you off the market?'

On Carson's last visit around three months before, Scott had watched with absolute hilarity as Carny had announced she was going to end Carson's single days by setting him up with a profile on Your Next Date and teaching him how to use it. Carson had

gone along with it for a bit of fun, but Scott was pretty sure he'd
then...

'Eh, deleted it the next day,' Carson admitted.

Yep, that was exactly what Scott had guessed.

'You're going to be single forever,' Scott sighed. 'You lucky
bastard.'

Carson bit into the well-done sausage on the tip of his fork.
'You don't mean that,' he said, grinning, then pausing his fork in
mid-air as he re-evaluated his mate's expression. 'Do you?' he
added, with obvious uncertainty.

Scott exhaled, then – elbows on the table – he lowered his
head and ran his fingers through his thick mop of dark blonde
hair. He kept it short at the sides and back, longer on the top, and
Carny made sure he navigated the dangerous line between
looking good and trying too hard, giving cutting but well-inten-
tioned advice, whether it was requested or not. 'Dad, that T-shirt
is, like, so last year. And send those jeans back to the nineties. I've
no idea why some of my pals fancy you,' she'd groan. 'I mean,
what's that about? I clearly need new friends.' Then she'd soften
it all by giving him a cheeky smile and he'd crack up laughing at
her cheek.

When he raised his gaze from the table, he saw that Carson
was still waiting for an answer. This was rarely chartered waters
for them. In over thirty years of friendship, they'd discussed jobs,
cars, houses, holidays, beer, aircraft and dissected every sports
league with the kind of analytical detail and insight that would
qualify them for roles as TV pundits. But feelings? Relationships?
Very occasionally and only in the late hours when alcohol had
blurred their inhibitions. Right now, he was entirely sober, but
the words were rolling out on a train of anxiety. 'I do. I can't make
this work any more, mate.'

'Make what work?'

Scott pushed his plate away, stomach too clenched now to eat. 'Marriage. Life.'

His friend's incredulity showed he wasn't taking this seriously. 'Yeah, because it's so hard having a gorgeous wife, a great daughter, and a nine-to-five job with a decent wage and enough free time to pretty much do what you want.'

'None of that is what I want,' Scott said simply, realising that saying it out loud was a visceral relief. Now that the words were out, more were tumbling behind them, his tones hushed so that his mother didn't overhear. 'Don't get me wrong, Kelly and I made it work, and everything was worth it to have Carny. I'd do it all the same way again to be her dad and raise her, but... you're going to think I'm a prize prick here... I feel like now that she's going out into the world my job is done.'

'Fuck,' Carson said, uncharacteristically short on words. 'What about Kelly?'

The smell of the food had gone from appetising to nauseating as Scott squirmed under the heat of the question he'd asked himself more times than he could count. 'Mate, I love her, but...' He stopped, digging deep for more. 'I married Kelly because she got pregnant when we were sixteen. I went into a job I hate because it helped support us. I'm not blaming anyone or moaning, but, you know... it's been this way for twenty-two years. These days, we're more like friends. We get on great, but are we madly in love? I don't think we ever were. I'm the only guy she's been with and vice versa. I've got to believe that she loves me in some way to have stuck around this long, but maybe she's just been waiting it out for Carny to leave too.'

Carson thought about that for a moment. 'Have you talked to her about it?'

'No, not yet. I didn't want anything to overshadow Carny's last year with us. I was going to talk to her tonight. Carny is going out with her mates after the party and Kelly's family will have headed off by then.'

'And what exactly are you going to tell her?' Carson probed, food long forgotten for them both.

'That I want to split. That I've taken voluntary redundancy at work. I finish up next week.'

Carson didn't even try to disguise his shock. 'Wait, you've what? You've done it already? Without talking to her about it? Fuck, you're an idiot. Come on, pal, she deserves better than that.'

A red rash of embarrassment started to creep around Scott's neck. It was a dick move. He knew it. When the directors at his company had asked for voluntary redundancies, he'd initially discounted it. After starting as an apprentice on the factory floor of Strathmold Auto, making parts for car interiors, he'd worked his way up, with the help of an Open University degree, to a management position. He earned a decent salary now, had a smart company car and thirty days holiday a year, but the thought of spending another twenty-odd years sitting behind the same desk every day made him want to put his head on his desk and weep.

On the day of the deadline for the voluntary redundancies, some kind of madness had taken over him. He'd done a bit of research and found out that with his length of service, his redundancy offer was a good one – a year's salary and he got to keep his full pension. It was too good to pass up. He'd wanted to discuss it with Kelly, but he knew she'd have argued about it, pointed out that it was a good job, with good money, and it gave them a comfortable life. She wasn't wrong, but that just wasn't enough any more and here was a way out. On the spur of the moment, he'd snatched the deal just minutes before the deadline, and planned to talk to her about it, but somehow...

'I know! But it just never seemed like the right time. Carny had her finals and then...' He cut himself off, hearing the cowardice of his own words. The truth was, he couldn't face the inevitable backlash, from his wife, his daughter, his mum, and even, yes, his mate, the one who was now looking at him like he'd lost his mind. 'Look, I'm not proud of any of this and I'll try to make it as painless as possible. I'm going to sign the house over to Kelly. The mortgage is just about paid off, so I'm not leaving her in the shit. I want her to have a good life – I just can't keep up the act that I'm the guy to share it.'

Carson's sigh didn't do anything for Scott's rising defensiveness. His mate wasn't letting him off the hook. 'And then what? What's your plan?'

Scott shrugged. 'Not entirely sure. I thought maybe I'd travel a bit. I always wanted to go to Nashville. Maybe play a bit of music. You know that's what I dreamt of doing when we were young. Between savings and my redundancy money, even after I've cleared everything off, I'll have enough to last a year, maybe two if I'm careful. The whole point is that I don't want any fixed plans. Every day since I left school, I've got up and done what was expected of me. I've worked hard, been a good dad, a decent husband... Now I just want to experience how it feels to wake up and do whatever I feel like doing.' He could hear how pathetic his gripes were. He sounded like a teenager trying to justify a gap year to his parents. Maybe if he'd had one of those, got all the wanderlust out of his system, then he wouldn't be in this situation now.

'You know that most guys who are going through this kind of shit just call it a midlife crisis and buy a motorbike or a yoga mat?' Carson remarked, obviously unimpressed, but defaulting to humour as they'd done in every serious situation their whole lives.

Scott lifted a bit of toast, glad of a break in the tension. 'Yeah, I thought about that, but I'm terrified of bikes and I'd look like a tit with a man bun. Pretty sure my mum would cut it off while I slept.'

Stretching back in his seat, hands on the table, Carson let out a low, slow whistle, but said nothing. He'd always been the less talkative of the two. Scott was pretty sure his mate would have his back no matter what, but he realised the feeling that was making him sweat for the second time that morning was a blast of insecurity and he needed to hear Carson tell him he'd stand by him. 'What you thinking there, big guy?'

Carson hesitated for a moment, ramping up Scott's anxiety. 'Mate, whatever you need to do, I've got your back. And Kelly's. I'll try to help you both in any way I can. But, yep, I think prize prick just about covers it.'

Scott felt his stomach unclench just a smidgeon. 'Wise. Profound. Thank God you're here. If you ever leave the RAF, you're a shoo-in for work as a motivational speaker.'

The two men sat in silence for a moment, both of them absorbing the discussion.

'Is it the sausages?' Sonya said with suspicion, making them both flinch at yet another silent ninja entrance. Damn those fluffy slippers. 'The butcher was shut, so they're the supermarket stuff. God knows what's in them.'

It took the men a moment to realise she was trying to get to the bottom of why the plate of breakfast ingredients was still sitting in the centre of the table, barely touched.

'Sausages are great, Mrs B,' Carson assured her, holding up the half-eaten one on the end of his fork. 'We just got distracted talking about... football.'

'Ah, nothing changes. You two were always the same,' she said fondly, ruffling Scott's hair and letting her slippers head a retreat back to her room. 'But bloody hurry up because your Kelly will hit the roof if we're late. Big day today, son. Big day.'

Big day indeed. It was the day that they would celebrate their gorgeous, smart, brilliant daughter's graduation. It was the day that they would say goodbye before she flew the nest. And today was going to be the day that Scott dropped the pretence of contentment and told his wife that he was leaving her.

3

KELLY BASSETT

At first, Kelly wasn't sure what had woken her. Perhaps it was Carny's arm, now stretched across Kelly's torso? Or maybe the sun streaming through the gap in the curtains that she'd forgotten to close before they'd fallen asleep?

A bang from downstairs told her differently. Kelly knew with absolute certainty that it was her brother-in-law, Rick, already up and causing chaos in Kelly's spotless kitchen. Not that her kitchen was always so immaculate, but some kind of hostessy duty compelled her to clean for three days before her family stayed over, and besides, it had been a welcome diversion from the stresses of the last couple of weeks.

'If it pisses you off, tell him to stop bloody doing it,' Scott would say, every time they came to visit and Rick rose at the crack of dawn and then took over the kitchen. It was a chef thing, her sister would tell her. It was always on the tip of Kelly's tongue to answer back that, no, it was an asshole thing.

Not that she disliked her brother-in-law. Quite the opposite. Their relationship was... complicated. Next-door neighbours as kids, he was her oldest friend, her person, long before he got his first Michelin star, long before he opened his own restaurant and long before he married her younger sister. When they were teenagers, they'd even dated for a while before she called it off and started going out with Scott. It was the right decision. Every time she looked at her daughter, she knew that.

Her gaze went to Carny, lying next to her. Her beautiful, self-assured, girl. In the waking hours, her daughter was a quick-witted, independent, impressive young woman, but now, asleep, her long brown hair fanning around her make-up-free face, she was still Kelly's little girl and looked barely older than she had when Kelly would tuck her in, read her a story, then kiss her forehead goodnight.

The thought made tears pool inside her bottom lids and she swallowed back the lump of nostalgia in her throat. *Pull it together, Kel*, she chided herself. *Get a grip.*

Carny murmured, then rolled over, still in a deep sleep, as Kelly lifted her daughter's arm and slid out of bed.

Not that she'd have vocalised it, but she was glad that Scott had stayed at his mum's house and given her and their daughter the perfect final night together under the same roof. Snuggled up in bed after everyone else was asleep, armed with popcorn, Kelly in a pale grey onesie and Carny in a Britney Spears T-shirt, they'd watched *Legally Blonde* for the millionth time.

She'd miss this. Every moment of it. As mother and daughter, they'd come through the slammed doors of puberty, the teenage sulks and the period of discovery, when Carny was finding out who she really was, and now they were something different. Friends. She just hoped they'd still be as close despite the miles between them, the excitement of Carny's new life, and the fact that Kelly might be about to drop a bombshell into their family's future.

That was for later though. She wouldn't allow anything to

spoil Carny's day, her last as their child under their roof, before she got on that flight tomorrow morning to start her new life in London.

Kelly knew she was luckier than some mums. Carny had stayed at home while she was studying theatre at the Glasgow College of Performing Arts, so Kelly had had her girl with her for twenty-two years. Now, she was going, it was time to slap on a smile and be happy that her daughter had landed the job of her dreams.

How times changed. Kelly had taken the first job she could get after Carny was born, as a receptionist in a local estate agent, the same one that she managed now, more than twenty years later. It hadn't been her passion or the job of her dreams, but she'd made a success of it and she enjoyed it. For Carny, her new role as an apprentice set designer in a small London theatre was so much more than that. It was the career she'd always wanted, one she'd studied for, worked towards for years, and Kelly couldn't be more thrilled that she'd achieved it. Even if it did mean living four hundred miles apart. That thought made her stomach lurch, and she paused, inhaled, waited for the feeling to pass.

When it did, she pulled on a robe from the back of the bedroom door, then made a pitstop at the bathroom to brush her teeth and pull her long tawny hair up into a high ponytail. She'd usually be applying her make-up and getting ready for her Saturday morning viewings by this time, but she'd taken this whole week off to spend with Carny. Rubbing a quick layer of moisturiser over her face, she knew she could still pass for thirty – a birthday that had been in her rear-view mirror for eight years. Although, much as she might look thirty on the outside, right now, she was so tired that she felt a couple of decades older on the inside.

Shirking off the thought, she made it to the hallway outside her bedroom, surprised when she spotted her sister, Sabrina, sitting on the top step. Their mother had been a fan of *Charlie's Angels* back in the seventies and Kelly and Sabrina had been two of the original detectives in the show. If Kelly had been a boy, there was every chance she'd have spent her married life dealing with the inevitable bind of being called Bosley Bassett, after the male on the team.

Sabrina caught her eye and budged over to let Kelly join her, a facsimile of countless times as children when they'd sit on the top stair in their parents' terraced house, reluctant to go downstairs because they could hear one or both of them on the warpath. It had been a blessing when they'd divorced. And an even greater shock when they'd realised that they missed the marital disharmony and remarried ten years later. They lived in the Lake District now but hadn't made the trip north because they said they were minimising their carbon footprint. Kelly had told them she absolutely understood, but she wasn't sure she did. Missing their granddaughter's celebration because they didn't want to make a three-hour drive? It made no sense to her at all. But then, she thought, desperately pressing on the lid of that can of worms, understanding her parents' self-absorbed, disconnected ways had always been a challenge.

'Morning, sis. Did you sleep okay?' Sabrina and Rick had slept in Carny's double bed.

'Yeah. Right up until Gordon Ramsay got up and went to work downstairs.'

Kelly playfully nudged her sister's shoulder. They were almost six years apart in age, and Sabrina had gone to college in Florida on an athletic scholarship when she was a teenager, planning to study for a business degree and then return home. However, she'd ended up marrying her college sweetheart and staying there for five more years. The two women had only got close after Sabrina's marriage broke down and she'd returned to the UK with only a suitcase, a devastated heart and a bitter taste caused by finding out her husband had been sleeping with a waitress at their local bar for months. Now, especially this morning, with both of them make-up-free and with the same ponytails in their chestnut hair, they could be twins. 'Is there a reason you're sitting here instead of lying in bed or going down there to join him?' Kelly asked gently.

'I'm psyching myself up,' Sabrina confessed. 'If I go down there, he'll give me jobs to do and I don't think I can handle the pressure. He lost two sous chefs last week. One of them spray-painted "Chef is a c.u.n.t." on the staffroom wall before he left. I think he's misunderstood,' Sabrina added, making them both giggle, as it was so clearly untrue. Rick was hot-headed. He was a perfectionist. He could be wholly unreasonable. And no, it wasn't a complete surprise that the c word would be used in his biographical information. 'You've got a lot to answer for, Kelly Bassett,' Sabrina added tartly, pulling out the often-used rebuke.

Kelly didn't argue. She was the one who'd reintroduced Rick to Sabrina when she'd come home from the USA. The last time he'd seen her younger sister, she'd been an eighteen-year-old kid, but by the time she returned she was a gorgeous twenty-eight-year-old woman. Their chemistry had been instant and they'd married within the year. Sabrina accepted him for all his flaws and eccentricities, while he encouraged her to loosen up and enjoy life – Kelly could see they were good for each other.

'Any word from Mum and Dad?' Sabrina asked, pivoting to a different subject.

Kelly nodded. 'They're definitely not coming. Mum says it's too far and they don't want to waste petrol as that puts money in the pockets of the oil and gas companies that are secretly running the government.'

Sabrina looked surprised. 'But I thought they'd bought shares in BP?'

'They have, but only because they're hedging their bets. Dad's obsessed with preserving resources because he says there's about to be some kind of energy apocalypse. Apparently it might be something to do with Brexit, the Dalai Lama, China, and Elvis is probably involved too.'

'Sounds about right,' Sabrina agreed. They were well used to their parents' conspiracy theories. They were the only kids in school whose parents built an underground bunker next to their whirligig. 'Let's do a DNA test and see if we're actually theirs. I honestly have my doubts. People keep telling me I'm a dead ringer for a young Joan Collins. It's not too late for me to expose the truth and get in her will.'

Kelly managed to keep the volume down on her giggle. 'You're also a dead ringer for our mother, so I wouldn't hold out much hope.' She put her head on her sister's, so they were like two buildings leaning into each other for support. 'I'm glad you're here.'

'Me too,' Sabrina told her. 'Just tell me the plan so I'm not late and I can make sure our temperamental chef is ready on time.'

Without lifting her head, Kelly ran through the itinerary. 'Okay, Scott, Carson and Sonya should be here around twelve o'clock for a pre-party refreshment, then we'll leave at around one o'clock. You're taking Sonya to pick up Scott's grandad and I'll head straight down to Loch Lomond with Scott, Carny and Carson. Carny was one of the organisers, so she just wants to get there early to make sure everything is going smoothly. I'm really looking forward to it, although I could quite happily have stayed in bed for another couple of...' The wave of nausea was upon her before she even realised it was coming, and she almost dislocated Sabrina's jaw as she leapt up and darted to the bathroom behind them, throwing herself over the toilet bowl, no time to even close the door behind her.

No. Not today. Bugger.

Stomach empty, retching finally over, Kelly slumped on the floor and rested the back of her head on the tiled wall behind her.

Only then did she see that Sabrina had followed her into the room and had closed the door behind her. No escape. Now she was sitting on the bath, staring at her with something between confusion and dread.

'Tell me it's food poisoning?' her sister begged, her voice so much smaller than it had been just a few moments before.

'I don't... I don't know,' Kelly stuttered, all too aware that her answer had the potential to break Sabrina's heart.

'But it might not be?' Sabrina asked, unwilling or unable to flat out ask what she needed to know.

Kelly thought about lying to save her sister's feelings, but what was the point? They knew each other inside out and Sabrina wouldn't be fooled. Lying would only make things worse. She shook her head gently, aware that any sudden movements could cause another rush of nausea. 'Might not be,' she admitted, as much to herself as to Sabrina.

Sabrina wasn't letting go. 'Are you late?'

The cool porcelain of the tiles was beginning to make the queasiness subside. 'Just a few days.' This was the fourth morning in a row that she'd thrown up before breakfast. It was time to stop kidding herself and face the reality.

'And you weren't going to tell me?' The pain was written all over Sabrina's face.

Kelly went for uncomfortable honesty. 'I guess I didn't want to think it could be true. I was going to wait until after today, then find out for sure before I said anything. I'm so sorry, Sabrina. You know I would never do anything to hurt you.'

'I know that. Bloody hell, I wish I'd gone downstairs and let Rick put me in charge of sausages,' Sabrina said, and Kelly appreciated the attempt to lighten the mood, but she knew her sister would be dying on the inside. Sabrina and Rick were on their third round of IVF and she still hadn't fallen pregnant. It had been their sole focus for the last three years, it had cost them every penny of profit from Rick's restaurant, the one that Sabrina worked so hard in too. Sometimes Kelly worried that the emotional strain would break them. So far, they were hanging on, but only just. Yet here she was, thirty-eight, with her daughter about to leave home and the very real possibility that she was pregnant again.

'What does Scott think about it?'

Kelly's cheeks began to burn again. 'I... I haven't told him.'

Sabrina's eyes widened. 'Why not?'

The big question. One that Kelly had asked herself a dozen times over the last week. Why not? Perhaps because over the last few months, maybe a year, he'd been so distant that sometimes it felt like the man she'd been married to for more than half her life was a stranger. He'd been so disinterested, so quiet, so disconnected, and she couldn't understand why. An affair would have been the obvious conclusion, but not only was that not in Scott's nature, but he never went anywhere without her or Carny, so she couldn't see where there would be the opportunity. In the end, she'd put it down to the fact that Carny was moving out and he was having some kind of empty-nest reaction, maybe some sort of midlife crisis, but when she'd tried to talk to him about it, he'd insisted nothing was wrong. She knew he was lying. They'd only made love once in the last six months, an encounter she'd instigated out of guilt after she'd done something so unthinkable she didn't ever want to revisit it. And she definitely couldn't tell Sabrina about it now or ever.

'I guess I wanted to wait because I'm pretty sure it's a false alarm and I didn't want to freak him out.' The first part of that sentence was a white lie, but the second part was oh so true.

'You do know how babies are made, right?' Sabrina, true to form, went right to the heart of it. 'Have you had unprotected sex?'

'You're hilarious.' Despite the sarcasm on both sides, Kelly knew it was a justifiable point. 'You know that after my surgery we didn't think I'd ever get pregnant again,' she reminded her sister of that awful time, just a few years after Carny was born. A ruptured cyst on her left ovary. Surgery. Forced removal of the damaged organ. They'd been told that there was still a possibility she could conceive again. For a decade they had lived in hope, but when nothing happened, she'd let the longing go, accepted the situation and counted their blessings for their one healthy child. Now, almost twenty years after the op, it was almost impossible to comprehend that reality could be drawing a different picture. 'So we've never used contraception. Just figured it would never happen.'

Saying it out loud, she could hear just how silly it sounded, yet it was the truth. After five years, ten years, fifteen years, the thought of another child had evaporated and it had ceased to be something that she gave headspace to. Until now.

Sabrina's sigh was long and soft and Kelly had a twinge of anxiety as to where they were going to go next with this. Was it going to wreck the rest of the day? Would Sabrina be able to put this out of her mind and celebrate Carny?

'Well, we're not going to sort this out sitting here,' Sabrina announced, getting up off the edge of the bath. 'You need to know for sure.'

'Yeah, but there's no way to do that today. I don't have a pregnancy test and I definitely don't have time to go get one.'

'I have one with me,' Sabrina said, so quietly that Kelly had to rewind in her head to check she'd heard right. Sabrina registered her confusion and offered an explanation, 'My period is due tomorrow, so I brought a test with me.'

'Oh, honey...' Kelly said softly. She had no idea they were waiting for that kind of news this weekend. She should have been a better sister these last few weeks, but she'd been so preoccupied with a dozen other things.

Sabrina cut her off. 'It's fine. Really.' Kelly didn't believe her, but kept quiet and listened. 'The test has two in the packet. I'll go get it and...'

Rick's voice: 'Sabrina, are you in the bathroom? Breakfast is on the table. And hurry up because I've made egg white omelettes and they taste like shoes when they get cold.'

Kelly, still kneeling on the floor, had another flashback. Her hanging out the window with a St Moritz cigarette when she was fifteen, a ten-year-old Sabrina beside her, awestruck at her big sister's sophistication, until their mother banged on the door, summoning them for dinner.

'Just coming,' Sabrina replied with her very best breeziness. 'Give me two minutes.'

'Okay, and can you wake Kelly and Carny too?' He obviously had no idea the sisters were in there together.

'Will do,' Sabrina answered, as Rick's steps descended back downstairs.

'Okay, I can't do a test while he's getting agitated about us coming for breakfast. There's no way I can pee on a stick with that kind of anxiety.'

Sabrina nodded. 'Yep, I get you. Right, breakfast and then we'll do it, okay? I'm sorry if I'm pushing you, Kells, but I need to know. I know this isn't about me, but I can't go through the whole day wondering if you're pregnant. I just can't.'

Kelly reached over and took her sister's hand. 'I understand. I do. After breakfast it is, but not here. My en suite. You go on down, and I'll go wake Carny.'

Sabrina nodded, then opened the door a little to check the coast was clear. Kelly let her go, then waited for a moment so Rick wouldn't catch them if he was in the hall. Kelly took Sabrina's perch on the side of the bath.

Damn it. This wasn't supposed to happen yet, but here it was. Today was the day she was going to find out if she was pregnant. Today was the day she might break her sister's heart. And today was the day she may have to tell her husband that they had a baby on the way.

The only thing she definitely wasn't going to tell him was the most important thing of all. That for the last twenty-two years, she'd been in love with someone else.

4

HARRIET BASSETT

As always, Harriet was awake long before the lovely nursing assistant came around with the morning teas. This was her last morning on the geriatric ward of Glasgow Central Hospital, and it wasn't just the dread of going home that had kept Harriet awake most of the night. Marg, in the bed next to her, had been coughing her lungs up and Jenny, in the bed across from her, had been shouting names in her sleep. Harriet had no idea who Jimmy, Fran and David were, but they were haunting Jenny's sleeping hours. She wanted to ask, but Jenny was rarely lucid when she was awake, and there had been no visitors to her bedside in the month that they'd both been on the ward.

'Good morning, pet,' Betty, the cheeriest nursing assistant Harriet had ever met, greeted her as she reached over to put Harriet's tea on her bed table. 'A wee cuppa for you. Did you sleep well?'

Harriet nodded. 'I did, thanks, Betty.' No point in being honest about it. No one wanted to hear someone complaining first thing in the morning. Or any time of the day for that matter. If there was one thing she'd learned in her eighty years, it was that the best way to get through life was just to smile and make the best of it. Don't make a fuss. Don't waste time complaining about something that can't be changed. That was one of her Dennis's most frequently quoted sayings. Not that he'd always lived by it right enough. He was always quick to say if he wasn't happy about something. Harriet had loved him for over sixty years, and he was a loyal, decent man, whose heart was in the right place, but my god, he could be difficult. Especially after the accident.

Harriet closed her eyes as she felt a lump form in her throat. *Silly old fool*, she told herself. All these years later and still it made her heart leak pure sorrow.

'Are you okay there, Harriet?'

Harriet's eyes flashed open and the corners of her mouth automatically turned up. The month she'd spent on this ward had been a blessed relief thanks to the absolute gem of a woman standing in front of her now: senior charge nurse Yvie Danton.

'I'm good, Yvie. Just resting my eyes. Thinking about all the things I'll need to catch up with when I get home this afternoon.'

Harriet didn't think she'd fooled Yvie for a second. One thing she'd learned about Senior Charge Nurse Danton was that nothing got past her. The younger woman had the most acute sense of instinct and empathy, and Harriet had watched as she'd gone the extra mile again and again to make sure everyone got the best possible care. Harriet was going to miss her. In fact, she was going to miss them all. If anyone had told her years before that she'd be happier in hospital than anywhere else, she'd have thought they were crazy. But that was before Dennis had succumbed to a brutal stroke and passed away suddenly last March. Before she'd spent more than a year at home, absolutely alone, realising that decades of his insistence that they kept themselves to themselves had left her with not a single person in her world that she could talk to. They had no family in their lives and although she'd had a few friends over the years, she'd outlived them all, except for the one or two who were in nursing homes, their minds lost to the cruelty of dementia. Even the lovely neighbours they'd had for decades had either moved out or passed away, replaced by young families or professional couples who had no time to pass the day with anything more than a hurried smile if they saw her at the window. Her weekly trip to the shops, weather permitting, was the only time she had spoken to anyone and even then, the assistants at the checkouts were in such a rush.

That's why, for over a year, she'd gone without human contact. Without chat. Without meaningful communication with another living soul. Harriet Bassett was absolutely alone.

It was difficult to say when the darkness had set in and she'd realised that she couldn't go on, that the endless months of loneliness, including a Christmas and New Year of absolute solitude, had broken her. There hadn't been a conscious decision. It had just been a matter of lethargy. After the first anniversary of Dennis's death, she had been too tired, too jaded, to keep swallowing the cocktails of pills that kept her heart working, stopped her bones from seizing, numbed her nerve endings to the pain of her joints, so she'd just stopped taking them. Let them pile up.

For the next few weeks, she'd woken up every morning, surprised and more than a little disappointed to see that she was still in the land of the living. That's when the fates had intervened. On her last day at home, as she'd carried her breakfast over to her chair in front of the fire, she'd felt herself take a dizzy turn. Stumbling, she'd reached out to clutch onto the dining table to restore her balance, missed, fell, cracked her head and passed out, fracturing her hip on the way down.

By some stroke of serendipity, the window cleaner had come

that day and saw her lying there. He'd called an ambulance and come in through her open bedroom window to unlock the door.

When Harriet woke, she'd initially been saddened that she hadn't slipped away quietly, and horrified to discover she was in hospital, but that fury wore off as the post-surgery painkillers had taken effect and she'd been put into the geriatrics ward with five other women. Over the next couple of days, she'd noticed a change in how she felt when she woke in the morning. There was always a hello and a smile from one of the other women. And the staff took such good care of her. Everyone from the cleaners to the consultants had a kind word, even when they were rushed off their feet and exhausted from trying to find beds for the constant waves of new arrivals. It wasn't perfect. Years ago, the lack of privacy would have filled her with horror, but after over a year of living in a world where the only person she saw was her reflection in the mirror, Harriet absolutely welcomed every glance, every chat, every warm meal and every laugh, and most of those came from Nurse Yvie.

'Well, I see you've managed to do it again,' Yvie proclaimed, a twinkle in her eye as she made the same joke they'd shared every morning for the last four weeks.

'Wake up looking ravishing?' Harriet quipped, laughing, patting the bottom of her hair. It had been a riot of thick, dark curls when she was a young woman. Now it was almost white, although it was still curly, especially after Yvie had given it a lovely blow-dry in her break last night. The long forgotten feeling of being pampered had been blissful.

Yvie nodded, as if it went without saying. 'That's the one. I don't know how you do it. Are you all packed and ready to go home? I think your transport is coming after doctor's rounds and after the pharmacy staff have been up to give you your discharge medication, so probably around lunchtime. Occupational health are all geared up and they'll be in to see you once a day.'

Just hearing Yvie say it out loud made Harriet's stomach flip. She wanted to go anywhere but home. Back to those four walls. Back to staring at the TV, because her eyes got so tired when she read now. Back to the loneliness that came with living alone, as a woman who was once a mother but no longer had any family in her life. Harriet knew she couldn't do it again. She didn't want to feel that aching, gnawing dread of waking up and having no one to speak to except an exhausted home carer who was rushing in and out because she had another thirty patients to see before the end of the day.

No, Harriet had a plan. Or rather, she was going to have another go at her original plan. As soon as she got home, she was going to stop taking all her meds. This time, she'd stay in bed, wait it out for as long as it took. Hopefully, before too long, she'd slip away in her sleep, and the hellish ache of loneliness would be gone. In the meantime, she had a few hours more in the outside world today and she was going to enjoy it.

'I was thinking about you yesterday,' Yvie told her, as she straightened Harriet's blanket and refilled her water jug. Given her job title, Harriet guessed she was in her early thirties, but with her generous curves, her pale blonde hair and beautiful, Rubenesque face she could have been younger.

Harriet nodded sagely. 'I believe George Clooney always says the same thing. He's obsessed with me.'

Yvie's chuckle made Harriet's heart swell. The biggest joy of the last few weeks was finding out that she could still make people laugh, still contribute something to a conversation. She'd run out of interesting conversation with Dennis some time back in the eighties. Or maybe the nineties. And he wasn't one for filling the house with friends or meeting people on holidays. He always said he was happy with just the two of them and Harriet had learned early in their marriage that it was pointless to argue. Now, well, she even missed biting her tongue to keep the peace.

Yvie lifted Harriet's chart with one hand, and slipped a pulse oximeter onto Harriet's index finger. A month on the ward had given her a whole new medical vocabulary, as well as a whole new affection for the nurse with the glint in her eye who was agreeing with her now. 'Completely understandable. He's wasted on that totally gorgeous, super-intelligent, highly accomplished human rights lawyer that he's married to. He could be home with you and a bit of *Britain's Got Talent* on the telly.'

'Doesn't know what he's missing,' Harriet mused, rewarded when Yvie giggled again. Her curiosity was piqued though. 'Why were you really thinking about me then?'

Yvie glanced up from the clipboard where she was jotting down the readings from Harriet's notes. 'Oh. It's a bit of a long story. I've told you about my sister, Verity, the teacher...'

'The one you love dearly but who drives you crazy?' Harriet had loved hearing all the antics of Yvie's large family and had encouraged the charge nurse to share her stories.

'In fairness, that could apply to all my sisters,' Yvie joked. 'Marina is so bossy she could mobilise an army to invade an enemy nation, and Zoe is so loved up and besotted with her new fiancé that I'm fairly sure she farts love-hearts,' she said, her deadpan delivery making Harriet smile again. 'It's Verity who is the primary school teacher. She loves the children she teaches but has a general disdain for most adults. Anyway, she has been teaching for about ten years, but she's always kept in touch with most of the students in the first class she ever taught, which is a bit of a wonder because our Verity is usually completely devoid of sentimentality and she has the social skills of a plant.'

Harriet didn't say a word, happy to listen. Yvie's stories were always like this – they went off in ten different directions but always came back to the point eventually.

'Where was I going with this?' Yvie paused. 'Oh yes! Today, one of those students is throwing a swanky garden party to raise funds for Glasgow College of Performing Arts and Verity is forcing me to go with her. She says if I don't, she's going to start uploading one childhood pic of me every day to Facebook. No one needs to see that. If you put them all together it's like one of those diet shows in reverse,' she shuddered. 'Anyway, when Verity was blackmailing me, she mentioned the name of the student who's throwing the party. Guess what it is?'

'Clooney?' Harriet asked, still confused as to where she fitted into this picture.

Yvie's chuckle woke Marg in the next bed, who, in one fluid motion, started coughing again, then scanned the room, put her head back on the pillow and fell asleep. 'No, it's Bassett! Isn't that bizarre? I've only heard that surname twice in my life – when I met you and then again when Verity told me about the party. Have you got a young relative who is around twenty-two and just about to graduate with a degree in theatre studies?'

Harriet's curiosity grew. The only other people she knew of with that name were... It pained her to think about. It was so long ago.

She forced herself to keep her voice strong and casual, to conceal the fact that her stomach was lurching yet again. She was never going to keep her breakfast down at this rate. 'The only other people I knew of with that name was my husband's brother and his family. Haven't seen them for over twenty-five years.'

Yvie stopped and perched on the side of the bed. That's why Harriet had taken a shine to her. She was never too busy to take an interest in her patients. Although, for once, Harriet was wishing that she'd move on and let it drop.

Yvie didn't.

'Was there a fallout?' she asked gently.

Harriet nodded. 'It's a long story.' She was hoping that the prospect of a drawn out saga would send Yvie running, but she just sat patiently, giving Harriet no choice but to go on. 'Dennis's brother, Jonathan, married my best friend, Anthea. We were always together, the four of us. Inseparable, really. But then… well, there was a rift. A long time ago. We never saw them again.' Harriet took a hanky out from the sleeve of her pale blue bed jacket and blew her nose.

Yvie was quiet for a moment, pensive, before asking, 'Didn't you tell me you have no family now, Harriet?'

'Yes. I suppose I don't think of them that way because it's been so long since we spoke.'

'So maybe after all this time, it might be possible to build a bridge? I could do a little garden party investigation to see if these are your relatives?'

The thought of it made Harriet's heart begin to thud so loudly that she was sure Yvie must be able to hear it. She'd never agreed with Dennis's decision to cut Jonathan and Anthea and their family out of their lives after the accident that changed everything, but he'd been absolutely rigid in his decision and wouldn't hear a single argument against it. At the time, Harriet had to admit, she was in no fit state to try. Even now that he was gone, she probably still wasn't. 'No, Yvie. I think we should let sleeping dogs lie.'

'Are you sure? It would be no bother to do some nosing around when I get there. I've watched every episode of *Line of Duty*, so I feel fully qualified for undercover work. Or, even better, you could come with us and suss it out for yourself. It's a fundraiser, and we've got an extra ticket because my mother was supposed to come but she can't make it.'

Harriet's heart was like a train now. Thank goodness she'd already taken her medication or she was fairly sure it could explode. It was a chapter that closed so long ago, yet it immediately threw up the very same feelings she'd had back then.

She dabbed her eyes with her hanky this time. 'Thank you, Yvie, I appreciate the offer, I really do, but some things are best left alone.'

Yvie nodded, then gave her a grin, doing that thing she was so good at – lifting the spirits. 'I understand, Harriet. I really do. I'd happily disown my sisters half the time. Don't even get me started on my mother.' She was laughing properly now, and Harriet was so grateful to her for dropping the subject. 'Anyway, I'm leaving just before noon, so I'll come say goodbye before I go. Give you time to come up with a speech about how much you'll miss us. Or to change your mind about coming to the party. We can always hide you behind a plant pot if you don't want them to see you before you suss out if you know them.' With a raucous chuckle and a squeeze of the hand, Yvie was off to spread joy to Marg in the next bed.

Harriet tucked her hanky back under her sleeve and let her head rest on her pillow, glad the bed was raised to almost a sitting position. Usually she'd read a book now. Perhaps do a newspaper crossword. But nothing, she knew, could hold her attention this morning. Not now that the door to her worst memories had been opened.

Jonathan. Dennis. That day that changed everything.

She could see them all down to the most minute detail: what they were wearing, what they were saying, what they were laughing about, and then the argument that had followed, the one that had allowed the true love of her life to storm out the door, to get into a car, to drive away. The man in that car had been her twenty-five-year-old son, Leo. That night was the last time she'd seen him alive.

To her absolute horror, Harriet couldn't press the stop button on the movie that had just begun in her mind.

Even though she hadn't been there when Leo had died, her imagination had recreated every detail. Every action. Every skid. Every crash. Every scream.

Now, every moment of pain from then until today was consuming her, pulling her back down into the well of darkness she'd existed in for far too long.

No more. She couldn't live with nothing but memories of all that she'd lost. It was time to go. It was time to be with Leo again.

Today, Harriet knew, was going to be the first day of the final chapter of her life.

10 A.M. – NOON

5

MAISIE

Maisie screeched her battered Mini to a halt outside the steel roll-up shutters at The Carrot Schtick warehouse. Janice and Jane were already standing there, like two forty-something, rotund mob bosses, only slightly scarier. First cousins, the women both used the same jet-black hair dye on their similar bobbed hair-styles, and accessorised with excessive jewellery, unique wardrobe choices and a general air of cynicism. They also made her laugh until her sides hurt.

'Och, it's you, love,' Janice said, fanning her face with her hand. 'Thank God yer here and we can get out of this heat. It's flipping roasting. Like the menopause all over again.'

Maisie chose not to point out that it was only around sixty degrees, and while that constituted high summer in Scotland, Janice's plight was made worse by the fact that she was wearing a furry cardigan that could keep Eskimos warm in the winter.

The two women had been with Sissy from the start and Maisie adored them. They knew their stuff, could rustle up a buffet at an hour's notice and let nothing stand in the way of getting the job done. Unfortunately, they also had the tact and tolerance of an irritated, authoritarian dictator, so it was usually best to keep them one step removed from clients. It was an executive decision after a very wealthy housewife, throwing a fortieth birthday lunch for 100 of her closest friends, overheard Janice saying, 'Forty, my arse. If she had that face lifted any more, her knickers would be doubling as a face mask.' Thus Sissy's desperation for Maisie to oversee the provision of the finger food today.

'Sorry, ladies! Don't shoot the messenger...' Maisie pleaded.

'Put yer AK 47 back in yer handbag, Janice,' Jane quipped, with a wink to her cousin.

Maisie grinned, relieved they weren't actually pissed off. She'd once played a serial vigilante with awesome fighting skills in a pilot that never made it to screen, but even that hadn't prepared her for the wrath of Janice and Jane. 'Sissy has gone into labour...' she began to explain.

'Oh dear Lord, that lassie's poor vagina is in for a day of it,' Janice sighed. 'Mine's never been the same since ma Kevin was born. Doctor said it was the biggest head he'd ever seen.'

Jane, always the more reserved of the two, rolled her eyes. 'Let the lassie finish, Janice. Honest to God, the size of yer lady bits is nothing compared to the size of yer gob.'

'Right. Yes. Okay. How's Sissy doing? The rest of her, I mean – not just her vagina. How far along is she?'

'She's not sure. Contractions just started a couple of hours ago. She's going to keep us posted throughout the day,' Maisie continued, trying to regain her train of thought. 'So I'm her stunt double and working with you today. The temp staff are meeting us there, so we just need to get everything loaded, transported to site and set up. Can you two take the van and I'll follow in my car?'

Jane nodded. 'No bother, hen. We prepared everything last night, so it'll take no time at all to get it moving.'

Maisie put her head on Janice's shoulder, trying not to sneeze as the mohair tickled her nostrils. 'Be gentle with me today, Janice. I've got the hangover from hell and the thought of going to Lomond House...'

The penny dropped. 'Ah, jeez – that's where that dickless bawbag, Nathan, did a runner...' Janice began.

Maisie cut her off, loath to endure a blow-by-blow account. 'Indeed it is, but we're not talking about it. We're loading food and you two are my emotional supports for the day. That may be the scariest thought I've ever had.'

Janice wrapped her arms around her and gave her a hug. 'We'll look after you, don't you worry. Now, get a move on before I faint and cause an earth tremor.'

It was exactly what Maisie needed. No overt sympathy. No coddling. Just a reassuring squeeze and a hint to get on with it.

In half an hour, they had the van fully loaded and Janice and Jane set off on the forty-five-minute drive to the shores of Loch Lomond.

Maisie punched in the alarm code and was just about to press the enter button when she remembered. The cake. In the cold storage. She ran back into the warehouse, opened the door to the refrigerated cold room and stepped inside. This was the first time she'd been in here in months because Sissy usually organised all the loading while Maisie went straight to the venues to prepare. That might explain why she didn't know that on the middle shelf, right at the end, her wedding cake stood as beautiful and perfect as it had been on the day, only a couple of months ago, that it was supposed to have been consumed. The sight of it punched her bang in the ribs. Four tiers. White royal icing with a single trail of deep red flowers cascading from the top to the bottom, an interwoven M and N engraved on the middle tier. She'd had no idea that Sissy had kept it. Maisie wasn't sure how to feel about that, although there was no denying it was so beautiful that it would have been a waste to bin it.

There was no telling if it was the cold air or the shock that had taken every bit of air from her lungs, but Maisie had to get out of there. She grabbed the huge white box to her right, backed out, kicked the door closed with her foot and then ducked under the half-open shutters to put it in her boot. Hands shaking, she went back in to set the alarm again, then, to a soundtrack of beeps, pulled down the shutters and locked them.

In the car, she switched on the ignition and the sound of Smooth Radio blasted out. When she'd arrived, it had been 'Before He Cheats' by Carrie Underwood – the ultimate empowerment song. Now it was 'Ain't No Sunshine' by Bill Withers. It had been one of Nathan's favourite songs and his cover of it had been one of the highlights of his set. He often shouted Maisie up onto the stage to sing with him, an earlier, much skinter, less impressive version of Bradley Cooper and Lady Gaga in *A Star Is Born*. All that training in musical theatre hadn't gone to waste. She'd loved it every time, and just thinking about it, Maisie felt a piece chip off her heart.

Hands on the wheel, she inhaled and exhaled deeply at least half a dozen times, using the calming techniques that had served her so well on the stage.

She pulled out of the car park and turned right, switching on to automatic pilot as she drove along a road she'd travelled on many times before – including a day just like this last autumn. On that unusually warm September morning, Nathan had been behind the wheel and she had been in the passenger seat, flip-flops kicked off, her naturally sallow skin even darker.

That day she'd been in a pensive mood. She'd just spent the weekend with her sister, Hope, and the biological family that Hope had found thanks to a search on a DNA database. They'd both been adopted as babies by wonderful parents but had surrendered to curiosity when they reached their twenties and technology offered them the prospect of some answers. Both Hope and Maisie had submitted their DNA test kits at the same time. Hope had struck the jackpot, eventually finding her father, mother and a whole rake of relatives. Maisie had struck out. Not a single match. Nothing.

Hope's new family had embraced her as part of theirs, but Maisie couldn't help the twinge of sadness. Hope had exactly the same eyes as her father. Some of the same mannerisms as her mother. Maisie still had no idea where her ebony waves, her emerald eyes, her sallow complexion, came from. She'd always wondered if she had Italian heritage. Or maybe Spanish or Middle Eastern. The combination of dark skin, jet black hair and green eyes had her baffled. She'd grown up in a home where she looked starkly different to her paler skinned, lighter haired family and although her mum and her late dad had been the best parents anyone could ever want, and they'd given her and Hope wonderful childhoods, it still just felt like there was something missing. Who was she? What was her heritage? And why had her parents given her away?

'What are you thinking about?' Nathan had asked as they'd driven down the coast road, past Dumbarton, past Luss, until they were curving around the side of the loch.

'I'm thinking this is a pretty isolated spot we're going to and you could easily bump me off,' Maisie had answered, unwilling to put a downer on the day by discussing the sadness that consumed her every time she thought about her burning need to find her biological family. Nathan already knew how she felt. Just like she knew him so well too.

He was a Londoner, and she'd met him in their first week at RADA. A few one-night stands had quickly turned into a relationship that lasted all through college. They'd moved into a tiny studio flat in Clerkenwell, skint but blissfully happy. They'd both been studying for a BA in Acting, but Nathan had started up an indie rock band in his first year and he soon realised that's what he wanted to do with his future.

He also decided, for a while, that his future didn't include her. She'd been heartbroken when he'd left to tour with his band at the end of their final year, telling her that it was time for them to chase their own dreams. The only thing that slightly soothed the pain was that she'd understood his need to give it a shot. Nathan was a talented musician, whereas Maisie's loves were the stage and screen. It was inevitable that their paths would hit a fork in the road.

Over the next few years, they'd kept in occasional touch – the odd text, some emails, a few drunken late-night phone calls – until a couple of months before, when he'd appeared on her doorstep, the band dissolved due to 'creative differences', and begged her to take him back. There had never been any question that she would refuse. He was the love of her life and they'd picked up exactly where they'd left off. In love. So easy with each other. And it helped balance out the loss she felt every time she watched her sister laugh with the relatives who had claimed her.

'Nah, I was going to bump you off but decided kidnap was a better option. I'll release you if you promise...' his words had tailed off.

'Promise what?' Maisie had asked, laughing.

Nathan didn't reply, instead he'd suddenly swerved on to a short slip road off the carriageway and headed through two massive iron gates. The Lomond House Estate was a National Trust property on the bank of the loch, a stunning Victorian mansion in glorious gardens.

'How did you know about this place?' she'd gasped, as the wheels came to a crunching stop on the gravel pathway.

'I asked Hope where your favourite place on earth was, but I couldn't afford the flights to New York, so I asked her where your second favourite place was. She said it was here.'

'It is,' Maisie had replied, his thoughtfulness making her emotional. 'Isn't it beautiful?'

Nathan had scoped the view, then leaned over and kissed her, drowning her in the intoxicating feelings that she'd missed so much when he was gone. 'I already had a beautiful view,' he'd murmured, mid-kiss.

Maisie had frozen, pulled back, the giggle rising from her gut with unstoppable force. 'Did you really just use the corniest line I've ever heard on me?'

His face was full of mischief. 'Did it work?'

The giggles still wouldn't stop. 'Under normal circumstances it wouldn't, but since you brought me here, I'll forgive you. Just don't do it again.'

He'd sagged with exaggerated relief. 'Thank God, because I'm shite at them.'

Maisie had landed bit parts in a couple of romcoms over the years, but she didn't particularly get the genre. Too slushy. Too cute. Too predictable. She'd choose comedy over romance any day of the week. But this... this was the stuff of slushy movies and love songs. The tingly feelings. The complete honesty. The laughs that came with knowing each other inside out.

They'd climbed out of the car and Nathan had reached for her hand as they'd walked across the grass to the edge of the water. She'd packed a picnic for their mystery tour, but first, Maisie wanted Nathan to see why it was one of her very favourite places. The grassy lawn, the wild summer flowers along the banks, the crystal-clear loch and the incredible view of the hills on the other side of the water. If there was a heaven on earth, this was it.

There was a huge stone just where the loch lapped across the pebbles of the shore. Maisie climbed on top of it while Nathan kicked his shoes off and took a few steps into the gently ebbing water.

'Holy crap, this is deceptively cold,' he'd groaned as he turned to face her, raising his hand to his forehead as he'd squinted against the sun. The bottoms of his jeans were getting wet, but he didn't seem to notice. 'You asked what I was thinking earlier...'

It took Maisie a moment to catch up. 'Did I? When? Oh yeah, I did. You're right. Were you thinking about football? Or Ariana Grande? Even if you were, do me a favour and lie. I'll believe any old bollocks you want to tell me,' she'd joked.

'I was thinking I love you,' he'd said earnestly.

'Not bad,' she'd answered, chuckling again. 'Keep going though. Forget what I said earlier – this place demands full-scale romance. Lay it on thick. I'll be Julia Roberts at the end of every romcom ever. Just a girl. Sitting on a rock. Asking a boy to tell her slushy stuff while she's trying to remember if she packed potato salad in the picnic.'

'And I was thinking I want to marry you,' he added, the slight choke in his voice just adding to the moment.

Damn, he was good. The last few years touring with the band had definitely brushed up his performance skills.

Amused and impressed, Maisie gave him a round of applause. 'Ryan Gosling should be bricking it. I think you could have a future on screen.'

At first, she'd thought he was squinting against the sun again, but then she'd realised that his expression was something else.

He'd leaned forward, kissed her. 'I'm not acting. I want to

marry you. If you don't say yes, I'm staying in here until my feet turn blue.'

'Smurf feet,' she'd quipped, still not absorbing the reality of... It hit her and she suddenly jerked her body back. 'Did you just ask me to marry you?'

The lips she'd just been kissing were a few inches away now. 'I did.'

'Because I'm Julia Roberts?'

He'd leaned in again, so close she could feel the heat from his chest. 'No. I want to marry you because you're Maisie McTeer. And you're perfect for me.'

'But... you're a musician. You'll join another band, spend your life on the road. How would that even work?' Even as she was saying it, her heart was soaring. He wanted to marry her. He was choosing her. And that felt better than she had ever imagined it would.

'I'm done with it,' he'd shrugged. 'I'm going to figure out what to do next, but I know it'll be here, and I know it'll be with you. Please say yes. Say yes,' he'd whispered.

She did. In that moment, the banks of Loch Lomond had been the setting for the most perfect, beautiful romcom moment of her life.

Months later, she would return, only to find herself in the romantic equivalent of a horror movie, the one where the leading man puts a stake through the heart of the heroine and then goes on the run, taking their future with him.

That's why she hated this place, why the very thought of being there today was making her want to hit the margaritas again.

She wasn't ready to be back there, to face her failure and crack her heart wide open again.

Swerving her Mini, Maisie pulled into a lay-by and screeched to a halt, sweating, heart pounding, fingers shaking.

Shit, shit, shit.

She couldn't do it.

But then... if she didn't, did that mean that Nathan had taken something else from her? That he'd won again, by tarnishing her favourite place forever? Not to mention, causing her to let down her best mate, an act of treachery that would undoubtedly lead to Sissy threatening violence with a breast pump.

Come on, Maisie, you can do this. Think of it as an act. Today you're acting like a stable, happy individual who hasn't had her future trashed by a horrible bastard.

After a few deep breaths, she calmed herself, then indicated, pulled out and continued down the road.

Somehow, for Sissy's sake and for hers, she was going to get through today, even if it broke her.

Which it probably would.

6

KELLY

It had been a real struggle to force something down at breakfast, but she didn't want Rick to think she didn't appreciate his efforts. She must have chewed that egg white and tomato omelette for a good five minutes before she could swallow it, all the while trying to ignore the anxious glances being thrown her way by Sabrina.

The thought of hurting her sister horrified her. God knows, Sabrina had been through enough. She'd been devastated when she'd discovered that her first husband had been getting more than chicken wings and a prime seat for the Superbowl at their local bar. Within a week, she'd come home penniless, with just the suitcase she'd gone there with, and she'd moved in with Scott and Kelly for a year while she rebuilt her life.

'Here you go, my love,' Rick said, as he put a plate in front of Sabrina and kissed the top of her head. For all his temper and his volatility, Kelly knew that he loved her sister. She'd known it since soon after she'd introduced them, but she'd be lying if she said it hadn't required an adjustment on her part. Rick had gone from being one of her oldest friends to her sister's husband in such a short time. In fact, they'd rediscovered each other in this kitchen.

They'd met a few times when Sabrina was a teenager, but Sabrina barely remembered him. Rick, exhausted and frazzled after losing a packet on the roulette tables, had popped in for an early-morning coffee with Kelly, when Sabrina had emerged from the spare room in her dressing gown, eyes bloodshot, after yet another night of sleepless hours and tears over the demise of her marriage. She'd slumped down at the table and Rick had handled it in the only way he knew how – he'd got up, raided Kelly's fridge, then made her sister coffee and French toast and insisted she eat it. After that, it had become a regular thing. Rick's occasional visits had become weekly, sometimes twice a week, as he and Sabrina fell in love. After a few months, she'd moved in with him, and gone to work in the restaurant, using her degree in business management to take care of all the jobs Rick's creative mind hated. Happy and clear-headed, he'd cleaned up his act, cut down the booze, forced himself to work less hours and focused on the woman who had changed his life.

'Am I missing something?' he asked, and Kelly flicked back to the present and saw that he was standing in the middle of the kitchen, his eyes going from Sabrina to Kelly, and back again. 'Isn't today supposed to be a celebration? You two look like someone died. What's happened?'

Sabrina threw Kelly an apprehensive glance and Kelly got the message immediately. *Don't say anything. Let it lie. Let's not talk about this right now.*

Kelly shrugged. She had zero acting skills, but she gave it a try. 'Just trying to come to terms with Carny leaving tomorrow,' she said. 'I'm thinking I might numb the pain by taking up smoking, drinking and gambling.'

Rick nodded thoughtfully. 'I thoroughly recommend it. That got me through most of my twenties.'

Carny came into the kitchen, now wearing a T-shirt that

announced, 'Don't hate me 'cause I'm a babe', paired with tiny jean shorts, her long limbs tanned to the colour of caramel.

As always, her daughter's relentless happiness made Kelly smile. Carny was bold, creative, brave and genuinely didn't give a toss what anyone thought of her. She was so sure of herself, so happy in her own skin and in her sexuality. She'd come out to Kelly and Scott when she was fifteen and announced that she was planning to track down Beyoncé and ask if she swung both ways. She'd obviously caught the end of Rick's statement. 'What got you through your twenties, Uncle Rick?'

'Yoga,' Rick answered, quick as a flash, his cover-up breaking the tension in the room.

It was going to be okay, Kelly told herself, going for another five-minute omelette chew, while Carny regaled Rick and Sabrina with her plans for her first week in London, which seemed to be fairly balanced between museums, galleries and other cultural activities, and sampling as many bars, cafes and coffee shops as possible so that she could swiftly establish her favourite social destinations.

Kelly had gone straight from school to a marriage, home and baby. She'd enjoyed her life, but she'd never stop being in awe of Carny's independence and confidence to live life on her own terms.

'So, tell us all about this party then, Carny.' Sabrina prompted her, and Kelly sighed with relief that she didn't have to make conversation for a few minutes. Instead, she could just listen to her daughter, enthusiasm oozing from her every word.

'The drama department is skint, so me and a dozen or so of my mates who were all in our final year decided to throw an epic fundraiser after graduation. We're all going our separate ways, so it's a kinda cool way to say goodbye. We're doing the same show we did for our end-of-term performance – "Music Through the

Decades" – and we're using the set I designed for it. We were going to do it in the grounds of the college, but one of the guys knows the family who own Lomond House, and they agreed to let us have it there for free, as long as we organised the food and bar. We figured the nicer the place, the more dosh people would spend, so hopefully we'll make a decent amount. Uncle Rick's bar bill alone should pay for a new set of costumes for the next show.'

Rick nodded solemnly. 'I'll do my best. I'm a charitable kind of guy. Just remember to scoop me up at the end of the day.'

No one noticed that Kelly was so distracted that she joined in the laughter a second or two after everyone else.

Last bite of the omelette swallowed, she lifted her mug of coffee off the table. 'Scott, his mum and Carson will be here around noon, so I'm just going to go start getting ready.'

'I'll come with you,' Sabrina blurted, jumping up and knocking her chair over in the process. She sheepishly lifted it back up and slid it under the oak bench table. 'I mean, can you do my hair for me, Kell?'

'Eh, sure.'

Carny shook her head with mock despair. 'You two are going to be like those old inseparable sisters who end up living together with forty cats and finishing each other's sentences.'

'No, we're—' Kelly started.

'Not,' Sabrina interjected, then wondered why Rick and Carny found this hilarious. Kelly was just grateful that it let them leave the room without creating suspicion.

She traipsed up the stairs, Sabrina right behind her. Her bed was still a riot of pillows and blankets when Sabrina plonked herself down on it and handed Kelly the test kit. Kelly stared at it for a moment. Only when she had a shot of pain in her mouth did she realise that she was chewing her bottom lip.

'I don't know if I'm ready for this. We could always do it later. Or wait nine months and see if anything drops,' she joked weakly.

Sabrina tossed a cushion at her. 'Good plan.' Her words oozed sarcasm. 'Or you can be a grown-up and go do the test before your sister passes out from stress.'

'Okay, I'll do that then.' Kelly retreated into her bathroom on trembling legs and sat on the loo. The last time she'd been in this position, she'd been a sixteen-year-old, with a boyfriend the same age and she'd been absolutely terrified. Her mum and dad had freaked out when she'd eventually told them, but, thankfully, Scott's mum, Sonya, had stepped in and calmed everyone down, promising to help them take care of everything. Her mum was sure Scott would bugger off and leave her, but he hadn't. They'd made it work, and everything had turned out okay. Mostly. Surely they could do that again. Scott would come round to the idea, they'd stick together and they'd raise another amazing kid. Wouldn't they?

'Have you done it?' came a voice from the bedroom.

'Don't pressure me. I can't pee on demand,' Kelly argued, deciding not to add that she hadn't taken it out of the packet yet.

'Turn on a tap. That always works for me.'

Okay, there was no avoiding this. She wasn't sure if she was more terrified that she was pregnant, or more terrified that she wouldn't be.

It had been over twenty years since the last one, but pregnancy tests hadn't changed much. After a quick scan of the instructions, she peed on the stick and then put the cap back on.

Back in the bedroom, Sabrina was on the edge of the bed, clutching a pillow to her stomach. 'Well?'

Kelly sat down on the cream furry rug in front of her sister. 'It takes a minute to work. Are you okay?'

'No,' Sabrina said honestly. 'I know that's so selfish of me and makes me a complete cow, but I'm not. All these years and it hasn't happened for us. Rick says he doesn't mind, but I'm sure he does.' Her eyes were pools of water now. 'And it just seems like a fucked-up world if you're pregnant when you weren't even planning another kid...' She stopped to gulp back a sob. 'And I'm desperate for one, yet I can't do it. Shit, I haven't even asked... do you want another baby?'

Another wave of nausea was rising, but Kelly wasn't sure if it was the omelette, the anxiety or the abject fear of crushing Sabrina. 'I... I don't know. Yes. I think. We'd figure it out somehow once we got over the shock. I'm just sorry this is happening like this and hurting you. I really am.' she said, apologising again.

'Please don't,' Sabrina countered, drying her eyes and trying to get a grip on her emotions. 'You haven't done anything wrong. It's just me. The IVF hormones have turned me into a wreck and I'm taking it out on you. I'll be happy for you, I promise.'

Kelly wasn't convinced. She wasn't even convinced she'd be happy for herself. 'Really?'

Sabrina tried a rueful laugh. 'Eventually. If you have another kid, it'll be someone else to do the shopping for us when we're eighty and living with our cats.'

They fell into silence for a few moments.

Sabrina cracked first. 'Okay, that must be a minute. Look and see what it says.'

Kelly took a deep breath as she picked up the test from the floor beside her, turned it over and stared at it. And stared. A bit longer.

'Jesus, Kell, you're killing me. What is it?'

Kelly slowly, almost trance-like, turned the test around. 'It's positive.'

Over the thunder clapping in Kelly's head, she heard Sabrina take a desperate intake of air and then expel it in a whimper.

'I'm so sorry—' Kelly began, but Sabrina hushed her.

'Don't. It's me who should be sorry. I've made this all about me, when it should be all about you. Can I blame the hormones for turning me into a self-centred cow?'

Kelly nodded, forcing a smile. 'Absolutely.'

'And if I ask you to give me the baby, that's the hormones talking too. Just putting that out there. So how do you feel? Are you happy?'

Was she? Kelly had absolutely no idea. For months she'd been living in dread of the empty nest, dealing with an overwhelming feeling of loss, both as a mother and a wife. She and Scott had made their marriage work by committing to it for Carny's sake and they'd been happy. At least, they'd been happy until Scott had pulled so far back from her that she'd hit the lowest point in her life a few months ago.

She blocked out that thought before it took hold in her head. What she'd done that night had been a mistake that she never wanted to think about again. It had been a one-off error of judgement. Maybe this was the universe forgiving her, giving her a way out, telling her it was going to be okay, once again giving her and Scott the gel they needed to stick together.

'Happy, I think,' she said cautiously, then put her head on her knees as a new feeling started in her gut and spread like lava to the nerves under every pore of her skin.

'Kelly...? Bugger, you're shaking. Is it the shock?'

Kelly shook her head, throat tightening, tears falling. Who was she kidding? How could she live with herself if she didn't tell Scott the whole truth? What she'd done wasn't just some minor incident that she could brush off and wipe from her memory. It had been a betrayal. One that would break his heart. He didn't deserve that. But how could she tell him now? And how could she tell the sister who was sitting here hurting?

She couldn't.

'No, I just think it's the thought of telling Scott,' she spluttered, fudging the truth. 'I don't know how he'll react.'

Sabrina nodded thoughtfully. 'Do you think he'll be pleased?'

'I think so. He's been such a great dad to Carny and he's been struggling with her leaving, so maybe this will cheer him up.'

'When will you tell him?'

Kelly picked up the pregnancy test, then stretched over and slid it into her top drawer, where she kept everything that was precious to her. 'I don't know. I don't want today to be about anything except Carny and celebrating her and then saying goodbye. So maybe tonight. Maybe tomorrow.'

'Do you think you'll be able to wait until then?'

Kelly shrugged. If there was anything she was an expert in, it was waiting. Hadn't she already waited for an eternity to admit her feelings to the person she truly loved?

Now, with a new baby, she was going to have a different kind of love in her life. One that would love her back. And maybe, somewhere along that path, she'd find her feelings for Scott again too.

She just had to take the first step and tell him.

7

SCOTT

'Right, you two, let me see you,' Sonya joked, scanning them from top to toe, just as she used to do when they were kids and going to a school disco. 'Och, I suppose you'll do. Scott, son, I'm glad you're already a father because those trousers can't be good for your swimmers.'

Scott flushed, despite the fact that he'd had a lifetime of being mortified by Sonya's candour. Okay, so the trousers were pretty tight, but Carny had chosen them and she'd assured him they were in fashion these days. At least both the trousers and his mum's dig had given Carson a laugh. His mate had been pretty quiet since their conversation earlier.

'Thanks, Ma. Your concern for my testicular health is noted. Good to see you're climbing right over those boundaries again.'

He didn't even want to contemplate how his mother would take the news about his plans for the future. Sure, he was a grown man and more than capable of running his own life with no judgement or involvement from a parent. Unfortunately, no one had informed Sonya of that.

It had always just been the two of them, after his dad did a runner when his mum was pregnant, so they'd always been especially close. He loved her and her opinion mattered to him. Most of the time.

No matter what, though, much as he knew his mum would take no prisoners, she was the kind of woman who would fight battles for her family and stand by them until the end of time. She'd proved that when he and Kelly were barely sixteen and expecting Carny. Sonya had taken them in and then helped take care of Carny so they could both go to work full-time. She'd given them every penny she had, while they saved like demons to buy their first house when Carny was five – the same three bedroom semi-detached that they still lived in now. They'd got it for a good price because it was in the same street as Sonya's house and she knew the seller, so they did an off-market deal. It had needed a total renovation, but they'd done the work as they could afford it, with Sonya pitching in with practical help, money and childcare whenever she could. Over the years since then, they'd repaid her, but Scott would always be grateful that she did everything she could to bail them out and help them when it mattered. He just hoped she'd support him when she found out his plans.

The three of them walked the two hundred metres along the street to his own house, his mother in her finery of a pink dress and matching coat, complete with the kind of hat he'd only seen on royalty. She was a vision of class and elegance, until the eyes reached her feet and were confronted with the sight of her furry slippers. Her shoes were in her bag, ready to put on at the last minute when they got to the garden party.

Scott used his key to open the front door and they went straight down the hall to the kitchen. He'd just fitted it last year. They'd decided to skip their usual summer holiday and spend the money on the house instead. Much as he felt like a complete dick for admitting it to himself, even back then, a year ago, he hadn't wanted to spend two weeks away pretending to be the perfect husband, when Carny was going in to her final year of college and he'd already started thinking that his opportunity to leave was on the horizon.

'Morning all,' he greeted the welcome party in the kitchen.

Carny was at the kitchen table chatting to Rick, already dressed for the party, wearing a fifties-style red dress, with a shawl neck and a flared skirt. She'd familiarised him with that description when she'd first put it on to show him. She'd also taught him the terms 'bloody great big fascinator', 'killer heels', 'hair like Kim Kardashian after two hours in the salon' and 'make-up that was contoured like a pro', when describing the rest of her ensemble for today. Looking at her now, he could see she'd absolutely pulled that all off perfectly.

Next to her, Rick was in black trousers and a black shirt, his signature look when he was out of his chef's whites. He'd been around for so long that, just like Carson, Scott thought of him as part of the family – the errant brother who was wild as a teenager, went off the rails in his twenties, and then married a good woman and sorted his life out. The one thing he'd always respected was Rick's career. There was no denying his reputation for being explosive and hot-headed, but even when he was winding down after a long day in the kitchen by blowing every penny of his money at the casino at 3 a.m., tanked up on Scotch, he'd still got up at the crack of dawn to get back to work in his restaurant. Rick had achieved so much, despite being wild and irresponsible for a large chunk of his life. Scott could only imagine what he'd have been able to achieve if he'd been sober for those years.

Carny's cheeky face was the first one to respond with a huge grin. 'Dad! Oh, thank God. I was calling the whole thing off if you didn't show.'

In life, his daughter may be short on conservative clothing

and discerning behaviour, but she'd never be short on sarcasm. And that would only ever be a good thing.

'As if I'd miss it,' Scott fired back, living up to their usual, affectionate verbal sparring. 'I mean, I would if I'd had a better offer, but you're the only option I had today.'

Carny was still laughing when his mum made a beeline for Rick.

'Hello, love, how are you?' Sonya boomed, following it up with a huge hug. The handsome, wayward chef was a bit of a Glasgow legend and Sonya loved taking her pals along to his restaurant.

'Uncle Carson!' Carny bellowed, getting up and throwing her arms around him. When she finally released him, she took a step back, glanced at Rick, then returned her gaze to Carson and groaned. 'Oh bollocks, I've spent my whole life telling both of you that you're my favourite uncle, and now you're both in the same room. I'm going to have to choose. The one who offers the most money gets the title.'

Scott's laughter almost made him spill the coffee he was pouring into his mug. In some ways, Carny had aspects of Kelly's personality – her practicality, her soft side – but when it came to her sense of humour, she was absolutely a chip off his mother's sharp, sarcastic block.

Kelly was going to be lost without Carny's funny, chatty presence around the house. And now, he was bailing on his wife too. The thought sent a wave of nausea surging up to his throat. Christ, how could he tell them? Every time his mind started to consider their reaction, he'd just stuck his head in the sand and blocked it out. He was going to have to face it pretty soon. More nausea.

Carny was all about... what was it they called it? Yolo. You only live once. So maybe she'd understand his need to chase his dream. Although, Kelly and Carny were so close, she'd be furious with Scott for hurting her mother. And Kelly would be devastated. Or would she? Things had been off with them for so long that maybe she'd be glad of the release. Or was he just telling himself that to assuage the guilt?

He was so deep in thought he almost jumped when Kelly and Sabrina came into the room. Sabrina gave him a quick hug and hello, then headed towards the fridge.

'Hi, babe,' Kelly greeted him, and he couldn't miss how gorgeous she was in a sharp cream trouser suit that he knew would turn heads. She'd always been a stunner. Full disclosure, it was why he'd fallen for her when they were kids. God, how naïve they'd been, but what else did they know at fifteen? They had no concept of character or compatibility, just raw attraction that they interpreted as love. Maybe it was, in a way. He'd definitely fallen for her personality pretty soon afterwards, and they had to have been compatible to last this long. Even now, he still felt like he loved her. Just not enough to stay.

She stretched up to kiss him and he saw that although her hair and make-up were done to perfection, she looked tired and there was definitely some tension in her eyes. Scott wasn't too surprised. Letting go of Carny was going to be difficult for them all.

'Hey, honey,' he said, giving his wife a peck on the lips. 'I'll get some drinks organised. What can I get you?'

'Just a coffee, thanks.'

'You don't want a glass of wine before we go? My mother's already on the gin. She'll be doing a conga by the time the buffet is served.'

His mum broke off from flirting with Rick. 'Scott Bassett, you're not too old for a bollocking, you know. You don't want to get on my bad side.'

Scott's laughter was just a little bit hollow. Once again, he had the sinking thought that everything he was planning to do would put him well and truly on his mother's bad side. She loved Kelly, and had treated her like a daughter since the day they'd broken the news that she was pregnant. This was going to tear bits off her heart.

'You tell him, Sonya,' Kelly interjected, laughing, as she stole his coffee mug from him. They both took it black, no sugar. Surprisingly, she took one sip, then wrinkled her nose and gave it back. 'Think I'll have tea instead. Hey, Carson, how are you?'

Carson, who'd been standing over at the fridge chatting to Sabrina, came over to give Kelly a kiss on the cheek. 'I'm good,' Carson told her. 'You look great.'

On any other day, Scott would have been oblivious to weird vibes, but he couldn't miss the way Carson avoided eye contact with Kelly when he greeted her. Shit. If she sensed something was off, she'd want to know what was going on. He knew he'd made a mistake telling Carson so early in the day. His mate was great, but he was hopeless in situations like this. Scott should have known that he wouldn't be able to look Kelly in the eye, knowing what was about to happen.

Just a few more hours. They just had to get through the day, then they could sit down and talk properly, he could explain what he'd done and pray that she would understand. It was for her sake too. She should be with someone who adored her, who would make her truly happy and treat her like the special woman she was. He made a mental note to repeat that thought when he spoke to her.

Thankfully, the weird moment between Kelly and Carson was cut short by the ring of the doorbell. Scott was just about to go and answer it when, 'I'll get it,' Kelly chirped. He let her. Anything to keep a bit of distance between her and Carson.

Carny came to his side and wrapped her arms around his waist, snuggling in for a hug. 'How are you doing, Dad? Have you booked a therapist for the separation anxiety you're going to have tomorrow?'

If only she knew.

'He's on speed dial,' Scott shot back, laughing. Breaking the news to his daughter wouldn't be easy either. He was hoping that Kelly would come down to London with him and they could tell Carny face to face, assure her that they were still going to be a family. That would never change. They just needed love and honesty.

'Scott?' Kelly's voice behind him sounded strange, quizzical.

As he turned to face her, she took another step towards him from the door and it was only then he saw that she was holding a large brown envelope, her face a mask of confusion.

She glanced down at the envelope again, then back at him. This time, when he followed her gaze, he saw that the envelope was open and a few sheets of paper were sticking out.

'I opened this before I realised it was for you,' she told him. Not that it mattered. They'd never had an issue with opening each other's mail.

'What is it?' he asked, still unconcerned. Nosiness and curiosity had now spread and everyone else had stopped their conversations and were waiting too.

'It's... it's...' She gazed down again, as if checking that she wasn't mistaken.

He did too, and that's when he spotted the name of his company at the top of the covering letter. Shit. Shit. Shit. He knew exactly what it was.

'It's a letter from your work,' Kelly said, a challenge in her voice and in the blaze of her eyes.

Oh No. No. No. No.

This could only be one thing. HR had told him they'd forward the paperwork to him, but he'd assumed it would be via email or their online portal. Who even used normal mail any more?

'Kelly, I—'

There was no stopping her. 'And I'm no lawyer, but I'm pretty sure it's documentation laying out the terms of your redundancy. The one it says that you've already agreed to. Something you want to tell me?'

What had he been thinking, just a few moments before? Something about how they'd be fine as long as they had honesty? He had a pretty strong feeling that he was going to find out sooner than expected how that was going to work out for him.

8

HARRIET

Harriet wondered if this was the sort of nightmare that made Jenny call out in her sleep.

For years, she'd blocked the memories from her mind, yet now here she was, on a bright ward on a sunny summer morning, eyes closed and watching it play out again like a movie in her mind.

Her son, Leo, had been such a handsome young man. It was immodest to say, but he'd absolutely taken after her side of the family. Harriet's father had been a Gurkha in the British army and had come to the UK at the start of WW2 for a joint training course in the Cairngorms. Her mum had been in the land army, and they'd met on a base, fallen madly in love and married within weeks. Leo looked a lot like him. Just like Harriet, he'd had an unusual mix of her father's Nepalese colouring, his chiselled cheekbones and full lips, and her Scottish mother's piercing green eyes. If Dennis's genes had made an impact, it was in his height and in the stubborn single-mindedness that could be both a blessing and – in the case of her husband, but not her son – completely bloody infuriating to live with.

That said, she'd loved Dennis dearly throughout their lives together. It was difficult to say why – on the face of it their personalities were so different. Harriet was far more outgoing, Dennis an introvert, but in the way that opposites attract and different qualities balance each other out, they'd just worked.

They'd met on the first day of her first ever job, when she went to work as a junior typist in an accountancy firm. Dennis had been her supervisor, and she'd been attracted to his quick mind and his calm authority, his absolute surety and confidence in his decisions. Her father had been the same way, so it was all she'd known. Dad had made the decisions in their family, and her mum adored him, so – old fashioned as it was – Harriet felt an ease and a comfort in Dennis's strength and his firm resolve because she knew that everything he did and said was, in his mind, his way of showing his love.

However, the characteristics that made him a great boss hadn't always been so effective in their personal lives. Harriet was always happy to go along with Dennis's ways – it was just the way of things back then and she hadn't questioned it – but their son hadn't always shared her quiet acquiescence. Leo didn't see that his dad's authoritative manner came from a place of care and protection. As a teenager, he'd challenged his father, announcing that he wanted to leave school when he was eighteen, to go travelling, that backpacking thing that the young ones did. Dennis had put his foot down, said no, told him it was far too dangerous. Instead, Leo had gone to work for Dennis's brother, Jonathan, as an apprentice electrician. He'd loved the work, loved the freedom, and even though it was only an apprentice's rate, he loved the money he was bringing in. The only thing he didn't love was that Dennis still had a say over his life. 'My house, my rules,' Dennis, never one to shout, would say with a quiet finality that couldn't be challenged.

'It's like living with a dictator,' Leo would moan to her when Dennis was out of earshot, only half kidding.

It was inevitable that Leo would rebel. The only surprise was that he didn't do it until he was twenty-five. By that time, he was fully qualified, earning a decent wage and saving for a flat. It had been a choice of saving for a car or his own place. He could always use their car if he needed it, so he'd prioritised the deposit for his first property. 'Another six months, Mum,' he'd told her. 'Another five months.' 'Another four.' 'I reckon January, Mum,' he'd announced that December, and when he'd said it, her heart had cracked. She would miss him desperately. Dennis wasn't much of a talker, preferring to read after dinner, or perhaps watch a bit of *Panorama* or the nine o'clock news. Harriet would usually sit in the kitchen, watching her soaps on the tiny portable TV with the circular aerial that was propped beside the fridge, then she'd go into the living room and sit beside her husband, and sometimes they'd hold hands across the sofa as they read.

No, he wasn't an easy man, but she'd loved him and he'd loved her too, in his own way. It was a way that worked for them both, even if she did have to run interference with Leo, to keep the peace between a father who was too strict and overprotective, and a son who was a grown man and desperate to break out on his own.

She had no doubt Leo's countdown to moving out had been hastened by the girlfriend he was seeing back then. After a couple of months, he'd announced, 'You'll love her, Mum. I'll bring her home at some point, but I don't want to terrify her by meeting the old man too soon.' He'd said it in a light-hearted way, but Harriet knew there was a grain of truth there. Dennis wasn't keen on meeting new people and no doubt he'd barely say a word to the girl when they met her. It was understandable that Leo wasn't keen to bring her home. Besides, they were young things –

they were too busy out enjoying themselves to meet parents, and quite right too.

Months later, the girlfriend still hadn't been introduced, but Leo was full of plans. One night, a week before Christmas, he came into the kitchen, bright eyed and happy. 'I'm going to take Mandy to see the Christmas lights at George Square tonight,' he'd told Harriet. 'I've been promising her all week, and she's going home to her parents in Edinburgh for Christmas, so this is the last chance we'll have to go. I just need to see Dad about borrowing the car.'

Dennis was in the other room with his brother Jonathan, the two of them having a pint and playing cards. Jonathan's wife, Anthea, her closest friend all their days, would usually come over too, but she'd gone into town with her daughter, Meredith, to catch the late-night Christmas shopping opening at C&A.

Harriet had turned down the TV in the kitchen, so she could hear the discussion, pretty certain that she already knew how it would play out. It had been snowing all day, and then the temperatures had dropped again, freezing the slush that was already on the ground.

'Dad, can I borrow the car? I just want to pop into Glasgow for a couple of hours,' she'd heard Leo say.

Dennis's response had been swift and decisive. 'Son, it's freezing out there. The roads will be treacherous. Just leave it for tonight.'

'Oh, come on, Dad, it's important. I'll be fine. The gritters will have been out already and the roads will be clear by now.' The drive to Glasgow would take about twenty-five minutes from their home in Weirbridge, a good ten minutes on country roads to get to the motorway, then another fifteen minutes into the city.

'Is it no' time you loosened the strings, Dennis. He's a grown man, for God's sake.' That came from Jonathan, who was a couple of beers down and always happy to stand up to his older brother, especially when he was losing to him at cards.

Dennis didn't waver, didn't raise his voice. 'The roads are too dangerous,' he'd repeated. 'Now play your hand and don't be interfering.'

'Dad, come on…' Leo had begged.

Dennis had laid down his final word. 'I said no. It's not a discussion.'

Sighing, Harriet had closed her eyes tight shut, then opened them and headed to the fridge. Maybe some tinned salmon sandwiches and a bit of Swiss roll would put that lot in a better mood.

A banging noise, like a hand slamming on a table, made her stop dead.

'Jesus Christ, Dennis, he'll be fine.' Another noise now. The clinking of metal. Keys. 'Here you go, pal, take my car,' she heard Jonathan say. 'I'm going to get a taxi home tonight anyway. I'll need a few more beers to get through a night with this one.'

It was obvious he was referring to Dennis, pressing his buttons as usual. Typical brother stuff. She was about to go in and calm things down when Leo flew past her, kissed her on the cheek on the way to the door. 'I'm away before he gets out that chair and comes after me,' he'd said, his laugh full of mischief. 'See you soon, Mum. I won't be long.'

He was at the door by the time she'd shouted, 'Drive safe. Love you, son.'

'Love you too, Mum,' he'd replied from halfway down the path.

Abandoning plans to intervene, Harriet had turned the TV back up to drown out the sound of the two men next door arguing, and then gone about making those salmon sandwiches.

The brothers had eventually stopped bickering, but she'd stayed in the kitchen for the next few hours, quite happy to let them get on with it and do her own thing. She'd finished watching her soaps, then switched to an episode of *Taggart*, getting her knitting out and carrying on with the sweater she was making for Dennis's Christmas present, while she made at least three wrong guesses on the trail of the on-screen murderer. A talk show came on next and she'd happily watched that too.

The titles had just rolled when the front doorbell rang. She got there first, opened it to see two police officers standing there.

'Mrs Bassett?'

Bewilderment had turned quickly to fear, which twisted her vocal cords so tight, she could barely get out a strangled 'yes'.

'Can we come in?' the older of the two officers, a man in his fifties with a kind face, had asked her. The furrow of his brow and the sympathy in his voice told her that something was wrong. Terribly, terribly wrong.

'No,' she'd said. Later she would think that was incredibly rude, but in that moment, something in her head was screaming that if she didn't let them in, then they couldn't tell her bad news. And if they couldn't tell her bad news, then it hadn't happened.

'Come in, officers. Harriet, stand back and let the men come through.' Dennis was behind her, in the living room doorway, only the slight tremor to his words giving a clue that he had a bad feeling about this too.

The policemen waited until they were in the living room, sitting on the sofa next to each other, Dennis in his usual chair, Jonathan over at the dining table, face ashen.

'Earlier tonight we attended the scene of an accident, on the back road, just outside town. A car skidded off the road, then rolled down the hill to the gulley at the bottom. We went to the home of the car owner, but no one was there.'

Jonathan didn't speak up, paralysed with fear. By now, they all knew what was coming.

'The driver of the vehicle had a wallet in his pocket, and his driving licence was inside. Leo Bassett. Listed at this address.'

Harriet was making a sound now that she didn't recognise. A whimper. Like a wounded animal.

'That's my son,' Dennis had said quietly. 'Is he okay? Has he been taken to hospital?'

The older cop took the lead again. 'Mr Bassett, I'm so very sorry to tell you this, but your son passed away at the scene.'

To this day, Harriet had no memory of what happened next. It was a blur of pain as she hit the floor to the sound of wails, which she was sure were hers.

She found out later that Dennis had to be pulled off his brother by the officers, who probably had no idea why he was screaming, 'You killed my boy. You bastard, you killed my boy,' to a catatonic Jonathan.

Eight days later, they'd buried Leo in the cold frozen ground, at a funeral attended by friends and a few mourners from Harriet's side of the family. No one from Dennis's family was allowed to come. By that time, they'd found out that the car's brakes were worn, that it had failed an MOT, and that Jonathan had decided to wait until after Christmas to get it repaired. He'd let their son drive a death trap. Dennis had never forgiven him and never spoken to his brother or his family again. He'd been absolutely adamant that she wouldn't speak to them either. Not that she'd wanted to. She was so utterly grief-stricken, she couldn't imagine ever wanting to speak to anyone again, not even her friend Anthea. She'd ignored all calls and callers, and eventually the phone and the door were still.

That night, Harriet had lost her boy and the man she married, replaced with a shell of a person who never truly recovered from the death of the son he loved. At the same time, she'd also lost her brother-in-law, her best friend, her niece and the family life Harriet had loved. Her whole world, gone.

Over the years, Harriet had wondered many times how they were, but contacting them wasn't an option, so she never had, not even twenty odd years later, when Dennis had taken his last breath.

She thought again about what Yvie had said. The other Bassetts. Could it be Jonathan and Anthea's family? Harriet tried to do some calculations. If the young woman Yvie mentioned was just graduating, she would have to be their granddaughter. Which would make her Harriet's great-niece.

Something about that thought made her smile. Did she still have family out there somewhere? Could that really be true?

Harriet opened her eyes, just as Yvie passed the end of her bed.

'You okay there, Harriet? You're a bit flushed. Shall I take a blanket off your bed?'

Harriet shook her head, her brain racing with connections, then decisions. Maybe it wasn't too late to lay ghosts to rest. Maybe if she wasn't going to be around much longer, she should use this time to forgive the conflicts from the past. 'Yvie, did you mean it when you said I could tag along to that event with you this afternoon?'

Yvie nodded. 'Of course. It probably breaks several hospital policies, but as long as you're fine with it, I'd love you to come. Verity isn't exactly a laugh a minute, so at least we'll have a giggle.'

'Well, then...' Harriet could hear the words coming out of her mouth, but she just couldn't believe that she was saying them. 'I think I'd very much like to come.'

NOON – 2 P.M.

9

MAISIE

Sissy's fourth text in an hour made Maisie's phone ping.

Sissy to Maisie: Is it all under control? Did you remember the itinerary and memorise all the details on the event plan?

Maisie fired off a quick reply to Sissy: Dear Control Freak, you asked me that ten minutes ago and the answers are still yes, yes, and yes. How are you doing? Has the business end kicked into action yet?

Sissy to Maisie: I'm only a couple of centimetres dilated. They've said it could be hours yet. Contemplating squeezing Cole's nuts so he can share the pain.

Maisie to Sissy: I think that's what got you into this situation in the first place.

A laughing face emoji came back and Maisie replied with a kissing face, then locked her phone.

Sissy's woes and setting up the buffet had both been much-needed distractions. It was difficult to wallow in heartbreak when her best friend was discussing her husband's testicles, while Janice was thundering towards her armed with a tray of coronation chicken canapés. Maisie hadn't had to seek instructions as to the actual location of the buffet area for the outdoor event. When she was planning her wedding, she'd been delighted by the beautiful old pavilion, situated on the lawn, just a few metres away from the edge of the loch. Built in Victorian times and restored to its former glory, it had been enhanced with concealed fridges, food warmers and a prep area.

At one end, a couple of the regular agency staff – mostly students on summer break – were setting up the bar, while, at the food end of the pavilion, Maisie was adding the final touches to the trays of gastronomic delights with Janice and Jane. It was quite a spread and they had, as always, laid everything out with the kind of presentation that made the whole thing look far more expensive than it actually was. Not that the organisers had scrimped on the food. There were salmon and prawn blinis. Chicken in many different forms: satay skewers, Cajun wraps, wings in hot spicy sauce. There were thin-cut slices of roast beef and beautifully presented bowls of pasta and salad. There were gluten-free options, vegan delights and in the centre was a six-foot-long slate packed with fruits, desserts and sorbets, preserved in ice troughs and arranged to look almost like art. Maisie knew her presentation probably didn't have Sissy's expert touch, but she had to admit, it was a pretty good attempt.

Out on the lawn, the serving staff were showing no sign of wilting under the midday sunshine, working swiftly to furnish the dozen or so large round white metal tables with condiments and cutlery. The guests were arriving at 2 p.m., and they were pretty much organised and ready to go with an hour to spare.

Maisie was on the verge of congratulating herself when the

phone in the back pocket of her yellow capri pants vibrated again. Pulling it out, she yelped and stabbed at the green button.

Sissy's face filled the screen, then widened out as Cole came into the shot, letting Maisie see that not only was he holding the phone, but Sissy still appeared to have a camelesque hump under her T-shirt.

'This baby doesn't want to come out,' Sissy wailed. 'It would be so much fucking easier if it was a zip-type operation. Unzip. Baby out. Zip up until the next time. I'll also need one for my hoo-ha because THERE'S ABSOLUTELY NO WAY ANYTHING IS EVER GOING IN THERE AGAIN!' she thundered, staring murderously at Cole. Maisie couldn't be sure, but the phone seemed to be trembling in his hand. Sissy turned back to the camera, 'Anyway, you've got thirty seconds until the next contraction to tell me again that everything's okay and you're not destroying my company's reputation.'

'Everything is okay and I'm not destroying your reputation,' Maisie assured her, as commanded. 'Please don't worry, I've got this. I feel helpless though. I should be there holding your hand and giving you some moral support. Or eying up cute doctors and trying to suck your gas and air.'

Sissy emitted something that was between a snort and a wince. 'Oh God, don't make me laugh. It cuts right across my martyrdom. Need to go, I'm... Aaaaaargh!!!'

The screen went black and before she could pull herself together, Maisie felt a wave of deflation, or maybe it was just that last night's margaritas had finally left her system and her emotions were coming out of their alcohol-induced fog.

She checked her watch. Forty-five minutes before the first guests would begin to arrive. There was to be a short welcoming speech, then food, then bar service for the rest of the afternoon and into early evening. After clearing up, she'd be lucky if she was away from here by eight o'clock tonight.

'Jane, do you want to take a break just now, before the crowds descend? We're just about ready here and I'll finish up and keep an eye on everything.'

'Sure thing. You good for a break, Janice?'

Janice put a lid on a tagine of Moroccan lamb and nodded. 'Thought you'd never ask. Can I just check though,' she addressed Maisie, 'on a scale of one to ten, how likely is it you'll fire us if we slip into the spa up at the main house and don't make it back for a couple of hours?'

'Janice, I love you, but I'm hot, sweaty, I smell of prawn cocktails, my best friend, aka our boss, is in labour and the last time I was here I was wearing a white dress and about to discover that my fiancé had done a bunk. It's fair to say I'm a woman on the edge and the chances of me losing it if I find you sipping Prosecco in a jacuzzi are pretty high.'

Janice gave this due consideration, then shrugged. 'Quick ciggy and a cuppa in the van then?' she deadpanned to Jane, who, like Maisie, was trying to keep a straight face. 'Perfect. You know those jacuzzis play havoc with your varicose veins anyway.'

With that, the two of them wandered off in the direction of the car park.

Maisie checked on the bar staff, who were unpacked, stocked up and ready to go too, then fired off a text to her sister. Hope would still be on shift at the hospital, but she usually took a break around now. If not, she'd get it when she'd finished her twelve-hour shift. Junior doctors were supposed to have regulated hours now, but given the overtime that Hope put in, the policy clearly wasn't working.

Maisie: Hey. Sissy in labour. I'm covering her event. At Lomond

House. Please bring home drugs that will make me forget all trauma.
Or make me a size 10. Love ya xx

She pressed send, and almost immediately a text popped into
her inbox. Hope had thumbs like speeding bullets.

Hope: Oh crap, that's a nightmare. You okay? Can't bring drugs as
will lose job and end up destitute. Will Prosecco do? Try not to crum-
ble. You've got this. Sending hugs. Love ya back. X

Maisie had a mental image of Hope's beautiful face rear-
ranging into a frown. Despite being completely different in every
way, and an age difference of a couple of years, they had been
close their whole lives, and especially since they'd moved in
together a few years ago. Even if Hope wasn't her sister, she'd still
be her favourite person.

Maisie: Prosecco acceptable. Not crumbling yet but avoiding all men
in case one accidentally proposes then stands me up. Apparently, it's
a thing they do. See you later xxx PS is it definitely a hard no on the
drugs?

Hope: If you need me, call immediately. I'll find a way to answer. It
was his loss. The twat. Xx

Phone back in her pocket, Maisie thought about joining
Janice and Jane in the van, then changed her mind when her gaze
went to the rock down at the water's edge, the one she'd been
sitting on when Nathan had proposed.

When she'd arrived here earlier, she'd told herself that she
would just avoid looking at the spot. Now, though, her feet began
to move, as if some invisible, sadistic force was pulling her

towards it and any resistance was futile. When she reached it, she felt the warm breeze coming off the water. The sun was high in the sky, yet she shivered as she remembered the last time she was here.

She couldn't say whose idea it had been to get married at exactly the same spot where they'd got engaged. It was probably hers. Nathan's predominant role in planning the wedding had been to put the soundtrack together for the ceremony and the evening reception.

The irony was, she'd have been happy to wait, but it was Nathan who'd pushed to go ahead with the wedding. He'd moved into the flat with her and Hope, which worked well because Hope spent her whole life at the hospital anyway.

In hindsight, Maisie wondered if she was his rebound option, the one he came to after the band split up, searching for familiarity and purpose and, more than that, the security of being somewhere he could belong. He'd never been close to his family, who struggled to accept that he wasn't joining the family construction business, and had pretty much cut off all ties with them. So if he didn't have his family and he didn't have his band, then what was left? The girlfriend he'd been with for a few years before he upped and left after college. Was that it? Was she just a fall back plan? Had he even truly loved her or had his fragile performer's ego been dented and erupted in a volcano of need for something he could count on? Or was she giving him too much credit and he was actually just a traitorous dickhead?

Of course, back then, she hadn't stopped to analyse any of this, too busy with the eternal hustle of earning a living as a performer.

As always, she'd spent that year they were together alternating between several different jobs. Aside from the occasional stint helping out at the college, there had been the recurring guest spot on a Scottish soap, where she played Fatima Khan, a kickass community activist. Then there had been the three-part series in which she played Angela Orb, a heroin-addicted identity thief. And an advert for thrush cream, which no-one ever mentioned, but it did get her many furtive glances as shoppers in the middle of the supermarket realised where they'd seen her before. Running up to Christmas, there had been the panto gig – *Aladdin* – and yes, it was more realistic to have a female genie because she got shit done. And, to supplement it all, she did private one-to-one drama lessons for bored children who desperately needed a creative outlet and whose parents desperately needed a couple of hours of peace. Even though the last year and a bit had ended in personal disaster, at least her career was tracking upwards. All she needed now to get to the next level, was to land the part she'd auditioned for in the new Netflix show.

Nathan, meanwhile, had spent the time writing songs and submitting them to his rake of contacts in the industry. His band had never found huge commercial success, but they were well known in the music world and he was respected for both his voice and his lyrics. He just needed to land one big sale and his songwriting credentials would be solidified. In the meantime, he spent way too much time 'accidentally' bumping into Lewis Capaldi every time the singer was back in Scotland.

Work aside, though, they spent every moment together. They'd go for walks, they'd sunbathe in the garden. As autumn turned to winter, they'd watch movies on rainy afternoons and they'd just generally exist in their own little bubble of bliss. Christmas had come and gone in a whirlwind of 'Look behind you' and 'oh no, it isn't', and then, just after she'd taken off the pointy shoes and genie robes for the last time, Nathan had pulled her down on to his knee as she'd delivered a coffee to his writing corner in the bedroom. 'Let's get married.'

Maisie had curled her arms around his neck. 'I think we've already done this bit. Remember the whole 'gorgeous day at the loch' thing?'

His hand had snaked up her jumper, making her shriek with laughter. 'You're such a smart-arse,' he'd teased. 'But you're my smart-arse. What I meant was let's set a date. Let's plan the wedding. You. Me. Somewhere beautiful.'

It had to be The Lomond House Estate.

Sissy had provided the catering as a wedding present, and they'd kept the rest of the costs down by making everything simple. Before Maisie and Hope's adopted father had passed away, he'd left a fund for his girls' weddings and it had covered everything else.

They'd booked the ceremony for the last Sunday in April and they'd both had mental images of them standing outside, next to this stone, under a gazebo decked with fairy lights that they'd erected just for the occasion, with fifty of their closest friends and family gathered. Her mum would walk her up the aisle, her bridesmaid, Hope, would be on one side of her, and her matron of honour, seven months pregnant Sissy, on the other. They just needed a warm, spring evening, and it was, right up until Nathan sent in the clouds.

Looking back now, as she'd done every single day for the last two months, Maisie still couldn't pinpoint when the unease began. When Nathan's money ran out and they had to live off her earnings? Or when his old record company bought one of his songs for an up-and-coming star and they'd had a slightly tense celebration because it wasn't a big enough deal to lift his mood, which had become darker as the weeks had gone by?

A shout from Jane interrupted the searching of her soul. 'Maisie, that's us back, love. Janice has had two cigarettes and a chocolate éclair, so she'll probably manage a couple of hours of a sunny disposition.'

As Maisie started back towards them, she immediately brightened her face and plastered on a smile. She hadn't won that role of 'carefree, happy secretary concealing a troubling itch' in that thrush commercial for nothing. 'Excellent. I'll notify the United Nations that they can stand down a peacekeeping force,' Maisie shot back, making Jane hoot and Janice harrumph.

As she walked away from her very own stone of crap destiny, she tried not to look back to the spot where her heart had been broken. She'd turned up. She'd been there. Ready to marry the man she loved.

And that man?

He'd been somewhere else altogether.

With auspicious timing, Scott's Apple watch buzzed to signify an incoming text. A rapid glance told him it was from the HR department at his work, informing him that they'd mailed the redundancy contracts. That was absolutely no bloody help to him now, given that everyone in the room was staring at him, waiting for his reply to Kelly's question, the one that had been a challenging, *I'm no lawyer, but I'm pretty sure it's documentation laying out the terms of your redundancy. The one it says that you've already agreed to. Something you want to tell me?'*

Silence. Not a sound. Until he heard Carny break the stillness with a hushed whisper to Carson. 'Is it just me, or is this like one of those programmes on telly where someone gets caught cheating and they're trying to decide whether to hide in the wardrobe?'

Carson didn't reply, but Scott could see his friend's eyes widen with horror. Shit. His best mate was a guy who'd actually faced war zones with impeccable calm and bravery, and now he was totally giving off panic vibes and reinforcing Scott's fear that this had become a hostile situation with no obvious escape route.

'What's going on, Scott?' His mum this time, and he could swear he could actually feel his bollocks shrivelling inside him. There was only one way out of this and, no, it wasn't going to make him feel proud – he was going to have to lie.

'Look, I was going to talk to you about this,' he stammered. 'I don't know what wording they've used, but it's just an *offer* of redundancy. I haven't agreed to anything. I just asked them to put it in writing out of curiosity, you know, in case you fancied taking the lot and blowing it all on a house in the sun.'

'Nice save, Dad,' Carny said under her breath, to him this time.

Scott didn't react, keeping his eyes trained on the clear and present dangers: Kelly and his mum.

He saw Kelly's eyes narrow, as if trying to implement some Jedi mind warp shit to detect if he was telling the truth.

He took the chink of uncertainty and ran with it. 'I was just exploring options. I'll run you through it all when we get back tonight.'

Christ, he was a dick. Why hadn't he thought this through? How the hell had he thought he was going to get away with this without exploding the lives of the people around him. The offer of redundancy had just come so quickly and he'd made a snap decision, thinking entirely selfishly.

'Och, you'd be crazy to leave that job,' his mum offered. 'You're set up for life there.'

Now wasn't the time to point out that that was the problem. He'd been with the same woman for all his adult life. He'd lived in the same house for all his adult life. He'd been with the same company for all his adult life. The thought of none of that changing until he reached old age and popped his clogs filled him with absolute horror. He couldn't do it. But, right now, he couldn't argue with a mother wearing the natty combo of a large hat and furry slippers either.

'I know, Ma. I was just... you know... curious.'

He could see from Sonya's face that she wasn't convinced, not one little bit. The woman could spot a lie at a hundred metres wearing a sleep mask and a canvas hood. He also knew that she wouldn't cause a drama on Carny's big day.

'Aye, well, that's understandable I suppose. Isn't it, Kelly?' she said, her words letting him off the hook, her expression telling him this wasn't over.

Kelly didn't look too sure, but she tossed the papers on the kitchen worktop and shrugged it off. 'Okay, we'll sort it out later. I'll be... I'll be right back.'

With that, the colour drained from her face and she bolted out of the room. A second later, he heard the door close on the downstairs bathroom. Shit. He was definitely going to have to come up with something fast to get them through the day and give him time to do this properly.

Avoiding Carson's unimpressed glare, and his mother's suspicious gaze, he threw his arm around his daughter's shoulders and reached for his coffee, wishing now that he'd gone for something stronger.

The conversations started up again around the room, but Carny was saying nothing, just looking up at him expectantly.

'What?' he asked, trying his best to look innocent.

Carny kept her voice low so she couldn't be heard. 'Nothing. It's just that I'm getting a weird sense of déjà vu from the time I told you I'd had my first kiss with the nerdy boy who lived at the end of the street, when I'd actually been snogging the face off Angie Vickers and I'd already let her feel my boobs.'

He sighed. He could just about live with lying to his mum and Kelly, but not to his girl, and especially not now that she was a grown woman whose trust meant more to him than anything else.

'It's a long story, Carny. I promise I'll fill you in later. Now can we just get on with celebrating your day and leave all the serious stuff for another time?'

'Sure, Dad. But you know… if something's wrong, you should talk to Mum. She's been acting really weird lately and I think there's something up with her too. She burst into tears twice last night when we were watching a movie…'

'Was it a sad one?' Scott asked, puzzled. Kelly was not at all weepy or emotional. She was one of those people that sailed along on an even keel and avoided drama. It must have been something heart-breaking to make her…

'*Legally Blonde.*'

Shit. That couldn't be good. The dawn of the empty nest must be having an even greater effect than he thought. If that was the case then his news was going to make it so much worse. Nope, hadn't thought that through either.

'I'll go check on her now, just make sure she's okay,' he announced, guilt beginning to crush his chest.

He headed out into the hall, a long narrow space that was lined with the three guitars that were his prize possessions: an Epiphone Hummingbird Pro, a Gretsch Rancher and a Breedlove Discovery Concerto. His fourth beauty, an acoustic Fender, lived in the boot of his car so that he could head to a quiet spot and play in his lunch hour if it was a dry, music-playing kind of day. Other guys might collect football trophies or spend their spare cash on flash cars, but for Scott, his guitars were his passion and his motivation. He used to play them in the box room until Kelly had turned that into a dressing room, so he'd hung them here to remind himself, every day, that the time was coming when he could put one of them in a case and go play, just travel for a while, a guy and his guitar.

He'd tried to explain it to Kelly a few times, but she didn't get it and had absolutely no interest in the music so she didn't take his pipe dream of living in that world seriously at all. Suggestions like 'Audition for *Britain's Got Talent*' didn't help. That wasn't the point. He knew he wasn't good enough to be a star, or to bump Garth Brooks off a stage, but he just wanted the freedom to explore that life. To live in Nashville. To spend his days playing wherever he could and his nights in smoky bars, listening to other bands and singers. It was a crazy dream, but it was his, and it was so close, he could almost hear the twangs... He could also hear the dulcet tones of his mother telling him not to be so bloody daft, but he ignored that voice and concentrated on the good stuff.

The bathroom door clicked, and Kelly came out, a yelp of surprise when she almost crashed into him. He saw that she was a whole lot paler than she'd been ten minutes ago, and he could smell the strong tangy mint of mouthwash.

'Hey,' he said. 'I just came out to check on you. Are you okay? Are you sick?'

Before she could answer, Sabrina poked her head out of the kitchen door. 'Everything all right out here?'

Scott picked up something in her voice: a wariness, maybe a touch of anxiety. Damn, those redundancy papers must have upset her too.

'I'm fine, sis. I'll be back through in a minute.' The way Kelly said it made it clear that she was closing down any further discussion, so, with just a little hesitation, Sabrina backed up into the kitchen and closed the door behind her.

"Kelly?' Scott prompted again, then repeated his last question. 'Are you sick?

She shrugged him off. 'Yeah, just got a bit of a dodgy stomach. Think I've got a bug. Too much popcorn with Carny last night.'

His emotional intelligence radar had never been particularly acute, but he knew it was more than that. Had the redundancy letter caused this? Kelly had never been someone who threw up when she was stressed though. Maybe bulimia? He'd read that was an epidemic these days.

No, it wasn't that. It was something more obvious.

'I know what's wrong, Kell,' he told her, feeling like a complete arse for not paying more attention. Being some kind of idiot was becoming an all too common theme for him these days.

Her expression changed, and the two little lines between her eyebrows got deeper. 'You do?'

He wrapped his arms around her, kissed the top of her head. He didn't want to be married any more, but they'd shared more than half their lives and he could honestly say that, in a different way than Carson, she was his best friend. He'd always love her. And he hoped that, when the dust settled, they'd still be as close as they'd been since the day they met. 'I do. Sorry, I know it's obvious. Carny leaving is going to be hard. For both of us. She's the best thing we've ever done.'

He felt Kelly's breath on his chest, and then heard something that sounded like a sob.

Bugger, Carny had warned him, but he hadn't seen her cry for years and it tugged right at his heart. This whole situation must be completely overwhelming for her.

'Hey, hey,' he comforted her, ignoring the feeling of a growing damp patch on his shirt. 'It'll be okay.' He pulled back and looked down to see huge pools of tears in her eyes. What had he been thinking? He'd been so focused on how his own life would look after Carny was gone, so determined to make the changes that he'd dreamt of, that he hadn't truly thought through how Kelly would feel. He'd even managed to convince himself that she'd find someone who really loved her and wander off into the sunset.

Shame burned in his chest and something else was there too: realisation. He couldn't leave her, today or tomorrow or next week. He was going to have to stick around for a while and make sure she was okay, give them both time to process the transition in their lives and find a way forward that would cause as little pain as possible for them all. He owed her that.

He rested his chin on her head. 'Look, Kell, I know things haven't been great for a while, but I'm here for you and, one way or another, we'll get through this.' Over her shoulder, his eyes fell on the Hummingbird guitar and he exhaled slowly. 'We'll get there. It might take a while, but we'll get there.'

'I know,' she murmured, loosening her grip and lifting her chin again. 'But, Scott, I need to talk to you. Just for a few minutes. Can we go upstairs and...'

Panic exploded in his gut. He thought he'd got away with the explanation about the redundancy papers, but obviously she wanted to discuss it further. Not now. This wasn't the time. He just needed to get out of this...

'Are you two okay?' Like the bro-code cavalry, Carson had come through the door from the kitchen at exactly the right time, and now he was taking in Kelly's tears and Scott's anguish, and Scott could see he was trying to compute what this meant. The potential for a wrong word or a misdirected gesture of sympathy was huge.

'Carson! Yeah, we're fine. Just... you know. Anyway. Let's... Let's...'

It was Kelly who took control, wiping her face and regaining her voice. To Scott's astonishment, it was as if Carson's presence had snapped her out of her gloom and turned off her tears. 'Let's round everyone up and get going, Carson,' she said, with eerie calm. 'I'm just going to fix my make-up and I'll be back down in five minutes.'

With that, she jogged upstairs and he heard the bedroom door closing behind her.

'What the hell happened? Did you tell her?' Carson demanded, his voice low so that he couldn't be overheard by anyone in the next room.

Scott shook his head wearily. 'No, mate. Man, what have I done? I don't know what the fuck I'm doing. It's just... I don't know if I can go through with it.' He leaned back, resisting the urge to bang his head off the wall.

Nope, he had to get it together. This was ridiculous.

He exhaled, shook off the mood. 'Come on, let's go. I'll think about it later. And Carson,' he said, putting his hand on his pal's shoulder as they headed back to the kitchen, 'thanks for the save, pal. For someone who's eternally single, you did good there. You know, mate, I think you'd be so much better than me at this marriage stuff,' he joked, trying to get some upbeat positivity into the day. 'If you ever want to trade places, I'm down for it.'

He was kidding, of course. He just didn't think to wonder why Carson wasn't laughing.

11

KELLY

The atmosphere in the car during the forty-minute drive to Lomond House had only been lifted above the tension of, say, a hostage situation, by Carny's cheery chat.

'I still can't believe we got this venue free,' Carny told them.

'How did you wangle that then?' Scott asked, and Kelly could sense that he was trying his best to be upbeat. He'd seemed a bit rattled by that letter earlier, but she was sure that, like her, he was just wired at the prospect of Carny leaving tomorrow. There was no way Scott would leave that job – he'd worked too hard for too long to quit. She dismissed all thought of it as Carny went on, 'It's owned by Letisha's aunt. Remember Letisha? She's the absolute stunner who played Diana Ross in the "Music Through The Decades" show. We had a thing for five minutes last year, until she ditched me for Mariah Carey. If only Diandra, who played Whitney Houston, was gay, we could have hooked up and our double dates would have had the best tunes ever. Anyway, Letisha's aunt got us a great deal with the caterer, and she said we could have this venue free, as long as we allowed her to film the performances and use them for their marketing. They're trying to attract more outdoor concerts and stage shows. We've brought a scaled-down version of my "Music Through The Decades" set, and we're doing highlights from the show. Between the upmarket location, the performances and the food, we knew we could charge at least thirty quid a ticket, and the bar should make good money too. Our fundraising target is ten grand, so feel free to get wellied, Dad. You too, Uncle Carson. Mum says she's driving home, so I'm counting on you both to boost our funds.'

Kelly tuned out and left them to it. Scott was asking the questions, genuinely interested in every detail of their daughter's plans for her first couple of weeks in London. Sometimes Kelly wondered if he was living vicariously through Carny and her new life of travel and theatre. Scott was definitely the one who'd passed on the wanderlust and the love of the entertainment world. He was the one who'd organised countless trips to theatres, to concerts, to shows, to any kind of performances that he thought they'd enjoy. It was definitely his thing.

There had been times over the years, usually after a few beers, when he'd talk wistfully about how he would have loved to have travelled and tried to make a go of it as a musician. He had a good voice and she had to admit he'd been pretty sexy when he'd played in a country band in high school. It wasn't her kind of music, but she'd been in thrall of his passion for getting up there and singing his heart out.

In the first year they were together, skint, with a toddler to take care of, both of them grafting in new full-time jobs, he'd left the band and his musical interlude had become nothing more than an occasional murmur of fond reminiscence. Over the last couple of years, he'd talked about it more, but, of course, he always followed that up by saying that he'd never have swapped their lives and their family for a pipe dream, so she was pretty sure it was just a bit of midlife shoulda, woulda, coulda.

Wasn't that kind of nostalgic 'what if' something that she knew all about?

Beside her in the back seat, Carson hadn't said a word in the last half-hour. When they were piling into the two cars, she should have paid more attention, but she was so drained from the conversation with Scott and distracted by saying goodbye to Sonya, Sabrina and Rick, who had gone ahead in Sabrina's Range Rover to pick up Sonya's father on the way. At eighty-one, Carny's great-grandad was still relatively strong and sprightly, and they were lucky to have him with them.

Not so lucky, however, on the resulting car seat allocations. Scott was driving, with Carny sitting next to him in the passenger seat, winning shotgun position because in his Golf hatchback there was more room up front for – in Carny's words – her bloody great big fascinator. That left Kelly, at exceptionally close quarters in the back with a six foot three, Royal Airforce flight engineer who, coincidentally, had the width of those blokes on the volleyball court in *Top Gun*, and who was emanating awkward tension from every pore.

She'd hoped to avoid this. Suggesting that Scott and Carson stay with Sonya last night had been a deliberate ploy to keep some distance, not between her and Scott, but between her and the guy whose thigh was now pressed up against hers.

'Mum. Mum!' Carny interrupted her thoughts, although it took Kelly a moment to catch up.

'Sorry, sweetheart, I was miles away.' Carson's hand was on the seat between them now, so close she could touch it.

'I was just saying, maybe you and Dad and Gran can come down to London for Christmas? If the show is still running, I'll need to work over Christmas and that means I'll be on my own and I'll have to go home at night and wallow in loneliness and self-pity.'

Kelly couldn't help but laugh. 'I think the chances of you wallowing are pretty low, but we couldn't take the risk. Of course we'll come.' As the words left her mouth, she gave an almost inaudible, involuntary gasp. Christmas. If her timings were correct – and she was positive they were – then she was around two and a half months pregnant now. Probably as a result of her surgery twenty years ago, her periods had always been sparse and irregular, but the fact that she'd only had one opportunity to conceive made her certain of her dates. If she was two and a half months gone, that meant the baby would be due at the end of January.

She let that sink in for a moment. Christmas. Eight months pregnant. And only a few weeks later they'd have a new baby. A whole new start. It was going to turn their lives upside down and she still had no idea how Scott would react. But then... hadn't he shown earlier how much he cared about his family? Even though things hadn't been great between them for a while, he'd still held her when she'd been upset and told her everything was going to be okay. At that moment, she'd felt like the worst person alive. He wouldn't have been so lovely if he knew what she'd done.

Carny turned around in her seat again, almost losing the fascinator out of the open window. 'Will you come too, Uncle Carson?'

Kelly's stomach clenched and she had a real fear that she was about to vomit in the back of Scott's Volkswagen Golf.

Carson didn't miss a beat. 'I'm not sure if I'll have leave. There's a good chance I'll be deployed overseas again by then.' Relief. He'd handled it well. Right up until he added, 'But if I'm around, then sure, of course I'll come.'

Kelly closed her eyes, trying to fight down the nausea that was bubbling away in her gut right next to the guilt.

No amount of purging was going to rid her of that.

Nor would it rid her of the mental image of Carson's face that night.

Despite trying to keep the memory at bay, it flooded into her mind in technicolour. Ten weeks ago. Middle of April. Carson had called early in the morning to say that he was going to be travelling from Lossiemouth, the RAF base in the North of Scotland, to RAF Cranwell, where his regiment was currently based. He had a free night on the way down and, like countless times in their lives, he was going to stop in to see his mates. Plural. Scott and Kelly. He may have been Scott's oldest friend, more like a brother to him, but Kelly had known him since they were kids too.

He'd arrived around lunchtime, and Kelly's first thought was that it was the happiest she'd seen Scott in months – 2020 had been a tough one, and it had spilled over into the first few months of 2021. He'd been zoned out. Pissed off. For a while she'd even wondered if he was depressed. Their intimacy was gone – he'd barely touched her all year and, the truth was, she wasn't that bothered. Their relationship had been stale for a while, just one of those low points in the Ferris wheel of marriage. It would get better again. It always did.

Due to a deployment in Cyprus, it had been a year since Carson Cook had walked through their front door, so, naturally, that merited a celebration. Carny had plans to stay over with a girlfriend that night, but she'd joined them for dinner, a riotous feast of Chinese food and wine, with the entertainment provided by Carny's insistence, egged on by Kelly and Scott, in setting Carson up with a dating profile.

'Uncle Carson, you're a catch!' she'd proclaimed, before taking his phone and demanding he unlock it so she could 'spread the word'.

'She's so right,' Kelly had agreed, feeling the delicious warmth of a couple of glasses of Prosecco. It had been so long since they'd had one of these totally relaxed nights with great food, loads of laughs, and one of their best mates, that she was a bit giddy.

They'd howled over suggestions for Carson's profile. 'Awkward, bit of a tit, hopeless with women,' was Scott's suggestion, spluttered out between gales of laughter.

'Dad, you're about to be banned from the table. And not just because you're wearing those ridiculous cowboy boots and making us listen to Tim McGraw's Greatest Hits.'

That had set them off again.

Kelly, meanwhile, was trying to focus on the task in hand. 'I think you should say, "Kind, humble guy, great sense of humour, impressive career, good heart".'

'You missed out "banging body",' Carny had remarked, typing furiously with her thumbs.

Carson had put his head in his hands, creased with laughter, as Scott yelped in mock outrage, 'Carny! That is just waaaaaay wrong!'

'Why? Dad, I'm a lesbian, but I'm not blind.'

To more cackles and comically heated disputes, they'd finished setting up the profile and Carny gave Carson a tutorial on how to use it. Kelly could see he was just going along with it for the fun of it and that there was no way he'd use it. She knew he'd had a few relationships over the years, but none of them had gone the distance, most of them burning out because his job meant he was never in one place for long. He liked it that way, he'd told her a dozen times. He just wasn't the kind of guy who needed commitment or the other things that came with a serious relationship.

After Carny had left to go and meet her girlfriend, Carson had tossed the phone to one side as Scott disappeared for a few seconds and came back with two guitars. Par for the course. This inevitably happened when they got together and alcohol was involved.

'Here we go,' Carson had whistled. 'My annual opportunity to look crap next to you,' he'd teased Scott. They'd both taught themselves as teenagers, but only Scott had continued to play regularly. Still, Carson could strum a tune, especially if it was one from the past.

They'd moved to the sofas and Kelly had poured more wine, popped open more beers and sat on the floor, her back against the couch her husband was sitting on, across from his closest friend, and sang along as they'd relived their favourite songs of their teenage years. It had been one of the best times of Kelly's life, when they were still crazy in love, and they would put Carny to bed and sit up late, no money to go out, already living adult lives, consumed with optimism that they'd make it work. Back then, she'd worshipped her husband, too young and naïve to realise that it wasn't a straightforward process, that you could love more than one person, that you could realise after the fact that you'd let the love of your life go and it was too late to get them back. As she sang along on that night back in April, as a thirty-eight-year-old woman who had learned lessons and realised truths, she now knew that to be true.

Scott had been the first one to crash out. Drunk, tired and happy, he'd called it a night and headed up to bed in the early hours. Once upon a time, they'd always gone to bed together. That hadn't happened for a long time by then.

Carson was lying on the couch, hands behind his head, his white T-shirt a stark contrast against the tanned skin of his arms. Kelly should have followed Scott's lead and followed him up to bed. She didn't.

'Tell me, then, I want to know,' she'd asked him playfully. 'How come you've never fallen in love, Carson Cook?'

He'd had many beers, and they'd obviously taken him to the tipping point where his bravery was higher than his defences. He'd shrugged, his eyes half closed, sleepy, 'Maybe all the good ones are already taken.'

There was something in the way he said it, something that made her put her wine glass on the coffee table between them. In one movement, she was kneeling on the floor beside him, so close she could see his chest rising and falling, hear his breath, feel a pull towards him that she couldn't stop, suddenly aware that it had been a long, long time since Scott had touched her, and even longer than that since she'd felt this turned on.

It was almost like an out-of-body experience. She was there, but she was watching as her face slowly moved towards his. When her lips met his, he let out a low, guttural groan that made her breasts harden, her pulse quicken and...

His eyes flew open and he pulled his head back. 'Shit! Kelly, no!' His voice was anguished, tortured. 'We can't do this.'

As she'd moved back towards him, their eyes locked, their faces just a few inches apart, every cell of her body longed to touch him again. She settled for fingertips, very softly tracing a line across his bottom lip. 'If you tell me to stop, I will,' she'd whispered. 'Tell me, Carson. Is that really what you want?'

12

HARRIET

The morning had passed in a bit of a whirl that had left Harriet feeling... well, quite excited. In the last sixteen months, she'd left her home once, and that was a month ago, in an ambulance, being transported to the hospital. For over a year before that she'd barely spoken to a soul. Day by day, she'd felt something slowly die inside her, like a plant deprived of light and water until living was no longer an option. Today, just for the moment, someone had opened the curtains and poured crystal-clear water on the soil. It was probably going to be a complete waste of time, but Harriet's curiosity and longing for something real, for someone to connect to, had compelled her to do it. Besides, the truth was, she didn't want to go home.

After she'd agreed to go to this fundraising event, Nurse Yvie had been like a whirlwind. She'd called someone in management – Harriet couldn't remember the title – and got authorisation to cancel the transport that was supposed to have taken Harriet home at noon. Apparently, they'd said it was highly irregular, but they'd allowed it when Yvie explained the circumstances and assured them she'd take full responsibility. She was so grateful to

Yvie for going above and beyond, just to brighten an old woman's day.

They'd made a new plan. When Yvie finished her shift, she would take Harriet home to change for the party, then they'd collect her sister on the way to Lomond House. The location had been a delightful surprise. She'd never been there, but she'd heard that it was beautiful.

What a turn of events from the day she'd envisioned when she woke this morning. Now she was going out. To an event. With a lovely young woman who would take care of her. More than that, today she might find out that she still had a connection to other living souls in this world. It was such a long shot, but she had nothing to lose. Being realistic, there was the strong possibility that Jonathan and Anthea were no longer alive. If by some miracle they were and she found them today, she just hoped that, wherever he was, if Dennis was watching her now, that he'd forgive her. In her heart of hearts, she knew that Leo would say that there was nothing to forgive. He'd never been one to hold on to bad feeling, fights or grudges.

About an hour before, Nurse Yvie had popped her head round the door of the ward. 'Right, Harriet, that's your transport cancelled and I've sorted out your discharge papers, so I'm just going to clock out, nip to the staffroom for a quick shower, and then I'll be back to collect you. We've plenty of time to stop by your home so you can drop your stuff off and change, and then we'll be on the way.'

'On the way where?' piped up Marg from the next bed.

Harriet had decided weeks ago that Marg was in for both a knee replacement and treatment for acute nosiness. Only the first one had been successful.

'Bingo,' Harriet had answered back, in hushed tones. 'I slipped her twenty quid and she's sneaking me out.'

'Harriet! You're going to get me sacked!' Yvie had exclaimed, laughing. 'Marg love, Harriet is going home today. It'll be you next,' she'd added, trying to cheer Marg up.

With that she'd gone and Harriet had swung her legs round to the floor. She'd reached into the locker at the side of her bed and transferred all her sweets and magazines over to Marg. 'Here you go. It's been a pleasure spending this time with you, Marg.'

Marg had nodded. 'Aye, it has. But let's hope we don't find ourselves back here any time soon.'

Harriet didn't want to say that she was almost certain that wouldn't happen. She wasn't coming back because she wasn't going to be around long enough for a return journey. Not that the other woman would understand. Unlike Harriet, Marg hadn't spent the last year of her life, day in and day out, staring at four walls – she lived with her daughter and her family and she had a whole network of other adult children and grandchildren who called her, who cared. That was worth living for.

Harriet had just finished packing the few things she had into plastic bags, when Yvie, now dressed in a lovely bright yellow summer dress that suited her generous curves, returned with a wheelchair.

Harriet smiled. 'You look very smart, dear. I almost didn't recognise you out of your uniform.'

'I know!' Yvie said, with a wink. 'I'm like a supermodel the minute I take it off. I'm sure those scrubs add fifty pounds. Right then, I know it'll break your heart to say goodbye to these bland walls and brick-hard beds, but are you ready to go?'

This morning, Harriet would have said no, that she wasn't ready to leave the cocoon of the ward, but now the prospect of a day out had eased her departure. She said her goodbyes with a cheery smile.

Yvie wheeled her to the car park and helped her climb into

one of those cars that was more like a small minibus. Strange, because Harriet was sure she'd told her that she didn't have a family, so why would she need a car like this?

'I run a couple of support groups,' Yvie said, pre-empting the question as she helped Harriet find her seat belt. 'One for people suffering from anxiety, and the other is a bereavement group.' She turned the key in the engine. 'We like to take trips sometimes, so I splashed out on this old jalopy. It's a bit rough round the edges, but it does the job. A bit like me,' she giggled, as they pulled out of the car park. 'I'll stop at a shop on the way and nip in for some milk and bread and essentials and we'll get you all sorted.'

'I'm so grateful for your kindness, Yvie. I can't tell you how much you've helped me today and how happy I am to be going out.'

'Och, it's nothing, Harriet. I'm glad of the company. And anyway, you won't be saying that when you meet my sister. Seriously, she could haunt a house.' From anyone else that would have sounded bitchy, but Harriet knew that from Yvie, it was just a bit of humour to brighten the day.

It only took a little over twenty minutes, with a quick stop, to reach her home and it was surreal pulling up outside it. Sixty years she'd lived there, since just a few weeks after she'd married Dennis. Of course, back then it was a council house, but like most of their neighbours they'd bought it in the nineties, planning all kinds of alterations to make it their dream home. They'd never made any of them. After Leo had died, they'd lost all interest.

Opening the door now, she felt no comfort, no happiness to be back. It had been a family home, then a refuge of sadness, then, in the last year, solitary confinement.

'You go and get changed then, Harriet, and I'll put this stuff away,' Yvie said kindly. 'Point me in the direction of the kitchen, but if you need any help, just shout.'

Once again, Harriet counted her blessings for this girl. Coming home alone today, facing this bleakness by herself, would have been torturous. Her hip ached a little, but it felt good to be moving. Walking slowly and carefully, she made her way from the living room to her bedroom. It used to be the dining room, but when Dennis could no longer manage the stairs, they'd moved everything down.

All was exactly the way it had been when Harriet left. Her cardigan was on the back of the chair, her glasses on her bedside table, her slippers beside the bed. She sat down on the old stool in front of her dressing table and almost gasped when she saw her full reflection. She looked rounder and there was a tiny bit of colour in her cheeks. That was what happened when you got three meals a day, instead of the titbits she'd lived on before she went into hospital. There was no pleasure in cooking for one and she'd completely lost interest in food. A piece of toast or a tin of soup had been as much as she could manage.

Now, though... She stared at her reflection for a moment more. Tomorrow, that life would be hers again, for as long as it took, but today? Today was going to be something special. She was going out, with a lovely lady, and she was going to make it count.

Opening a drawer in the dressing table that had been closed for many years, she took out her make-up bag, her perfume, her pearls and she applied all three. A bit of mascara, some powder, a little blusher and then the red lipstick that was the perfect enhancement to her caramel skin, just a light coat so that it wouldn't run into the tiny creases around her mouth. Since she was a child, her mother had told her to moisturise every day and it had served her well.

Her make-up completed, she pulled her hair into a sleek bun at the back of her neck, then donned the pearl earrings that matched her necklace. Gingerly, wincing slightly at the stiffness in her hip, she got up and went over to her wardrobe. She hadn't been one of those women who had ten dresses for every occasion, not since her dancing days with Dennis were over. No, she had a dress for weddings, one for birthdays or parties, one for funerals, and a couple of daytime dresses that hadn't seen the outside world in a long time.

She was about to take out the plain purple shift dress that she'd often worn to church, when she stopped, and her hand moved to the left, to a hanger that was at the very end of the rail, shrouded in white sheeting with buttons down the middle. With fingers that didn't work as well as they used to, she undid the buttons one by one, and let the white protector fall, revealing a frock in the palest blue silk, with tiny white flowers embroidered across the hem. The top of it was modest, with a boat neck and long sleeves, little pearl buttons on the cuffs, and the skirt was a gentle flare that ended just below her knees. It had been her bridesmaid's dress for Jonathan and Anthea's wedding, over fifty years ago. Now it would be called vintage.

Before she could change her mind, she slowly, hanging onto the back of her chair for support, took off the soft trousers and jersey top she'd worn in the hospital and gently pulled on the dress. A lump formed in her throat when she caught sight of herself in the mirror and saw that it still fitted perfectly as it had that day. It was a million memories and a million years ago, but right then, staring back at herself, was the same Harriet.

When she'd worn the dress the first time, it had been with high stilettos in the same fabric, but they'd been given to a charity shop years ago, for fear that they were a one-way trip to the fracture clinic. From the shelf in her wardrobe, she took out a pair of low white pumps and a matching bag. She was ready. If today was going to be the last party of her life, she was going to do it in style.

She heard the creak of the door opening.

'Harriet, are you all right in…? Holy shit, Harriet! Oh my goodness – I mean, sorry about the swearing – but – oh my goodness again… Harriet, you're beautiful! That dress is incredible!'

The strange thing was that she actually felt it. 'Just something I threw on, but I think it'll do,' she said, blushing.

'Oh, it abso-bloody-lutely will,' Yvie agreed. 'Let's get going then. That dress needs a public appearance. If it was a size 20, I'd have mugged you for it by now.'

An hour after she'd come back home, Harriet was leaving again, a different woman. Yvie's arm slotted through hers, supporting her as they walked down the path to the car, then she let go. 'I can do it,' Harriet said, before climbing into the car on her own this time, touched that Yvie was grinning from ear to ear as she watched her. 'Okay, but we've got the wheelchair in the back, and we can use it whenever you feel you need it,' she said, closing the door, then going round the van to jump in behind the wheel.

After ten minutes or so, they stopped outside a modern block of flats and Yvie pressed the horn. A few seconds later, a tall, thin woman with long red wavy hair and a frosty, unamused expression marched towards them. Harriet's first thought was that these two women couldn't be more different – there wasn't a shred of similarity between them.

'I know what you're thinking, Harriet,' Yvie quipped, gesturing in her sister's direction. 'Nicole Kidman with PMT.'

They were still laughing when the other woman got into the back of the car. 'What's funny?' she asked, her gaze going from Yvie to Harriet, before a bulb went on and she joined the joke.

'Wait. Did she just tell you I looked like Nicole Kidman with PMT?'

'I'm afraid I can't lie. Yes, she did,' Harriet said sincerely.

'Traitor,' Yvie hissed, giggling.

'Thought as much. I would have much preferred brothers. I'm Verity and you must be Harriet. It's lovely to meet you.' Now that the new arrival was grinning, Harriet could see that she was younger than she'd first thought, maybe early thirties.

The car started to move as Yvie got them on their way.

'You too, dear. Thank you so much for allowing me to come along.'

'Not at all! You're very welcome. I'm sure Yvie told you that we had an extra ticket, because our mum can't make it. Actually, I'd originally bought four tickets, but my sister Marina refused to come. She said she's been to enough fundraisers to last a lifetime.'

'You must let me give you the money for the ticket, dear,' Harriet offered.

Verity looked horrified. 'Absolutely not. I was very happy to support the cause and to see the work Carny has been doing. She's a really talented set designer, and I'm not just saying that because she's my former student. She was in the first class I ever taught and she's kept in touch with me all these years. Such a lovely girl. And such a funny coincidence that she shares your surname. Yvie explained to me that you wondered if she might be part of your family that you lost touch with.'

'Yes, but I do realise that's very unlikely,' Harriet added hesitantly. 'Still, it's all rather exciting.'

'It sure is,' Yvie agreed. 'And in the meantime, I get to spend the day with one of my favourite women. That's you, Harriet. My sisters are way down the list,' she teased, earning a playful flick on the back of the head from Verity.

Harriet thought about probing further, asking if Verity knew anything more about the girl's family, but she stopped herself. She didn't want to learn anything that would end this adventure or crush her hopes just yet. She'd always known this was a long shot, a needle in a haystack, but she wanted to enjoy the excitement for a little longer.

'I do hope that this girl...'

She'd forgotten the name already. Aging was a terrible thing.

'Carny...' Verity said gently.

'Yes, Carny, is Jonathan and Anthea's granddaughter. Or maybe a cousin. Dennis and Jonathan had a load of relatives that they didn't keep in touch with. It could be the child of one of those.' A cousin would do. Someone. Anyone. A connection, no matter how tenuous. But if it was indeed their grand-daughter...

That thought made her pause for a moment, her throat suddenly tight. If Leo had still been alive, he'd no doubt be a father by now. Would she have had her own grandchildren? Also the fallout would never have happened, so would she have a full house for Sunday dinner, with the lost side of their family, and her grandchildren running around? The pain of that picture in her mind must have made her shoulders sag, as Verity suddenly leaned forward from the back seat and touched her arm.

'I hope you won't be disappointed if it's not them. My sister is the eternal optimist. She grew up thinking she was going to marry Brad Pitt.'

'There's still time,' Yvie shot back. 'Especially now that he's single again.'

The banter between them lifted Harriet's spirits. 'Please don't worry. As I said, I understand how improbable this is. If today just leads to a day out with you two lovely ladies, then I'll be happy.'

Verity nodded, clearly pleased with that response. After a few moments of companionable silence, she leaned forward again. 'Harriet, please don't think I'm being nosy...'

'You are nosy,' Yvie said.

Verity ignored her. 'But do you mind me asking... How did you and your family lose touch?'

Harriet thought about making up a story, then decided against it. What happened was her truth and she suddenly felt the need to share it. 'I'm afraid it's a long story...'

And it was. It took her the rest of the half-hour journey to explain it all to them. There were tears and there was some laughter too, but mostly, there was just listening, and Harriet felt something in her soul lighten with every word she spoke.

The history ended just as they pulled into the car park at Lomond House and Yvie immediately snapped the engine off and reached over to squeeze Harriet's hand. 'I'm so sorry you lost your son, Harriet. And your husband too. Please, please, if you can find the time, I'd love you to come to our bereavement group. We have lovely people there and I think you'd find comfort and friendship too.'

Harriet bit her tongue before she admitted that finding time wasn't going to be part of her future. She blocked out the thought. That was for later. 'I might just take you up on that. Thank you.'

Satisfied, Yvie let her go, just as Verity, who'd already got out of the back seat, pulled open Harriet's door.

'Are you ready for this, Harriet?' she asked, holding out her hand to help Harriet out of the car.

Harriet lifted her good handbag, and hooked it over her arm. 'Oh yes, dear, I'm more than ready.'

2 P.M. – 4 P.M.

13

MAISIE

The buffet was all set up and under cover, the bar was organised and her waiters and waitresses were already in position, next to the organisers' table, serving wine and orange juice to the first guests as they arrived. A band had set up on a raised platform near the pavilion, a sight that made Maisie smile. That had been her once. Maisie's parents had saved every penny they had to send her to RADA in London, and she loved performing, but she'd enjoyed working behind the scenes on the college productions and workshops too. She recognised most of the students on the stage finishing up their soundcheck. They'd all performed in the last big show before the end of term – a celebration of music through the decades. Maisie had helped them polish their vocals and stage presence. Not that they needed much coaching – they were outstanding talents and the show had been sensational.

Just seeing people from her own world eased a little of the angst that was still crushing her heart and for a second she thought about blowing off the whole catering supervision and just asking to join the performers for a couple of hours. She did very little musical theatre now, focusing on drama instead, but she still loved to belt out a tune. Only the thought of the pain Sissy would inflict on her for doing so dissuaded her.

As if some kind of psychic warning had been relayed, Maisie's phone immediately pinged with a text from Sissy.

Sissy: Have you ruined my company yet?

Maisie: Absolutely. I'm going on the run with Janice and Jane and 300 mini hamburgers.

Sissy: Don't make me laugh cos I've lost faith in my bladder.

Maisie: Soz. Have you shot that baby out of you yet?

Sissy: I think it's barricaded itself in.

Maisie: Please wait until I get there. Around 9 p.m.

Sissy: If it's not here by then you'd better bring suction cups and a Dyson.

Maisie: Will do. Love you xxx

Cole (on Sissy's phone): She says 'Aaaaaaaaaaaaaaaarrrrgghhhhhhh!' (having a contraction). Will call you if any news.

Maisie slipped her phone back into her pocket and headed over to the pavilion for a final check. The organisers didn't want the buffet opened for another hour, but a few of the serving staff were tasked with passing round canapés, which Jane and Janice were now expertly arranging on trays. Maisie joined in, impressed as ever by the speed and efficiency of the cousins.

Jane raised a hopeful eyebrow. 'Any word from Sissy?'

Maisie filled them in on the gist of last text exchange.

'And how're you holding up, love?' Janice asked her, with her trademark juxtaposition of flippant concern. 'If you're having murderous thoughts, can I suggest you take them out on that twat over there who's asked me three times if he can sneak a beef wellington off the buffet.' She nodded to a gentleman who was standing with the organisers, but his eyes were trained on the food area. 'I mean, I don't know what bit of "Only if you want to lose your bollocks" he doesn't understand.'

Maisie let out a deep sigh as she turned to look pleadingly at Jane. Just when her hangover had been beginning to ease off, she had a feeling she was about to encounter another kind of headache. 'Tell me she's kidding?'

Jane shook her head mournfully. 'Sadly not. You might want to take ten per cent off the bill.'

'I'm no grass, but I'm shopping you to Sissy,' Maisie said in her best tough-girl voice.

'Och, I reckon I could outrun her,' Janice said, unconcerned. 'She'll no' be wanting to chase me with her lady bits in tatters.'

Thankfully the band started tuning up at that moment and drowned out the ladies' raucous cackles.

Maisie carried on helping to load trays, passing them out and then getting ready to replenish the ones that would soon come back. Sometimes these functions had a gradual build-up of people, but it seemed like all 200 had pulled into the car park at the same time: men in suits, some in just shirts, women in everything from simple summer dresses and trouser suits, to beautiful outfits that wouldn't be out of place at a royal wedding. Oh, and there were hats, loads of them, which made her heart swell. She blamed her inner forties movie star for her love of great headwear.

'Are you really okay?' Jane asked, as they worked.

Maisie nodded. 'Apart from the remnants of a killer hangover, I'm fine. And then I'm not. And then I'm fine again. It seems to be changing on a minute-by-minute basis.'

'Can I ask you something?' Jane went on. 'Tell me to piss off if you don't want to answer.'

'Only if you tell Janice not to kill me,' Maisie said, earning pursed lips of warning from Janice.

'Did you have any idea he wasn't going to show? Any clue at all?'

How many times had she asked herself that same question? And how many times had she wondered how she could have been so blind?

'None,' she answered Jane's question truthfully. 'If anything, he was the one who was pushing to tie the knot. At least, he was at the start. We researched all the different ways we could do it, but we kept coming back to here, because this was where he'd proposed.'

'Och, the bastard,' Janice murmured. Maisie was beginning to wonder if she should find a way to alert Nathan that he might want to hire some personal security.

'When we set the date for April, I'd thought we were still good. I thought he was happy. Actually, that's not true. He'd started to get... I don't know... restless, is probably the best way to describe it. After the band split up, he was so sick of all the fighting and friction that he swore he was done with it. He wanted to focus more on songwriting, so he stayed at home writing music for over a year with no big success. By that point, it was as if he was going stir-crazy. He had no money coming in and he was stuck in the house. I think that's probably when he began to realise that he missed life on the road.'

'Aye, that happens to them,' Janice said mournfully, as if it was a situation she was familiar with.

Jane groaned. 'For the love of God, don't get her started, Maisie. She swears she once snogged one of those lads from Wet Wet Wet and then he did a runner the next day.'

'I bloody did!' Janice argued. 'We really had something that night. He just couldn't give up life on the open road. Not even for me.'

'What did you have, Janice?' Jane bickered back. 'Other than sore feet from the dancing and a bit of indigestion from the kebab on the way back to your place. I'm telling you, he wisnae one of the band. He was probably a plumber from Bridgeton who'd sussed that a minor case of identity theft could get him a shag.'

Janice's expression turned thunderous, so Maisie quickly intervened before strawberry tarts were weaponised. 'Eh, I thought we were talking about me and you two were helping me to work through my pain?' she demanded, cutting them off and forcing a couple of reluctant stand-downs. '*Anyway,*' she pressed on, 'I was still oblivious that he was having doubts right up until the day. I mean, like I say, I could see he wasn't over the moon with life, but I thought it was just career stuff. Actually, and this makes me sound like a fool, I thought the wedding was the thing that was keeping him going. Don't say it, Janice – I'm already fully aware that I was a clueless tit,' she warned.

Janice didn't bite. 'No, love, you weren't a tit. You just loved him. Like I said, it happens.' She shot her cousin a warning glare, challenging her to cast doubt on her Wet Wet Might Not Be Wet experience again.

Maisie felt a heavy stone settle in her stomach. He'd hurt her. There was no way to minimise that. She just wished she knew how to get over it.

Jane pushed a tray of prawns on oatcakes with Marie Rose dip to the front of the counter. 'If it's any consolation, I thought you handled it like a champion that day.'

Janice and Jane had been there. Actually, they'd been here. Right here. The two of them thrilled to be in charge of the food for the fifty guests. They'd kept it small, just immediate family and a few of their mutual friends. To everyone's surprise, a couple of weeks before the ceremony, Nathan's old bandmates had pitched up with a bottle of Jack Daniel's and an olive branch. They'd even offered to play during the ceremony and at the reception. Maisie had been so thrilled when they'd sorted out their differences, sure that it was just what he needed to cheer him up – right up until she discovered there may have been ulterior motives involved.

On her wedding day, the first clue that there was a problem was when the guys from the band didn't show to set up and do a soundcheck. But, as she got ready in one of the beautiful rooms in the main house, she hadn't been too concerned. They were rock and roll guys. Sticking to schedules wasn't their strong point.

'They're a nightmare, that lot,' she'd told Hope, who was simply stunning in a cream floaty dress, with daisies in her hair. As an overworked doctor who spent her life in scrubs, her sister didn't get much time to play dress-up, but she'd gone full-scale feminine for the occasion. Sissy, at seven months pregnant, was wearing a loose flowing kaftan in the same shade. Maisie's dress was a little more unorthodox. She'd decided it was crazy to spend a fortune on a frock she'd only wear for a day, so she'd got in touch with a friend who worked in the costume department at one of Glasgow's biggest theatres and gone for a rummage in their storerooms. The result was a gorgeous, ethereal gown that was exquisite in its simplicity. Ice-white georgette, falling from one shoulder, it swept to the floor and made her look like a princess. Which was the whole point, given that it had been worn to a royal ball for three years by Cinderella in the Christmas panto run.

Sissy had offered her services. 'Look, how about I sing when you walk down the aisle. I can do a mean version of any Little Mix song. Your choice.'

Maisie had collapsed with laughter. 'Thank you, but it's fine. It's no big deal. All that matters is we're getting married. It's not going to spoil the day if a couple of rockers are too wasted to show up and sing "You're The Best Thing That Ever Happened to Me".'

She'd checked her watch. 'Okay, let's go. Nathan will be wondering where we are. Can you call Cole and...'

With perfect comic timing, Sissy's husband, Cole, had burst in the door at that very second, the slam of the wood so loud Maisie had almost missed the ping of the incoming text on her phone.

Almost.

Cole went first. 'I don't want to worry anyone, but I just got a weird text from Nathan.'

'Saying what?' Sissy had demanded, hands on her hips, her stomach way out in front.

Cole's expression was pure bewilderment as he pulled out his phone and read from the screen. 'All it says is, "Please take care of her. I'm sorry."'

'What? Take care of who? What's he sorry for?' Maisie had asked, grinning, positive that this was some kind of prank or hiccup. Then she saw the text on her own phone.

I'm sorry. I love you. I just had to go. Nx

Now, two months later, Maisie unconsciously popped a shrimp tempura in her mouth as she finished recounting the words of that little nugget of pain to Janice and Jane.

'That was it?' Jane exclaimed. 'That was all he said?'

'That was all he said,' Maisie confirmed, swallowing down a second shrimp tempura without even registering it. Food had soothed the soul many times over the last couple of months. Unfortunately, it hadn't done much for her waistline, but she'd worry about that when she was only being cast as Shrek or Pavarotti.

Janice had stopped work now and was staring at her, agog. 'Did you ever speak to him afterward, to find out what had happened?'

Maisie took a deep breath. 'No,' she admitted, then watched as both women's jaws dropped.

Janice went straight to astonished horror. 'Never? He jilted you and you didn't call to give him a piece of your mind?'

Maisie exhaled, then took another cleansing breath, aware she'd need full oxygen and a steady voice to share the next bit. 'No. He tried to call me a few times, but I wouldn't answer. What was the point? It wouldn't help anything. It was done. What does it matter why he went?'

For the first time ever, Janice's mouth was opening and closing but nothing was coming out.

Jane stepped in with a more compassionate, gentler version of Janice's outrage. 'Because there's no... there's no... och, what is it you young ones say when something is done and dusted.'

'Closure?'

'Yes! There's no closure. You're right. It doesn't matter why he left, but it matters that you didn't give him a piece of your mind for doing it. No, no, no. You don't let people treat you like that, love. Why did you accept that?'

'Because...' Maisie stopped in her tracks, reached for another shrimp tempura, and yes, she knew she was eating her pain away. They were right though. Why had she just accepted Nathan ditching her? Why? Why hadn't she spoken to him, demanded answers, held him accountable? The answer was floating in the darker skies of her mind. She hadn't fought for him or for answers because there was no point trying to force someone to want you. She'd known that her whole life, ever since she was old enough to understand that her parents had left her. Gone. They'd never come back and even now, all these years later, they hadn't tracked her down. And, oh God, that stung. With Nathan, it had been easier to bring down the shutters, block it out.

But Janice and Jane were right – she had so many questions

and if she didn't get answers, then how would she get closure? How could she ever move on? Was she just going to spend her whole life being terrified that the next person she loved would leave her?

'Excuse me, young lady!'

Maisie swallowed the last bite of her shrimp, then turned her attention to the source of the voice. 'Yes?'

'I see you're eating from the buffet,' pointed out the slightly irate, pink-in-the-face gentleman in the cream linen suit, who'd been eyeing up the food since they arrived. 'Therefore, I think it's only right that I should be served one of those beef wellingtons.'

Maisie smiled sweetly. 'Sorry, sir, the buffet isn't open yet.'

'But that's ridiculous,' he blustered. 'It's not as if you're doing anything else with your bloody time.'

Out of the corner of her eye, she saw Janice hear this, puff up and step forward, like a boxer about to go into the ring. Damn. This wouldn't end well.

Maisie leaned over, so that she was closer to the obnoxious git. 'Sir, I mean this in the most polite way. Bugger off. And then, when you've done that, bugger off again. Now, if you'll excuse me, I've got a very important call to make.'

With that, she turned on her heel, pulled out her mobile phone, clicked on her contacts and found Nathan's number.

Then she called him.

14

KELLY

The sound of the gravel crunching as they pulled into the car park at Lomond House shut down the scene that had been replaying in Kelly's mind for the last two and a half months, but it didn't delete the image of Carson's expression as she'd asked him whether he wanted her to stop kissing him.

'Mum!' Carny, standing beside her, held the car door open. 'Honestly, Mum, you're in a fog these days. If the roles were reversed, you'd be searching my bags for marijuana or tequila.'

'I would never do that – that's such an invasion of privacy!' Kelly objected, resolving to get a grip and stay in the moment.

Carny was going for amused cynicism. 'Really, Mother?'

'Okay, but only once a month and I was careful not to leave traces.'

'Mum, I knew. You always tidied my tampons.'

A florid-faced, suited gentleman getting out of a Volvo Estate next to them almost choked as he overheard the end of that conversation.

'Did we miss something?' Scott asked, as he and Carson came

round from their side of the car to a coughing bloke and Kelly and Carny in fits of giggles.

'Nope, nothing at all,' Carny said, with utterly convincing innocence. 'I think that bloke had something stuck in his throat.'

Kelly felt her laughter turn into a wince of pain somewhere in the solar plexus. It was less than eighteen hours before her daughter was going to board that 8 a.m. plane to London tomorrow morning. How was she going to get by without seeing this girl... no, this *woman*... every day? Without listening to Carny's daft jokes and sharp put-downs. The house would be so quiet. At least for the next six and a half months.

She'd almost told Scott about the baby earlier, but Carson had chosen that moment to interrupt them. In hindsight, she was glad and relieved that she had put it off for a little while longer. This day was for her daughter and nothing should overshadow that.

She linked arms with Carny as they made their way from the car park, across the lawn, to the area that had been set up to greet the guests.

Two members of the official college fundraising committee had offered to come along and help out, allowing all of the drama team who'd organised the event to relax and enjoy it. They were sitting at a table at the roped-off entrance so Carny stopped to have a chat with them and check all was going well. Happy that no disasters were afoot, Kelly handed over the family tickets. Scott and Carson headed straight off to the bar, while Kelly and Carny strolled across the lawn, passing two waiters with trays of drinks. Carny thanked them and lifted two white wines.

'There you go, Mum. I know you're driving home, but you can have one, can't you?' Her shoulders slumped a little as she handed a glass to Kelly. 'I've just realised this is our last day on the bubbly together. If I'm not singing "Wonderwall" and telling you how much I love you by six o'clock, there will be something far wrong.'

'Just another normal weekend night then,' Kelly teased her, wondering how she was going to get away with not actually drinking the alcohol in the glass. Another thing she hadn't thought through. Between the sickness, the baby, the close proximity to Carson and the prospect of her daughter leaving tonight, this really was a motherload of a day. In every sense of the word.

Scanning the gorgeous gardens, she could see many of Carny's friends and their families were already here. Just to the right of the pavilion, Kelly noticed that the stage had already been set up – a crazy collision of pop art and photographs from over the years, all of them on the faces of LED edged-cubes that could be spun to represent a specific decade. Carny had designed a full-size version for the end-of-term show and it had been spectacular. Kelly watched as she cast a critical eye over it now, then subtly nodded her approval. She'd spent hours here yesterday setting it all up and was clearly still happy with how it looked.

The full musical performance would come later, but for now, there was a band on stage. Kelly had seen them before. It was a group of twelve from Carny's year group, who'd merged a jazz band with a female vocal trio to form a fifties-style group who took current songs and gave them an old, jazz twist. Right now, they were doing a slow, jazzy cover of 'Don't Cry', a song she used to love, by Guns 'n' Roses. It was one of the first tunes Scott had learned to play on his guitar a million years ago. It was a bizarre moment, a random choice and for some reason it made her feel better. This was all going to be okay. The Scott she married was still there and they'd be fine, just like they'd been for the last twenty-odd years. If she could go back would she make another choice? Maybe. In hindsight. But that wasn't how life worked.

'Excuse me, have you seen a very talented set designer who owes everything she has to her favourite primary school teacher?'

Carny spun around and threw her arms around the red-headed woman who'd joined them. 'Miss Danton, you came! I'm so chuffed. And you're right. Those nativity sets we made started it all. Cotton wool sheep and Lego baby Jesus will be my inspiration for life.'

Kelly waited until Carny had released her favourite teacher, then she stepped forward to hug Verity too. Ten years ago, as Carny went into her final year of primary school, Kelly's first impression of her new teacher, the recently qualified Miss Danton, had been that she was young, brusque and aloof. How wrong she'd been. After teaching Carny and a group of her friends that year, she'd kept in touch with them all through high school, even tutoring them when she thought she could help. It was after one of those tutoring sessions that Kelly had offered Verity a coffee and they'd ended up chatting in the kitchen for hours. After that, they'd gradually become good friends who went out once a month or so for a cocktail or two. Talking of which...

'You don't have a drink,' Kelly pointed out. 'Here take this one – I haven't drunk from it yet and I'm driving anyway.'

She could see that Verity was about to object, so she just went right ahead and put the glass in her hand.

'Did you get the voicemail I left on your phone earlier?' Verity asked, before taking a sip of vino.

'I didn't. Sorry. It was hectic this morning.'

If there was a prize for understatement of the year, it was waiting for her right next to a non-alcoholic beverage.

'No worries, it's fine. At least, I hope it is. I've got a bit of a story to tell you.'

'You're getting married!' Carny blurted.

Verity's lips pursed with disapproval. 'I'm single. No man on the scene for the last year. But thanks for reminding me.'

'New job?'

'Nope.'

'Pregnant?' Carny kept trying. That one caused Kelly to have a sudden coughing fit.

Verity was amused now. 'Did you get the part about there being no man on the scene? Bit of an anatomical impossibility there.'

Carny shrugged, playing along. 'I skipped all that stuff in science class. Too many bits of anatomy that held no appeal.'

'Tell me the story,' Kelly prompted, changing the subject, curious to know why Verity had been calling her. Over in the distance, she could see Scott and Carson propping up the bar. God, what a mess this was. 'It can't be any crazier than the way my day is going.'

Verity took another sip of wine. 'I'm not sure about that. My sister Yvie called me this morning...'

'The nurse?' Kelly asked for clarification. Verity had three sisters and Kelly hadn't met them, so sometimes it was difficult to keep track.

'Yes. The one that's Mother Teresa in her spare time. Anyway, you know she works in the geriatric ward at Glasgow Central, and she gets way too attached to her patients...' Verity said that like it was a bad thing. 'I mean, she brought two of them to my house for Christmas dinner last year.'

'There was clearly an imbalance of compassion distribution in the womb,' Carny teased her.

'I thought you didn't do biology?' Verity shot back a teasing dig, with pitch-perfect timing. 'Back to my point. She's had a lovely old lady on her ward for the last month – hip replacement – and it broke Yvie's heart that she didn't have a single visitor in all that time. Turns out she's got no family at all because of some fallout a million years ago, and...' She paused for dramatic effect. 'Her surname is Bassett.'

'You're kidding!' Kelly blurted, genuinely intrigued. 'I've never met anyone with our surname before.'

'Me neither. Yvie and I thought it was a bit of a coincidence! So... do you have any long-lost family members?'

Kelly was genuinely puzzled, and more than a little choked up at the thought of the old lady being alone. 'I have no idea. I'd need to ask Sonya. Or maybe Scott would know. Although, if she's a Bassett, then Carny's grandad would be the best person to ask and he's coming today, so that's perfect. Is it pathetic that I really want her to be related to us?'

'Mum, are you filling up again? What is wrong with you?' Carny shook her head, amused and surprised that Kelly was being so emotional.

She wasn't the only one. Kelly saw that even Verity was looking at her curiously.

'Allergies,' Kelly shot back, brushing it off, while blinking back the tears.

Verity covered up Kelly's embarrassment by steering them back to the point of the conversation. 'I hope she's related to you too. It's heart-breaking that she's got no one in her life. She's such a lovely lady and she's had a terrible time.'

Kelly swallowed, clearing her throat. 'Can you give me her number and I'll call her? I'd love to find out more.'

'Actually, I can do better than that. The reason I called you was to let you know she was coming along with us today. We had a couple of spare tickets because my mum and one of my other sisters dropped out. I hope that was okay?'

'Of course it is! Where is she?'

Verity nodded. 'She couldn't stand for too long, so she's sitting over at a table near the buffet with Yvie. Shall we go over?'

This was just what Kelly needed. A distraction. Something to keep her busy and out of Scott and Carson's way for a while.

She was just about to agree, when she spotted Sabrina and Rick coming towards them and waved. Even at a distance, she could see Sabrina had been crying, her gorgeous face an incongruous frame for bloodshot eyes and red-rimmed lids.

Behind her, Rick's shoulders were practically up at his ears and his forehead was ravaged with lines of stress, or fury, or some other emotion that definitely wasn't positive.

Kelly's spirits dropped like a stone. When they were growing up, living in the same street in Houseburn, the next village along from where Scott and Carson grew up in Frewtown, that was exactly the expression Rick had right before he did something that would get him grounded for a month. Hopefully, whatever it was, he'd save it for later and not bring it to a breezy garden party with two hundred students, parents, grannies and grandads all decked out in their finery.

As if they were mocking her, the band switched to 'Saturday Night's Alright For Fighting' by Elton John.

Carny spotted them too, but thankfully she was too giddy on life to notice the black cloud above them. 'Aunt Sabrina! Where's gran and GG?' Carny had called her great-grandad that since she was a little girl.

'They've gone to the loos,' Sabrina answered, and Kelly saw that her sister was forcing cheeriness. 'Your gran said to say if she calls you come quick because it means she needs help with her Spanx.'

'Great,' Carny deadpanned. 'It's just one moment of glamour after another. Anyway, wait until you hear this. We've got a whole

Long Lost Family situation going on here.' She paused, turned to Kelly. 'Did I tell you I used to really fancy Davina McCall?'

'You didn't,' Kelly replied, 'but I kinda guessed. You spent a whole summer watching her exercise DVDs while sitting in your pyjamas on the couch eating chocolate digestives.'

Carny nodded solemnly. 'Gained eight pounds, but it was worth it.'

Sabrina, meanwhile, was clearly confused as she greeted Verity with a hug. She'd joined Kelly and Verity many times for cocktails, so they already knew each other pretty well. 'We're related to Davina McCall?'

Verity rolled her eyes. 'You lot make my crazy family look sane. No, you're not related to Davina McCall, but you might be related to...' She was still talking, but Kelly had lost concentration, because a hand had come from behind and grabbed hers. Before she even turned around, she knew who it belonged to.

Taking a step back, she scanned the others to make sure they were otherwise occupied. Sabrina was totally focused on the revelations Verity was sharing with her, while Carny was scanning the crowd for her grandmother and great-grandfather.

Another step back, then she slowly spun around to face him. His expression had changed now. Before he'd been emanating fury. Now he just looked hurt.

'You're pregnant?' her brother-in-law and oldest friend whispered, his eyes locked on hers.

He knew her so well, she barely had to move her head to signal to him that he was right.

'Fuck,' was his reply, but he was smart enough to keep his voice low and his expression impassive. 'And you didn't think to tell me?'

Kelly's stomach was on a spin cycle again. 'I just found out this morning and...'

'Yeah, I heard,' he hissed, eyes blazing, his irritation building again. 'Sabrina just told me all about it. Fucking hell, Kelly, I don't believe you! It's been the only thing on your sister's mind for years and she's devastated.'

'I'm sorry. It wasn't deliberate. You know that.'

'I know, but it doesn't help. Fuck.' He ran his fingers through his collar length hair. 'Look, Kel, I know our relationship is... complicated.'

That was one way of putting it.

'But neither of us want Sabrina to get hurt. She just said to me that I would have been better spending my life with you because at least then I'd have kids.'

Kelly almost buckled with the pain of that. No one knew the full story of her feelings for Rick. Hearing him say that, and the way he was looking at her now, was forcing her to confront an alternative reality.

This whole situation had the potential to break them all. Because for over two decades she'd been holding open a door to a different life, too scared to take a step through and see what was behind it. More than anything, her heart wanted Rick to take that step with her.

15

SCOTT

'That's what I want to be doing,' Scott said, using his beer bottle to gesture towards the band.

Carson lifted his bottle from the bar. 'Singing Elton John songs at a garden party?'

Scott gave him a dig in the ribs. 'Take the piss all you like, but I just want to give it a shot. Am I crazy?'

Carson took a swig of his lager. 'Absolutely.'

Scott grinned. 'Appreciate the support.'

There was a pause for a moment that neither of them felt a desperate urge to fill. Carson was the kind of mate who could sit by your side all day, fishing rods in a river, and not feel the need to prattle on about stuff that didn't matter.

Surprisingly, Carson broke the silence first. 'Are you definitely going to make the break, then? Definitely going to leave all this?'

While he pondered his answer, Scott stared at the water a few metres away. This place was stunning. He'd had no idea it even existed. It was the kind of place you'd bring someone you loved, to have a romantic weekend, or even to propose. It was so far removed from his own proposal to Kelly. In fact, there hadn't actually been one. A pregnant sixteen-year-old has a way of galvanising your actions. One night he'd come home late after band practice and she was waiting on his doorstep. They'd been seeing each other for about a year or so, and yeah, they were crazy about each other. Every now and then, he'd get a bit jealous because she was always hanging out with that Rick bloke who lived next door to her, but other than that it had been pretty epic. He had no idea what love was meant to feel like, but he was fairly certain this was it – although that might have been swayed by the fact that they'd finally started sleeping together a few months before and it had blown his mind. Yeah, it was definitely love, the kind that made him want to see her all the time. That's why his first reaction when he'd spotted her sitting on his step was to be glad she was there. His reaction to what she was there to tell him had been something else altogether.

It was no surprise that he'd gone straight to panic, freaked out and spilled the whole story to his mother. In fairness to his mum, she'd been great. It had always just been the two of them and he knew that while she might give him a good bollocking when he fucked up, she'd always stand by him and help him figure stuff out.

Back then, his mum had given him a choice, said that she'd help him take care of his responsibilities even if he didn't want to continue the relationship with Kelly. She'd even said Kelly could come and live with them, whether they were together or not. It was an option, but not the one he took. His dad had walked out on his mum when she was pregnant and she'd never been able to trust another man after that. She'd had a few short-term flings over the years, but she'd never loved again. Scott had gone through his life seeing the consequences of what his father had done, viewing him as the lowest form of pondlife for deserting them. He wasn't going to be that man. A combination of pride and the way he felt about Kelly had taken him down a different path.

Relieved that history wasn't repeating itself, that her son wasn't taking the same cop out of desertion as his dad, his mum had helped them with the deposit for their house, then chipped in on the mortgage payments too. She'd also looked after Carny while Scott was at work in the factory and Kelly had her first job as a receptionist in an estate agency. Somehow, they'd all pulled together and they'd made it work.

Until now. Or, rather, until a few years ago when he'd realised that his whole life was going to be the same, day in day out, until he died, no doubt keeling over while sitting at a desk doing a job he hated.

The sound of the band transitioning to Stevie Wonder's 'Superstition' snapped Scott out of his memories and back to a foggy recollection of Carson's question.

'What did you ask me? Sorry, my head is scrambled today.'

'I asked if you're still going to make the break. You had a lucky escape with those redundancy papers this morning, but Kelly is going to find out and you should tell her first.'

Scott's shoulders slumped. 'Nah, I think I need to change the plan. I'm going to ask my work if I can delay the redundancy. I realised this morning how crap life is for Kelly right now. Losing Carny will be devastating for her and I think it's got her so stressed she's making herself ill. When I saw her crying, my heart broke. You know Kell – she's not one for drama and tears, so this has to be killing her. How can I leave her when she's like this? I just can't do it, so I'm thinking I'm going to stick around for a couple more months and wait until she's got used to life without Carny being there every day.'

Carson was staring down at his bottle. 'And what if she never gets used to it?'

'Christ on a bike, big man, are you trying to depress me? What happened to Mr Cool, Calm, Positive Thinking?'

'He got stuck on that dating app Carny set up,' Carson said, breaking up the heavy stuff with humour as always.

They ordered up two more beers, then continued their conversation.

'Do you think there's any chance...' Carson paused, clearly searching for the right words. 'That maybe she wants out of the marriage too? Maybe she wants to see what other things life has out there?'

Scott thought about that for a moment. 'I doubt it. She's always seemed happy...'

'So have you,' Carson pointed out.

'You're right. I guess I'll find out. But not today, not tomorrow, not next week. I'll give her as much time as she needs to work out the whole empty nest thing.'

'And what about your dream?' Carson asked. 'Can you handle putting it on hold again?' Ouch. That one stung.

Scott thought about it. 'Like I said, I don't see that I've got much choice. It's the right thing to do. We've been married for twenty-two years and she's never let me down, never done anything wrong. I owe her for that.'

A few blokes who obviously had the same notion for a beer came up to the bar then and stood right beside them, making it impossible for them to carry on having a private conversation. This seemed to bother Carson. Weird. It wasn't as if anyone knew them here. Why would he care if anyone overheard him? But obviously it did, because he wrapped it up.

'Look, I think we need to talk about all this later,' Carson said, sounding irritated. 'This isn't the time or place and I've got a couple of things I need to tell you.'

Scott really hoped it wasn't bad news because right now

Carson was giving off 'someone is dying' vibes. He decided he didn't want to wait until later to find out what his buddy had to say. 'Come on, mate, you can't leave me hanging on that. What things?'

Carson was visibly relieved when Carny appeared and caused a diversion before he had to answer.

'Should have known you two would be propping up a bar somewhere,' she ribbed them.

Carson agreed. 'We're just doing our best to help you get to that ten thousand fundraising target. As well as acting disturbingly true to type.'

That made Carny grin. 'You sure are. I appreciate the fact that you don't set your behaviour standards too high for me to aspire to. Dad, I...'

Scott saw her gaze flick to a woman who had just slipped behind the bar. It wasn't politically correct to judge someone on their appearance these days, but damn, she was beautiful.

Carny spoke again, to the woman this time. 'Maisie?'

Maisie turned around and threw her arms out. 'Carny! Come here, you gorgeous babe!' It seemed she hadn't got the political correctness memo either, he thought as the two of them hugged. 'You've no idea how good it is to see you,' she was saying now. 'Take me away from here and let's drink too much and make really bad choices.'

Carny found this hilarious. She disentangled herself and then raised a mischievous eyebrow. 'Maisie, meet my dad and my Uncle Carson.'

'Oh shit! I'm sorry!' Maisie's cheeks flushed a gorgeous shade of pink. 'I didn't mean the bit about drunken bad choices. I was just...' She stopped, then crumbled into laughter. 'How about I just stop backpedalling and try to distract you both with cheap compliments about how you look too young to be her dad and uncle?'

Scott nodded thoughtfully. 'That would work for me. Carson?'

His mate didn't hesitate. 'I think I'd be all in on that too.'

'Excellent!' Maisie beamed, then leaned forward, elbows on the bar. 'Gents, you both look waaaayyyyy too young to be grown-ups with an adult daughter and niece,' she proclaimed loudly, then turned it down a few notches, 'How was that? Suitably fawning?'

'I bought it,' Carson shrugged, laughing.

Scott nodded. 'Yep, me too.'

Carny sighed. 'Honestly, what are you two like? Sometimes I've no idea how I made it to adulthood.'

It struck Scott that this was the first time he'd actually laughed all day.

'Dad, Uncle Carson, this is Maisie McTeer. Singer, actress...'

'Gorgeous babe?' Maisie suggested.

'And gorgeous babe,' Carny added. 'Maisie has done lots of work with us at college.'

'I just do the easy, showing-off bit,' Maisie interjected. 'Whereas your daughter is incredibly talented. Her sets on our last show were brilliant.'

Scott nodded in agreement. 'She is. She gets it all from me.'

Carny laughed as she shot him down on that one. 'Dad, it took you two days to build an IKEA wardrobe and three doors have fallen off the kitchen you fitted last summer.'

'As I was saying, she gets it all from her mother,' Scott recanted, grinning. Now that he was looking straight at this woman's face, something was niggling him. His eyes narrowed, as he tried to place her, then he blurted, 'Hang on. Aren't you in an advert on TV?' She flushed and he mistook it for bashfulness. 'No, you're great in it! It's for... for...' He was clicking his fingers, which was a small mercy because it stopped him from slapping himself when the answer came to him. Shit. He remembered now. Thrush cream. Yes, he was a mature adult who should be able to discuss such things in a reasonable manner. But no, he was never going to be mature enough to discuss lotion on the privates of a woman he'd just met. Thankfully Carny interrupted him before he had to say it out loud.

She moved swiftly on, turning back to Maisie. 'What are you doing here today? I hope you're performing?'

Maisie sighed. 'If only. It's a long story. My friend has a catering company and sometimes I help out. Today she was supposed to be organising this, but she went into labour this morning...'

'Very thoughtless of her,' Carson observed, deadpan.

'Exactly! No consideration for me at all. Anyway, so here I am. Lucky me. Can I interest you gentlemen in a slice of beef wellington?'

Before they could answer, they were rudely interrupted by a vision in pink.

'Carny...'

'Gran! I've been looking everywhere for you. And GG, it's so good to see you. Thank you for coming.' Grandad slipped his walking stick over his forearm and then hugged her. Scott could still remember when Carny had been tiny, and only beginning to speak. His grandad had suggested that Carny call him GG because it was easier to say. It had stuck all these years. GG. Great Grandad.

Scott shook his grandad's hand, then went in for a hug. 'Grandad, you're looking great.' He wasn't being glib. His grandad was in his eighties and he still had a penchant for good suits and well-polished shoes. Today he was in cream chinos, a navy blazer and a Panama hat. He was the most stylish gent in the garden.

In the midst of all this, Scott noticed that Maisie had moved over to talk to two women who were behind the counter along at the buffet. He made a note to track her down later and ask her about her career. He'd never actually met someone who performed for a living, so he was genuinely interested.

His mum threaded her arm through his. 'We just bumped into Kelly and Sabrina and they were telling us some crazy story about a long-lost relative. Have they been on the drink?'

'No,' Carny exclaimed. 'That's why I've been searching for you. My old teacher, Verity Danton, has a friend, an elderly lady, who lost touch a long time ago with her family.'

'Why does she think that she's related to us?' Grandad asked.

'I know it's a long shot, but her name is Bassett, so she was just hoping there was a connection,' Carny explained, before something or someone caught her eye. 'Actually, that's them over there, sitting at that table.'

Everyone's heads swivelled in the direction of a table with three women sitting at it.

'The one who looks like Nicole Kidman is my old teacher, Verity, and the blonde lady is her sister, so the elderly lady... oh my, I love that dress...' Carny got pulled off track and had to reset. 'The elderly lady must be the one who's looking for her family.'

Scott squinted as he tried to get a better look. 'What do you reckon, Grandad? Is she one of us?'

16

HARRIET

Harriet was having an absolutely lovely time. In fact, it was the nicest day out for as long as she could remember, even if she did feel slightly like she'd gatecrashed someone else's party. They'd sat in the sun all afternoon, had wonderful iced drinks, listened to superb music, watched all the proud parents and the thrilled youngsters wander by and, oh my goodness, the chat between these two sisters made her laugh. Such an interesting dynamic. It made her wish, not for the first time, that she had siblings of her own.

Today had taken such an unexpected turn. When she'd woken up this morning, she'd thought she would be back home by this time, sitting in her chair, staring at the four walls, silently screaming with every passing minute. Even if this was a futile endeavour, if there was no family here to find, she'd still be glad she came. It was the perfect last day out.

'Yas! Incoming! There's Carny, and look, I think she comes bearing grandparents,' Yvie said, her gaze going over Harriet's shoulder.

Harriet's heart began to thud at a rate that couldn't be good for a woman of her vintage. Perhaps she should have taken extra medication today. At least Yvie was on hand to rescue her if she passed out.

She wanted to turn around, she really did, but fear gripped her. She wasn't sure what scared her most: the prospect of finding her brother-in-law and her old friend, Anthea, or the prospect of it not being them.

She sent a silent message up to Dennis. 'I'm sorry.' There was no doubt he'd see this as a betrayal. He'd gone to his grave hating his brother for what he'd done. The thing was, Harriet had never quite felt the same way. She would have forgiven Jonathan. In fact, in a quiet corner of her mind, she held the thought that if Dennis hadn't been so stubborn, so controlling, so damned rigid, and had just let Leo use their car, then they might not have lost him at all.

'Hi!' Yvie was saying now to the people who were approaching, so they must be close.

'You found us,' Verity added warmly. 'Come, take a seat.'

Harriet sensed the new arrivals right behind her now and took a deep breath. This was it. The moment of truth.

She raised her head, to see a beautiful, smiling young woman, maybe in her early twenties, with the most fabulous vivid red dress and a wonderful headpiece, her long, caramel hair falling in waves down her back. Next to her, a young man, maybe in his late thirties. Then a woman in pink, with a wonderful smile and a kind face. And then... a gentleman. A very smart, elderly man in a striking white hat.

'This is our friend, Harriet,' Verity added.

Harriet barely heard her, too busy searching the face of the man in front of her. He stepped forward, held out his hand. 'I'm John Bassett. It's a pleasure to meet you.'

Harriet's heart stopped thudding, and instead it cracked wide open.

John Bassett. Not Jonathan. It was a different man. This wasn't her brother-in-law, these people weren't her family, and despite her sermon to herself only a few moments ago about not minding if she didn't find them, she felt her hopes shatter like the glass of a fallen vase.

Everyone was silent, and she realised that they were waiting, holding their breath, desperate to know.

Harriet reached out and shook his hand. 'I'm Harriet Bassett. And it's a pleasure to meet you too.'

Everyone else around them visibly slumped.

'Oh no!' the young girl in the red dress said sadly. 'You don't recognise each other? We're not who you're searching for?'

Harriet was touched that this lovely young lady seemed so disappointed.

'Gutted!' muttered Yvie.

Harriet felt the same way. 'I'm afraid not. The Bassetts I was looking for were Jonathan and Anthea. I did think it would have been rather an unlikely – but wonderful, of course – coincidence.' It was taking every ounce of strength and discipline she had to remain calm and give no inkling at all of the fact that she truly wanted to cry.

'Mr Bassett, please have a seat.' Yvie offered one of the two free chairs to the gentleman. 'And Mrs Bassett...'

'Please call me Sonya. I'm John's daughter, and Carny's gran.'

'Sonya,' Yvie repeated, 'please join us too. It would be lovely to talk to you for a while, even if there's no family tree to discuss.'

Mr Bassett sat on the chair next to Harriet, while the younger man said his goodbyes and explained that he'd left a friend at the bar.

The young woman – Verity had called her Carny – leaned

over and kissed her grandfather on the cheek. 'I'm sorry, GG. I was so hoping we had a dozen more like you out there.'

'Ah, pet, you know they broke the mould after they made me,' he told her with a cheeky glint in his eye.

Harriet warmed to him immediately and couldn't help but smile.

John turned to her, shaking his head sadly. 'I'm afraid I've never come across a Jonathan Bassett in all my years. I'm so sorry we couldn't give you any answers today.'

'Maybe some things are best left to lie,' Harriet said, knowing that to be true. If ever there was a sign that she was on a fool's errand, this was it. Time to give up any silly notions of family and accept that she was the only one left.

In the meantime, it was a summer day and she was in beautiful surroundings with lovely people, so she was going to suspend her sorrow and make the most of every minute.

'Ah, I'm heartsore,' Sonya announced. 'You know, I watched a programme on telly last year with that Ant and Dec and they did those DNA things and discovered they were related to a whole village in Ireland. Oh, and they were related to each other and didn't know that either.'

'I saw that too!' Yvie joined in. 'Didn't one of Dec's newfound cousins have a helicopter?'

'They did!' Sonya chuckled. 'Harriet, can I ask... do you have a helicopter? Because if you do, then I'm more than happy to change my dad's name to Jonathan and we can make a go of it.'

Beside her, John was roaring with laughter. What a wonderful sound. A whole family laughing together. It had been so long... And no doubt they'd be on their way now that they had no reason to stay here.

Right on cue, Sonya stood up, and Harriet felt her disappointment swell for a second time. She was right. Off they'd go and...

'I'm just going to nip to the bar and get us all some drinks. I won't be a sec. Dad. What would you like?'

'Lager for me, love,' he replied, hooking his cane on to the table and sitting back in his chair, making himself comfortable.

'We're fine thanks, Sonya,' Verity cut in, holding up a half full glass of wine.

Sonya nodded, then turned to Harriet. 'And what about you, Harriet, what can I get you?'

They weren't leaving. They were staying. These lovely people were very happy to sit here and pass the time of day with her.

Harriet suddenly felt so emotional it was a struggle to keep her voice steady. 'I'd very much like a gin and lemon, if that's not too much trouble.'

'It's no trouble at all, Harriet,' Sonya replied. 'Back in a tic. Come on, Carny, you can give me a hand to bring the drinks back.'

'No worries, Gran. Mrs Bassett...' she turned to Harriet, 'can I just tell you that is the most sensational dress I've ever seen. You look spectacular. I know it's vintage, but is it original?'

Harriet nodded, feeling, for the first time in many moons, rather special. 'It is. It was actually my bridesmaid dress for a wedding almost sixty years ago.'

The young woman's jaw dropped. 'Can I take a picture please? I just want to keep it in my mind so that I can try to recreate it.'

'Of course,' Harriet beamed, then felt herself blush as Carny whipped out one of those fancy mobile phone things and snapped away.

When she was done, she hugged Harriet. 'Thank you. I love it.' Then Harriet watched as she slipped her arm through her grandmother's and off they went to the bar. What a wonderful girl. She'd have given anything to have that kind of love in her life. It was yet another reminder of how alone she was, but she fought back the feelings of sorrow and regret. She could let the sadness come tomorrow. Right now, she was going to make the most of this wonderful day.

'Well then, Harriet,' John said, leaning forward slightly as he started to chat. 'Tell me about yourself. Did you ever go dancing at the Locarno when you were young? Ah what a place that was.'

'I did!' Harriet gasped, delighted to hear the name of a club she'd loved as a youngster. 'In fact, I used to drag my husband there back when we were first courting. He wasn't one for dancing, but he indulged me.'

John was a picture of astonishment. 'I'll be damned. That's where I met my Glenda in 1963. Harriet, I bet we were there at the same time. Do you remember...?'

That's how it started, both of them on a tidal wave of nostalgia. Sonya and Carny brought back the drinks, and Sonya rejoined them. Carny quickly explained that she couldn't sit back down. 'Sorry, but I have to make sure everything's ready for the main show. Someone has to stand behind the stage and spin those cubes to the right decade. Gotta love the glamour of show-biz.' With a chuckle and a hug for her gran, she skipped off.

'We're just going to get some food, Harriet,' Yvie announced about ten minutes later. Or was it twenty? In the giddy joy of sharing her memories, she'd lost track of time. 'Can we bring you back a plate? You too, John?'

'That would be wonderful,' she agreed. And it was. Hospital food had been an improvement on her year of toast and soup, but this was a feast. She didn't have a huge appetite, but she nibbled at every treat, chatting as she did so, heart soaring with happiness.

Harriet was mid-sentence when the leader of the band took to the microphone and thanked everyone for coming to raise funds for the theatre department and announced the start of the main show, 'Music Through The Decades'. There were eight or nine of them on stage now, with a full horn section and strings. Her happiness soared to absolute bliss when he declared that they were starting off in the fifties, and they struck up the opening chords of their first song – 'All I Have To Do Is Dream'. One of her very favourites. She used to listen to the Everly Brothers singing that song until she wore away the grooves in the vinyl record.

For a moment, words escaped her and John must have spotted her captivation with the song, as he leaned towards her.

'What do you say we have a dance, Harriet?' he asked, gesturing to the wooden square in front of the stage, a makeshift dance floor that had already seen a few people twirling round it.

'Dad!' Sonya yelped, incredulous but definitely amused. 'The last time you danced you pulled a muscle.'

'I see your pulled muscle and raise you a hip replacement,' Yvie piped up, looking pointedly at Harriet.

'Aye, well we can just sway a bit,' John retorted. 'If we get stuck, we'll call for medical attention. Stand by in case we need you.'

'Aye aye, captain,' Yvie saluted.

Harriet wasn't sure she could do it. She hadn't danced in decades. However, the thought of causing a fuss by refusing outweighed the fear of actually doing it. She took Yvie's outstretched hand, utilising the support to pull herself up, then swapped it for John's. They strolled over to the dance floor, and they swayed. In the one spot. Feet fixed to the ground. Bodies just moving a fraction from side to side. And Harriet loved every minute of it. When the song ended, they stayed up for another, 'Blueberry Hill', and John made her laugh by singing the words. Still, they swayed.

'Come on, lass, let me walk you back to your seat,' he said, when that one ended.

Another gentle stroll took them back to the table. Harriet lowered herself into the chair and thought how she felt ten years, maybe twenty years, younger than she had this morning.

Yvie shook her head and nudged her sister. 'You realise we're getting outdanced by a couple with a joint age of 161?' she observed. 'I really need to work on my social life.'

Harriet took another sip of her gin. She'd been nursing the one that Sonya had brought over, wary of overdoing it and having any reason to have to go home early.

John was chatting to Sonya now, Yvie and Verity were on the dance floor, and she took a moment to gaze around her, desperate not to miss... She stopped, rewound a second, her gaze now searching frantically for a face she'd just seen in the crowd. She couldn't put her finger on it, but there was something so familiar about it, so astonishing and yet...

Her eyes darted around, still trying desperately to locate the face she'd just seen in the midst of the guests. She couldn't find it. Had she imagined it? Was it a trick of the light?

Her search was so intent that John noticed the change in her demeanour. 'Is everything okay there, Harriet? You look a bit pale. Was it all that swaying?'

Harriet forced her eyes to be still, her heart to slow down, her shoulders to relax, as she chided herself. One gin and she was seeing things.

'I'm absolutely fine, John,' she told him, choosing to blur the truth. Because whatever would he think of her if she blurted out that she thought she'd just seen a ghost?

4 P.M. – 6 P.M.

17

MAISIE

Maisie still felt rattled after the phone call to Nathan, but she distracted herself by doing a tour of the event, making sure that plates were being cleared away, empty glasses collected, and desserts were circulating to both the guests who had nabbed tables and the others who preferred to stand and mingle. Everything was running like clockwork – mostly, she knew, because Jane and Janice were queens when it came to managing a buffet, and the bar and waiting staff were all well-trained professionals they'd worked with many times before.

Happy everything was under control, she plonked herself down on the grass and pulled out her phone. No new calls. No new texts. On an impulse, she sent a WhatsApp to her agent, Francine, a jaded, cynical yet weirdly motherly woman who'd represented her since she left RADA.

Hey... any word from Netflix? If you're looking for me, I'm just sitting around, clutching at straws. 😂

The reply was swift.

Nope.

Francine was a woman of few words.

Sighing, Maisie went for someone who would at least put a couple of endearing xx's at the end of a text conversation. She wasn't going to tell Sissy that she'd called Nathan because she knew what the reaction would be and she was too young to die.

Maisie: Update? Am I an aunt yet?
Sissy: Still refusing to come out. If Cole tells me to breathe through the pain again, I'm amputating his willy. Going by his logic, he won't feel it if he thinks happy thoughts.
Maisie: Good plan. I'll bring baby to visit you in jail.
Sissy: Yer a pal. Love you.
Maisie: Love you back xxxxxxx

She knew she was right not to tell Sissy what she'd done. She wasn't going to be responsible for the baby coming out to the sound of even more swear words.

Instead, she texted Hope. Her sister would be home by now, back for some sleep and a shower before returning to the hospital tonight for another shift. She was three months into her rotation in A&E, and the department was swamped, especially on weekend nights.

Maisie: News – I called Nathan. Got closure. Time to move on.

She jumped as the phone immediately started to ring. Hope.

Maisie didn't even get a chance to say hello before her sister bellowed, 'What do you mean you called him? What did you say? What did he say? What was the shitbag's excuse? What closure?

Tell me every word you said!' Hope shot the words out like bullets.

'I didn't say anything. It was his answering machine, so I hung up.'

A confused pause. 'So how did that give you closure?'

Maisie pulled at a piece of grass and tried to get the next bit out without her voice breaking. No, she would not cry. She would not. 'It was a woman's voice on his answering machine.'

'Oh, sis, I'm so sorry. Are you in bits?'

'Weirdly, no. I think all these weeks I've been waiting for him to appear at the door. But hearing the woman's voice... I'm done. Something snapped. I think I've had post-jilted PTSD and I'm going to find a way to get over it and get my life back.'

'Yaaassss! You're badass, you know that?' Hope exclaimed, in her best gangsta voice.

Maisie chuckled. 'You should never use slang. It's like Mary Poppins telling someone to fuck off.'

'I know. I just felt the occasion merited it,' Hope explained, giggling. 'I'll wake you up when I get home tomorrow morning. I'll bring you breakfast. Any requests?'

'Brad Pitt. And a Post-Jilted Support Group.'

'I'll start with pancakes and we'll work on the rest,' Hope laughed. 'Love ya.'

'Right back at you,' Maisie told her, hanging up, then pushing herself up to her feet. The call was still making her brain cells whirl and she was sure she could still hear the echoes of the woman on the answering message's voice. So Nathan had met someone else. Maybe he'd met her before they'd split. Maybe that's why he'd bolted. What did it matter? All that mattered now was that she didn't waste another moment of her life on him. She just needed to work out how.

Back at the pavilion, she saw that Carny's dad and uncle were still propping up the bar. 'You still here, gents? Lovely to see you're embracing the culture of the day.'

'I find beer to be exceptionally cultured,' Scott replied archly.

She was grateful these two were there – their easy chat and sarcastic humour had been a welcome distraction from the woes of her day. In lieu of thanks, she racked up another two bottles on to the counter. 'On the house. You can never have too much culture.'

Janice just happened to walk behind her as she did it. 'I'll be reporting those freebies to Sissy,' she said, in the manner of snitch who had a direct line to the mob boss.

Maisie feigned horror. 'No, please, I'll do anything.'

Janice raised an eyebrow. 'A bottle of Tia Maria and I'll forget I saw anything,' she deadpanned, then bustled back over to replenish the vegan chocolate cheesecakes.

'Scott!' a voice from over at the tables shouted, and the three of them glanced over to see a woman in pink, holding up an empty wine glass, flashing a beaming, questioning smile.

'My mother,' Scott explained, with an amused shake of the head. 'She also likes a bit of culture. Usually with bubbles in it. Back in a sec. I'll go see what the others want.' Off he went in the direction of his family.

Maisie did another quick scan of the area. The tables were all pretty clear, the serving staff were doing their rounds, and over at the buffet, Janice and Jane were beginning to clear away the appetisers and entrées, just leaving the sweet stuff for those who'd yet to indulge. She was about to go and give them a hand when she realised that Carny's uncle was staring into his bottle like a man with the whole world on his shoulders.

'I'd say penny for your thoughts, but you look like it would take more than that. I could organise a whip-round...?' she offered, trying to make him smile.

It almost worked. He managed something between a smile and a grimace. 'Thanks, but you'd be better with a bank loan.'

'Oh, that's not good. Bad day?'

'Something like that. Anyway, sorry, I'm not usually a miserable git.'

Maisie wiped down the countertop as she chatted. 'That's what all miserable gits say.'

She felt it was a small victory that that made him laugh. Hope had pointed out many times over the years that Maisie's inherent need to cheer people up was some kind of weird character blip. And once she started, she couldn't stop. Plus, this guy was nice and talking to him was keeping her mind focused on non-Nathan stuff, so it wasn't exactly a hardship.

'Point taken. I'll henceforth suspend my miserable git-ness for the rest of the day.'

She took a bow. 'Excellent. Then my job is done here. You can repay me by making small talk for the length of time that it takes me to clean this bar.'

The sudden expression of determination on his face told her that small talk might not be his area of expertise. He was definitely attractive though. She caught herself – what was she doing? Half an hour ago, she'd decided to move on with her life and already she was eyeing up another guy? Must be the heat and the whole post-jilted PTSD thing. If she'd done this two months ago, she could have saved herself much pain and the cost of a whole lot of margaritas.

Oblivious to her inner monologue, he blurted, 'So do you come here a lot? Oh God, did that sound like a bad nightclub chat-up line?'

'It did. You clearly need non-miserable practice.' She was finding his awkward sweetness kind of endearing. If there really was a post-jilted support group, she could ask them if this was normal. They could all sit around in their wedding dresses or morning suits, discussing the lasting effects of some duplicitous twat or twat-ess bailing out on the I do's. Actually, that might make a really cool premise for a show. She stretched over and grabbed a napkin from the buffet, then pulled a pen from her pocket.

Carson's eyebrows raised. 'Are you going to give me notes? Your top five tips for cheery conversations?'

He was funny too.

'No, I just got an idea and I need to write it down or I'll forget it. It's a thing. I'm one of those people who keeps a notepad beside the bed in case I get blinded by inspiration for a script during the night.'

'Does it work?'

'No, but it's handy when I wake up hungry and decide to make shopping lists,' she admitted truthfully. She made a quick note on the napkin. Jilted Support Group.

'Jilted support group?' he asked, reading it upside down. 'Okay, I so want to hear what that's about.'

Maisie felt her cheeks heat up. How was she to know that reading upside down would be one of his specialities? Other than the cute smile. And the kind face. Aaaargh, what was happening to her? She hadn't had so much as an iota of interest in a single member of the male sex since that day. She was losing it. This madness had to stop. Right now. There was no way she was going to offload her woes to a complete stranger. Absolutely not. That would be completely pathetic. Although... wasn't she moving on? Taking her life back? Telling her truth?

'See that rock over there,' she heard a voice saying, while the part of her brain that was in charge of her gob sent out an alarm and screamed at her to stop talking. Moving on was one thing, cornering an unsuspecting bloke with a sob story was another.

Carson followed her gaze, obviously unsure where this was going. Poor guy.

She still had time to stop herself. Abort mission...

'I got engaged there in autumn last year.' Dear God, why was she still talking?

'Eh, congratulations?' he said, with a tinge of uncertainty, clearly picking up that this wasn't a straightforward situation.

'And then a couple of months ago, I was here again to get married.'

A realisation was dawning in his increasing expression of trepidation as he made connections between 'married' and her note on the napkin.

'It was a beautiful afternoon and my family was here and I had on Cinderella's frock...' That might have been an unnecessary detail – he just looked confused now. 'And my fiancé saw none of that because he didn't show up. His name was Nathan. If you ever meet him, please punch him in the face.' Adding that last bit was a last-ditch desperate attempt to sound glib and stop terrifying the poor guy. He was probably horrified that he'd got trapped in this situation and trying to find a way to escape to a Portaloo until she was gone and it was safe to come out.

Yet... she was suddenly aware that she was being prevented from repetitively wiping the bar top because his hand was on top of hers.

'Shit,' he said quietly. His small talk game wasn't improving, but she was almost undone by the sincerity in his voice when he added, 'I'm sorry.'

Okay, this had to stop before she was sobbing into his chest. Time to deploy the acting skills that had won her several TV roles, a couple of panto gigs, an eight-month run in a touring production of *Chicago* and that advert for thrush cream that she'd dropped from her CV. Let's do this.

She pulled back her shoulders in a casual shrug. 'It's fine, honestly. It was a bit of a nightmare at the time, but at least I found out before it was too late to get a refund for his ring.' The last bit was said in her best comic tone, lest he think she was a materialistic horror. 'Anyway, I just got an idea for a sitcom about a support group for people who'd been jilted. If it ever happens, I'll make sure his character ends up with an STD and it'll make me feel so much better.'

He seemed to buy her breeziness, because he was laughing again, and he'd taken his hand off hers. Situation salvaged. Emotional equilibrium recovered. They could let this conversation die and he could skip off to the Portaloo now, then they could leave here with nothing more than a bit of embarrassment (her) and an amusing anecdote to tell down the pub about a chronic over-sharer who got royally stood up on her wedding day (him). Except, he was still talking.

'And what would happen to the girl? In the show?'

'She marries Channing Tatum, gets a starring role in *Grey's Anatomy* and lives the rest of her life in Malibu next door to her very best friend, Julia Roberts. I might just have told you all my deepest fantasies. I don't seem to be able to stop talking.'

'I see that.' He was teasing her. Maybe that was his way of dealing with uncomfortable situations. She had a feeling she'd just added another line to his anecdote. How had she managed to go from STDs to Channing Tatum?

Please, if there's a God, make this stop. Find a way. A bolt of lightning would be good right around now. A distraction. Anything.

'Maisie!' a panicked voice interrupted the thought. Apparently the Gods of Awkward Situations had got their act together and sent Carny, who had just materialised through the crowd and was now standing next to her uncle, slightly breathless. 'We have a situation,' Carny announced.

Maisie wanted to wholeheartedly concur, but she had a feeling Carny was on a different page.

She leant forward on the bar, oozing relief at being rescued from her severe foot and mouth episode. 'Tell me.'

'Tamsin has just thrown a hissy fit and took off.'

'I'm going to need more than that,' Maisie countered, completely confused. Who was Tamsin, why did she throw a hissy fit, where had she gone, and what was Maisie supposed to do about it?

'Tamsin! The blonde who played Stevie Nicks in the seventies decade of the show. She had a blowout with her boyfriend and she's stormed off. No idea where.'

'Okaaaaaaay.' Maisie wasn't getting this at all, what did this have to do with her?

'We chose a Fleetwood Mac song as the finale for the whole show! We've been rehearsing it for weeks and it's all synched with a highlight film we're playing on a huge screen beside the stage, so we can't change it. We desperately need a new Stevie to get up there and sing "Landslide",' Carny switched from delivering a news report to a slightly more beseeching tone. 'A Stevie that's already here. And knows the song. And who'll save the day.'

The penny dropped. 'When do you need her?'

'Like, now.'

Maisie made a quick calculation – stay here, torturing this poor man with her troubles, then help Janice and Jane pack up the buffet, or go up on stage, sing a song she loved, one that was all about getting over heartbreak.

What would Stevie Nicks do? She would go her own way.

'Janice,' she shouted. 'Woman the fort. I'll be right back.'

18

KELLY

'What are you two talking about over there?' Sabrina had tried to sound casual. Kelly could see the anxiety in her expression. It wasn't difficult for anyone involved to read the situation. Kelly was pretty sure she could map it out from start to finish. In the car on the way over, Sabrina would have been ruminating over the fact that Kelly was pregnant. If Rick had noticed she was quiet, she'd probably have brushed off his concern because she wouldn't have wanted to discuss it when Sonya and Scott's grandad were in the car. They'd have waited until they arrived here and they had a private moment. Sabrina would have made Rick promise not to say anything, and then she'd have blurted out the whole damn story. When she'd finished telling him everything, they'd come to join the rest of the family, at which point Rick had completely overlooked his promise of silence and tried to corner Kelly about her situation only a few feet away from several family members.

'Nothing. Nothing at all,' she'd answered her sister's question with loaded innocence.

This was officially Worst. Case. Scenario. And there was only one way to deal with it. With a smile on her face, as if nothing was at all amiss, Kelly had blocked any further discussion by moving away from Rick and stepping right back into the family group, positioning herself shoulder to shoulder with her sister. Rick had then made some excuse about going for a drink and stormed off. Discussion averted. For now.

Stomach churning, nerves tighter than the guitar strings up on the stage, she'd stuck to Sabrina like glue for the next hour, trying her best to fill the time and keep everything on neutral territory by introducing Sabrina to a couple of the officials on the college fundraising committee. She'd met them a few times over the years at various events and had even managed to get her bosses at the estate agency group to sponsor some prizes for the end-of-term awards. Desperate to pass the time on neutral territory, Kelly had engaged them in conversation with Sabrina about future fundraisers and then floated the idea of holding an event at Rick's restaurant.

Sabrina, ever the professional, was all in on the idea, and they spent the best part of an hour exploring every possibility that the bombastic Mrs Cameron-Smith, the head of the committee, threw her way.

The tension knot in the back of Kelly's neck was finally unravelling, when Rick snapped it back to a gobstopper by reappearing, eyes bloodshot and wobbling slightly, making it clear he'd spent the last hour in a one-on-one with a tray of alcohol. Goddammit. This wasn't good. An anxious sister. A drunk brother-in-law. A whopper of a secret. And Mrs Cameron-Smith, the biggest gob in the West of Scotland.

Kelly knew she had to avert the potential for disaster.

'Rick, would you mind coming to the buffet with me? I just want to bring back some nibbles for everyone.'

Sabrina broke off from her conversation about whether

helium balloons would signal that the potential fundraiser wasn't environmentally aware. 'I'll help...' she offered, obviously desperate to escape.

Kelly forced herself to adopt a breezy smile. 'No, it's fine. I only need one extra pair of hands. We'll be back in a sec. Have you told Mrs Cameron-Smith about your vegan menu?'

'Vegan menu?' Mrs Gobby-Smith exclaimed to Sabrina. 'Oh, the students in the Vegan Society will be thrilled. I was just telling the rest of the committee...' And off she went again, this time extolling the virtues of a plant-based diet to Sabrina, who had adopted a fixed grin and an interested expression, while surreptitiously digging her heel into Kelly's foot. If it wasn't for the whole relationship-destruction potential of the situation, Kelly would have found this hilarious.

Rick, meanwhile, immediately realised what she was doing and went along with it. 'Sure,' he agreed, then took a couple of steps into her sister's orbit. 'I won't be long, darling. I'll bring you another drink on my way back.'

Cutting through the crowd, they headed off in the direction of the pavilion, but as soon as they were out of Sabrina's eyeline, Kelly searched for somewhere they could speak in private, without being seen. To the left, near the Portaloos, she spotted a large catering van with 'The Carrot Schtick' emblazoned on the side. That would do.

Rick followed her, his alcohol levels slowing him down a little. When they reached the van, Kelly glanced around. Only people going to the loos could see them, and they'd probably just assume they were a couple taking a break from the crowd.

Hot and weary, she sat down in the shadow of the van, leaning back against the side of it. Rick sat down in front of her, his gaze averted.

Kelly had no idea where to start. After a few moments, she went with, 'I'm sorry.'

Rick finally met her gaze and Kelly felt something inside her curl into a ball of regret and sorrow.

She'd expected recriminations, but to her surprise, he seemed to deflate, the heat fizzling out of his demeanour. 'Ah, fuck,' he said wearily. 'We both know it's me who should be apologising to you. I'm sorry, Kell. I just... I just wish you'd told me before Sabrina found out so that I could have prepared her a bit,' he said. His words were a little slurred, but she could feel that he meant them. 'This whole infertility process has just about broken her and I can't bear to see her hurting.'

'I would have, but I didn't plan what happened this morning. You know, I'd never hurt my sister.'

His eyes met hers again and she felt a heat rise in her chest.

'I know. It's just... it's been hard on her. She's been through hell with the IVF. She'll be fine, it's just been a shock.'

'I get that. Like I said, I'm sorry.' Kelly knew she was saying the right words, but the hairs on the back of her neck were beginning to bristle. Rick had been her best mate for most of her life, and now his only concern was for her sister. No 'how do you feel about it'. No 'congratulations'. In every lifetime, she would let that slide, avoid confrontation at all cost. Maybe it was hormones. Or his fury with her earlier. Or perhaps the tension with Carson. Or the thought of Carny leaving tomorrow. But when the fuck was he going to check in on her and ask if she was okay? If she was happy? Sad? Completely fricking terrified? How was he the only one in all these years to be allowed to blow up, freak out and she always had to be the calm, accepting shoulder and defuser?

She took deep breaths, trying to control a bubbling anger that was threatening to burst its barriers.

'Is that it?' she spat, before she could stop herself.

Rick reeled at the venom in her voice. He opened his mouth to speak, but she got there first.

'Really? That's it. It's all about Sabrina? Not a single fuck about me? How am I doing, Rick? Huh? How am I doing? How would you even know, because clearly I'm totally fricking insignificant in this picture now.'

Barriers burst. Bubbling anger everywhere. And as soon as she'd done it, she realised she'd lit Rick's touchpaper of volatility. His explosion matched hers.

'Are you serious? It's all about Sabrina because *she's my wife.*'

'And I've been your closest friend your whole life! Doesn't that count for anything?'

'I don't know, Kell, does it?' The alcohol he'd consumed was making him fire back at her. He was drunk. He was mad at her for upsetting his wife. This was a time to de-escalate, yet, she couldn't.

'What? How can you say that to me? For years, I saved your ass, picked you up, smoothed things over every time you were too drunk or too angry to get yourself out of a situation. What do I get for that, Rick? Put on a shelf because someone more important came along?'

'Are you kidding me? Someone more important? Talk to me about being replaced by someone more important, Kell. Talk to me about that. Talk to me about how you ditched me, ditched *us* for Scott. Getting fucked over when someone else comes along is something I know all about.'

This time it was Kelly who reeled, utterly astonished at what she'd just heard. 'What? Rick, we were fifteen! We were kids! What the hell are you talking about?'

'I'm talking about years of having to watch you play house with Scott. You replaced me first. So did I go off the rails? Yeah. Because you know what, Kell? It's much easier to deal with the person you're in love with being with someone else when you're wasted on Jack Daniel's.'

She felt like she'd been slapped. The anger fractured into something else. Pain. Her voice went from fury to the gut-twisting wail of the wounded. 'Noooooo, don't say that. Don't say that. You were never in love with me. Never once did you ever tell me that.'

'BECAUSE YOU WERE MARRIED!'

Two women going into the Portaloos heard his raised voice and stopped, stared, clearly trying to work out if this was a situation that required intervention. The stunned silence must have assured them that all was fine and they carried on into the cabins.

It took Kelly five seconds. Ten seconds. Fifteen seconds to process what he'd just said and what it meant.

He'd been in love with her. All that time.

Her emotional balustrade snapped again, and this time when she fell, she landed on bitterness.

'How long? How long were you in love with me?' she enunciated every word with clipped fury.

His emotions had ricocheted too. His anger lowered, so did his voice. 'Until I met Sabrina.'

'You fool,' she said. 'You absolute fool.' The senselessness was almost too much to bear. All those years wasted.

'I don't need you to point that out. Spent enough time thinking that myself. Daft bastard, in love with someone he can't have.'

A tear. A single one, rolling down her cheek. Sorrow, regret and frustration that even now they couldn't get on the same page, even now he misunderstood her. If only they'd communicated better, maybe he would have told her and she could have had the opportunity to be honest with him too. Perhaps even make the changes and give themselves a shot at a different life. One in which they'd be together.

'No. You weren't a fool for loving me. You were a fool for not telling me. Because, my friend, for way too many years I've been in love with you too.'

The shock of saying it out loud, for the first time in her life, caused her whole body to tremble. It was almost as if saying it had made it real, but no... In her heart it had been real for a long, long time.

She could remember the first time she'd realised it. Or maybe it was the first time she'd admitted it to herself. Carny's eighth birthday. Back then, Rick had already opened his first restaurant in the city centre, and, like every year, he'd insisted that they let him organise her party. He was a nightmare in those days. Heavy drinking. Crazy nights out. Wild parties. Beautiful women. Yet, through it all, he'd show up at their house once or twice a week, drink coffee and talk, play with Carny, cook them dinner, sometimes just sit on a chair in the garden and watch the sunset. Kelly always thought it was just the antidote to the life he led, the tiny intervals in his week that reminded him who he was, in a time when he was garnering acclaim for his work, and notoriety for his behaviour outside the kitchen. To the rest of the world, he was the maverick, wild, Glasgow chef, a gastronomic genius and hard-living party guy. Kelly knew better. To her, he was just Rick. The boy who'd grown up next door. The wild one who used to walk her home from school, then go and flirt with the girls in the years above them. The one who always had her back, unless he was drunk on cider or ditching school to go and sunbathe in the local park with a beer and a packet of cigarettes. The one whose name she would write in her diary for years, until they finally got together when she was fourteen and he was fifteen. The one whose brotherly friendship had become an on/off teenage romance, right up until she'd met Scott at the village youth club.

If Rick was the wild guy, Scott was his opposite. A good guy.

Decent. It helped that he was gorgeous and half the girls in school fancied him, but he barely noticed because back then he was all about his band, his guitar, his music. Then he was all about Kelly.

At the band's gigs, Scott would sing songs by Simply Red and Robbie Williams, and people she'd never heard of like Johnny Cash and Randy Travis. And when he'd sung their songs about love, he'd search her out in the crowd, and she'd feel like the most special girl in the room. He'd had big dreams back then – and he'd given up every one of them when they'd found out she was pregnant. Yep, a good guy. Decent. For the first few years, she'd truly thought she was in love with him and then gradually things had changed. Full-time jobs. Rent. Bills. An adult life by seventeen, and by the time they were twenty-four, they had an eight-year-old child and an amicable friendship where the excitement and passion used to be.

And Rick? More and more, Rick had become the guy she lived vicariously through, the one that made her feel she had a connection to life, to excitement. He was worth every drama and every exploit and all his flaws.

Friends. Nothing more. Until that night in the restaurant.

Rick's restaurant was usually closed on a Monday night, but as always, he'd opened it just for them so they could hold Carny's ninth birthday party there and Kelly was grateful for it – relieved they didn't have to spend money they didn't have on soft play parties or cinema trips for all Carny's friends. Instead, Rick let them decorate the restaurant, he provided the food and brought in one of his staff to help with setting up and then clearing everything away.

That night, after the candles had been blown out, and twenty little girls had been collected by their parents, Kelly had hugged him, said goodnight and she'd held a sleepy Carny's hand as they left, with Scott carrying a stack of gifts her friends had brought for her. They were halfway to the car, when Kelly had realised that she'd lost her bracelet. 'Damn. You go on to the car with Carny and I'll just quickly run back.'

'No problem. Hope it's there,' Scott had said as she took off in a sprint, retracing her steps to the restaurant.

The door was open, so she'd gone into the empty room, through to the kitchen, into Rick's office and...

The nails digging into his bare back had been the first thing she'd seen. Then his buttocks, hard, tight, undulating back and forward, in perfect synchronicity with the groans of pure pleasure and encouragement coming from the woman he was making love to on his desk. The waitress. The one he'd brought in to help with the party.

Kelly had backed out, ran to the car, breathless, stunned, jealous and, she realised with horrified shock, devastated that it wasn't her. There wasn't a single night since then that she hadn't thought about that moment, there wasn't a single time that she'd made love to Scott without closing her eyes and picturing it, there wasn't a single day that she'd doubted she was in love with her best friend, the one who'd gone on to marry her sister.

Even now, as she sat on the grass on the banks of Loch Lomond, pregnant and emotional, the irony was devastating. She'd always thought that her true feelings were the one secret between them. Now she realised that his were too.

'Why? Why didn't you tell me?' The temperature was back up, his voice anguished, insistent.

'Because I thought if I told you the truth that I'd lose your friendship.'

Before he could answer, her gaze settled on Scott, walking towards the car park.

Rick saw him too, and almost instantly he was on his feet, the sudden action making him sway again.

'Scott!' he shouted, waving at his brother-in-law.

'What are you doing?' Kelly murmured, panicked.

He glanced down and, for the first time, he looked at her like she was a stranger. 'I guess we both fucked up... and we both have to live with it.'

He turned away, walked back towards the party, passing Scott just a few metres away now. Rick didn't say a word to him.

Kelly winced as Scott frowned, stared at the back of a departing Rick and then turned to face her, his expression one of confusion. 'What's up with him? And why are you crying?'

'Because...' she stopped, held her breath, then sagged with resignation. What was the point of keeping up the pretence? 'Scott, come sit down for a minute. I've got something to tell you.'

19

SCOTT

Scott was having trouble processing what Kelly had just told him. 'You're pregnant?'

No. This had to be a joke. Some twisted prank. She couldn't be pregnant. How could that even be possible?

'I'm pregnant,' she repeated quietly, with more tears.

Like a whodunnit movie, rewinding then replaying so that the audience could spot all the clues that they'd missed, Scott's mind connected all the signs that he'd failed to recognise. The tears. The changes in her mood. He'd even put some of it down to her fear of the whole empty nest thing. He was a clown. An actual fricking clown.

'But... how? All these years? How? How can that be? I thought we couldn't? Why now?' He was aware that he was just throwing out words, but his brain was refusing to form coherent thoughts.

Kelly was chewing on her bottom lip. 'I don't know why. I can't explain it. I just... I just am.'

'Since when?' His brain was like a car engine on a frozen morning, continually trying to restart, and only working a little more each time. How could it be? They'd made love maybe once this year, a couple of months ago...

'A couple of months.'

Shit.

For years after they'd had Carny they'd hoped for another child, but it hadn't happened. Kelly had been told that the op she'd had to remove her ruptured cyst had probably made it impossible. After that, they'd stopped thinking about it. Even when they were still having regular sex, they'd never discussed contraception, never given it a second thought. Fuck, how could he have been so stupid? How?

'Scott, you're scaring me. You look like you're about to pass out.'

'I'm sorry, Kelly. I don't know what to say.'

That's what came out of his mouth. Inside his head, all he could hear was fuck. Fuck. Fuck. Fuck.

This couldn't be happening. Not now. Not when he had made the decision to change his life, to go and find happiness on his own terms. This was karma. Deep down inside, he'd known that it was a dick move. Now karma was paying him back.

The sound of a sob made it through the blasts of the bombs exploding his future and he opened his eyes to see Kelly was crying again.

He leaned over and put his hand on hers. 'Hey, hey, hey, it's okay. I'm sorry, I'm being a dick. It's just – Christ, I can't believe it. When did you find out?'

She sniffed and then wiped her tears away with the palm of her hand. 'This morning. I was sick.' Crap, she was crying again. 'And... and... Sabrina saw me.' She couldn't get the words out through the sobs.

He budged over and put his arms around her and let her cry, big, heaving, choking shudders of distress. His heart couldn't take it. Their relationship had drifted into something more like friendship years ago, but he still loved her, still cared for her. They'd been together more than half of their lives – he wasn't going to let her suffer on her own.

'And she had a pregnancy test with her, so we did it and it was positive. I didn't want to tell you earlier because I needed... I needed to think. And I didn't want this to ruin Carny's last day.' Her words were coming thick and fast now, as if they were falling out of her in a mad rush before the sobs came and jammed them again.

'It's okay,' he stroked her hair, his chin resting on the top of her head, just like they'd done this morning. That already seemed like a lifetime ago. 'Kell, it's okay. I've got you.'

With another sniff, she lifted her head and dried her face again. 'I don't deserve you,' she said, in a voice so sad, so heartbreakingly desperate.

That twisted the knife of guilt. No, she deserved someone better. Someone who, just a few hours ago, wasn't planning to do a runner and leave her. Someone who was nothing like his dad. A guy who wouldn't take off without so much as a glance over his shoulder.

His thoughts were beginning to find some kind of coherence again and there were questions that he hadn't asked yet. 'How do you feel about it?'

She shrugged in his arms, then straightened up so that they had eye contact. 'Shocked. Scared.' For a split second, he wondered if there was any possibility that she wouldn't want to keep the baby. That was a whole other minefield of pain that he couldn't even think about. 'Excited too,' she admitted, smiling for the first time since she had broken the news.

To his surprise, there was a twinge of relief. She was excited. She wanted to keep the baby. He knew that he would have supported her either way, but, in reality, he wasn't sure if he'd be able to live with that decision, not when they were already a family, with a home and everything they needed to give their son or daughter a good life.

A home that he was planning to sign over to her as a parting act of gratitude for the years they'd spent together.

Kelly was watching him. 'What about you? Are you horrified?'

He exhaled. How could he answer that? There was no way to go even close to honesty without devastating her. For a moment he thought about coming clean and telling her everything. That's what a guy with integrity would do. That's what Carson would do. His mate was the most honest, straight-up guy he'd ever known. If this was him, he'd absolutely do the honourable thing and take responsibility for the situation.

The truth was that he wasn't horrified at the thought of having another child. He was horrified by the fact that it had taken away the future he'd been planning for a year now, the one that he'd been counting down to, fantasising about, the one that had kept him going for every soulless day of going to the same job, in the same car, from the same house, with a wife he was no longer crazy about. That was the trade-off. The choices. And he knew already that actually the choice had already been made.

He wasn't his father.

All his life he'd done the right thing, lived up to his responsibilities and tried to be a decent dad. If he had to go back, he wouldn't change a single thing, or make one different decision. He'd thought he was ready to start a new chapter, but someone had just flicked the pages back to the start. There would be no redundancy. No travel. No Nashville dream. Maybe this was the universe telling him that he was where he was supposed to be.

'Och, sorry! Don't mind me. I was just going to pop these trays into the van. Didn't realise you were having a conflab here.'

A woman with jet black hair and a vape hanging from her mouth had appeared, carrying a towering pile of silver trays. She proceeded to lean over them and slide open the door of the van, then toss them in.

'What a day, eh? That band was fabulous. They were doing hits of the sixties and me and my cousin Jane were like Martha and the Vandelas down there. I haven't moved that much in years. I'll have rigor mortis by tomorrow. That's what they call it when your body seizes up, isn't it? Or is that the thing that happens when ye pop yer clogs?'

Scott tried his best to formulate an answer, but he couldn't get his jaw to function.

The woman slid the van door closed, then appraised the scene in front of her. 'Are you two okay? The pair of you look like someone's died,' she wittered, with a chortle that emphasised that she thought that was a ridiculous notion.

After a couple of seconds, her laughter dried up.

'Aw, bollocks, *has* someone died? Have I just put ma foot in it? I'm always doing that, it's an affliction.'

Kelly finally found her voice and rushed to reassure the stranger. 'No, no! Sorry, no one's died. The opposite actually. We've just found out we're going to have a baby. Another one. Twenty-two years after our last one. It's a bit of a surprise.'

The woman almost combusted with relief and delight. 'Well, that's lovely! Although, if you weren't trying, then you'd think that by your age you'd have the hang of that contraception palaver.'

It was clearly meant to be a joke, but it fell flat, mostly, Scott knew, because she was right.

'Aye, done it again,' the woman said wearily. 'Clearly too soon for the contraception jokes. Tell you what, I'll nip back to the buffet and grab you a couple of strawberry tarts. They'll take the edge off until the shock wears off.' With that, she bustled off back to the party.

She was wrong. This was the kind of shock that would take a whole lot more than strawberry tarts to get over.

'Are we going to be okay?' Kelly was trying so hard to put a brave face on this that Scott couldn't do anything but reassure her.

'Sure we are. Of course. It'll just take a minute to get used to the idea.'

She moved back into his arms and they sat in silence, both trying to adjust to their new reality.

All Scott could hear was strawberry tart woman's voice in his head, asking if someone had died. The only person that was no longer with them was the new version of Scott, the one he'd hoped to become. And he was going to have to accept that there was no way to bring him back to life.

20

HARRIET

Harriet felt a tinge of sadness as she realised the event was coming to a close. She'd managed one more sway with John. Her hip was aching, and her feet were sore in these shoes, but it had been worth it.

She'd be lying if she said she wasn't sad that this lovely family weren't related to her. She'd had such hope and, despite the baggage of the past, it would have been so wonderful if it had transpired that way, but she was going to have to settle for nothing more than a smashing day with very enjoyable company.

John and Sonya had sat with her all afternoon, Scott had joined them earlier for a while, and even the granddaughter, Carny, had pulled up a chair and they'd had a very nice chat, right up until someone came and told her there was a problem with the band. She'd gone off to help sort whatever the issue was. These days, the young ones were called... Oh, what was it? Harriet wracked her brain. Snowflakes. That was it. Something to do with them being entitled and high maintenance, but that was all rubbish as far as she was concerned. Every youngster she'd met here today had been charming, the waiting staff had been terrific, and as for the band, they'd managed to get an eighty-year-old woman to move to music for the first time in decades. That took something special.

Her mind flicked back to that strange episode earlier. What on earth had come over her? She'd caught a glimpse of a face in the crowd, and it had been so startlingly familiar that it had given her a bit of a funny turn. She had no idea why. It had been a young face, a woman, yet although Harriet felt some sense of recognition, she was positive it wasn't someone she knew. Och, she was losing it. Her medication must be playing tricks with her mind. Or maybe it was the start of something. Dementia. Alzheimer's. Well, she wasn't going to be around long enough to find out. The prospect of losing her faculties or having to rely on others to help take care of her filled her with horror. No. That wasn't how she wanted to go.

In some ways, today had made it even more impossible to go back to the life she'd been living since Dennis died. How could she sit in that house, day after day, alone, when outside this was what the world was like? People were meeting and talking and dancing and laughing. There was joy and there was love, and all of those things just made her feel the emptiness of her life and the emptiness of her heart so much more acutely. Humans weren't designed to live in a vacuum, so while it had been a wonderful day, alas, now it was almost time to go. It was close to six o'clock and the college rector had just given his speech of thanks and congratulations and then handed back to the band for the final song.

'Are you okay there, Harriet?' Yvie asked, as she returned from the car with a blanket. She brought it around to Harriet and tucked it over her legs. That cheery smile had barely left Yvie's face all day. She was a special one, that girl. One of those people whose care for others shone out from her.

'Thank you. You're so kind. All of you are, actually. Thank you for allowing me to join you for the day. It's been such a pleasure and I've thoroughly enjoyed it.'

'The pleasure's been all ours, Harriet,' Sonya replied.

'It certainly has,' John agreed, popping his Panama hat back on to his head. 'I reckon we upstaged the lot of them on that dance floor. John Travolta and Olivia... Whassername.'

'Newton John, Dad,' Sonya said. 'Oh, remember those rubber trousers she wore in *Grease*! I always fancied a pair of those, but I was worried that from the back, I'd have looked like a pile of tyres.'

'I feel your pain, Sonya,' Yvie quipped. 'Mine were tractor tyres.'

Harriet remembered the movie. She'd gone to see it with Dennis. Jonathan and Anthea had taken Leo for the night – he must have been about seven or eight – to let them have a rare night out. She'd been singing those songs for months afterwards, sometimes having a dance in the kitchen with Leo as she prepared dinner. Dennis would roll his eyes, but Harriet knew that inside, he found it amusing.

She felt a twinge of nostalgia. Those had been wonderful times. And if her life now was the price she had to pay for the twenty-five years that she had her boy, she'd gladly pay it in this lifetime and in the next.

'Bloody hell, what's our Carny doing up there?' Sonya blurted.

Harriet turned a little in her chair to see Carny, up on the stage that she'd designed, microphone in hand. 'Ladies and gentlemen, we have a very special treat for you now.'

'I really hope she's not going to sing,' Sonya murmured. 'I love her dearly, but her voice sounds like a combine harvester.'

'We chose our final song tonight because it's about growing older, about moving on and saying goodbye, even when it hurts.

That's how we all feel about ending our incredible time at the Glasgow College of Performing Arts.' There was a rousing cheer from a group of her fellow graduates when she said that. 'Anyway, we have a very special guest for the final number. Some of you may recognise her from TV shows or pantos, or an advert that she'll kill me if I mention...' There was a ripple of laughter. Harriet figured it must be an inside joke. 'However, we know her as a very talented actress and singer who gives up her own time to work with the students in the theatre department. Ladies and Gentlemen, Maisie McTeer!'

The band struck up the opening bars of a song that Harriet recognised immediately. 'Landslide'. Fleetwood Mac. She'd first fallen in love with it back in the seventies, but years later, after she'd lost Leo, she'd listened to it endlessly. Every single time another piece of her heart had chipped off.

Now, tears sprang to her eyes, and she was forced to blink them back. *Don't listen*, she told herself. *Ignore it*. Maybe if she struck up another chat with John, she could block it out and hold herself together.

She was about to turn back to face the table when... She stopped. Every muscle in her body freezing as the same sensation she'd felt earlier consumed her once again.

That face.

It was the same one she'd spotted through the crowd, but that time it had been a fleeting glance. Now she could see it more clearly.

The young woman – damn, she couldn't remember what Carny had called her – was standing in the centre of the stage, her beaming smile dimming slightly as she closed her eyes and took a breath, ready to sing the first words of the song.

Harriet took in every bit of her. Her jet-black hair was a mass of waves and curls, pulled back with combs, highlighting her exquisite face. The shape of her jawline. Those undulating cheek-bones. The two dimples on either side of her mouth. The dark, creamy skin. The full, russet lips.

And then, as she sang the opening line, she opened her eyes and Harriet had to hold onto the arms of her chair to steady herself. Even from this distance, Harriet could see that her eyes were light.

She wasn't just looking at a performer on stage. She was looking at herself from sixty years ago. She was looking at Leo from twenty-five years ago. There was such a similarity, such a familiarity, it was breath-taking.

Of course, she was being ridiculous. That medication really did have a lot to answer for.

Carny returned to the table, but Harriet barely registered her, unable to take her eyes off the stage. That voice! It was almost hypnotic. Intoxicating. Mesmerising. Every single person there had stopped what they were doing, drawn in by her words.

The song seemed to last for ever, yet for no time at all, and when the final note was sung, Harriet was fairly sure she had forgotten to breathe.

And then it was over. The crowd burst into riotous applause, while the singer gave an appreciative bow, then waved as she ran off the stage.

'Wow, she was amazing. What a perfect end to the day. Shall we hit the road then, Harriet? Harriet?' Yvie's voice eventually broke through her trance, but she couldn't reply.

Instead, she reached towards John's granddaughter. 'Carny...' Words were escaping her. She couldn't formulate a sentence in her head. She regrouped. Tried again. 'Carny, that young lady who sang. What did you say her name was?'

'Maisie McTeer. Isn't she brilliant! I think she's going to be a star one day. She's lovely though – not a diva bone in her body. I totally fangirl every time I see her. Don't say it, Gran...!' She rolled her eyes to Sonya. 'No, she's not a lesbian, and no, I haven't been out with her.'

Harriet had no idea what half of that meant, but it didn't matter.

'Do you think...' Harriet paused, unaware of what she was even trying to say. 'Do you think I might be able to meet her?'

If Carny thought it was a strange request, she didn't show it.

'Of course. Hang on and I'll just go grab her for you. I think she's over at the bar. She was talking to Uncle Carson there.'

With that, she got up and headed towards the pavilion. Harriet turned in her seat and saw the young woman about fifty metres away, grabbing some glasses off a table as she passed it and then depositing them on the bar, before slipping in behind it. Carny reached the same spot just a few seconds later.

To her bewilderment, Harriet realised she had butterflies in her stomach. This was so ridiculous. Crazy. How could a total stranger have such an effect?

'Are you okay, Harriet?' Yvie asked. 'Is that someone you know?' She'd obviously heard Harriet's exchange with Carny.

'No. I mean... I don't know. I'm not sure.'

The butterflies got even more frenetic as Harriet watched the woman glance over, nod her head, and then, arm in arm with Carny, start walking towards them.

'Shame about that lassie not being a lesbian. Her and our Carny look great together,' Sonya remarked.

'They do,' Verity agreed.

Harriet couldn't speak. She was holding her breath again and now she felt a little light-headed.

When they reached the table, they stopped right in front of her.

'Everyone, this is Maisie. Maisie, you know my gran, Sonya...'

'You were spectacular up there, pet. Do you do private functions, because I'd love you to sing at my fiftieth birthday party next month.'

'Gran, you're fifty-eight,' Carny said, giggling.

'You only count the round numbers,' Sonya chirped.

Harriet watched Maisie nod, smile, laugh. 'I'd be happy to. Carny has my number, so just text me the details and we'll set it up.'

'Smashing,' Sonya beamed. 'Now we just need to get a few of those topless waiters and we're sorted.'

Carny brushed right over that. 'Excellent. Another moment of woke awareness, Gran,' she teased. 'Okay, Maisie, this dapper gentleman is my great-grandad. And this gorgeous lady here is Harriet. Harriet, this is Maisie.'

Harriet had just lifted her arm, just begun to move her hand in Maisie's direction, when a loud ring cut through the air.

Maisie immediately jumped, then burst into action, pulling a phone out of her back pocket. All the young ones had them now. In Harriet's day, you just went to see your pals – none of this texting business.

'I'm sorry!' Maisie blurted. 'It might be my best friend. She's in labour. I'm so sorry, but I need to get this, in case she's about to pop. It was lovely to meet you all. I hope you've enjoyed your afternoon.'

With that she was off, phone at her ear, moving swiftly back to where she came from.

The disappointment was crushing, but why? Why on earth did Harriet mind that a woman she'd never met before didn't have time to talk to her? This was the most bizarre day ever.

'Not someone you know then, Harriet?' Yvie chirped.

Harriet shook her head, tried to keep her voice light and nonchalant. 'No. Mistaken identity.'

'Och, that's a shame. Are we ready to go then? I'll stop for some fish and chips on the way home, Harriet. You barely ate anything today.'

'Too busy dancing,' John said warmly. With that, he reached over to the little vase in the middle of the table, took out a tulip and handed it to a shocked Harriet. 'For you. For being my dancing partner,' he explained. 'I don't know about you, Harriet, but I thoroughly enjoyed myself.'

Harriet glanced one more time at the distant figure of Maisie McTeer. Every bone in her body sagged and it was a struggle to find her voice, but eventually she managed it. 'I did too, John. I'm just sorry it's all over.'

It was. It was all over in more ways than one.

6 P.M. – 8 P.M.

21

MAISIE

Maisie didn't recognise the number. Crap. Must be a nurse at the maternity hospital. Or maybe Cole had forgotten to take a charger and their phones had died. Or maybe it was Francine, with news about the Netflix job and because it was the weekend, she was calling from a different number. Or maybe...

'Maisie?'

No.

Oh God.

No.

'Nathan.' It was a statement, not a question. His voice would seem to have supernatural powers, because at the very minute he'd said her name, it felt like someone had taken a baseball bat to her chest and knocked out her lungs. *Breathe. Just breathe.*

'Yeah. I... em... Did you call me? I saw a missed call from your number.'

Crap. She hadn't even read the digits of the incoming call properly and his name hadn't flashed up because she'd deleted his number. When she'd called him earlier, it had been from memory.

From the noise in the background, she guessed he was in a car or maybe on a tour bus. It was no comfort that he sounded a bit apprehensive. Her legs turned to marshmallow, and she was suddenly aware that she was in the middle of a crowd of people, and this wasn't a conversation she wanted to have here. Or anywhere. But especially here.

'Can you hang on a second?' she said, trying to come across as together and confident, but she had a definite feeling she sounded more like the devastated wife in those movies who tries to keep the kidnappers on the phone longer so the FBI can trace the call.

Turning left, she cut through the remaining partygoers and nipped down to the edge of the water, just along from the pavilion, where Janice and Jane were busy packing everything up.

Slumping down on the edge of the grass, she realised she was sweating, so she kicked off her shoes and stuck her feet into the water, gasping when the cold assaulted her toes.

'Maisie? Are you okay?'

Oh the irony. He'd jilted her at the altar, humiliated her, destroyed their future and shredded her heart to the point that she couldn't get out of bed for two weeks – and only then did she get up because Hope was threatening to drag her by the ankles, yet now she let out a tiny gasp and suddenly he was Mr Care and Concerned.

'I'm fine,' she said, trying to get the words out through gritted teeth. Why now? She'd been moving on from him for at least... oh, maybe two hours... and she felt like she was right back at stage one of the grieving phase, which, if she remembered correctly, was right between devastation, heartbreak and wanting to throw darts at his photo.

She had no idea what to say next, until she remembered his earlier question.

'Yes, it was me. That called you.'

'Okay.'

Christ Almighty. She had seen this man naked. They had spent endless hours discussing everything from international politics to the merits of peas versus beans. He'd bought her tampons. They'd picked their kids' names (Faith and Charity – but only because they were mocking her sister, Hope). Yet now, she couldn't think of a single thing to say to him. She contemplated just giving the phone to Janice and letting her issue death threats.

He went first. 'Where are you?'

'Err, this is going to sound pathetic, but I'm at Lomond House. At the water.'

He groaned. 'I knew you'd remember the date.'

Hang on, what? She tried to compute. She'd been so hungover, and then so hectically busy all day, that she hadn't given a second thought to what the actual date was.

She tried to compute. The second of July. No, the third. Oh crap... Cue another skelp across the chest with the baseball bat.

'Actually, I'd forgotten, but thanks. I've just realised.'

Today was the anniversary of the day they'd first met each other, on an introductory visit to RADA. How could she not have realised that?

He must have thought that the significance of today had somehow moved her to come to the place that had so much significance for them. The thought gave her just a tiny spark of confidence. At least she wasn't here, staring at her engagement ring, weeping tears of devastation.

'I'm here because I'm working. For Sissy. She was catering a garden party, but she went into labour this morning, and she's gone to hospital, so I'm her stunt double.'

What are you doing? Stop joking with him. Stop being nice. He is Satan's spawn.

'Sissy's in labour? Wow. That's amazing. Is Cole with her?'

'Of course. Why wouldn't he be? He's not the type to do a runner.' It was out before she could stop herself. He deserved it.

There was a sigh. 'I guess I am,' he said tightly.

'I guess you are.'

Another silence. The cool of the water was bringing her heart rate down, and she could see in her peripheral vision that people were hugging, saying goodbye, leaving.

'Maisie, I'm sorry.'

Wow. An apology. Only two months late.

'Why?'

'Why am I sorry?'

'No, why are you saying this now?'

'Because I tried to tell you at the time and you wouldn't pick up or respond to my texts. I've called you a hundred times. You've blocked me, haven't you?'

'Deleted your number.'

'I figured. And I was too chickenshit to just appear on your door. But now I've finally got you, I can tell you; I'm so sorry.'

Maisie could hear the sincerity in his voice and she tried to ignore it. He'd gone to RADA too. Music was the passion he'd chosen to pursue, but he was also a trained actor. This could all be one big performance. Anyway, what did it matter that he was sorry? That didn't cancel out what he'd done. It didn't bring their future back. This was pointless.

'Okay. Appreciate the apology,' she said curtly.

'Wait, that's it?'

'What else do you want?'

'Maisie, you called me today. I thought it was because you wanted to talk. Wanted to give me a chance to explain.'

'I was... Actually, I don't know why I was calling. I got it into my head that I needed closure and that I would get it if I spoke to you, but this isn't helping. It really isn't. It's just making me hate you.'

Her tone was getting heated now, the tension ramping up, the way it had done on the couple of occasions that they'd had blowout arguments. There hadn't been many at first, but in the last couple of months of their relationship, they'd become more frequent. But then, didn't everyone bicker when they were organising a wedding? With them, it had always started small. A dig. A niggle. A difference of opinion over something stupid, like what they were going to binge-watch, or what they were going to have for dinner. So many things took on an importance that hadn't been there before. Cups left on tables drove her mad. He'd lose the plot when she shaved her legs in the shower. Sometimes they had to postpone an argument because Hope had come home from a shift, and they didn't want to have an atmosphere in the house when her sister was, quite literally, putting her life on the line to help people. It put their petty squabbles into context, and then Hope would go back to the hospital for her next shift and they'd kiss and make up and all would be good again until the next time she shaved her legs.

In between all that, though, they'd had so many good times and she'd actually been grateful for the challenges. She'd seen them as a test of their relationship, and she was sure that they'd passed. Shame he'd chalked it up as a fail.

Maisie realised she was holding her breath, waiting for him to rise to her bait, so it was unexpected when he gave a sad reply of, 'I deserve that.'

Oh. Right. Wind. Out of sails.

'You do,' was all she could manage.

Another awkward pause.

'Look, Maisie, can we meet? Tonight? I can't do this on the phone. I need to see you, to explain what happened.'

'You're in Glasgow?'

'No, Edinburgh. We were playing here last night. But I can come to Glasgow to see you. I'll just grab a cab.'

That threw her completely. She'd seen stuff on social media about the band, and how they were back together, so she'd assumed he was on the road or out of the country, or back in London. She'd completely missed any announcement of an Edinburgh gig.

'We're picking the tour back up this week, so we're flying to Amsterdam tomorrow morning.'

That set her pulse racing again. He was here in Scotland. If she wanted to, she could see him, touch him. She caught Janice waving at her and that took her thoughts in another direction. She could stand up to him, shame him for what he'd done. Get that closure she'd been talking about earlier. But...

'Who's the woman?' she blurted.

'What woman?'

'On your voicemail. When I called you earlier, it was a woman on your voicemail message saying you weren't available. It's none of my business, but I guess I'd just like to know how quickly you moved on.'

'It's just someone from the record company. It's nothing. Just a friend who was larking around. It's not what you think...'

'How do you know what I think?' she challenged, irate again, fairly sure she didn't believe a word he said.

'Because it's probably what anyone would think.' He sighed. 'Maisie, help me out here. I want to see you. I want to explain, and I want to say sorry. You deserve that. And...' he tailed off, and she could hear that the words had got stuck somewhere.

'And what?' she prompted.

'And I miss you. Fuck, Maisie, I miss you so much. See me. Let me explain.'

Wow. Just when she thought that him jilting her on their wedding day was the biggest shock he could deliver, he'd just hit her with another one that came close on the Richter scale.

'You miss me?'

'Every day. See me. Please.'

Holy crap. Say no. Say no. Say no.

'I can't.' Close enough.

'Maisie, give me a chance. Five minutes. You can. Just choose to do it.'

'No, I mean, I actually can't. I'm going straight to the hospital to be with Sissy as soon as I get away from here.'

'Afterwards. Any time. I could come to the flat. I don't care if it's the middle of the night...'

'No!' Even if she wanted to, she couldn't do it at the flat. It was too invasive. She'd only just stopped seeing him lying on their bed, making coffees in the kitchen, playing his guitar in their bedroom. Those memories were only now a little blurred in her brain. She didn't want to bring them into focus again. And besides, if Hope found him there, she couldn't trust her sister to be in the same room as Nathan without practising her surgical skills on his bollocks. 'Hope is at the flat,' she lied. 'And my mother. They're having a movie night.'

That would rule out the possibility of him just showing up. He might want to see her, but there was no way he was brave enough to face all three of the McTeer women at the same time.

'Right. Well, how about...' He hesitated, and she could hear his mind whirring. 'Is Sissy in Glasgow Central?"

'Yes.' She wasn't sure where this was going.

'The coffee shop in the hospital, then. It's in the main building, on the ground floor and it's open all night. The one we went to when Stix fell off the stage and got concussion.'

Bizarrely, that made her smile. Stix was the drummer in the band. At one of their Glasgow concerts, he'd gone to the front of the stage to throw his drumstick into the crowd. Unfortunately, he'd slid on a pair of knickers someone had thrown on the stage, lost his balance and taken a header down a good ten feet to the front row. After four hours in A&E, he'd been released, and they'd all ended up in the coffee shop at the hospital until dawn, most of it spent taking the piss out of Stix for his epic rock and roll fail.

Nathan hadn't finished. 'I'm in the studio just now, but I could get there about ten o'clock and I'll wait. All night if I have to. Just come and find me and give me five minutes. Please.'

Say no. Say no. Say no.

'Okay.' Damn it.

She didn't have to see him. She could change her mind and leave him with nothing but a hundred-quid taxi bill to show for his travels from Edinburgh to Glasgow. That was typical Nathan. Too much of a rock star for public transport.

'I'll meet you at ten, unless Sissy is giving birth at that exact moment.'

'Yes! Great. I'll be there. And Maisie...'

'What?'

'Thank you.'

She hung up. What had she done? Why had she agreed?

It took a moment before the obvious answer presented itself. Maybe her love for him wasn't in the past tense.

22

KELLY

Scott's reaction to the baby had been pretty much as she'd expected: shock, stunned reasoning, then acceptance and support. Not too dissimilar from the reaction he'd had when she'd first fallen pregnant over twenty years ago.

Back then, they'd had something else though – they were head over heels in love and besotted with each other. Maybe that was long gone, but it had been replaced by something else: they were a family. It had worked for them so far, and there was no reason it wouldn't work for the next twenty years.

The truth was, though, there was only one man she was in love with, but she could never have him. Hearing him say that he'd been in love with her too might have been the most painful thing she'd ever heard. Her mind was still exploding every time she replayed his words. How could she not have known? Why didn't he tell her? It was too late now, she knew that. There was no world in which she would hurt her sister. He was untouchable – and that gave her only one way forward. She would make it work with Scott and they'd continue to be a family. Rick would still be in her life and so would her sister. It wasn't ideal, but it was the only scenario that worked, and it was the one that was best for the baby.

The baby.

Just thinking that set off a gush of excitement. All those years she'd been desperate for another child and it hadn't happened. This was fate evening things out. She couldn't have Rick, but she could have the child she'd longed for. It was a deal she could live with.

Scott's arm tightened around her waist as they walked back towards the rest of their family. She could see Sonya and Grandad, saying goodbye to the people they'd spent the afternoon sitting with. Carny had told her that the woman Verity and her sister had brought along wasn't a relative after all. It was a shame. Maybe they could still keep in touch with her though, since she didn't have anyone else.

Her gaze went to the other side of the lawn. The fundraising committee had finally dispersed, but Sabrina was still there, deep in conversation with Rick. They hadn't yet noticed that Carny was heading for them, bottle of champagne in hand. She had every right to enjoy herself. She'd earned it.

But God, she'd miss her. She'd been her whole life for so long. Sometimes she wondered how she and Scott would survive without their daughter gluing them together. Now she had the answer. One glue was going, but another one was on the way.

She was so busy watching Sabrina, Rick, and Carny that she wasn't paying attention to what was now going on to her left. Sonya and Grandad were heading their way, Sonya deep in conversation... with Carson. Crap. The one person she'd been trying to avoid all day.

'Kelly, my love, we're off now. We're just going to go and say goodbye to Carny, and then Sabrina and Rick will drop Grandad and me home.'

That had always been the plan. Sabrina and Rick would drop them off, then come back to Kelly's house for a curry. Carny was going out with friends straight from here, so Kelly would drive Scott and Carson back to their house too. They'd all have dinner, then Carson was taking the sleeper train down to London. She had a couple more hours to keep out of his way, and then he'd be gone. She could do it. After all the trauma today, she could deal with anything.

'Are you sure you and Grandad don't want to come over for a curry as well? You know you're very welcome,' Scott offered, getting in there just before Kelly was about to say the same.

Sonya yawned. 'I know, love, and thank you. But Grandad's bones are aching and I'm desperate to get my bra off and my jammies on and watch some telly. Think *The Voice* is on tonight. Can't go wrong with a bit of Tom Jones.'

Laughing, Kelly nodded her agreement. 'Okay, well, we'll walk with you to your car.' She was so grateful that – as always – they'd showed up for Carny, and keen to make sure they both got in the car safe and well. And yep, there was a part of her that wanted to see Rick, desperately hoping that he'd calmed down and could at least act normally around her. She had no idea how they could move forward from all this, but for her sister's sake, she had to try to smooth it over.

'Babe, I'll be over in a minute, I'm just going to go get the pint I left at the bar earlier. Carson, mate, come keep me company. Mum, I'll see you later,' he said, giving Sonya a kiss on the cheek, before giving Grandad a hug. 'I'll be round during the week to watch the football, Grandad.' It was their weekly thing. On a Wednesday night, after work, Scott would take round fish and chips and some beer, and he and Grandad would watch the footie together. Sometimes, especially lately, Kelly had got the feeling it was Scott's favourite night of the week.

She kissed him on the cheek. 'Don't be long, honey. I'll wait for you two in the car.'

Sonya took her arm and gave her a squeeze. 'I'm holding on for support – a couple of glasses of wine and the world is spinning.'

Grandad gave a loud chortle. 'A couple of glasses? More like six.'

Sonya put her other arm through his. 'Aye okay, old man. Honestly, the sooner you lose your marbles, the better.'

That set Grandad off again. Kelly adored their relationship. They teased each other mercilessly, but it was all from a place of love.

They traipsed across the grass towards the car park and Kelly locked eyes on Sabrina and Rick, already standing in front of their Range Rover, waiting for GG and Sonya. She could see that her sister looked strained and Rick... He turned the other way and wouldn't meet her eye. Kelly's blood ran cold. Had he told Sabrina about their conversation? Had he admitted that he'd been in love with Kelly? Or, worse, had he shared Kelly's revelation that she was in love with him?

God no. That couldn't happen. She was about to lose Carny, she couldn't lose Sabrina and Rick too.

When she reached them, Sabrina immediately went into fluster mode. 'Kells, we've decided just to go home instead of staying at yours for a curry. After we drop Sonya and GG off, we'll come back and collect our stuff, then just head off.'

No, no, no. What was going on? Kelly tried to make eye contact with Rick, but he wouldn't even glance in her direction. Had he shared everything and completely screwed her relationship with Sabrina?

'Really? Oh, please come. I was so looking forward to...'

'No.' It was said with a steely glare and such firm resolve that cold waters of panic flooded through Kelly's veins. He'd told her. How could he? He wasn't even trying to be civil or to find a way to deal with this.

Sonya chimed in. 'I hate to be high maintenance, but can we get going then, Sabrina? If I don't get to a loo soon, you'll need to stop the car on the hard shoulder for me. I'd rather pee in a bush than go to those portable toilets. I'm always terrified someone will tip it over while I'm in there. And don't get me started on the perils of wet seats.'

'Thanks for that, Gran. I'm going to need therapy to get rid of that mental image,' Carny teased. 'But thanks for coming today,' she told Sonya, giving her a huge hug. Carny had insisted that she didn't want to do one of those big goodbye scenes at the airport tomorrow morning, so this was the last time she'd see her gran and great-grandad before she left. That's probably why she was hanging on to Sonya like her life depended on it.

Kelly was grateful that the goodbyes were covering the uncomfortable vibes between her and Rick, but her heart was hurting as she watched her girl. She swallowed back tears – for Carny, for Sonya, for all of them. She hated goodbyes.

'Right, you,' Sonya finally said, untangling herself. 'Call me every day on the FaceTime. If you don't, I'll send out a helicopter to search for you and they'll only embarrass you when they pull you up on that hoist thing...'

'I will, Gran. Please come and visit me. Lots.' They hugged for a few more seconds, before Sonya released her again, letting Carny say her goodbyes to GG. 'Eh, did I see you flirting with that lovely lady earlier, GG? She just drove off in a car that looks like the Popemobile.'

Grandad chuckled. 'Just being polite, young lady.' he blustered.

'Okaaaaaay. Well, I think you should go for it, GG. Make a new friend. I think she liked you.'

'Understandable, really,' GG joked. 'I'm regarded as a catch down the over-eighties' club.'

Much as he was joking, Kelly realised it was the first time she'd ever seen Scott's grandad blush. He gave Carny another hug and then climbed into the car. She tried to meet Sabrina or Rick's gaze, but neither would make eye contact. Instead, they both just got in the car, not even glancing back as Kelly and Carny waved goodbye.

When they were out of sight, Carny sighed. 'I'm going to miss them so much. Why can't I have dysfunctional families like all my friends? It would make goodbyes so much easier.'

Kelly bit her lip. If only her daughter knew just how dysfunctional they really were.

'Do you think there's anything wrong with Aunt Sabrina and Uncle Rick, Mum?' Carny wondered aloud. 'I think they must have had a blowout this morning because every time I spoke to Aunt Sabrina today, she looked like she'd been crying. Come on, Mum, what's going on? You two share everything.'

Including being in love with the same man, Kelly added in her head. Sabrina knew. She was certain of it now. How would they ever get past that? How could they ever come over for Saturday night dinner, or Christmas, or birthdays, or summer barbeques and long weekends away, if Sabrina was constantly worried that Kelly was lusting after her husband? And what if she told Scott? She wouldn't. Would she?

'I've no idea. Maybe they did have an argument this morning. You know what they're like though – they'll be madly in love again before the day is done.' Kelly wasn't sure that she believed that. Wasn't sure she wanted to.

'Yep, you're probably right. You know you four have got a lot to answer for. All these happy marriages are nauseating. How am I supposed to live up to decent levels of jaded cynicism when I come from perfectly normal parents who barely have a cross word? You should be ashamed of yourself, Mum. You've ruined me.'

Despite her angst, Kelly laughed. 'I'm sorry, hon. How about I throw a plate or something at your dad before you go. I mean, I'll make sure I miss him, but you'll get the effect.'

Carny contemplated the suggestion. 'I suppose it's a start. As long as it's a dinner plate. Hardly worth the effort otherwise. Where is Dad?'

Kelly could barely concentrate on the question, too chilled by Rick and Sabrina's behaviour. It took everything she had to summon a nonchalant smile. 'He's just grabbing his beer and then he and Carson are meeting me at our car.'

'Okay, I'll come say goodbye. The others aren't ready yet anyway. They're still packing up.'

Carny took her hand and they made their way towards the car on the other side of the car park. On the way, she peered over and saw that, in the distance, Scott and Carson were still standing at the bar, deep in conversation. So much for grabbing his beer and coming straight back.

Another thought... If Sabrina and Rick weren't coming back to their house for dinner, then it would just be her and Scott and Carson. Everything inside her groaned. Today was the day that just kept on giving. That was going to be the most uncomfortable couple of hours. She and Carson still hadn't spoken about that night, and what had happened between them, but it was definitely causing tension. How could it not? Just another thing to add to her list of regrets. The only comfort was that she knew Carson wouldn't say anything to her husband. He loved Scott too much. He'd never hurt him.

God, make this day be over. Maybe she could suggest Carson get an earlier train tonight, and then she and Scott could just put their feet up, watch a movie and talk about the baby. Get used to the idea. Begin to make plans.

Before they reached the car, a van screeched to a halt in front of them and Carny's friend, Letisha, poked her head out of the driver's seat. 'You coming, Carnage?' she bellowed, laughing as she used the nickname Carny's friends had given her. 'Oops, sorry, Mrs Bassett. Didn't see you there.'

'Need to go, Mum. I've got my keys. I'll be back at some point during the night or in the morning to get my stuff before I go to the airport. Love you, Mum.'

Kelly felt the warmth of her hug as she cuddled her. 'Bye, my love. Have a great night.'

'Will do.'

With the crunch of wheels reversing on gravel, they were gone. Kelly made for her own car, climbed into the driver's seat and let her head fall back on the headrest.

What. A. Day.

She'd discovered she was pregnant.

She'd devastated her sister, who'd been trying for a baby for years.

She'd told her sister's husband that she'd spent half her life in love with him.

She'd broken the news about the baby to her husband.

And she'd done all of that while twisted in angst about her daughter leaving home.

Now? Now she was sitting in an almost empty car park waiting for her husband and his best friend – one that she was avoiding out of shame over what they'd done.

They were nowhere in sight now. And she had no idea what was keeping them.

23

SCOTT

'Kelly is pregnant.'

He hadn't even made it halfway across the lawn before he'd blurted it out. In fact, he didn't even want a beer – it was just the only excuse he could think of to get away for five minutes before his head exploded.

'What?' Carson spluttered. 'You're kidding.'

Scott felt a moment of solidarity from his mate, who looked just as stunned and shocked as he was.

'I wish I was. At least, I think I do. Fuck, I've no idea what I think. My head is scrambled. I can't believe it.'

They were still walking, on autopilot, only coming to a halt when the bar stopped them.

'Are you still open?' Scott asked the women who were standing further along, clearing away buffet trays. There was no sign of the one that was there earlier. He hadn't seen her since she got up to sing. He just hoped the women eyeing him with disapproval were either nice or empathetic to a crisis. 'It's an emergency situation that requires alcohol,' he added wearily.

'It's yer lucky day – I'm in a good mood,' one of them said, coming towards him.

'Christ, that's a first,' the other woman snarked. 'Stand by for a blue moon, an eclipse and for that loch to split down the middle for a bloke with loaves and fishes.'

On any other day, Scott would have found them hilarious, but right now he just needed a drink. 'Can I have a Jack Daniel's please? A double.'

'Make it two,' Carson added. 'Thanks.'

There was a raised eyebrow behind the bar, but in fairness to her, the woman didn't say a word, just served the drinks. Carson gave her a twenty-quid note and told her to keep the change.

Scott pulled at his tie, then realised he wasn't wearing one. The tightness around his neck was pure tension and it was choking him. He picked up his drink and knocked it back in one go, then put the glass back down on the bar and ran his fingers through his hair, resisting the urge to tear it out.

Carson was standing with both hands on the bar, leaning into it, head bowed.

'Christ, mate, you look as shocked as me,' Scott said, vocalising his thought from a few moments before.

Carson lifted his head. 'Are you sure? About Kelly?'

'She just told me that she did a pregnancy test this morning and it was positive, so yeah, pretty sure.'

Carson was stretching his neck from side to side now, the way he used to do right before any important event: a free throw in basketball, an exam in school, asking a girl out. 'Did she say how far gone she is?'

Scott was wishing he hadn't downed the JD, because now he really wanted another one. 'A couple of months.'

'Jesus.' Carson turned back to face the bar, head down again.

'Mate, you're not helping here. What the fuck am I going to

do? Actually, don't bother answering that, because I already know.' Weariness and frustration oozed from every word. He really, *really* needed another drink. As if catching onto some paranormal transfer of thought, the women over at the buffet glanced up at him, and without saying a word, the one who'd served them came back over, lifted the JD bottle again and poured another two fingers into their glasses.

This time he put twenty pounds on the bar, but she waved it away. 'Call it a freebie, son. From what I can see, it's medicinal and prescriptions are free in Scotland.'

The simple kindness gave him a lump in his windpipe. Or maybe he was still psychosomatically choking.

'Rewind,' Carson told him. 'What are you going to do?'

'I'm going to withdraw my redundancy and stay here and bring up my kid,' Scott clarified, as if it went without saying. In his mind it did.

'And what about all that stuff you said this morning? About how you weren't in love any more. You were planning to leave. Just you and your guitar and a whole new life.'

The choking sensation was getting even stronger.

Scott took a sip of the second drink, aware that if he knocked this one back there was a very good chance he'd vomit. 'Cancelled.'

'You're not going to go?'

'Of course I'm not going to fucking go. I can't leave my wife when she's pregnant. Seriously? If that's the kind of guy you think I am, mate, you don't know me very well.' He knew he was diverting his anger, projecting it on to Carson, but he didn't know what else to do with it.

Carson took it on the chin and came back at him, choosing his words more carefully. 'I had to ask. This morning you're saying you've spent years counting down to the day you can go, and now the clock's been turned back on that by what? Sixteen years? Eighteen?'

'Fuck. I'll be halfway through my fifties by then. Too fucking late.' Scott's future passed in front of him. Eighteen years from now. Same job. Same house. Same car. Same wife. Kid going off to college and suddenly he can leave again. Only he's fifty-six and he knows he can't jack his whole life in for some crazy dream because it won't be long until he's retired and he'll need somewhere to live and a pension. That'll be it. His whole life. Gone.

'But why? Look, Scott, I know how you feel about this stuff. You can't repeat history, can't abandon your kid. But you're not your dad. He pissed off, left you and your mum and he didn't take any share of the responsibility. That's not you. There would be nothing to stop you from finding a way to do both: to live the life you want but still be a good father. Plenty of other people are separated, divorced, but they work out a way to share the kids.'

Scott thought about that. Actually, it had gone through his mind when he was sitting with Kelly and she told him the news. But...

'I can't. Carson, we've been together twenty-two years now. She loves me. And in a way I love her too. I can't let her down, I'd hate myself and I'd spend every day feeling like shit.'

'What if she didn't?'

Carson spat the words out so quickly, Scott struggled to decipher them.

'What if she didn't what?'

'Love you. What if she was messing around? What if she wasn't loyal to you?'

Scott hated hypothetical questions because they served no purpose here, but he went along with it anyway. 'Then, yeah, I guess that would change things. But, come on, it's Kell. This conversation is pointless because you know she'd never do that. Never...'

'She did.'

Two words. Spat out. And they just hung in the air.

'What?' Scott wasn't grasping this at all. Were they still being hypothetical? They had to be. But why was Carson so agitated, so pissed off? Scott had a really bad feeling that he was reading the map, but it wasn't giving him the whole picture.

Carson seemed to shrink before him, as if someone had opened a valve and sucked out the air. 'I'm sorry, mate. I love you and I can't let you derail your life on a lie.'

Scott's internal temperature was going in the other direction. His head was a pressure cooker and Carson's words had just added so much heat it was about to explode. 'Carson, I swear to God, if you don't start making sense, I'm gonna deck you.'

Carson exhaled wearily. 'Something happened. Between me and Kell.'

Scott tried to speak. Nothing came out. This couldn't be happening.

He tried again. 'What do you mean, "something happened"?'

No reply. Carson was just standing there, head back, as if he was looking to the skies for answers. That's when Scott lost it. For the first time in his life, Scott lost control and the target of his fury was his best mate.

He launched himself forward, got two hands to Carson's chest and pushed him backwards while simultaneously getting right in his face. 'You slept with my wife?' he roared. Another push. 'You slept with my fucking wife?'

'Bloody hell, Jane! You get that one, I'll get the other,' he heard the woman behind the bar shouting as she started racing towards him. For a woman of her age and size, she moved like a whippet. None of which he cared about right now. He pushed Carson again and this time he stumbled as he went back but caught himself before he fell. Scott pulled back his fist and only now did Carson put a hand up to defend himself.

If he'd been rational, he'd have considered that Carson was a trained military operative who could take him out with one punch, but logic wasn't playing any kind of part in his thinking right now.

Carson raised his hands in a surrender gesture. 'No! I didn't sleep with her, I swear. It was a kiss. That was it. Nothing else.'

'You fucker,' Scott snarled as he moved forward, fists flying outwards until...

It was as if he'd suddenly been cocooned by a cage of steel. His arms were pinned to his side by a force from behind, while a woman had jumped in between them.

'That's enough!' she bellowed. 'Jesus, you're grown men! Stop acting like twats! And you,' she focused on Scott, 'settle yourself before Janice takes you down. You okay there, Janice?' she asked the person behind him, the one who was holding him in a vice.

Scott felt a breath on the back of his neck. 'Aye fine, love. I'll be even better when Jackie Chan here calms the fuck down.'

Scott knew there was no chance of escape. He wasn't going to go quietly though. He still had things to say to Carson. Heartfelt things. 'You piece of crap,' he spat.

Carson had both hands out in a calming gesture. It wasn't working. 'I don't blame you for hating me, but I swear we only kissed. I just needed you to know so you had full disclosure before you decided to give up the life you wanted.'

'Who made the first move? Huh, Carson? Who did it?' Scott had no idea why that was important to him, but he wanted to know.

He watched as Carson hesitated, then said, 'I did. It was me.'

'You fucking snake...' He tried to lurch towards him, but the arms holding him back were too strong.

'Scott, enough,' Carson begged. 'I'm so sorry. Come on, man, let's go home and we can talk about it, sort this out.'

'Home? Fuck off. I tell you what to do. You really want to be a mate? Go and get my wife, and you and her get out of here and leave me the fuck alone.'

'Don't be crazy, Scott, come on. We're not leaving you here.'

'Oh, so now you're concerned about my well-being? You weren't so fucking cautious when you were kissing my wife. So go on. Be the good guy. I'm asking you to do something – go and find my pregnant wife...'

'Oh dear God, if you'd mentioned that before, I'd have let you punch him,' the woman who was holding him muttered.

Scott carried on regardless, but he was calmer now, exhausted. 'And take her home. I need time to think and I can't do that with either of you anywhere near me. Just go, Carson. We're done here.'

Something, he wasn't sure what, finally got through. Carson sighed, shook his head, surrendered the fight and walked away.

The woman behind Scott loosened her grip, let him go, while the one who'd got in between them gave him a sad smile. 'Right, champ, looks like he got the message. So what's the plan now then?'

What was the plan now then?

Scott had absolutely no idea.

24

HARRIET

As Yvie helped her into the car, Harriet reflected that saying goodbye to the family who had been gracious enough to spend the day with her had tugged at her heart. So silly. She'd only met them a few hours ago, and yet she'd felt like she'd known them for years. Meeting strangers was something she'd always avoided, mainly because Dennis had preferred to stick with family. After Leo died and his relationship with his brother fractured, his avoidance of new people had soared to new levels. For twenty years, it had just been the two of them and Harriet had gone along with it because she couldn't bear to add more pain to his wounded soul. Somewhere along the way, she realised now, she'd forgotten about her own.

It was too late to change it. The only thing worse than the solitude would be causing a burden to other people, foisting her needs on them. If anything, today had, in some way, proved that point. Her happiness had only been possible because these two young women in the front seats had made it happen and depending on other people wasn't something that she could ever come to terms with – especially now that it was patently obvious that she was losing her marbles. Her reaction to that young singer had been visceral, so extreme that it defied logic or comprehension. Harriet had always prided herself on her sharp mind and her pragmatic personality – the thought of both those features diminishing filled her with nothing but fear. The prospect of living like that was terrifying.

'Are you okay back there, Harriet?' Yvie chirped from the front seat.

'Oh I am, dear. You know, I can't thank you enough for what you've done for me today. You've made an old lady very happy. And slightly tipsy. I don't think I've had three gins in the same day since the turn of the century.'

Verity twisted round in her seat. With her long red hair and the colour in her cheeks from the afternoon sun, Harriet thought she was exquisite. 'Well, you deserved them today. I'm so sorry that the Bassetts weren't the family you'd been hoping for. You must be so disappointed.'

Harriet paused to muster the appropriate reaction. Yes, she was beyond disappointed, but as always, she wasn't going to spoil everyone's day by moaning about something she couldn't change.

'I am a little,' she acknowledged, for it was inconceivable that she wouldn't be. 'However, that's life, isn't it? If I've learned anything in my hundreds of years on this planet...' that made Verity smile, 'it's that life doesn't always work out the way you want it to. There's always a blessing to be found, though, and today, my blessing was spending time with you two wonderful women.'

'We're the lucky ones, Harriet!' Yvie countered. 'We've had a smashing day. Watching you and John doing a *Strictly Come Dancing* made my jaws hurt from smiling. If he were forty years younger, I'd have been pulling on my Spanx and my dancing shoes and begging him to teach me a few moves.'

Harriet knew what Spanx were. They'd had a whole discussion about them on the ward one day, when Yvie was bemoaning their evil. Ah, who'd be a young woman nowadays? Reading the magazines that Marg's daughter had brought in every day, Harriet had learned that for many of them, it was a torturous affair. They sucked in their stomachs with those restrictive garments, they had injections that froze some bits of their face and filled out other bits, they tattooed their eyebrows and wore eyelashes that could brush floors. Oh, and – quite incomprehensibly – they had an obsession with making their bottoms bigger. In Harriet's day, they'd been obsessed with making them smaller. Funny how the world turned.

'Ah, yes, he was quite the gentleman,' Harriet agreed, feeling the corners of her mouth turn up as she said it. He'd been an absolute treat. When Harriet watched the humour and teasing between him and his daughter, she'd decided that he was very lucky to have his family, but they were just as lucky to have him. 'Must be so lovely for his family to have his company.'

To her surprise, her words brought a tear to her eye, which she quickly wiped away, hoping neither of the girls had noticed. Time to change the subject and move it on to safer ground, after all, this may well be the last opportunity she had to talk. To speak. To actually exchange words. In no time, she'd be back home and then it would be back to just her and four walls. No discussions. No interactions.

Last year, during the endless months of isolation, she'd actually forgotten what her conversational voice sounded like. It wasn't the same when it was just echoing off the walls of empty rooms. The only consolation was that this time, she knew there was an end in sight. It wouldn't be for long. And hopefully she'd slip away before the pain of the solitude or the worry of a confused mind became unbearable.

'Must be wonderful for your family to have you too. I'm so grateful for your kindness today. Your parents must be so proud of having such lovely girls.'

Harriet may have been preoccupied by her thoughts, but she couldn't miss the silence that her comment met, nor the curious glance Verity gave her sister.

Yvie kept her gaze firmly on the road in front, but she was the first to speak, anchoring her words with a rueful sigh and, Harriet thought, a slight wobble of tension in her relentlessly cheerful tone. 'Ah, well, if only that was the case,' she said. 'Our mother, well, she dances to the beat of her own drum. The reason she couldn't make it today is because she's currently in… actually, I'm not sure where she is. She announced she needed to feed her soul and went off to trek Nepal with her very bendy yoga instructor.'

'She doesn't keep in touch?' Harriet asked, appalled that any mother could do that.

'No,' Verity answered this time. 'She's never been one for playing happy families. Our dad was though…'

Oh dear. Past tense.

'I'm sorry. I didn't realise he'd passed away.'

'When we were kids,' Verity said, matter of fact.

Harriet did a quick calculation. If he'd died when they were kids, he was probably a young man. A memory of Leo, kissing her, waving goodbye, walking down the path to the car played on fast forward in her mind. Death was sad. But the death of a person who has not yet lived their life was a different level of tragedy.

'He committed suicide. He had a lot of issues that weren't talked about back then. Depression. Alcoholism. It'll never stop being a heartbreak. That's why I formed our bereavement group – the one I was telling you about earlier. I wanted to reach people who had suffered a loss, who were feeling the pain that we felt when we lost Dad.'

Harriet felt like she'd been slapped. Suicide. How broken, how desperate that poor man had to have been to leave his children. And how brave those children must have had to be. She saw now why there was a such a strong sense of humanity in these two women. Verity was a teacher, one who had welcomed her company without question today. And Yvie, quite simply, had the biggest heart of anyone she'd ever met. Their father's suicide clearly hadn't defined them, but perhaps it shaped the women they'd become. That would be his legacy.

What legacy would Harriet leave behind? she wondered. Nothing. Not a single footprint to be walked by people she loved, because there was no one left to take the steps.

It was time.

'I'm so sorry for you both,' she said, truthfully. 'I've always chosen to believe that Leo is somewhere near, watching over me. I don't know if that's true, but it's what I needed to get me through the days.'

'Actually, I chose to believe that too, Harriet. I think Dad is out there somewhere, and he can see us live our lives. And yes, I think he's proud of us.' Harriet saw Yvie shoot a cheeky glance at her sister. 'Or at least, proud of me. He probably thinks you're nippy and prone to judgement.'

'Seriously?' Verity punched Yvie in the arm.

Yvie yelped. 'Ouch! Dad saw that. He says you've to say sorry and buy me dinner.'

Harriet felt a pang of envy for their ability to soothe each other, to make each other laugh, to lift each other back up.

She turned to look out of the window and saw, to her disappointment, that they had just pulled into her street. A few seconds later, Yvie manoeuvred the car into a space outside her home and switched off the engine. This was it, Harriet thought. Day over. Her last hurrah had come to an end, but goodness, it had been fabulous while it lasted.

Harriet leaned forward in her seat, put her hand on Verity's shoulder in front of her. 'You two are wonderful. Thank you. From the bottom of my heart.'

'You're so welcome, Harriet. It was great to meet you. Take care of yourself. And if you ever fancy another day out at a party, we'd be delighted to join you.'

Harriet squeezed Verity's shoulder, then reached for the handle to open the door.

'Wait a sec!' Yvie exclaimed, as she jumped out and came around to Harriet's side of the car, then opened the door and held out her arm. 'If you break your other hip falling out of my prestige vehicle, the NHS will sack me.'

Somehow, Harriet managed to muster a smile, but it faded with every step they took towards her front door. As they walked slowly up the path arm in arm, Harriet couldn't help feel that this was more than just a goodbye at the end of a day. It was far more likely that it was a last goodbye for them both.

At the door, Harriet fumbled with her keys, so Yvie kindly took them and let them both in.

'I'm just going to make you a cup of tea and a sandwich,' Yvie offered, slipping right back into nurse mode. 'And we can sort out your medication for tonight too.'

'Och, no, dear. Your sister is waiting in the car! On you go. I'll be absolutely fine.'

'I know you can do it all, but I'm here, so please let me help. Besides, it's good for Verity to have to wait a bit. Did you see the punch she landed on me in the car?'

Laughing, she bustled off into the kitchen and Harriet eased herself down into her favourite armchair, the one that Dennis had sat in every evening. When he'd died, she'd thrown out the old portable TV that used to be in the kitchen, and this was her spot for watching television now. It was ironic – she'd finally secured the best position and she'd give anything to have to sit in the kitchen again.

After a few minutes, Yvie came through carrying a tray with a mug of soup that she must have heated in the microwave, a corned beef sandwich, a caramel wafer and a cup of tea. She put it down on Harriet's little TV table, and then wheeled it across so that it was directly in front of her. 'There's your medication for this evening too, Harriet,' she said, pointing to the saucer that had four pills in the middle of it. One for her arthritis, one for her high blood pressure, one for her heart and another one for... she couldn't remember, but it always made her feel slightly woozy. 'I called in to the office and checked that your care worker will be here tomorrow morning. Apparently, one came to visit this afternoon while we were out. I told them I'd kidnapped you and taken you dancing. I don't think they believed me,' Yvie chuckled. 'They underestimate our powers, Harriet.'

'Yes, they do.'

'Is there anything else I can help with? I'd be very happy to come back later and help you get ready for bed.'

'That's very kind of you, but I'm fine. I need to get used to doing these things by myself, start as I mean to go on.' Yvie didn't need to know that she had no intention of going on for long. Already, just being back in this room, she could feel the loneliness begin to creep under her skin, feel the despair wrapping itself around her stomach.

Yvie took a pen out of her pocket and jotted a number down on the pad by the telephone. 'There's my number, Harriet. Please call me anytime. The next meeting of the bereavement group is a week on Wednesday and I'd love you to come. I can collect you and bring you home again, it's not a problem.'

Harriet knew that anything other than an affirmative answer would raise alarm. 'I would very much like to come. But please don't come for me. You've done so much for me already. I'll get a taxi.'

'Okay, well, the offer is there.' She reached down and gave Harriet a hug. 'You be good, no more dancing and call me if you need anything at all.'

'I will.' She knew she wouldn't.

'And I'll see you a week on Wednesday.'

'You will indeed.'

As Yvie waved goodbye, then left and closed the door behind her, Harriet knew that a week on Wednesday probably wasn't going to come.

8 P.M. – 10 P.M.

25

MAISIE

Maisie had got stuck up in the office in the main building at Lomond House for way too long and it had thrown her behind schedule. She'd only gone there to let them know that they were just about cleared up and finished, and to return the keys for the Pavilion, but the organisers of the event had been there too and they'd wanted to discuss the possibility of The Carrot Schtick catering a couple of other functions that were in the calendar. Maisie was delighted that they were so happy with today's service and she'd have good news to share with Sissy.

As she began to make her way towards the car park, she did a quick calculation. It was just after 8 p.m. She wanted to head home for the quickest of showers, so that would take about forty-five minutes to get there, then, say, twenty minutes for a shower, and then it was a half-hour drive into the city centre to the hospital. She'd easily be there by ten.

Nathan O'clock.

Once again, the thought unleashed a river of adrenaline that made her stomach swirl and her knees threaten to buckle.

While she walked, she fired off a text to Hope.

Maisie: Are you awake? If so, give me a call. Meeting Nathan later.
Need you to talk me out of taking a weapon. Xx

She kept walking, staring at the screen for a return text. It didn't come. Bugger. Hope must still be in bed. Night shift was hell on the time clock. Maisie could very slightly relate because when she'd finished an eight-month national tour with *Chicago*, performing six nights and two matinees a week, and then gone straight to a three-month stint on a soap, it had taken her body clock weeks to readjust to working during the day and relaxing at night. Not that she felt her job compared in even the slightest way to Hope's, on account of the fact that belting out 'All That Jazz' didn't come with the possibility that she would have to perform CPR, stitch up a couple of stab wounds, appease gang members hyped up on drink and drugs or dodge a potentially fatal virus. Hope was the one who kept people alive – Maisie was the one who entertained them.

Still no reply. She sighed, slipped her phone back in her pocket and continued making her way to the car park. Janice and Jane had finished packing up and were just closing the van doors when she got there.

'That's us good to go, love,' Jane announced, giving Maisie a hug. 'Smashing working with you today. I can't wait to get home and get my feet up with some pakora and a Baileys.'

'Aye, we're living the dream, pet,' Janice echoed, with a cheeky glint in her eye.

'Thank you, both of you,' Maisie said, hugging them in turn. 'See you at the next garden party or my next wedding, whatever comes first.'

'If it's yer wedding, I'll bring ma trainers,' Janice teased her. 'You know – in case I need to chase down the groom.'

Jane closed her eyes. 'Dear God, save me from this one,' prompting Janice to feign innocence.

'What? Still too soon?'

'Not too soon, Janice,' Maisie assured her, howling with laughter. 'I'll give you plenty of warning so you can get some training in and get your speed up.'

'Don't encourage her,' Jane sighed wearily. 'Anyway, let's go.' Then, almost an afterthought... 'Do you think Jackie Chan will be okay down there?'

'Who?' Maisie asked, puzzled.

Janice pointed over at the figure of a man, sitting on the grass down by the water. 'One of those blokes you were talking to earlier. They ended up trying to pummel each other and we had to split them up.'

Maisie couldn't hide her shock or her confusion. 'What? Who did? Where was I?' she asked, squinting to see if she could recognise him.

'It happened when we were clearing up and you were up at the main house. They knocked back a couple of large ones and then they got into it. I think they were fighting over me to be honest,' Janice said, flicking her hair back.

'Understandable,' Maisie agreed, still squinting, until her vision adjusted. 'Crap, it's Carny's dad. Is he on his own? Did they just leave him?'

'In fairness, he didn't give his mate much choice in the matter.'

'Aw, Jesus,' Maisie sighed. 'I'll go check on him. Make sure he's not about to wade on in there.'

'We'll wait...' Jane offered, but Maisie shooed her on.

'No, no, don't be daft. I'll be fine. He's my friend's dad and he's a really nice guy.'

'His mate wisnae saying that earlier. Right enough though, seems his pal was up to no good with his wife. It was like an episode of *Dynasty*.'

'Bloody hell.' Dammit, there was no way she could leave him now. If anything happened to him, she'd never forgive herself. She mentally added ten minutes to her schedule. She could just quickly check on him and still make it to the hospital for ten. 'Right, you two get off. I'll see you later.' She could see they were still hesitant to leave her. 'Go. Shoo. Look, there are still plenty of people sitting at the tables outside the main house and they can see me. I'll be fine.'

That, and the desperation to get home in time for *The Voice*, mollified them enough to go.

Maisie strode over to the water, glad that it was still daylight and that it had cooled down from the early afternoon heat. Scott had his back to her so she was almost upon him when he heard her.

'Scott? Are you okay?'

When he turned to face her, she somehow managed to contain her surprise with just a silent, sharp intake of breath. This afternoon she'd appreciated the view of the two attractive guys at the bar, but now this one looked awful. Red face, blood-shot eyes, his shirt crumpled, hair messed up. This was an '8 a.m. after a night on the town, then falling asleep face down on a sofa clutching a bag of chips and cheese' look, not a dad who had just spent the afternoon at a fab party with his family.

'If I said yes, would you believe me?' His voice was hoarse, as if he'd been yelling or crying. Maisie really didn't need this right now. She had places to go, an ex-fiancé to meet, a best friend to calm down before she amputated her husband's penis... but she couldn't leave this man when he was so clearly distraught. Not only was he her friend's dad, but it wasn't so long ago that she'd been sitting on this very grass, by this very water, with her heart breaking in two.

She sat down on the grass, pulled her knees up to her chin. 'Probably not. Are you here alone?'

He took a swig from the beer bottle in his hand. 'I sent everyone away. Couldn't face any of them. It's been a day to remember, that's for sure.'

She knew she had to keep him talking, try to draw him out of his shell. 'Okay, I need full statistics to grasp the magnitude of what's happening here,' she said softly, with just enough levity to perhaps cajole him into opening up. 'What age are you?'

He eyed her like she'd lost the plot. It was a distinct possibility. 'Thirty-eight.'

'Thirty-eight,' she repeated, thinking that made him thirteen years older than her and only about sixteen years older than his daughter. Wow. 'So, in thirty-eight years, where does today rank in the top ten of really shit days?'

A bit of a smile on his five o'clock shadow. This was progress.

'I'd have to say it's at the top. Numero uno,' he admitted, with a slightly manic lilt. This could go either way. He could go sad and despondent or full-scale crazy bitter shouting at the sky. Maisie figured the best thing to do was to work on the end game.

'Got you,' she was calmly matter of fact. 'I'm not asking you to tell me about it, but I just want to check if you've got a plan?'

Another swig of beer. 'A plan? For what?'

'Well, I'm pretty sure you live in Frewtown, yes?' He didn't contradict her, so she ploughed on. 'Well, it's going to get dark soon. And cold. You're about forty-five minutes from home. You're in the middle of nowhere, I doubt you'll find a taxi, and if you did it would cost you about the same as a good night out to take you that far. I'm literally going that way, so how about you let me give you a lift home?'

'I can't go home. My best friend and my wife are there.' Oh bollocks, he was going bitter. 'And today, she told me she was pregnant and he told me they'd had... a thing.'

That took her by surprise. This afternoon, she'd spilled her whole sob story to his mate, Carson, and he'd been so empathetic. He'd seemed like such a good, genuine guy and she'd even felt a few flutters of attraction to him. But then, she'd also loved Nathan. The alert button on her knob radar was obviously malfunctioning.

'I mean, what am I meant to do with that?' he groaned.

He had a fair point. 'I think you need to go home and talk to them.'

'I can't.'

'You can.'

'And you're an expert on such things?'

Well, hello sarcasm. Maisie could feel the ticking clock in her head. She had to move this along and, right now, she was getting nowhere. Time to get real.

'Actually I am. Do you know where I'm going tonight?' She didn't give him a chance to answer. 'I'm leaving here to go to meet the man I was supposed to marry a few months ago.' That got his attention, so she carried on. 'Right here, actually. He proposed to me over at that rock and that's where we were supposed to get married.'

His body language had changed and he was leaning forward now, elbows on knees. 'Supposed to?'

Maisie nodded, recanting the pamphlet edition of the story she'd told his friend earlier. 'I was here, in my white frock, flowers, my mother had on a hat, we were ready to go... but he didn't show up.'

'You're kidding!'

Why was that always how people reacted? In what universe would someone make up an amusing, rib-tickling tale about getting chucked at the altar?

'Sadly not. Today, he called me – actually, in a moment of insanity I called him, but it went to voicemail, then he called me back – and he wants to meet me tonight to explain, so that's where I'm going. Only, I can't leave you here because Carny is my friend and I feel a responsibility to make sure you don't crash out on the grass, roll over into the water and sink like a stone. So there you go. Even if you don't want to go home, do it for me, because if you don't, I'll never meet my ex, I'll never find out why he left me and I'll die a bitter old lady who hasn't had a functioning relationship for the last sixty years of her life.'

He blew his cheeks out, sat back. 'Has anyone ever told you you're pretty dramatic?'

That made her laugh. 'Kinda goes with the territory. But the bottom line is, if I can face him, then you can face whatever is happening with you – because there really isn't any option, is there? We can't avoid them forever.' She could see he was almost there. Almost. 'And anyway, didn't Carny say she was leaving in the morning? If you don't go home, you won't be able to say goodbye.'

He flinched at that thought and she almost punched the air. Direct hit!

'Okay, you're right,' he sighed, as, with a few precarious wobbles, he pushed himself up from the ground. 'How did you get so good at this?'

Easing out her groaning muscles, Maisie stood up too. 'I played a hostage negotiator in a TV show. But the gig after that I played a psychopathic serial killer, so we could have gone either way there.'

Maisie breathed a sigh of relief as they crossed the grass to the car. Mission accomplished. Even if she wasn't being entirely honest. She'd persuaded this guy to face the people who hurt him, but she still wasn't entirely convinced that she'd have the courage to do the same.

26

KELLY

Kelly couldn't look at Carson. Couldn't speak to him. They'd been in the car for forty-five minutes and she'd just kept her eyes on the road, her mouth shut and hands on the wheel. It was still daylight, didn't get dark at this time of year until after ten, but she concentrated on the road like she had no idea what was up ahead. That pretty much summed up her life too.

As they turned into her street, she felt the coiled spring inside her tighten even more.

Why? What reason could he possibly have had for telling Scott what had happened between them?

At first, she'd refused to leave Lomond House without Scott, confused about what had happened. After Carny, Rick and Sabrina had left, she'd sat in the car for almost fifteen minutes, waiting for Scott and Carson to come back with their beers. She was about to give up and go and find them when she'd spotted Carson, face like thunder, walking towards the car.

He'd wrenched the door open and climbed into the passenger seat. It had always been the plan that Scott would drive to the garden party and she would drive back. He'd thought she was just offering to be nice, but it was so she had an excuse for not drinking.

'We've to go on ahead. Scott is going to stay here a bit longer.'

'What are you talking about? Why would he want to...' She'd stopped, taking in Carson's expression, the tightness in his voice, the hunched-up shoulders and abject misery seeping out of every one of his pores. In all the years she'd known him, she'd never seen him look so utterly wretched. 'What's wrong, Carson? What's happened?'

'I don't even know where to start,' he'd said. 'But let's go. I'll tell you at home.'

'No. Why would I leave without Scott? Don't be ridiculous.' A chilling, terrifying sensation of dread and fear had made her skin prickle and she tried to scramble her mind for explanations. Had the two men fallen out? Had a fight?

Carson had turned his face towards her. 'Kelly, please.'

There was something else there. This wasn't just some minor situation, a boozy argument or a difference of opinion. There was something in his eyes: a devastation, something dark... She'd been avoiding him because she felt so guilty about what had happened that night. Now she realised that Carson's guilt was staring right back at her too. The fear exploded into panic.

'Carson, what have you done?' She didn't give him a chance to reply. 'WHAT HAVE YOU DONE?'

Thank God the windows were up in the car, because she'd just ramped up the volume.

'I told him what happened. Between us.'

Astonished, Kelly had slumped back in her seat, her eyes not leaving his. 'Why?' she'd whispered. 'Why would you do that?'

'I didn't mean to. It... it came out.'

'How, Carson? How does something like that just pop out?' Her eyes were on fire and the words were coming out like bullets.

This couldn't be happening. It didn't make sense. Carson was the most loyal, decent man, and much as she'd been embarrassed to see him, she'd had absolutely no thought that he would tell Scott what had happened that night. It just wasn't in his DNA. They were family and she knew he loved Scott too much to hurt him.

No. This wasn't happening. She'd grabbed the door handle and wrenched it open, jumped out. For a moment, she'd thought he might follow her, but he didn't. Picking up speed, she'd run across the grass in the direction of the pavilion. Scott wasn't there. Then she'd spotted him, sitting on the grass over by the water, head bowed, beer in hand.

Changing direction, she'd run towards him, almost reaching him when he'd lifted his head.

'Go home, Kelly. Just go home.'

Her first reaction had been to bluster. 'Scott, I don't know what Carson said, but it was nothing. A misunderstanding. Honestly, I...' The look of pure disgust on his face had stopped her in her tracks.

'Did you fuck him?'

'No! Of course not. How could you think that?' Oh God. She couldn't do this. Had she had sex with Carson? No, she hadn't. But both she and Carson knew that was only because he'd stopped her that night. Refused her. In the last two and a half months, she'd wondered so many times what would have happened if he hadn't. That wasn't something that her husband needed to hear, not now, not ever.

His shoulders had sagged with what might have been relief, exhaustion, devastation – it was hard to say. This was a different Scott. It wasn't her easy-going, laid-back husband, the reliable, dependable family guy who took everything in his stride and liked an uneventful, easy life.

This was a different man altogether.

'Babe, I'm so sorry. It was a stupid mistake. You know we'd never hurt you.'

'Do I, Kell? Because right now, I'm hearing things I definitely didn't know and it definitely fucking hurts. How do I know that you're not lying, that the baby isn't his? We've had sex once, Kell. Once this whole year. And you're telling me that's when you got pregnant. After twenty years of nothing?'

Kelly sank to her knees. 'Scott, I swear... on Carny's life... we didn't sleep together. This baby isn't his. It's yours. I promise you.'

'Your promises mean nothing,' he'd spat.

'Come home, babe. Let's talk about this. We'll sort it out...'

'No. You don't get to call the shots here. Go home. I'll come when I'm ready, but I want you to leave, take him with you, and then get him out of my house. Do you understand me?'

Perfectly. It didn't even need to be said. Defeated, she'd got up, backed away, paused...

'I'm sorry, Scott,' she'd said again, then she'd walked back to the car, climbed in, and driven home in silence, unable to bear speaking to the man who'd just thrown a firecracker into her marriage.

Now, as the car slid into the driveway at the house, she pulled on the handbrake and didn't even glance in his direction. Carson followed her out of the car and she let them in, threw her keys in the bowl on the console table by the door.

'Get your stuff and get out,' she spat, still walking, right down the hall into the kitchen. God, she was tired. Exhausted. The pregnancy test. The heartbreak of the conversation with Rick. Carny's graduation. Sabrina's pain. And now this. She just didn't have the energy for it. She was going to make a cup of tea and then she was going to wait for Scott to come home, and they were going to sort this out. Surely he'd forgive her? It was Scott. She was pregnant with his baby. He *had* to forgive her.

Sliding into a chair at the kitchen table, she put her head in her hands, waiting for the kettle to boil. Moments passed before Carson interrupted her thoughts.

'Kell?'

It was an effort to raise her head, but when she did, she saw him standing in the doorway, his holdall at his feet.

'Why, Carson? Why would you tell him that?' It was the same question she'd asked earlier, but this time the rage was gone. She was too tired for it.

'I'm sorry. I guess...' He paused, and it was almost as if he was trying to work out what to say. Surely it should be straightforward. There must have been something, some really, really, cast-in-stone, bloody massive reason that he'd felt the need to share the information. 'He's like my brother. I couldn't live with keeping it from him.'

It was a crap answer to a crap question. She could sense there was something more, that he wasn't telling her the whole truth, but she was too over it to care. It was done. The reasons didn't really matter.

Even through a haze of anger, she didn't doubt that he'd had reasons that mattered to him. In the lifetime that she'd known Carson, she'd never seen him make one shady move. It just wasn't in his character.

He was leaning against the doorway, as if counting on it to hold him up. 'He told me that you're pregnant.'

A weary sigh. 'Yup, seems like that's been the news of the day.' The kettle clicked off, and before she got up, he stepped over his holdall, took a mug out of the cupboard, made her a cup of tea. He didn't have to ask what she took in it, and for some reason that resonated with Kelly.

He placed it in front of her, then pulled out a chair on the other side of the table and sat down. 'Tell me what's going on,

Kell? I just want to understand. One minute you're kissing me and then... this. I don't get it.'

'I'm not sure I do either,' she admitted truthfully. She almost stopped there, but he was here and he wanted to listen to her, wanted to give her a voice, to understand. Something inside her needed to talk. 'The last couple of years... they've been rough. We've been so disconnected, like we were just living in the same world, but going through the motions of life, no blips, no dramas, nothing.'

Carson leaned forward, his elbows on the table. 'Isn't that a good thing?'

'Maybe, but Scott seemed... distant. Like he was a million miles away. I was dreading Carny leaving, struggling with the loss of purpose, and I needed someone to share that with, but he just didn't hear me. Didn't see me. And, before you say it, I know none of this justifies what I did. I'm just trying to explain. That night we kissed...'

Could she say this? Could she tell him the humiliating truth?

She took a breath. 'That night, it had been months since he'd touched me, since he'd heard me. I'd tried to talk to him about it, but he brushed me off every time. I guess I was feeling insecure, feeling crap about myself, just... lost. And then, I...' Kelly knew she had to say it, to acknowledge the truth, if she had any hope of salvaging this situation. 'Carson, I'm sorry. We both know it was all me. You didn't ask for it or see it coming. It's why I haven't been able to talk to you since it happened – because I made such an arse of myself. I think I was just trying to feel something that wasn't pain or dread. Pathetic as it sounds, I needed to feel wanted. Loved. To be touched. And there you were.'

Carson's smile was almost ironic. 'There I was.'

'Except... when you brushed me off, it felt – oh God – it felt so much worse. Like a physical pain. Rock bottom. Another rejection and I couldn't bear it. When I went up to bed, I woke him up and... well, I tried to numb the pain and, for once, he went along with it.'

Silence descended as he processed this.

'Kell, why do you want to be with him if you feel like this? It makes no sense.'

For a split second, she thought about giving him that last piece of the puzzle, telling him the whole truth, that she was in love with Rick. Why did she settle for the lack of intimacy with Scott? Because if she couldn't have Rick, then Scott was the second-best thing and she could live with that. She could take the hit, because other aspects of their lives together brought her so much joy. Their friendship. Their security. Their daughter. And now, the child that was going to make the next chapter of their life happy.

Instead, she went for the abridged version, the core of her truth. 'He's my best friend. And what we have isn't perfect, but it's enough.'

Carson disagreed. 'It's settling for less than everything.'

'No one gets everything, Carson. Life's not the fairy tale.'

There it was. That was it. The truth that she'd come to terms with, lived her life by, truly believed in her soul. No one gets everything.

Carson sat back, shook his head. 'But that doesn't mean you shouldn't try.'

There was no combat, no argument there, but still, Kelly couldn't let it lie. 'Are you trying, Carson? Because you don't have everything either.'

The flinch that crossed his face told her that she was right.

'I know, but I guess that's where we're different,' he shrugged. 'I don't want to come over like a self-righteous prick, but I don't want to settle for less than everything. And if that means I never find what I'm looking for, then I can live with that, because I tried. I hope you work things out, Kell, I really do, because I love you both.'

Kelly stared into her mug, saying nothing, as he pushed back from the table and stood up.

'I'm going to get out of here, so that you two can talk without him trying to kill me. I'm sorry again for telling him, Kell. I know it doesn't look like it to you, but I was trying to do the right thing.'

He picked up his bag, and as his footsteps in the hall receded, all Kelly could hear were his words, going round in circles in her brain, like bumper cars, crashing into every compromise she'd ever made, every sell-out she'd made herself believe.

'I don't want to settle for less than everything. And if that means I never find what I'm looking for, then I can live with that, because I tried.'

Maybe he was right.

But what if getting what you truly wanted would hurt everyone else that you loved?

27

SCOTT

Scott wanted to press a pause button on time because every passing moment was closer to getting home. The blur of the alcohol he'd knocked back earlier was almost gone and he didn't know if he was grateful or sorry he didn't have a bottle of Jack Daniel's in his hand. He'd never been much of a drinker, but today he was giving himself a pass.

Beside him, Maisie reached over and turned on the radio. It must be a retro station because he immediately recognised Fleetwood Mac's 'Go Your Own Way'. Shit. It was as if the whole world was trying to tell him what he had to do today and every message was different.

The sounds made his thoughts rewind to the Fleetwood Mac song he'd heard earlier in the day. 'You were brilliant back there, when you sang. You blew everyone away.'

'Thank you. I was glad Carny asked me. Sometimes when you're having a crap time, the only thing that makes it better is to go and sing your heart out to a song about having a crap time.'

'Profound,' he said, with mock gravity.

'Thank you. I'm thinking of putting it on one of those Instagram pages with inspirational messages.'

It seemed crazy to be laughing right now, but yet he was.

'Must feel so good to be able to do that,' he mused. 'A million years ago, I was in a band and I loved every minute on the stage.'

'Wow, what happened? Do you still sing?'

Damn, he suddenly wished he hadn't opened that box. If she'd asked him that question yesterday, he might have told her that he had plans to pick up his guitar again, but not now. Dreams gone. He tried to close the subject down. 'No, not any more.'

She reached over and switched the radio back off. 'Okay, we have about forty minutes left until you're home and we can sit in silence or you can talk to me. About anything. Up to you. And it's pretty unlikely that we'll bump into each other again, so I promise that whatever we talk about, whatever you say, the minute you get out the car it'll be forgotten. Done. This is like the car version of Vegas. What's said in the Mini stays in the Mini.'

There was a pause of indecision, swiftly followed by an outpouring of words as his mouth took over from his brain. 'I was going to tell my wife I was leaving her today, before I found out that she's pregnant.'

The car swayed slightly and a loud 'Holy shit!' came from the driver's seat, followed by, 'Sorry! But if you're going to land something that big, you might give me a bit of warning.'

'Noted.'

Maisie wasn't letting him get away with shutting down again. 'Okay, you're going to have to give me something more than that. I need details.'

'It's a pretty pathetic story,' he warned her.

'Scott, did you hear what I said about getting jilted? I do pathetic. It's my very favourite type of story.'

No wonder Carny liked this woman. Her kindness and sense of humour shone right out of her. Besides, he'd probably never see her again so he had absolutely nothing to lose by baring his soul.

'When I was sixteen, I was in the band and it was everything. I thought it was going to be my life and I was up for it. It was all I wanted.'

'Tell me you didn't have leather trousers,' she said, with a cheeky smirk.

His answer made her shriek with laughter. 'Two pairs. I interchanged them when they began to smell a bit off.'

'Oh, that's brilliant,' she spluttered. 'So what happened?'

'Kelly – Carny's mum – got pregnant. We moved in together, got married, I found a job, Carny was born... I carried on playing for a while, but it didn't work out. The rest of the guys went off to uni or got jobs and that was it. Game over. I've spent the last twenty odd years living that life, but now... Are you ready for the all-time biggest cliché?'

'Go for it.'

'I'm Midlife Crisis Man. Decided life's too short. I want to make up for lost time.'

'That's two clichés. Maybe three.'

'Oh, I've got loads more,' he assured her.

'Go right ahead, I'm here for them.'

So he did, kicking off with, 'For years, I've felt trapped, in a rut, but I didn't want to rock the boat while Carny was still at home.'

'Hang on – you stayed together for Carny's sake? I mean, she is one of the loveliest people I've ever met and I can see why you wouldn't want to upset her or break up your family, but I think you just hit the cliché motherlode.'

'And yet, still there's more. I'd worked it all out – how I could leave my wife, sign the house over to her, do everything I could to make it an amicable split, then I wanted to go to Nashville and… well… Free spirit. Open road. Rolling stone. Rhinestone cowboy.'

She grasped her heart. 'You're killing me.'

'I reckoned I had enough money to last a year or two, so I was going to take my chances. And I know how crazy it sounds, but, honestly, it's the only thing that's kept me going, kept me getting up every day, going to work.'

'How long have you been planning this?'

'About eighteen months, give or take. It was like a distant fantasy for years, then with Carny leaving home… I don't know how to describe it. It made me focus on what my life was actually like, what I wanted it to be. That's when I realised I had to do it,' he admitted. 'So I volunteered for redundancy in my job, and I was supposed to finish up next week. But now, my wife is pregnant again, so I'm withdrawing my redundancy and I'm back at square one.'

The whole time, they'd been keeping it light, mocking the reality, but that last bit stuck in his throat for the sheer brutal truth of it.

'Wait a minute, though. Didn't you say something happened between your friend and your wife?'

'Yeah, but to be honest, that doesn't change anything because that's not the point. They didn't actually sleep together. At least that's what they're both saying. So that means she's going to have my baby. I can't just up and leave – the guilt would kill me, knowing that I was deserting my kid, that I'd stayed for Carny, but not for this one. My dad left my mum when she was pregnant and I've spent my life hating him for it – I can't be that guy.'

'The fact that we're even having this conversation shows you're not that guy.'

That one hit home somewhere, but his head was too scrambled to work out why.

'And I know that, because I know someone just like him,' she went on.

'The arse who left you?'

That made her giggle. 'The very same. Strange thing is, you'd probably relate to him.'

'How's that?' he asked, doubtfully, pretty sure he'd have absolutely nothing in common with someone who was such an obvious prick.

'You ready for this? He's a singer in a band. Left me, got the band back together, went on tour.'

It was so bizarre, Scott had to search her profile to see if she was joking. Nope, he didn't think she was. 'Shit,' he exhaled, incredulous.

'Indeed.'

'Okay, now I need more details. I can't believe you let me drone on and then you've just swooped in with that. You've got about fifteen minutes to totally overshadow my pain.'

They should both be broken, wallowing in their pain, yet something in her was giving him a lifebelt, keeping him above water, as if they were keeping each other afloat until the coastguard got there.

'I'll do my best. Although, I'd like to point out that you've just put me on the clock and that's extra pressure.'

'You've got this. I've got faith in you.'

She took a deep breath and let loose. 'We'd been together on and off for years, since college. We were both chasing our own careers though, hustling to make it. I landed some good parts, he was doing well with the band, getting a lot of traction, especially in Europe, but they weren't breaking through and it got to them. They split up just before he came to live with me. Together.

Engaged. Jilted. All in the space of a year. That's like a really good first series in any show.'

Her attempt to make a joke at the end somehow made it even sadder.

'So what's happened since then? Because that's a lot, yet you seem like you've got it together.'

'Did you get the bit where I said I was an actress?' she asked with a smile. 'Nope, definitely not got it together. It brought up a whole lot of stuff that I was already struggling with. My sister and I were both adopted when we were kids, from different families. Our adoptive parents were amazing – my mum still is, but my dad died a few years ago. Anyway, last year, my sister and I did those DNA tests and she tracked down her biological family. It wasn't all hearts and roses – the woman who gave birth to her is a bit of a cow – but her dad and his family are amazing and she has this whole extra chunk of happiness in her life. My test didn't throw up a single match. Not one. So... I'm nowhere. And, if I'm honest, maybe that's why I clung to Nathan and maybe that's why it hurt even more when he left me.'

Scott added 'self-indulgent twat' to the list of labels he'd given himself today. He'd been so totally, utterly immersed in his own problems and now this woman, the one who'd laughed and joked, and tried to help him, tried to make him feel better, was giving him a playbook on picking yourself up and staying strong.

'So what happens now?' he asked her.

'Now, I'm going to the hospital to be with my best friend who is in there about to give birth. And meanwhile, my ex will be sitting downstairs in the hospital café where I've arranged to meet him. I've still no idea if I'll go through with it. I think I'd rather bang my head against a wall until I pass out.'

That made him laugh.

'Christ, Maisie, how are you still in one piece?'

She took her gaze from the road for just a second, turned to him, and as he saw her full face, he was blown away by the fact that even after telling him all that, she was still smiling. 'You already know.'

'I do?'

'I drink margaritas and I get on stage and sing Stevie Nicks songs.'

The street lights came on just as they pulled into his road. He checked his watch. Almost ten o'clock. Carson's train was at eleven, so hopefully he'd be gone by now. He'd barely processed the thought, when he saw his front door open, and Carson walked down the path, his holdall over his shoulder.

'There's your...' Maisie began.

'I see him.'

'Do you want to talk to him? I can beep the horn, attract his attention.'

'No.'

He watched as Carson carried on down the road, his back to them.

Scott unclipped his seat belt. 'Thank you for the lift. And for listening.'

'You're welcome. The minute you open that door, this conversation is forgotten, so I just want to say good luck. You know, before I forget that you're the all-time champion cliché guy.'

Without thinking, Scott leaned over, kissed her on the cheek. 'See ya later, Stevie Nicks. Hope you work everything out with the ex.'

He climbed out and waved as her Mini left the street, then turned, stared at the house he'd lived in all of his adult life. The dream of leaving had been good while it lasted. Now, he just had to work out how to make himself stay.

28

HARRIET

Pulling the photograph albums out of the mahogany sideboard under the window had almost ended her, but Harriet had refused to give up. Eventually she found the one she wanted and clutched it to her chest. The final collection of photographs from Leo's last year on this earth. She settled back in the chair, steadying herself, trying to summon up every ounce of courage that she had left. In the years since he died, she'd never once been able to bring herself to look at these photographs, and yet now, she felt an overwhelming need to see her son's face. Slowly, carefully, she turned the album over and opened the back cover, then flicked to the very last page.

The pain was almost physical as her eyes fell on the photograph of him taken on his birthday, just a couple of months before he died. She'd taken the photo herself and she could remember every detail of that night. They'd gone out for dinner, a rare treat because Dennis preferred to eat at home. It hadn't been anything too fancy, an Italian restaurant in the Merchant City that Leo loved.

'Mam, you'll love it. Mandy and I come here all the time. I

think that's why she loves me. That and my irresistible charm and good looks,' he'd added with a cheeky wink.

That had made her chuckle. It made her heart swell that he'd found someone who was making him so happy.

The dinner had been lovely and, afterwards, Leo had driven them all home. Dennis had gone up to bed, but Harriet had other plans. She went to the fridge, took out two little tubs of ice cream and held them up to him.

'Yassss!' he'd cheered, making her laugh. 'Come on then, Ma, let's go.'

They'd walked together, down to the end of the street and up on to the bridge that stretched over the river that ran behind their house. When they got there, they'd climbed on the wall, and sat, feet dangling over the side – just like they'd done every year since he was old enough to climb up without the risk of him toppling into the water.

When he was young, they'd gone in the daytime, but in the last few years it had seemed even more special at night, just the two of them, chatting, laughing, with no sound other than the water that ran below them. At one point, he'd thrown his head back and that's the moment she'd been reminded of when she'd seen that girl singing on the stage today. A bright, beautiful young thing, just like her boy.

Only a few moments after that, she'd taken the photograph. She'd popped one of those disposable cameras from the chemist's into her coat pocket and made him smile for his annual birthday picture. After it had been developed, she'd slotted it into the next empty page of this album. Leo's life. One photo at a time. Twenty-five images, taken a year apart. A book that had ended far too soon.

She lifted the picture out of the tiny white corners that held it in place and brought it closer to her, touching his face. 'Hello, son...' she whispered, tears dropping like rain down her face. Her boy. Her beautiful boy.

Her breath caught somewhere in her chest and she let out a silent scream, her shoulders falling forward as she clutched him to her heart.

For a moment she thought that was how she might go, right there, right then, and she welcomed it. Death didn't scare her, because it was just a walk to that bridge, and she knew Leo would be there, waiting for her.

She had no idea how long she sat there like that, but the daylight was dimming outside when she finally felt strong enough to move. She glanced at the medication that Yvie had left for her on the table beside her, then reached over, picked up the pills and...

No. She wasn't going to take them. What was the point? She had no more reasons to drag out her time on this earth, sitting here alone, day after day, until her mind or her body failed her. No. Enough.

Putting the pills back down on the table, she decided to let nature take its course.

She was about to push herself up from the chair and make her way to bed when the ringing started. It took a moment to register what it was. It had been so long since her phone had rung – maybe a year? Two? She only kept the line on in case she ever needed to call someone, maybe a doctor or the chemist.

Dennis had installed it on a shelf right next to his chair – the one she was sitting in now. She reached over and lifted the handset from the cradle.

'Hello?' A pause. Must be a wrong number.

'Hello? Is that Harriet?' A man's voice.

'Yes.'

'Harriet, this is John. Carny's grandad. We met today at the party. I was the twinkletoes that had you dancing.'

Harriet almost dropped the phone.

'Are you still there, Harriet?'

She realised she was going to have to try to summon words, before he thought her utterly rude and hung up.

'I am, John. And yes, of course I remember you. Although, dancing might be a stretch. Did we not decide we were swaying?'

He had a lovely, deep laugh. 'Aye, I think we did.'

Another pause and Harriet was flummoxed as to how to fill it. Thankfully John managed it first.

'I hope you don't mind me calling you...'

'Of course not, but, John, how did you get my number?'

'I looked it up in the phone book. It's an old one from years ago, but there aren't many of us Bassetts in there. You weren't hard to find.'

Harriet wasn't sure why she found that funny. Maybe because all those young ones used that internet thing these days, and yet here they were, two old codgers, managing perfectly well with their old-fashioned ways.

'The thing is, Harriet...' he went on. 'I fair enjoyed your company today. There aren't many of us left that remember the same things. And, well, it's not like we've got time to hang about and play it cool, as our Carny would say, so I was wondering if maybe you'd like to have dinner with me one night next week? Our Sonya said she can come and collect you and drop us off at a nice little restaurant I frequent regularly. They do a lovely meal, none of that fancy stuff that doesn't even fill your plate. I'd be very honoured if you would accompany me.'

'Oh.' It was all she could get out.

'I'll not be offended if you say no, Harriet, but, well, we have to live while we're still able, don't we? There's still a bit of life left in us yet.'

It was only when a tear splashed onto her hand that she realised she was crying again. Not the wracking sobs from earlier. Just a tear or two, and more from happiness than sorrow. She looked down to see the droplet of water had fallen right next to the photo of Leo and that's when she knew... This was his doing. It was a message. *Live your life, Mum. It's not our time yet. Be happy. I'll see you soon...*

'John, I would be delighted to have dinner with you. I'm free on Monday night, if that would suit you.'

There was a rustle on the other end of the line, then she heard him shout, 'Sonya! Can you be our taxi driver on Monday night? Harriet and I are going out for a bite to eat.'

The reply carried all the way back down the line. 'Of course, I can, Dad. Ah, that's lovely. But no drinking, drugs, or wild parties and if yer not home for midnight, you'll be grounded. Can't have you going off the rails at your age.'

'Tell her we can't promise anything, John,' Harriet heard herself saying. 'But we'll do our best.'

'Aye, I think we will. Harriet, you've made my day. I'll see you Monday and I'm already looking forward to it.'

'I am too. I'll be sure to wear my swaying shoes. Goodnight, John.'

'Goodnight, Harriet. Sleep tight.'

After she put the handset back down on the phone, Harriet put her hand to her mouth, too shocked, too stunned, to process what had just happened. It was another moment before she felt her cheeks ache and grasped that she was smiling from ear to ear. She looked at the photo that she was still clutching in her other hand. 'Thank you, son,' she whispered, before tucking the image into the pocket of her cardigan. She was going to keep him with her, for as long as she was here.

Her gaze then skirted to the table next to her, to the little pile of pills. Slowly, she reached over and picked them up, and then one by one, she put them in her mouth and swallowed them, washing them down with the water Yvie had left beside them. Maybe it wasn't time to make rash decisions about life just yet.

Harriet let the pills settle, her spirits absolutely transformed. What a day it had been. What a wonderful, wonderful day. It was all thanks to the marvellous Yvie, who had taken the time to care about her, to go out of her way to do something kind. She'd brought this delightful family into her life, people who loved each other, who laughed, who picked each other up and lived for today. Harriet couldn't be more grateful. She had woken up in hospital this morning with a heavy heart, and now she was going to bed lighter. She had a new friend. She had something to look forward to. She had... hope.

Now she was going to go to bed, and tomorrow she would get up and she would read a book, perhaps watch some television, maybe sit in the garden. And then she would look in her wardrobe and decide what she wanted to wear for her dinner on Monday night.

She was still smiling as she pushed herself out of her chair, then picked up the tray her dinner had been served on. She could leave it until tomorrow, until the carers that Yvie had organised arrived, but force of habit prevented her from doing that. Her Dennis couldn't bear to have things out of place or left lying where they shouldn't be. Every night before bed, they would tidy away anything that was lying around, make sure all the dishes were washed and dried and back in the cupboard. It was just his way and she hadn't minded. You didn't spend sixty years with someone without learning to live with their foibles.

With a hand on each side of the tray, she took a step forward, then another, a bit of a shuffle, feeling the ache of the stiffening of her hip. The doctor had said it might be like that for a while, so she knew she had to just keep going, keep walking and...

The sensation of falling was upon her before she could gather her thoughts and comprehend what was happening. Her foot. It had caught on something. The table leg. She'd forgotten it was there and she couldn't see it because she was carrying the tray. Only, she wasn't any more. Now she was falling and it was like slow motion as she watched the tray fly from her grip, sending her crockery and cutlery flying across the room.

Flailing desperately for balance, she reached out, tried to grab something, anything. She managed to clutch the edge of the table, but it gave her no balance as her moving weight toppled that too. She heard a scream she recognised, one of her own, and then she heard the thud, felt the pain as she hit the floor. For a split second, she thought she was fine. She could still think, and nothing felt broken or cut. She could get up, she was unharmed, she was...

She didn't even sense the table falling until it hit her, sending a searing pain through her head. She wasn't okay. She wasn't getting up.

The last image Harriet saw before her world went black was Leo.

He was waiting for her.

10 P.M. – MIDNIGHT

29

MAISIE

The hospital car park was surprisingly packed when she finally careered into the first space she encountered. She grabbed the box from the back seat and started running straight into the maternity building. She'd planned to go home, to shower, to waltz up to meet her new niece or nephew looking clean and sparkly, but the detour to take Scott home had delayed her, and then, two minutes after she'd dropped him off, Cole had called to say the baby had been born.

'Don't tell her what it is!' she'd heard Sissy, a little groggy, in the background. 'Just tell her to get here right now.'

'I'm coming!' she'd bellowed, spinning the car around and heading straight to Glasgow Central.

As the huge glass doors slid open and she ran into the reception of the maternity building, she spotted the clock on the wall. It was just after 10 p.m. Right now, if he'd kept his word, Nathan would be arriving at the café over in the main building. She didn't even want to think about that. If the whole, sorry, jilted, devastating drama of the last year had taught her anything, it was about taking care of the people who loved you, making them your priority and, right now, Sissy was way further up the list than the guy who had broken her heart.

Cole had told her they were on the fourth floor, room 412, so Maisie rushed to the lift and, juggling the box in her arms, managed to bang the button. 'Come on, come on, come on...' Ping.

The doors opened and she jumped in, pressed 4, itching the whole way as the steel box ascended. The baby was here, so strictly speaking there was no rush, but that was irrelevant. Her best friend had just given birth, and she needed to be with them right now.

After what seemed like a week and a half, the doors pinged open and she followed the directions, pressing the big red buzzer at the entrance to the ward.

A smiling nurse in navy scrubs answered the door. 'Maisie? Sissy told us you were on your way,' she said in hushed tones, and Maisie realised that there were at least a dozen rooms along the corridor, all of which probably had sleeping babies and knackered mums. 'It's supposed to be parents only, but we can sneak you in for twenty minutes,' she said kindly, gesturing to the door that said 412.

Maisie thanked her, turned to the side so she could get through with the box, and squeezed past. Juggling again, she opened the room door and...

Sissy. On the bed. Cole sitting on a chair beside her. And in Sissy's arms, the tiniest, most beautiful, sound-asleep...

'It's a girl.'

Girl.

'Oh Sissy, congratulations! I mean, you too, Cole, but she gets more for doing all the work.'

Maisie put the box down on the table and rushed to the side of the bed, hugging Cole, hugging Sissy, then staring, open-mouthed, at the gorgeous bundle in her arms. 'No way did you make that,' she whispered. 'She's far too perfect.'

'You're right. I got Cole to shag Margot Robbie nine months ago and she just dropped this one off.'

'Thought so,' Maisie said, deadpan. 'How are you feeling?'

'Bit tired, but I'm okay,' Cole answered, then veered backwards to avoid the daggers from Sissy's evil glare.

'If you want to stay married to me – and you need to because my vagina is ruined…'

'Yeah, Janice was worried about that,' Maisie interjected.

Sissy carried on making her point, like it was a completely normal comment. 'Then you'll go and get your two favourite adult women some coffee.'

While Cole took the opportunity to escape, Maisie climbed on to the bed beside Sissy, snuggling in, so they both had the same view of their new girl. 'She's perfect, Sissy. How are you feeling? Is it as amazing as everyone says?'

'If I go mushy, will you throw it back in my face in future moments of disagreement? Or tell Janice and Jane? Because those two prey on the weak.'

'Absolutely not. Lips are sealed,' Maisie assured her solemnly.

'It's amazing,' Sissy whispered, her eyes filling until she sniffed so loudly, she almost woke the baby. 'I honestly can't let her go. I can't put her down or take my eyes off her and I love her so much it's actually hurting my heart.'

Maisie sniffed next. Sissy was the toughest, most ballsy woman she'd ever met and yet here she was, turned to mush and absolutely devoted to this little soul who'd just arrived in the world. And yet... She didn't want to make this about herself in any way, but this just made it so much harder to understand how her parents could have given her away. She shook off the melancholy that thought brought with it.

'Her name! I can't believe I forgot to ask her name!'

'Marzipan. I named her after something special to me.'

'Tell me you're kidding,' Maisie spluttered, not entirely sure that she was.

'I'm kidding,' Sissy assured her, grinning. 'This is Freya Maisie Bane.'

'Really...?'

'Really. We named her after her godmother. It was you or Janice. You won the toss.'

'Oh my God, Sissy, thank you. I'll be the best godmother ever, I promise! I'll take care of her, and I'll teach her stuff, and I'll...'

'Will you babysit every Saturday night and have her for three weeks in summer so Cole and I can go to Ibiza and pretend that we're still cool?'

Again, Maisie was pretty sure she was kidding, but she'd only been a godmother for a minute and didn't want to get bumped off the title by making a wrong move. 'Absolutely.'

'I knew we made the right choice. Although, Janice would have taught her to arm-wrestle like a pro. Talking of which, how did today go?'

Maisie didn't get a chance to answer before the door opened and Cole came in with two coffees.

'Great!' Maisie decided this wasn't the time to fill Sissy in on all the drama. That could wait until a moment that wasn't a life-changing milestone in Sissy's and Cole's lives. However, it did remind her... 'There was only one slight problem,' she said, scrunching her nose. 'The buffet was perfect, the bar ran like clockwork, everyone was thrilled with our service, which is just as well because I was halfway here before I realised that...' She gestured to the big white box. 'I completely forgot to put the cake out. It was in the back of my car and totally escaped my mind.'

'You're fired,' Sissy sighed. 'Your godmother was great while she lasted, Freya,' she said to the sleeping child.

'But it does mean that we have cake to have with our coffee,' Maisie gushed, jumping up, determined to regain her popularity. She climbed off the bed, grabbed the box, opened it wide and... 'Tada!'

Two stunned faces stared back at her, before Sissy covered her daughter's eyes. 'Don't look, Freya,' she said. 'I'm just going to give you to Daddy so Mummy can kill Auntie Maisie.'

Maisie didn't understand. 'What have I...?' She cast her eyes to the box she was holding out in front of her and almost dropped it. There, in glorious yellow and pink, was the largest penis cake she'd ever seen. Maisie stared at the sponge phallus that had been made for the hen night. When she looked back at Sissy and Cole, both of them were absolutely buckled in hysterics. Maisie gingerly put the box back down on the table. 'I, er, seem to have picked up the wrong cake.'

'You think?' Sissy howled, completely helpless with amusement. The flush on Maisie's face didn't even subside as they drank their coffee to a soundtrack of Sissy giving a push by push account of every detail of her delivery. When she eventually got to the bit about 'shooting a human being from her birth canal' (Sissy's words), Maisie could see that her friend's eyes were getting heavy. Climbing off the bed, she put her coffee cup in the bin.

'You know, I think I'm going to quit while I'm ahead and leave you two to it.'

The nurse must have been on the same page, because at that moment she knocked on the door and popped her head in. 'Sorry. We're just going to lock the ward for the night.'

'No worries, I'm just leaving. Thank you so much for letting me come.' She ignored the fact that the lovely nurse was now staring, transfixed, at the cake. Probably not something that was particularly popular on a maternity ward. Flustered, Maisie kissed an amused Sissy, 'Love you. I'm so proud of you,' and then an equally amused Cole. 'Love you and proud of you too,' and then bent down to kiss her goddaughter. 'And I love you too. Sorry about the cake. I'll explain when you're eighteen,' she whispered.

'Twenty-one,' Sissy countered.

'Twenty-one,' Maisie agreed, before blowing them kisses and vacating the room, giggling her head off as she went. She was halfway down in the lift when she checked her watch. Almost eleven o'clock. Nathan. She wondered if he was still there. He'd never been one for patience, so she doubted it.

Breaking into a jog, she reached the main building in just a few minutes. Through the revolving door, straight ahead, turn to the left and then...

He was there. Sitting behind the glass wall of the café, nursing a cup of coffee. The rest of the place was deserted, except a table in the corner, a man and a woman, holding hands, their faces stained with tears. Whatever the reason they were there, Maisie could see it wasn't good. And yet, their fingers were entwined, their heads close together, almost like one person made of two halves.

The thought stopped her in her tracks. That was what she wanted. That's what she and Nathan should have had.

She took a step backwards, edged behind a pillar, so she was out of sight, but still had a view of him. She pulled out her phone and dialled his number, then watched as he picked up the phone on the table in front of him.

'Hello?'

'I need to ask you some things...'

She could see his surprise. 'Where are you? Are you coming?'

She didn't answer. It was her turn to ask the questions. 'Why did you leave?'

Maisie watched as he glanced around to see if anyone was in earshot, then his shoulders slumped as he leaned forward onto the table. 'I realised I... needed more. The guys in the band called, told me the record company had offered us a new deal, and they needed us to fill in at a gig that night. They wanted me back. I couldn't say no.'

'And what about me?'

'Maisie, for months I'd watched you doing your thing, hustling for jobs, just managing to cover the rent and bills. I hadn't sold a song for decent money. I was bored and I was frustrated. I needed to feel... alive again. I needed to do something for me, something that would give me the kind of life I want. I want success. Money. Excitement. A better life than the one we were living.'

Now she knew. It wasn't for another woman. Or because she'd done something wrong. It was all about him. 'So you just left me? You couldn't have talked to me, worked out a compromise, or a way that you could go back on the road but we could still have our relationship?'

'I know, I know. It was a shit thing to do, believe me I've beaten myself up about it so many times.'

'And now?' she asked, challenging him. 'What is it you want now, Nathan?'

'Maisie, I want you back. The band... it's not working. The guys are dickheads and it's just as bad as before. We're getting nowhere. I should never have gone back. I'm so sorry but I can fix it. I can quit. After the Amsterdam gig, I can come back and...'

Another noise in her ear interrupted his words. She checked

the screen. An incoming call. Hope. Without saying another word to Nathan, she disconnected and took Hope's call.

'Hey. I'm on a break. I was just checking whether I had to shake down some patients to raise the cash to bail you out?'

'Your patients' money is safe.'

'You didn't go and meet him?'

'I'm looking at him now. He's sitting in the café at the main building, but he doesn't know I'm here. I spoke to him on the phone though. He wants me back.'

'And what do you want, sis?'

Maisie was still watching him. He'd continued to speak for a few seconds, and now he'd pulled the phone away from his ear, puzzled as he checked the screen. Maisie wondered if he would get up and leave, but he didn't. 'I don't know.'

'Oh, hon. You know I'll support you no matter what. You do whatever you want to do, Maisie. But do the right thing for you. I'm on a break for the next half-hour or so. I'm in the staffroom at A&E. Come tell me what happens. Unless you kiss and make up – in which case I'm not bringing you pancakes in the morning.'

'That's emotional blackmail right there,' Maisie remarked archly.

'I know – I have no scruples,' Hope agreed. 'Love you, sis.'

'I love you too.' Maisie disconnected the call, stared at the man she'd been so sure was her future. It would be so easy to go over there, to take back what she'd had, but a scene was replaying in her head, and she could see herself, in the car, speaking to Scott. When he was a teenager, he'd given up his dreams because he refused to leave his child. Now, despite the fact that his marriage was over, he was prepared to give up his dreams for a second time, because he couldn't leave his child or his pregnant wife. That's what Maisie wanted. Someone who loved her enough to stay, no matter what.

Her phone burst into life again, Nathan's name flashed up, and she watched him press the phone against his ear, waiting for her to answer.

Someone who loved her enough to stay, no matter what.

The question was, could he ever be that guy?

30

SCOTT

Scott sat out on the front step for a few minutes, maybe more, to clear his head before he went inside to face Kelly. What was he doing? What the actual fuck was he doing with his life?

This was karma. He'd known it was shady, keeping his plans to leave Kelly under wraps until now, then springing it on her. And he had to acknowledge that he had been a crap husband for a long time now. He just hadn't wanted to be there any more. And instead of doing the right thing and talking to Kelly about it, he'd shut her off, detached from their relationship. That couldn't have been easy for her, especially as they'd known for months that Carny would be moving out this summer.

Still, though... she and Carson. What was that all about? How could they do that? And was it wrong that he was more stung over the fact that his best mate could do this to him than his wife?

His pregnant wife.

They were going to have another baby. He couldn't process how he felt about that. His emotions were firing all over the place. God, he loved being a dad. It had been the best thing in his life, without a doubt. And he was only thirty-eight, so it wasn't as if this was happening late in life and he was worried about keeping up with the kid when it got older. It was just that he'd thought those days were behind him. If this was twenty years ago, he'd have been made up. Fifteen years ago, same. Even ten. But not now, when his dream life was so close he could hear the music.

At the end of the day, though, it didn't matter how he felt or what he'd have preferred, because this was how it was, and he only had one real choice, one option he could live with.

Sighing, he got up, put his key in the door and went on in.

Kelly was sitting at the kitchen table, a cup of tea in front of her. No wine now. Not when she was pregnant.

When she raised her eyes to his, he could see the apprehension, the anxiety, and he wondered what that would do to the baby inside her. No more fighting. They were adults. He had to do this calmly, for the baby's sake.

'Carson is gone,' she said.

'I know.'

The ticking of the kitchen clock was the only hint that seconds were passing because right now he felt that time had stopped. Neither of them moving, no one speaking, just stillness.

'I don't know if I can do this right now, Scott,' she said, weary, all the fight gone. How had he not registered how exhausted she'd been over the last few weeks? 'So please, say what you have to say. I'm not going to argue.'

Pull the Band-Aid off, he decided. 'Why did it happen? With Carson? Do you have feelings for him?'

'No,' she replied, so forcefully that he believed her. 'It was a one-time thing. I'd had a few drinks. I was sad. Lonely. And it's no excuse, but I felt invisible. I'm taking all the responsibility for what I did, Scott, but you have to admit that I wasn't wrong in how I was feeling.'

'You weren't wrong.' He got up and opened the fridge, took

out a bottle of water. No more beer. This needed a clear head. 'Are we both going for honesty here though, Kell?' he asked, sitting back down.

'Yes.'

'Then you have to admit that things haven't been right for a long time. Years. I don't know when it changed – way back when Carny was a kid, I think. Fuck, we were kids too.'

It was telling that she wasn't contradicting him. She knew. She'd felt the same. He just wished that one of them had admitted it at the time.

She lifted her mug, took a sip of her drink, buying time until she answered. 'I know what you're saying, but we were happy.'

'Were we? Maybe at the time we thought we were, but come on, Kell, neither of our hearts were in it. It was comfortable. Pedestrian. Settled. That's it. We were settled. Can you honestly say that you woke up every morning and thought how much you loved your life?'

'No. But I loved our family and I loved you. I *still* love you.'

'I thought we were going for honesty, no?' he prompted, and then watched as the truth flashed across her face. She didn't argue the point. They both knew.

'What about some honesty from you then too, Scott?' There was a hint of a sneer in there, and he took it on the chin. 'What was going on with you last year, when you could barely look at me? Was there someone else? Or had you just checked out so much that I wasn't even worth a shred of effort any more?'

He lowered his eyes, stared at the bottle in his hands. 'There's never been anyone else.' He raised his gaze. 'But I was going to leave you.'

He'd always wondered if she had any idea, any hint of what he was thinking. The utter shock he saw in front of him told him that she didn't.

'You were going to leave? When? Why?' she gasped.

'Soon. I was going to tell you this weekend. I was waiting until Carny left. I've been waiting for years.'

'How did I not see that?' she groaned in disbelief. 'Where were you going to go?'

'I don't know. That's the whole point. I'd had enough of knowing, Kell. Since we were teenagers, we've known where we were going to live, where we were going to work, what we were going to do every weekend. Christ, we even knew when we would have sex. And that was all okay, because we were doing what we thought was the right thing: we built a stable life for Carny and it was what we wanted. We didn't fight, didn't hate each other. Like I said, we just settled. Until I didn't. It stopped being enough for me. I'm thirty-eight, and I haven't lived, not really. And I know you think this is my midlife crisis, but it's more than that. I realised I wanted a shot at a different life.'

'So you weren't just leaving me, you were leaving everything?'

'Yeah. My job, this house...' He gestured around him. 'I just wanted to take my guitars, go travelling, see where I ended up.'

She was eyeing him now like she didn't recognise him at all. 'Scott, you're an adult. You're not some kid who can go off backpacking for a year. You have a career. You have a life...'

'One that I don't want,' he bit back, raising his voice for the first time. He caught himself, took a breath, calmed his heart rate back down. He couldn't help contrast the difference between this reaction and the way Maisie had responded in the car. She'd got it. If anything, she thought it was crazy, incomprehensible even, that he *wouldn't* follow a dream. His wife wasn't even pretending to understand.

She banged her mug down on the table, sending tea splashing everywhere. 'So you were just going to leave? Just walk out on me after twenty-odd years? Wave goodbye and toddle off. Don't you think I deserve more than that?'

His voice ramped right up to match hers. 'I thought this was what we both deserve! I thought you deserve to be with someone who really loved you, someone you were crazy about too. And I thought, after a lifetime of doing the right thing, that I deserve to go and try to find the life I always wanted. I wanted to sing, Kelly. To play guitar.'

'Scott, all little kids want that stuff. They all want to be a football player. Or a rock star. Or a fucking astronaut. But they don't wait until they're almost forty and then jack in their whole lives to go do it.'

'Well, maybe they should!'

They stared at each other, both furious, both fighting to contain their emotions, to get their temperatures back down.

Kelly was the first to break the silence. 'Wait, did Carson know what you were planning?'

'No. Not until today. I told him this morning.'

'That's why he told you,' she said, with a bitter laugh.

He wasn't sure which page she'd turned to, but he wasn't on the same one. 'What do you mean?'

'That's why he told you what had happened between us. He was giving you an out.' For the first time her eyes filled and she threw her head back. 'Unbelievable. He threw us both under the bus to try to help you. What a fool.'

He got there. A little later, but he saw now what she was saying. Carson had been giving him some kind of justification if he still wanted to leave to pursue his dreams. His appreciation evaporated as quickly as it had arrived. The fact remained that he had kissed Kelly. That was unforgivable, no matter what he tried to do to make up for it afterwards. The pain of that conclusion hurt him more than anything Kelly could say to him.

Scott was suddenly bone-tired. Exhausted. Seeping fatigue from every pore. They were getting nowhere. They'd resolved nothing and he needed this conversation to be over. 'What are we going to do now, then? What do you want?' he asked.

'I'm having this baby, Scott.' she said with absolute determination.

'I would never ask you not to,' he countered immediately. 'Just like I didn't last time. I don't know if you believe me, but I don't regret it. I really don't. If I could go back, I wouldn't change anything.'

'Doesn't that tell you something?' she pressed.

'Yes! It tells me that I did the right thing. That *we* did the right thing. But that was then. I'm asking you what you want to do this time.'

He had no idea what he wanted her to say. Since the moment she'd told him, it had been going back and forward in his head. He couldn't live with leaving his child. But he wasn't sure he could live with what he'd need to give up to stay.

'I want us to be a family, to try to make it work. Maybe we can find what we had at the start, Scott. Maybe those kids are still inside us and we can find a way to start from scratch. Maybe that's why this has happened. I want to try, Scott. I think we owe it to each other and to our baby. Don't you?'

He stared at the table for a long time, before raising his head to face her. 'If you're asking me to stay, I will,' he said, resigned to his fate.

'I am,' she answered, with no hesitation. 'I'm asking you to stay and give us another chance at making us work.'

31

KELLY

Kelly watched the lights go out in Scott's eyes when she said it.

'Then I'll stay,' he said, decision made.

So how come neither of them felt like they'd won? Eventually they would, she told herself. They'd compromised before and they'd made it work for so many years. They could do it again. Couldn't they? She wasn't sure she believed what she'd said earlier about rediscovering their young love, but she was prepared to try. The reality was, she was out of options that she could live with. She'd already known that. She wasn't proud of how she felt about Rick, and she was pissed off with herself for telling him today. That had been such a bad move. If he'd told Sabrina, then... She shuddered. She couldn't even contemplate that. She couldn't lose her sister. She just couldn't. Even if Rick had wanted her now, it would come down to a choice between him and her sister, and she'd choose Sabrina every time. That was love, and so was the way she felt about this baby. She was going to give it the best life, the best family, the best father and that was the one she was sitting with now.

'I'm going to bed,' Scott said, getting up from the table.

She decided to go with him. Carny wasn't home yet, and there was no point waiting up for her. If she was due to leave at 8 a.m., she could be home any time between now and 7.55 a.m.

He paused. 'You're not planning to tell Carny about the baby before she goes are you?'

Kelly shook her head. 'No. I think we need to get used to the idea first. I thought maybe we could go down to London next month and tell her together? Maybe even take your mum and tell her then too?' She was trying her best to sound positive, to act like all this was normal.

Scott just murmured, 'Okay,' and headed for the door.

Planning to follow him, she'd just pushed herself up from the table when the doorbell rang. Change of plan. Her girl must have forgotten her keys. She was exhausted, but maybe she would climb into Carny's bed with her tonight and they could watch something on TV, just like they'd done last night in Kelly's room.

Her throat began to tighten and she recognised the signs. *Do not cry. Get a grip.* There had been way too many tears today already. If this was the last night with her daughter, then she was going to put a smile on her face, hug her tight and appreciate every moment.

'I'll get it. Carny must have forgotten her keys,' Scott said, vocalising her thought.

She opened the kitchen cupboard, searching for something for her and Carny to snack on while they were watching the movie. This pregnancy was turning her upside down, she thought, her hand automatically going to her stomach. Sick all morning, and the munchies all night. Her head was still in the cupboard when she heard the kitchen door opening.

'Hey, sweetheart, I'm just looking for something for us to eat. Is there anything that...'

'Kelly?'

Sabrina. She pulled out of the cupboard to see her sister, standing in the doorway, face utterly ashen. Oh God. Rick had told her that Kelly was in love with him. The idiot had actually told her.

'Sabrina, I'm so sorry,' she began, feeling a wave of nausea that wasn't being caused by the baby. 'I didn't mean to...'

'No!' Sabrina cut her dead, making her stomach lurch again. Panic. What was she going to say? How could she fix this? 'It's me who's sorry.'

Kelly was taken aback. 'What?'

They were still standing, facing each other, a couple of metres apart, like gunslingers about to take their shot.

Sabrina stepped forward. 'It's me who should be apologising to you.'

Okay, rewind. Recompute. What was she missing here?

'Why?'

'Because I was a complete cow to you earlier. You're pregnant and I should have been one hundred per cent supportive and I wasn't. I was pissed off and jealous and I took it out on you and I'm sorry. I'm happy for you, I really am. And I promise I'll be better. I'm going to look after you and do all the things I should have offered to do this morning. I'll come to those breathing classes with you, go shopping for baby stuff, anything you want, I'm there.'

The relief was so overwhelming, Kelly was almost giddy. 'You don't have to apologise, and you don't have to do all those things either.'

'I do. I want to...' Sabrina took a step forward and Kelly opened her arms, thinking her sister was coming in for a hug. She threw her by stopping and thrusting her hand out in front of her. Kelly took a second to register the thing in Sabrina's hand, the white stick, made of plastic, exactly the same as the one that she'd looked at this morning. 'Because when we got back home tonight, I did a test and I'm pregnant too.'

Kelly stared. And stared. Too stunned now to speak.

'Some day, huh?' Rick's voice.

Kelly glanced over to the door and saw that he'd joined them now too and was leaning against the doorway. Like a defib on a heart attack, it was enough to shock Kelly back to the present. She opened her arms, threw them around Sabrina. 'Oh, sis, I'm so happy for you. This is amazing. So fricking amazing!' She absolutely meant it. All these years, all that pain. Her sister needed this.

Over Sabrina's shoulder, Kelly's eyes met with Rick's. 'Thank you,' he mouthed, a sad smile.

He hadn't told her. She should have known that he wouldn't.

'Come sit down!' Kelly told her sister when she finally released her. 'I want to hear everything. I mean, I know you peed on the stick, but I want to know how you feel...'

'I will. I just need to go to the loo first. I think my bladder is in training for what's coming. Oh, I forgot – Scott said to tell you he's gone on up to bed. He looked exhausted. I didn't want to tell him our news in case you hadn't told him yours yet.'

'I have,' Kelly replied, trying to cajole her spirits up from the floor.

'Ooooh, how did he take it?' Sabrina asked.

'He's... processing.'

Her sister was so giddy with delight that Kelly wasn't sure she was taking anything in. 'That's good. Hang on, need to pee. God, my bladder has definitely heard I'm pregnant and given up already.'

With a smile that could light up a street, Sabrina dodged around her husband and nipped into the downstairs loo. Rick closed the door after his wife left, then came forward and met

Kelly at the table. This time, it was him who made the first move, wrapping his arms around her.

'Thank you,' he said again, keeping his voice low. 'I'm sorry about today. I was a dick. It's just... not always been easy.'

'I know that feeling,' she whispered, squeezing her eyes tight shut, trying desperately not to lose herself in his arms.

After a moment, he pulled back, so that he could see her face.

He was speaking in hushed tones, but she caught every word. 'I messed up, Kell. I'm sorry. I should have said something a long time ago. I just... I didn't know you felt the same.'

The crack in her heart, the one with his name on it, widened a bit more. 'We both messed up.'

'Yeah, I guess we did. But maybe that's because this was the way things were meant to work out. I love you, Kell. I always will. You're my centre. My balance. And there isn't a day in our lives that I won't love you or be there for you.'

She could see the truth of that in every crease and line of his face. 'I know,' she whispered, the crack splitting open a little bit more.

'You need to know, though, I love your sister with all I have. She's everything.'

'She's lucky to have you. And you're lucky to have her.'

He held out his hand. 'Friends?'

'Friends,' she said, taking it. They stood there like that for a few moments of perfect bliss, until Kelly broke the spell. 'Now, go and check she's okay,' she prompted softly.

He lifted her hand, kissed it, then walked away.

Kelly pulled her chair back out and sat at the table again, ready to resume celebrations when they came back.

Rick's words were still echoing in her mind. *I love your sister with all I have.* She couldn't remember the last time that Scott had said something like that about her. Couldn't remember the last time she'd felt his love, his all-consuming, deepest, heartfelt passion for her. The last time that he'd been desperate for her. That he'd said he couldn't live a day without her in his arms.

And she couldn't remember the last time she'd felt any of those things about him.

Another thought. Was that why her feelings for Rick had changed? Had she manufactured a fantasy about him because it made up for the feelings that were missing in her life, a life that she hadn't been prepared to change because she wanted to keep her family together? Maybe she needed Rick, not because she loved him but because thinking about him filled a hole in her life.

'I love your sister with everything I have.'

Maybe it was time that she decided not to settle for someone who couldn't say that about her?

Harriet forced her eyes open. She was so tired. Wanted to sleep. But she knew she couldn't. Where was she?

The floor was cold, the room even colder. She waited until her eyes adjusted to the light that was coming from a lamp a few feet away.

Her living room. A table lying on its side next to her.

She was scared to move, not sure if she could, unable to think straight, her skull thudding with every breath she took. The clock on the mantelpiece was ticking, but she couldn't lift her head, so she had no idea of the time, no idea how long she'd been lying there, no idea how much longer she could stand the pain.

This was what she'd feared. Another fall. Her body failing her. The last time she'd been knocked out and hadn't woken until she'd been taken to hospital. But that had been during the day, when there were people around, and she'd been lucky that the window cleaner had found her.

Now it was definitely night-time. No one was going to come until morning at the earliest and she had no idea if she had the strength to last that long. Maybe she'd been wrong before. Maybe this was her time to go.

Her lids had closed again when there was another noise. A scratching sound. Over at the window. She tried to turn her head to see who was there, but a searing pain shot across the back of her eyes, so she put her cheek on the floor again.

The noise stopped. Must have been a bird. Not help. This was it. If it was, she was at peace with it, as long as it made the pain in her head go away.

Another noise, at the back of the house now. A bang. A crack. Then thuds that sounded like...

'Harriet! Harriet! Verity, call an ambulance!'

Harriet forced her eyes open again, just as Yvie fell to her knees in front of her. Her fingers went immediately to her neck, checking her pulse.

'Yvie...' Harriet whispered.

Yvie's hand was on her cheek now, then her forehead. 'I'm here, Harriet, don't worry. Verity is calling an ambulance and we're going to get you to hospital. Can you squeeze my fingers? Can you tell me where it hurts? Are you dizzy?'

'Just my head. Pain. Yes, dizzy.' She felt the sensation of Yvie gently checking her arms, her legs.

'There's no blood and I can't feel any obvious breaks, but I can't move you until the paramedics get here with the proper equipment, in case you've hurt your neck or your back. Let me get a blanket for you and try to make you more comfortable.'

A couple of seconds passed and then Harriet felt the warmth of a blanket being wrapped around her.

'The ambulance is on its way.' Verity's voice now.

'Thanks, V,' Yvie replied.

Verity dropped to the floor now too, and Harriet could see her red hair and the blue of her eyes. 'How are you doing there,

Harriet? The ambulance won't be long. We've got you, don't worry.'

'Thank you,' Harriet whispered, her voice a little stronger now that the fear was beginning to subside. She wasn't alone. She had people here caring for her. She just needed to stay strong for a little longer and...

'Harriet, try to stay awake. Can you do that?' Yvie urged gently.

Harriet opened her eyes again. Yes. She could do that. Stay awake. Try to clear her head.

Verity scrambled to her feet. 'I'm going to go out front and wait for the ambulance.'

'Shout me when it's here,' Yvie asked.

'Will do. You know, your intuition freaks me right out sometimes. It's like some weird superpower.'

Harriet could hear the lightness in her voice, and it lifted her spirits. *Stay awake*, she told herself again. *Just stay awake.*

Yvie was tucking the blanket in around her, making sure no cold air could get in, then she lay down next to her, so they were face to face, noses just a few inches apart and put her hand gently over Harriet's fingers. 'Try to keep talking to me, Harriet,' she said softly. 'Can you tell me what happened?'

'I... I tripped. Lost my footing.'

'Okay, so it wasn't a faint? You didn't collapse?'

'No, I fell. With the tray.'

'Bugger. I knew I should have helped you to bed before I left. I'm so sorry.'

'Not... your... fault. It was mine. An accident. Why... why did you come back?'

She saw Yvie's little frown. 'I honestly don't know. Verity and I went back to my flat for dinner, but then... I don't know why, but I couldn't settle. Something just didn't feel right. I was worried about you. When you said goodbye earlier, something felt...' she paused, perhaps trying to choose her words. 'It felt like you thought we wouldn't see each other again.'

'I did,' Harriet told her, her voice feeling much stronger now. She felt a tear slide from her right eye on to the floor. Yvie saw it and wiped it away.

'Really?'

Harriet was worried she'd said too much, so she backpedalled a bit. 'I'm ancient. Not many years left,' she managed to joke.

'You've got plenty of years left, Harriet Bassett,' Yvie chided her. 'Anyway, the feeling that something was wrong wouldn't leave me. I told you earlier about my dad, do you remember?'

'Yes.'

'Well, all my life I've wondered if anyone could have saved him. If anyone had a feeling about him – not that he was going to kill himself, but just a feeling that something wasn't right. Maybe he didn't answer his door. Or someone heard a noise. I don't know. Just something that they ignored. And maybe if they'd checked on him, they could have saved him.'

Her words made Harriet so sad for her. 'I'm sorry that happened to you.'

Yvie smiled. 'Thank you. Sometimes I think this is why it did. So that I'd pay attention. The uneasy sense of foreboding was still niggling me when I was taking Verity home, we decided to swing by and just check on you. If the house had been in darkness, I'd have assumed you were asleep and I wouldn't have disturbed you. But when I saw the light on and the curtains open... that uneasy feeling again. Your neighbours must have wondered why two women were peering in your window at this time of night, but I'm glad we did. That's when I saw you on the floor. I smashed a little pane of glass in the back door to get in, but I promise I'll fix it,' she added with an apologetic grimace.

The corners of Harriet's mouth turned upwards. 'I think I forgive you. Just this once.'

'The ambulance is here!' Verity shouted from the hallway.

'There you go, Harriet. That wasn't too long. We're going to take such good care of you.'

The footsteps of the paramedics drowned her out, and the next few minutes – Harriet had no idea how long – passed in a flurry of tests, and checks and questions, until they were confident that it was safe to transport her. Yvie came with her in the ambulance, with Verity offering to stay behind to sort out the door and make the house secure.

At the hospital, she was whisked straight into A&E and then into a cubicle.

'Nurse Danton, are you actually bringing patients into us now?' A doctor with a long beard and a kind smile came into the room almost immediately, clutching a clipboard.

Harriet watched as Yvie laughed. 'Indeed I am. I feel I'm not busy enough, so I search out lovely ladies like Harriet here in the hope of getting some repeat business.'

The doctor worked efficiently and thoroughly, asking many of the same questions as the paramedics, and adding some more of his own, garnering information from both Harriet and Yvie. Harriet's head was so much clearer now, although it still hurt to the touch, and her body ached in some parts, but there were no sharp or persistent pains. She hoped that was a good sign. The most important thing was that she could think clearly again. It was such a relief.

'Right then, Harriet, the good news is that I agree with Nurse Danton, that nothing seems to be broken. That being said, you've got a nasty bump on your head and you've not long had that hip, so I'd like to X-ray both, just to be on the safe side. I also want to admit you at least overnight just to check there's no concussion. Is that okay with you?'

'Of course. Thank you,' she said, feeling overwhelming gratitude for the doctor, for the NHS, but especially for the nurse standing beside her, holding her hand.

'We're pretty backed up out there, got to love a Saturday night in A&E, but we'll get you over to X-ray as soon as possible.'

'I'll call admissions, and then I'll speak to my ward and organise a bed,' Yvie offered. 'I can take Harriet up there after X-ray. I've got my mobile if there are any problems when you see the scans.'

'Thanks, saves me a job. I'll speak to you as soon as they're through.'

The prospect of an overnight stay in hospital didn't thrill Harriet, but at least there was a comfort in knowing she was in familiar territory. Although, this time she didn't want to stay in more than one night, because she was determined she was making it to dinner with John on Monday.

Yvie pulled a chair to the side of the bed and sat beside her, reaching for her hand again. 'Can I ask you a personal question, Harriet?'

'After all you've done for me, you can ask me anything,' Harriet assured her.

A mischievous glint appeared in Yvie's eyes. 'Was my super-sharp intuition wrong, or was there a lovely connection between you and that nice Mr Bassett today?'

Harriet's eyes widened and she couldn't resist a coy smile. 'Well, it's funny you should say that...'

Despite the pain, despite the discomfort, despite everything that had happened to her that evening, Harriet managed to relay every detail of her call from John and their plans, relishing Yvie's response, which veered between delight and...

'Harriet, don't take this the wrong way, but I have to say I'm a bit gutted. I've just realised that you're eighty and you've managed to hook up a date today, and I've seen absolutely no action for months. I'm clearly doing something wrong.'

'Taxi for Bassett?' A chirpy porter with a delightful Irish accent, sporting a navy polo shirt and matching trousers, appeared in the doorway. 'Nurse Danton!' he exclaimed. 'What are you doing here?'

'Evening, Freddie. Don't ask – it's a long story,' she ribbed him, then turned to Harriet. 'This is Freddie, the fastest porter in town. But if you tell him anything, make it scandalous, because it'll be all over the hospital in no time.'

'I'd defend my honour, but she's absolutely right,' Freddie conceded gleefully, clicking the brakes off Harriet's bed. 'Right, let's get you to X-ray.'

Yvie held the door open as Freddie manoeuvred the bed like a Formula 1 car, out of the room and into the main A& E corridor. They'd only gone about halfway along, when Harriet felt a sense of absolute dread. She'd been so sure she was fine. Positive that she hadn't done herself any damage. But now she wasn't so sure because she had to be hallucinating. Standing just up ahead, talking to a member of staff in scrubs with a stethoscope around her neck, was the young woman from the garden party. The singer.

This couldn't be real.

She was getting closer. Closer still. She was definitely hallucinating. Concussion. It had to be.

She was almost upon her now, and as if sensing that someone was staring at her, the young woman turned, caught her eye, then...

'Stop!' Harriet blurted.

Yvie looked panicked as Freddie immediately pulled back and stopped. 'What's wrong, Harriet. Do you feel sick? Dizzy?'

Harriet was right beside the singer now, only a few feet away, as their eyes locked. The young woman frowned as if she were trying to place her, then Harriet watched as the realisation dawned and she said, 'We met... today... didn't we?'

The penny dropped for Yvie too and she answered for her. 'Yes! At the garden party. You sang the last song. You were amazing.'

'You sang?' asked the doctor she'd been talking to. 'I thought you were doing the catering?'

'I'm a multi-tasker,' the young lady shrugged, then turned back to Harriet. 'I think we were introduced earlier, but I'm Maisie. This is my sister, Hope,' she gestured to her bewildered companion. 'I hope you're okay?' she asked, taking in Harriet's predicament.

'I'm sure I will be.' Harriet could have stopped there, wheeled on, gone to X-ray and let this moment pass, but hadn't she already spent too much of her life doing that already? 'I thought you were spectacular this afternoon...'

'Thank you.'

'And I wonder if... If... I know this might sound very strange, but I wonder if I could show you something?'

If Maisie was startled, she didn't show it. 'Of course.'

Fumbling, Harriet reached into her cardigan pocket with trembling hands and pulled out the photograph she'd put there earlier. 'Would you mind looking at this. It's just that... I wonder if we might be related?'

MIDNIGHT – 8 A.M.

33

MAISIE

Maisie's heart went out to this lovely lady on the hospital wheelie bed thingy. She must ask Hope what the correct technical terminology was. Mobile bed? Wheelie mattress? Anyway, the poor soul must have been in an accident or had some kind of fall, because she was pretty banged up: dressings on her head, bruising on one side of her face, an eye that was swollen and already turning a dark, angry shade of pain.

Yet, she was smiling, holding out a photograph and gazing at Maisie with such nervous hope that she felt devastated that she was about to deliver a crushing blow.

'I'm sorry, but I'm afraid that's not possible,' Maisie said gently, wincing inside, feeling that she had to give a bit extra to cushion her words. 'I don't... I don't have any relatives... except my mum and my sister here, and to be honest, they're forever trying to disown me, so I promise you're having a lucky escape.'

Beside her, Hope was nodding her agreement. 'She's right. You don't want her. Totally high maintenance.'

The blonde woman who was with the elderly lady stepped in, tenderly placing her hand on the woman's shoulder. 'Och,

Harriet, if it's any consolation, you can have me. My mother wouldn't notice.'

Maisie felt a pang of solidarity. Anyone who dealt with sadness by trying to inject some gentle humour into the situation was her kind of woman.

'Move it along there, Freddie, you're causing a traffic jam,' bellowed a nurse, coming right up behind the bed, pushing a tall pole decked with all sorts of machines. Maisie had no idea what they were for but they looked like they could launch a space shuttle.

'Keep yer teeth in, Teresa, we're on our way,' Freddie joked, eliciting an eye roll and a harrumph of exaggerated disapproval.

'Please...' Harriet whispered urgently, still holding up the photo.

Maisie was about to take it, just to be polite, when the porter took off, manoeuvring Harriet's trolley bed thingy like he was in command of a Ferrari.

'Take care,' Maisie shouted after her, feeling awful that she hadn't been able to help. 'Will she be okay?' she asked Hope, who responded with a kindly shrug. 'I don't know, she's not one of my patients. She's in good hands though. I'm pretty sure that's Yvie Danton that's with her. She's the senior charge nurse up in Geriatrics. Anyway, I'll find out who she belongs to and see if I can check on her for you if you want?'

'Just if you've got time. I know you'll be slammed for the rest of the night.'

At the end of the corridor, just a couple of metres away, the swing doors opened, and the receptionist Maisie had met at the front desk came through. 'Dr McTeer, the very woman I'm looking for,' she declared.

'What can I do for you, Stephanie?' Hope asked brightly and Maisie marvelled as always that this confident, incredibly smart woman was her little sister, the one who had chosen this field because she'd had cancer as a kid and spent many years in hospital.

'There's a gentleman at reception asking to speak to you. A Mr Jackson. Says it's regarding your sister.' The receptionist's arched eyebrow of curiosity landed on Maisie at the end of that sentence.

Bugger. She should have known that Nathan wouldn't let it lie, that he'd come and track down Hope and try to plead his case, or get some answers, or whatever it was he needed to satisfy his ego.

'Ah great. Romeo isn't giving up,' Hope groaned. 'What do you want me to do, Mais? It's your call.'

Maisie swallowed, unsure what to say. Just a few minutes ago, when she'd walked away from the café in the general building, she'd been so sure, so confident that she was doing the right thing. She'd dashed over to seek some moral support from her sister, but she'd barely blurted out what she'd done, and they hadn't even made it to the privacy of the staffroom, when the lady on the go-faster wheelie bed had stopped to speak to them, so she hadn't yet managed to hear Hope's opinion or reassurance that she'd done the right thing.

Walking away from people had always been so difficult for Maisie. She was the person who forgave friends anything, who hung onto relationships long after they were done. She gave people second, third, fourth chances, unwilling to cut them off just because of their mistakes. It would totally be in her nature to forgive Nathan, but then what? Would she spend all her life worrying when he was going to jack her in again when he decided he 'needed' something else? Would his self-indulgence press her buttons now that she'd been on the wrong side of it? Or had he learned his lesson, and after a suitable period of grovelling, be given another shot at their love? If so, was she prepared to risk it?

'What are you thinking?' Hope prompted again.

A flashback to another moment from her car journey with Scott.

'I'm thinking, "what would Stevie Nicks do?"'

Hope grinned. 'And?'

Maisie nudged Hope's shoulder. 'I think when you get off shift, Stevie would want you and I to go and get those pancakes.'

Her sister's chuckle made everyone in hearing distance smile. 'Thanks, Stephanie,' Hope said, in her very best doctor's voice, 'but could you please tell Mr Jackson that I'm not available to speak to him tonight... or any night until the end of time?'

The chipper receptionist had no idea what was going on, but she was loving it. 'I'd be very happy to, Dr McTeer,' she replied before waltzing off. The details of this little interaction would be all round the staffroom by morning.

Hope repaid the shoulder bump with one of her own. 'I'm proud of you,' she said, giving Maisie a grateful glow. 'But I need to get back to work, because the pubs are not long out and it's about to turn into a crowd scene around here.'

Maisie sighed deeply. 'You should definitely think about getting a real job. All this saving people's lives is so overrated.'

Hope could match her underplayed sarcasm all day long. 'You're right. That advert for thrush cream was a level of giddy success I could only aspire to.'

Giggling, Maisie adjusted her bag on her shoulder, ready to go. 'Exactly! Right then, I'll get out of your hair.'

'Try not to have any more life-altering dramas before I get home,' Hope teased.

'I'll do my best. See ya la—'

It was the draught from Stephanie exiting the A&E door that

caused the movement that caught Maisie's eye, a piece of paper, or maybe a pamphlet, fluttering on the floor, next to a trolley of dressings. Her first instinct was to ignore it. She had no idea why she didn't.

She took a few steps forwards, scooped it up, realised what it was. 'Hope, that lady in the bed must have dropped...'

She froze.

Her words stopped.

The photograph.

The picture.

The man.

'Maisie? Are you okay? What's up?' The voice was in the periphery somewhere, but Maisie couldn't absorb it or formulate a reply, utterly transfixed.

The man in the photo.

'Maisie! What is it?' Hope was right next to her now and all Maisie could do was drag her eyes from the image and then slowly, like she never wanted to let it go, hold it out towards her sister.

As she took the photograph, Hope's face transformed, from a furrowed brow of concern, to wide-eyed astonishment. Her slow exhalation came with a whispered, 'Holy crap.'

Maisie was still staring at the image in Hope's hand, unaware that her sister's gaze was going from Maisie's face, to the photo, to Maisie's face again.

'Now I see why she asked you to look at this,' Hope affirmed. 'He's your absolute double.'

Maisie was nodding slowly, still trying to kick-start her reaction. Hope was right. The resemblance was uncanny. The skin, the eyes, the tilt of the nose, the little crooked cinch of the top lip, he even had her dimples. It was all she could do to force out a strangled. 'Who is he?'

'I've no idea... Wait.' Hope turned the photograph over.

On the back all it said was: Leo Bassett. Age 25.

Maisie repeated the name, hoping that something would come to her. 'Leo Bassett.'

Hope was pensive. 'I don't recognise the name. Does it mean anything to you?'

'No, nothing at all. Wow. It's so bizarre though. I've never...' Maisie couldn't get the words out.

'You've never what?'

'I've never looked like anyone before.' It had been such a common conversation between them growing up that she knew Hope would grasp how much that mattered. It had been one of Hope's biggest thrills when she'd met her biological family and saw resemblances for the first time.

'Dr Robertson,' Hope spoke to a tall, preoccupied gent in a white coat, who was standing at a nearby computer terminal. 'Do you mind if I take an extra ten minutes' break? I've got a family situation I'd like to deal with and I don't have anyone on the board at the moment.' Maisie had seen *Holby City* – she knew that meant Hope wasn't currently tending to any patients.

The doctor glanced over. 'Dr McTeer, have you taken your full break on any shift since you started working here?' he asked pointedly.

'Erm, no.'

'Exactly. I think we can spare you for another ten minutes.'

'Thank you,' Hope beamed, before grabbing Maisie's hand. 'Staffroom,' she hissed, pulling her towards a door further along the corridor.

They were the only people in the stark, white-walled room. Maisie saw there was a small kitchen unit with an inbuilt steel sink on one side, and a microwave and kettle the other. A fridge sat next to it, and in the centre of the room were eight chairs, positioned around a low white coffee table.

'I think you should call Mum,' Hope suggested, flicking on the kettle, then taking two mugs off the drainer.

Maisie shook her head. 'I'm not calling Mum after midnight on a Saturday night to say, "hey, I just saw a photo of some random bloke who looks a bit like me."'

Hope put her hands on her hips. 'He doesn't "look a bit" like you. He looks *exactly* like you after we did those Snapchat filters that show you what you'd look like if you were a bloke.'

It was a fair point, but... 'I'm still not phoning Mum. I'll see if I can track down that lady and ask her a few questions and I'll discover that there's no possible connection and I'll have forgotten about it by the time we get to the Pancake Shack.'

Hope was spooning instant coffee into cups now. 'You don't actually believe that, do you?'

'Of course I do! How could there be any other outcome?' Maisie blurted, challenging Hope's comment. In her head, she reinforced that thought. It was ludicrous to think there could be any other reason for this other than a weird coincidence. People didn't just bump into long-lost family members. That was the kind of stuff of soap operas, and only then because an uncannily large number of soap characters had a secret evil twin.

Over at the kettle, boiling water was going into the mugs now. 'Maisie, I know you're scared...'

'I'm not!' A realisation. 'Okay, I am.'

'But you know what you're like – you're not going to be able to stop thinking about this and it'll drive you crazy. Mum will understand. Actually, I think she'd be really pissed off if you didn't call her. And I'll grass you in a flash, so you're as well doing it.'

'Man, I'm glad I don't share your evil streak. I think this whole

Florence Nightingale do-gooder thing is a cover for your dark side.'

Hope slipped her mobile phone out of the pocket of her scrubs, unlocked it and thrust it into Maisie's hand. 'Call her.'

Maisie realised that she had no choice. If she were honest, that was probably a good thing because she absolutely didn't know for certain if she would do this on her own.

Sweeping the screen up, she went on to Hope's 'favourites' list, gratified to see that she was at the top. Her mum came next. Then there were many of her new family members: her dad, Aaron, his new wife, Aggs, then her myriad stepbrothers and sisters.

Maisie had three people on her favourites list – her mum, Hope and Sissy.

Her thumb took charge, pressing her mum's picture.

'Hope, are you okay?' her mum answered after just one ring.

'It's me, Mum,' Maisie corrected her, 'but you're on speaker and Hope's here too.'

'What's happened? Where are you?' This woman didn't share their DNA, but she'd been the absolute best mother they could ever have wished for and Maisie adored her.

'We're fine, I promise. Hope made me call you.'

The relief in her mum's laugh was instant. 'Ah, have you two been in at the cocktails? If you're phoning again to make me tell you the words of "Fernando", I'll have to go and get my Abba album.'

'Yeah, sorry about last weekend, Mum,' Hope said sheepishly. 'That was Maisie's fault. She spiked my drink.'

Maisie made the throat-slicing gesture to her sister, then took the lead on the call. 'It's nothing to do with Abba, Mum. It's a bit of a bizarre story. I met a lady today – I think her name is Harriet – and, well, long story short, she showed me a photograph of a man and asked me if I was related to him.'

'Oh, dear Lord, darling Why did she think that?'

'Mum, he's Maisie's absolute double,' Hope jumped in.

'Really? Did you ask her about him? Who is he? Can you go and speak to him?'

'I know nothing at all about him yet except that his name is...' she flipped the photo over again and read the name out loud. 'Leo Bassett. Does that mean anything to you?'

'No, my darling. You know that we were given no information at all when we adopted you. All we ever had was a little wristband with the name you'd been given when you were born.'

At exactly the moment her mum said that, Hope and Maisie made the connection.

The name she was born with. Her mum had told her a million years ago, when she was just a kid.

'Mum, can you tell me the name again?' Maisie asked, not trusting her memory.

'Of course, sweetheart. It was Leona.'

Leona.

Harriet's son was called Leo. So did that mean...?

Maisie didn't have time to finish the thought, because her own phone began ringing in her pocket. Dammit. It could only be one person. She needed to handle this herself. 'Mum, I'll buzz you back.'

She ended the call and switched from Hope's phone to her own.

'Nathan, enough. We're done. There's no point...'

'Maisie?'

A woman's voice. It took Maisie a minute to pinpoint it.

'Oh my God, sorry Francine! I thought it was someone else.'

'That fuckwit you used to go out with?' her agent replied, with typical blunt candour.

'Yes, that would be the very fuckwit I was referring to,' Maisie quipped, her mind way too distracted to absorb the fact that Francine was calling her late at night.

'If you go back to him, I'm dumping you as a client. Just saying. Anyway, I don't usually call my clients at this ungodly hour, but I just stepped off a plane... I'm in New York, darling... and when I checked my emails, there was one I thought you may want to hear about immediately. You got the part. The Netflix series. Lead role. Enough money to buy a new boyfriend every night of the week if you so choose. It's a guarantee for one season, with an option for a further five. I'll forward the contracts over tomorrow. Maisie?' Silence. 'Maisie? Have you fainted?'

'No, I'm still...' Maisie got three words out, before her brain shut down again. She'd landed the role, the kind that every jobbing actor dreamt about getting. The lead character. A gritty crime drama. A massive production budget. A fantastic script. Global distribution. And she might never know how good that would feel because she was fairly sure her heart was beating so fast it was close to exploding. Thankfully, Hope had heard enough and decided to intervene. She took the phone from Maisie's hand.

'Hi Francine, it's Maisie's sister, Hope. Maisie's faculties appear to have short-circuited at the moment, but if she still had the power of speech, she would tell you that she's delighted, and thank you very much for letting her know. She'd also like to say you're a freaking phenomenal agent for helping her land the role.'

Maisie could hear Francine laughing, something that didn't happen too often. 'Excellent. Just don't let her faint and do herself an injury. The health insurance isn't valid until she's signed the contract.'

With another chuckle, Francine disconnected, leaving Hope and Maisie staring at each other, both wide-eyed with beaming grins, until Hope broke the spell first, gave out a screech that was barely audible, so as not to have A&E security charging in here, and then threw her arms around her sister. 'You did it! Holy shit, Maisie, you did it!'

'I... did... it.' Maisie blurted, her brain kicking back in like a battery that had just been started with jump leads. 'I did it!' she repeated, with a voice higher than any note Stevie Nicks had ever hit.

The two of them were still entwined, still jumping up and down wearing inane grins, when the door opened and Stephanie, the receptionist, marched in. She didn't even raise an eyebrow at Hope and Maisie's behaviour, too keen to relay the point of her presence.

'Dr McTeer, he says he's not leaving until he speaks to you. Do I have your permission to call security? Or there are a couple of gang members in the waiting area who are itching for someone to fight – I could let them loose?'

Even in her shocked condition, Maisie was amused by Stephanie's deadpan delivery.

Hope sighed. 'Sorry, Stephanie. I'll call security and ask them to take care of him.'

'No, it's okay. I've got this,' Maisie's mouth said, as her brain scrambled to keep up. She had no idea what was fuelling her, but she couldn't stop herself. 'Back in a sec, sis.'

With that, she marched out of the room, down the A&E corridor and banged through the double doors into the waiting area.

Nathan stopped pacing when he spotted her storming towards him. She knew that look on his face. It was the one he got when he was pissed off because he wasn't getting his own way.

'Maisie! Can we go somewhere? We need to talk. We need to sort this out. Come on, baby...'

'Stop!' Maisie's objection was quiet but firm enough to make the two young guys with the face tattoos and the gold chains in the row of seats nearest them sit up and take notice. 'I just want to make sure I understand everything.'

'Can we go—'

'Nope, I want answers right here, right now.'

Nathan didn't argue, clearly shocked at this assertive version of his former fiancée.

'The truth is that you jilted me at the altar because I wasn't enough for you. Because you wanted money and success, and a different kind of life. And you didn't think that would happen with me.'

He shrugged awkwardly. 'Come on, Maisie, you know how it is. You're never going to get the fame and fortune thing with bit parts and adverts. And I wasn't making anything from music. One of us had to shake things up.'

'And how's that working out for you?' she demanded, with cool menace. 'Was it worth it? I thought you said that the band were dickheads and you were ready for chucking it again.'

'Yeah, I am, but...'

Shit. She saw it so clearly now. 'So really, just like last time, I'm the safety blanket you come to when you've got nothing else. And then, as soon as boredom sets in, off you go again.'

He had the cheek to react with indignation. 'That's a bit harsh, Maisie. I want to come back because I think we can make it work. I've realised what's important.'

She wondered if he actually believed what he was saying. It was all rubbish. She was sure of it. He'd come back to her last time because she was a port in a storm, where he could live for free while he tried to establish himself as a songwriter. When he'd got a better offer, he'd taken off without so much as a thought for the woman in the white dress, waiting for him at their wedding. His loss. More than he even knew.

'The thing is, Nathan, I'm not doing the bit parts and adverts any more.'

'You've given up acting? Not surprised really. I'm sure there are other things you could do that—'

Maisie cut him off. 'Nope, not given up acting. You see, I've just landed the part of my life. Lead role in a Netflix Original. A worldwide release, with more money than I know what to do with. Oh, and then there's the travelling. There will be lots of that. The production budget is huge. And then off camera, there will be the media work and the interviews, and I daresay there will be quite a social scene for the cast of a show that's pretty certain to be huge. So you see, Nathan – you did me a favour. If you hadn't dumped me, I might not have gone for this audition, and I might not have landed a gig that will give me the kind of life I always dreamt of. And now I can see that my dream life will be even better without a knob like you in it. Goodbye, Nathan. Don't call me. Don't text. Don't come back. I'm far too busy to deal with losers.'

With that, she turned on her heel and walked away, heading for the double door that Hope was holding open for her, to the sound of two blokes with face tattoos howling with amusement. She wasn't normally one for bitchiness or spite, but man, that felt great.

Today had been exhausting. She'd sung on stage. She'd landed an incredible job. And she'd just said a final goodbye to the man she'd once thought would become her family. But could she be about to replace him with another family she knew nothing about?

34

SCOTT

Scott woke up with a banging sore head and a mouth that was as dry as the grout he'd tried to insert between the bathroom tiles last summer. It was another DIY job that hadn't gone quite to plan.

He banged on the screen of his mobile phone to silence the 7 a.m. alarm he'd set before he'd gone to sleep the night before, then, groaning, he rolled over onto his front, and pulled Kelly's pillow over his head. She was already up. Or maybe she hadn't come to bed. He had no idea. He'd been pretty wasted last night. What a fricking day it had been. Last thing he remembered was letting Sabrina and Rick in. He hadn't even bothered asking them why they'd pitched up so late, he'd just made himself scarce and come to bed. He wasn't sure what was going on with them, but he'd had enough drama for one day. All he cared about was getting up in time this morning to say goodbye to his girl. He'd wanted to go to the airport with her, but she'd refused, saying she'd rather say goodbye at home. He knew her taxi to the airport was booked for 8 a.m. That gave them an hour together. That was, of course, if she was even home yet.

That question was answered almost immediately.

'Morning, sunshine!' Even through the pillow, he could hear Carny's singsong greeting.

'Sssssshhhhhh.' He managed to ease the bounce-back foam up just an inch or so from the back of his head. 'Didn't we used to tell you that children should be seen and not heard?' he croaked, desperate for water. Either his throat had grown fur or his voice box had cracked.

'Ooooooh, nice voice, Dad. You'd be great on the sex chat hotlines. Anyway, get up. Time to come say goodbye and beg me to stay. My taxi will be here soon. Don't clutch on to my ankles though, because I can't face plant in heels. I'll do myself an injury.'

Scott rolled over onto his back, catching sight of his daughter for the first time. The long caramel hair. The gorgeous face. The cracking grin. And... 'Are those the same clothes you were wearing last night?'

Carny nodded. 'Erm, yes. I got home five minutes ago. It was a great night though,' she beamed. 'I got led astray by a man.'

Scott squinted as he pushed himself up on to his elbows, trying to process that information. 'Sweetheart, are you coming out as straight? Only, that might take me a minute to get used to.'

Carny found that hilarious. 'Eeeew, no. I wouldn't know where to start. The man was Uncle Carson. He called me to say goodbye from the train station and I persuaded him to ditch the train and come out with us and then fly down to London with me this morning. We ended up in an all-night café in the West End with all my mates from the show yesterday. We made it all the way from the Beatles to Robbie Williams before we got thrown out and barred. I think "Angels" tipped them over the edge.'

There was way too much information there for him to process. The only bit he was managing to grasp on to was Carson.

Didn't get train. Flying down with Carny. Fuck. He could feel the rage rising again.

Thirty years of friendship, and they'd never fallen out, never doubted each other, and now this. Last night, he'd been going over it in his mind before he fell asleep and, sure, there was something to be said for Carson telling him what happened with Kelly, giving him an out, providing a justifiable reason for Scott to leave in search of the life he'd always wanted. That said, Scott had come to the conclusion that he'd only 'fessed up out of guilt, because the fact remained that Carson had made a move on his wife. Unforgivable.

Even more so now that he and Kelly had agreed last night that they were going to stay together and make another go of it. He didn't have much faith that they were going to make it work and get to the 'happy ever after' stuff, but he had to try, because he would never be able to look at himself in the mirror if he left her and the baby when she'd begged him to stay.

Again, fuck.

'Carny, love, go and grab your things and get organised. I just need to speak to your dad for a minute.' Kelly had appeared and was standing in the doorway. It crossed his mind that she seemed... calm. Her hair was pulled up into a messy bun and her face was scrubbed clean, giving her even more of a resemblance than usual to the young Kelly he'd married.

Carny's gaze went from one to the other. 'Have you two fallen out?'

'Yeah,' Scott said, at exactly the same moment that Kelly said, 'No'.

'Excellent,' Carny asserted, pushing herself up from the bed. 'Good work, parents. I'll be in my room sorting out my cases if you need a referee.'

She sang the chorus of 'Angels' all the way along the hall and into her bedroom.

Kelly waited until Carny's door closed, and then came over and sat on the edge of the bed as Scott forced himself up into a sitting position, eyes squinting against the sun that was streaming in through the window.

'We need to talk,' she said, calmly, almost friendly, her tone such a stark contrast to their discussion last night. Snapshots from yesterday kept popping up in his head like the flashbacks from hell. Shit, he'd lost it. Lost it with Carson, although he deserved it. Lost it with Kelly last night. Ranted like an idiot to Maisie, the singer who had given him a lift home in the car. Actually, that had been the only time in the whole day that he felt... himself. Like he could talk. Be open. Say how he felt and not be judged. Apart from the ranting idiot moments, that was. If he ever met her again, he definitely had to open with an apology. Although, he was pretty sure she'd cross the road if she saw him coming.

'Kells, we talked enough last night. We're good.' He didn't have the energy for it today. He was staying. They were going to give it another try. Talking it to death wasn't going to change that. He just wanted to get up, kiss his daughter goodbye, hug her tight and then come back to bed and sleep until his head didn't feel like someone had hit it with a mallet.

'No, we didn't. I wasn't completely honest with you.'

He couldn't work out what she was saying. 'You're not pregnant?'

'I am,' she rushed, obviously wanting to re-establish that fact. Whatever she said next didn't matter then, he decided. They were where they were. Any other details were irrelevant.

Her skin was pale, and he could see she was exhausted. Maybe after Carny left she could come to bed too. They could sleep, watch a movie... Even as he was thinking it, he knew he was trying to convince himself that they could have some kind of normal. No one was buying it.

'I wasn't honest about Carson.'

Sucker punch right in the stomach. 'So you did sleep with him?' he bit back before she could explain.

'No! God, Scott, we can't communicate about anything. It shouldn't be this difficult.'

'Preaching to the choir,' he acknowledged, energy gone again.

He watched Kelly adjust her posture and knew she was resetting, coming in for another try. 'I wasn't honest about what actually happened with Carson. I know you think he came on to me, but he didn't. I came on to him.'

Scott shrugged. 'What does it matter?'

'Dammit, Scott, please try to hear me.' There was no anger in her tone, only low-level exasperation. 'I came on to him. He was falling asleep. He had his eyes closed. I kissed him. As soon as he realised what was happening, he stopped me. He did absolutely nothing wrong. It was all me. You can be as angry with me as you want to be, but you need to stop being angry with him, because he's had your back the whole time. I'm sorry I didn't tell you last night, but... I didn't want to give you a stronger reason to leave.'

Scott processed her words, then processed again, making sure he had this right. Carson had been half-asleep. Kelly had kissed him. He'd stopped her. His mate hadn't betrayed him.

A rampant surge of adrenaline cleared his head and switched his energy on to high. His whole life might be a complete shitshow right now, but it had just got a little bit better. Scratch that. A lot better. He could sort out things with Kelly later, but God knows when he'd see Carson face to face again. He could be posted somewhere for months, years even.

Scott threw the duvet back, and jumped out of bed, just his

boxers on. He grabbed his jeans from the charcoal velvet chair in the corner, then pulled a T-shirt out of his drawer, hopping on one foot as he attempted to get a leg in his jeans at the same time.

'I'm going to the airport,' he said, breathless as he shoved an arm into his T-shirt.

'But Carny expressly said she doesn't want us to,' Kelly argued. 'She's already arranged to meet friends there.'

'I know, but I need to see Carson. He's getting the same flight.'

Kelly was shaking her head now, but he didn't care. She wasn't going to stop him. He had to make this right. Christ, he'd tried to deck him yesterday.

'You don't need to go to the airport.'

Here we go. Another fight.

'I do. I'm not doing this on the phone. He has to know I mean it.'

'You still don't need to go there...' she countered again.

He wasn't even going to argue any more. This was pointless. He was going. End of. He was tossing things out of his top drawer, searching frantically for matching socks.

'Because,' Kelly was still speaking, 'he's downstairs in the kitchen.'

Scott stopped. Gaped at her, open-mouthed. 'Why didn't you say that?'

She threw her arms up. 'Oh dear God, I tried.'

He took the stairs two at a time, landing with a thud at the bottom. When he opened the kitchen door, he saw Carson, leaning against the worktop under the window. He was in a black T-shirt and jeans and he had last night's stubble on his face. Scott knew that would be rectified the minute he got back on base. They'd always joked that Carson could go to sleep in a swamp and still wake up clean-cut and ready to work.

'Mate...' he started, then realised he had no clue what to say.

Any uncomfortable moment of emotional vulnerability usually resulted in one of them suggesting they go for a beer and the matter being forgotten. He decided to go for the direct approach. 'I'm sorry. Kelly told me you did nothing wrong.' It was all going well until he followed up with a challenging, 'Why the fuck didn't you tell me that yesterday?'

'Lose – lose,' Carson shrugged. 'I had to tell you about what happened, because you needed all the information before you decided whether to stay or go. But I wasn't gonna blame it on Kell, because... I don't know. She's my mate too. I was trying to do the right thing.'

'Even if it meant I tried to punch your lights out?'

Carson shrugged, grinning. 'Pal, you had no chance. I let you get a swipe in because I wasn't going to punch back. Had to let you think you had the upper hand.'

Inexplicably, without warning, Scott felt himself begin to laugh. Relief. That's what it was. Pure fricking relief.

He took a step forward, arms out.

Carson feigned horror. 'Are you gonna try to hug me? Because I need warning for all that soppy shit.'

Scott knew he didn't mean a word of it. 'Yeah,' he said, crossing the room. 'Brace yourself.'

'Stop!' Carson held his hand up and for a minute Scott thought he was going to object, going to throw another grenade in there just when every single iota of his being was bursting with relief that they'd sorted this out.

'Why? What now?'

'You know your T-shirt's on back to front? I've got standards for that soppy stuff.'

Scott threw his arms around his mate and hugged him, for way too long and way too hard, but he didn't give a toss.

A few seconds later, they were still standing there, arms round each other, doing those back bump things, when Carny and Kelly came into the room.

'Aaaaaw, cute,' he heard his daughter saying. 'Are you two absolutely sure you don't play for my team?'

35

KELLY

'Okay, have you got everything?' Kelly fretted. 'Did you pack your toiletries? Your chargers? Your...'

'Mum! I'm going to London, I'm not going trekking in Nepal. They have shops there. And electricity.'

'Please let us come to the airport with you,' Kelly begged again.

'Mum, I love you. I really do. But I'm meeting my mates there and I don't want to be worrying that you're sad. I'm only letting Uncle Carson come because he's promised to ignore me as soon as we get to the terminal building. I promise I'll be fine.'

Carson and Scott both lifted cases and took them out to the taxi as Kelly hugged her girl close. 'I know you will. I'm just going to miss you so much.'

'I'll miss you too, Mum. You know I'll end up FaceTiming you twice a day, phoning you three times a day and sending at least ten texts. I'll be at full-scale stalker level. You'll be begging me to stop by the end of the week.'

'Never,' Kelly said softly. This was it. Twenty-two years since a tiny bundle was placed in her sixteen-year-old arms, she was letting her go. In a way, they'd grown up together. 'Be good, my love. Have a great time. Party like crazy and work really hard. We're so proud of you. You're going to have a great life.'

'I already have a great life,' her daughter beamed, then hugged her again. 'I love you, Mum. Take care of Dad. And don't be having house parties or turning my room into a swingers' den as soon as I'm gone.'

Spluttering, Kelly was trying and failing to swallow back the tears. 'I'll tell your dad to hold off until next week then.'

'Good move. Just in case I come back and there's a stripper pole in my room. I'd do myself an injury.'

Kelly didn't want to say that, with her nausea, and her swollen boobs, she couldn't think of anything worse than swinging round a pole. She'd agreed with Scott that they would go down to London together to tell Carny about the baby in a month or so. Right now, she just wanted her daughter to know how much she was loved and to go out there ready to take on the world. There was an irony there. They'd tried to bring their daughter up to be fearless and independent, to think for herself and have a thirst for adventure. Then, when all those qualities equipped her to go off and make her own life, Kelly felt devastated to lose her. Nobody ever said this parenting stuff would be easy. And now she was going to get to do it for a second time and she was pretty sure that even if she avoided past mistakes, she was bound to make new ones. No matter what, though, she knew that, above all else, she was going to love this baby just as much as she adored her daughter.

A horn beeped outside and Carny released her and threw her backpack over her shoulder. 'I'll text you when I board. And when I land. And when I get to my digs. See what I mean about the whole stalking thing?'

Holding her free hand, Kelly followed Carny down the

hallway to the front door. Carson was already standing over at the taxi and Kelly gave him a grateful wave. He nodded back, acknowledging an unspoken truce between them. She knew he'd been surprised when she'd called him last night, right after Sabrina and Rick had left. She'd thought he would be on the train by then and she was hoping to persuade him to come back, but it turned out he'd already been in touch with Carny and his god-daughter had coerced him into changing his plans and he was in a taxi on his way to meet her.

They'd ended up speaking on the phone for the twenty minutes it had taken Carson to travel from the city centre to Carny's hangout in the West End. They'd talked it all through, from a place of friendship and love this time, apologised to each other, and then discussed how to handle things moving forward. They'd hung up with all fences mended, peace restored. Carson had been family to her since they were sixteen – it would take more than this to break them.

Kelly still wasn't sure what the tipping point had been in deciding to make the call in the first place. Maybe it was Scott's honesty or his willingness to stay with her, no matter what the cost to his own future. He wasn't perfect, but his selflessness had reminded her of the young boy she'd met and fallen in love with. Maybe now, a couple of decades and a whole lot of jaded cynicism later, they could all do with a bit of honesty and selflessness.

It had been a shock that he'd planned to leave her, but, yep, if she was honest, he had just cause. They both did. They'd both been coasting for so long, only giving a part of themselves to each other. Scott had kept his longing to escape secret, just as she had kept her feelings for Rick deep inside, in a place that was hidden from everyone else. If they were ever going to move forward, that had to change. They had to get honest and they had to want each other to be happy, had to try to give each other what they needed. In Scott's case, one of those things was Carson.

Yep, that had probably been the tipping point – the moment when she realised that Scott might come to terms with everything else in their lives, but he'd never be able to shrug off losing the guy who was like a brother to him. That's when she'd picked up the phone. And watching Scott now, waving at the taxi, laughing through the sadness she knew he felt about Carny moving out, she was glad that she'd fixed the injustice. She just wasn't sure she was done yet.

When the taxi was finally out of sight, they closed the door and made their way back into the kitchen. 'I'm just going to grab some water and go back to bed,' Scott said, taking a glass out of the cupboard and filling it from the tap. 'You look knackered. You going to go for a sleep too?'

He was right about her being tired. Last night, or rather, earlier that morning, she'd dozed for a couple of hours in Carny's bed, but mostly she'd stared at the ceiling, thinking everything through, taking a good hard look at herself and their situation.

'Maybe in a while,' she answered his question. 'I'm feeling a bit queasy, so I might wait till that passes, then check Carny's flight got off okay.'

As if some paranormal separation anxiety service kicked in, her phone pinged at that very moment.

Missing you already! Love you Mum. Tell Dad I love him too xx

She passed the message on, making Scott smile.

'You know, I think we did okay with that one,' he said, leaning against the sink now, taking a sip of his water. 'I'm going to miss her around here.' He glanced at the clock. 'Ten minutes in and I'm not sure I'm liking this empty nest thing.'

She appreciated his attempt to keep things cordial. He had every right to be furious, to be taking her to task, but he wasn't. In some ways, that was sadder. She'd kissed another man, and he was prepared to overlook it. Even if he was doing that for the sake of the baby, it still said so much. He was indifferent. The opposite of love.

They still had something that would keep them together – but maybe it was time to stop settling for less than everything.

'Tell me how it was going to work,' she began, then spotted his confusion and realised he had no idea what she was talking about. She tried again. 'The separation you'd planned. How was it going to work?'

She watched him slump. 'Kell, what's the point of going over it all? Let's just leave it, huh? Move on. Try to make this work.' Not one inflection in his weary tone made her think he was enthusiastic about that idea, yet he was prepared to do it.

Like fast-forwarding a show on Netflix, and realising you'd guessed the tragic ending, she saw the years ahead. Just like the last twelve months. Scott, detached, switched off, a great dad, but utterly miserable in every other aspect of his life, forcing himself to put a smile on his face every day despite knowing that he was no closer to the future he'd hoped for.

'Please,' she said. 'Just spell it out for me. I want to know.'

He blew the air out of his cheeks. 'The redundancy papers.'

God, was it really only yesterday that they'd arrived in the mail? It seemed like a lifetime ago.

'I'd already agreed to the offer. I should have told you, but I was just waiting for the right time. Actually, that's not completely true. I was bottling it and didn't want to say anything until Carny was gone. Anyway, you saw the amount they were offering. I was going to pay off the rest of the mortgage – we've only got a couple of years left on it anyway – and then sign the house over to you.

Then I was going to put enough money in the bank for your bills over the next couple of years. And whatever was left, I was going to take and live on it. I just wanted to live the old dream, Kell. To go to Nashville, to play music, maybe see if I could get the occasional open mic gig. I just wanted to know what that life felt like before I'm too old to enjoy it. I figured I could pick up some work when I'm travelling. Not fussed what it is. Working in bars. Anything.'

'After twenty years of working you were going to walk out and leave everything behind? You were going to have nothing to show for it?'

'I do have something to show for it,' he argued. 'I've got a family I love and who love me back. That's more than a lot of people get.'

His stoicism crushed a little bit of her soul. All anger over him agreeing to the redundancy was gone now. All she cared about was choosing the right path forward.

'What about you, Kell? What is it you really want?'

She was so surprised by his question; it took her a moment to formulate the answer. It had been so long since they'd talked with this kind of openness, she was out of practice.

What did she truly want?

She took a breath, determined to give a truthful answer. 'I want to feel completely loved by someone who loves me with everything they have.'

A flicker of embarrassment crossed Scott's face, but he said nothing. She knew he wasn't going to claim to be that person. He wasn't going to lie. The decision she'd come to during the last few sleepless hours had been the right one.

'I think you should go,' she said, knowing she was going to have to get this out before she changed her mind.

'What? Why? How can I? We've already established that we

have a kid on the way and that means I've got responsibilities. I'm not bailing out on them.'

'You don't have any responsibilities yet,' she came back. This was what she'd been thinking through during all those hours staring at the light on Carny's ceiling. 'Hear me out.' He didn't argue, so she went on, 'Take the redundancy. Pay off the mortgage. But don't sign the house over yet. Take what's left and go and do your thing.'

'I can't...'

'You can. I want you to. Look, we need to compromise. I desperately want this baby and you're its dad, so it's going to need you around. But I want other things too. Like I said, I want a partner who adores me...'

'Kells, I'm sorry...'

'That wasn't a criticism. It works both ways, Scott. We both know that the way we feel about each other has changed. It's not enough any more.'

For a moment she thought about telling him how she felt about Rick, but she didn't. There was no point putting that out there. They'd both made the decision to move on. That could stay in the past for both of them.

'Go to Nashville. Our baby isn't going to be born until January, so you've got at least six months to go and see what that life is like and find out if it makes you happy. And when the baby is born... I don't know what happens then, but we'll figure it out. If you decide to come home, Carny's room is empty, so we can figure something out, share the house, I've got no idea, but we'll make it work.'

With every word, she could see that his head was lifting higher, his shoulders were coming up, he was breathing deeper, as if a massive, crushing weight was being lifted off him.

'Are you sure, Kells? Really sure?'

'Yep. I'll come with you when we tell your mum and Carny. We need to make them both understand that this is what's best for both of us. For all of us.' Kelly got up from her chair and went around the table to him, taking the outstretched hand he offered her. 'We've had a good life together. We've made the best of it and we've taken care of each other. I don't want that to stop now, whether we're together or apart. We're family.'

'We are a family, Kell. We always will be, no matter where we are or what we're doing.'

'I know... and sometimes...' A great big, choking sob caught in her throat as she thought again about Carny's taxi disappearing down the street. 'Sometimes, with family, you have to let each other go.'

36

HARRIET

Harriet had déjà vu. As always, she was awake long before the lovely nursing assistant came around with the morning teas and, just as always, it had been another restless night on the ward. Marg, in the bed next to her, was still coughing her lungs up and Jenny, in the bed across from her, had been shouting names in her sleep again. And, strangely, all of that made Harriet feel at home.

'Morning, Harriet!' It was Betty, with her tea. 'What a shock to see you back here this morning. You must have fair missed us if you had to do a wee bit of impromptu gymnastics to get here,' she joked. 'Yesterday must have been some day.' Harriet was sure Betty broke at least a dozen of all those new-fangled rules about what was appropriate to say to patients, and Harriet absolutely loved her for it.

And yes, yesterday was definitely, as Betty said, 'some day'.

Replaying it in her mind, she didn't know quite where to start. The highlights had been extraordinary. Yvie, that absolute treasure, being so thoughtful. The garden party had been wonderful. Meeting John had been delightfully unexpected and his phone call... well, it wasn't an exaggeration to say that had been one of the most pleasing surprises of her life. Although, she did wonder if she might have to postpone their dinner, given that she was somewhat battered and bruised.

She didn't want to dwell on the darker moments. Going back to the house alone. Deciding not to take her pills. Falling on the floor. Although that physical pain didn't even come close to the unbearable grief of opening her photo album and seeing Leo's face there. The same face that she'd seen earlier that day, when the young lady had sung on the stage. The memory of that was making her heart race yet again. It had been so uncanny. So... Another thought came to her. She'd brought the photo with her! She was sure of it. And now she had an irrepressible longing to look at it again.

'Betty,' Harriet called to the nursing assistant who was over by the sink, filling up Jenny's water jug. As soon as she was finished, she bustled over.

'What can I do for you, my pet?'

'Last night, Nurse Yvie gave me this nightdress to wear, but I wonder if you wouldn't mind helping me to find my cardigan. I was wearing it when I came in.'

'Ah, it might have gone down to the laundry, Harriet. I hear you took a right nasty fall. Let me have a look...' She pulled open the door of the slim wardrobe behind the bed and began to rummage.

If Harriet had been wearing a pulse monitor, the beeps would have quickened instantly. The photograph. It had been in the pocket. She couldn't lose it. It was the only copy, and there was no negative, no way to recreate the image of Leo's face on his twenty-fifth birthday. The thought of losing it was unbearable. It would utterly, utterly break her heart.

'Here it is!' Betty announced, triumphant, and Harriet almost cried with relief. 'I'll pop it down to the laundry later, Harriet – unless you're getting out of course. I'll check with the charge nurse after breakfast,' she said, laying it down on the side of her bed and marching off to carry on with her morning tasks.

Harriet sagged against the pillows, waiting for the adrenaline to settle. Only when she was sure she could lift her head again without feeling dizzy did she reach for the cardigan, slip her hand into the pocket... no, must be the other pocket... no, must be...

The panic shot through her yet again. It wasn't there.

Breathe, she told herself, as her chest began to tighten, *just breathe.*

She had to find it. She wouldn't rest until she did.

'Are you looking for this, Harriet?' Yvie. She'd been so fretful; she hadn't even noticed Yvie coming into the ward. Yet, there she was, like an angel, standing at the end of the bed and she was holding...

Harriet burst into tears. 'Oh Yvie, my photograph! I thought I'd lost it. Thank you so much. I'm... I'm... I'm a silly old fool, that's what I am – look at me weeping again. Where did you find it, dear?'

Yvie sat down on the edge of her bed, just as she'd done almost every day for the last month. 'Well, that's a bit of a story, Harriet. You must have dropped it in A&E, when Freddie the porter was rushing you to X-ray. Oh, and all your results came back – nothing broken. You're going to be absolutely fine.'

'Thanks to you,' Harriet said softly.

'All part of the NHS service,' Yvie joked.

Harriet tried to remember leaving A&E. Wasn't that when she saw the young lady... the singer... Yes, she'd met her again here at the hospital last night and it had been such a shock. Or had she? Harriet wasn't sure that she hadn't been dreaming. Or possibly concussed. After the X-rays, Yvie had brought her up to the ward and helped her to bed, and she'd been so completely exhausted, so overwhelmed with everything that had happened, that she'd gone out like a light.

Perhaps it was a dream after all.

Yet... it had seemed so real. The girl's face had been so familiar to her, every feature and line a recreation of one that she had seen before. It was all coming back to her now. She'd tried to show her the photograph, but the girl didn't take it.

'A visitor to one of our doctors down there found it,' Yvie went on, 'and she brought it up last night, but you were already asleep.'

'Can you please ask your doctor to thank her friend...'

'Actually, it was her sister,' Yvie prompted and Harriet could see that Yvie was watching her face for a reaction. What was she missing? Yes... It came to her. The young woman was with a doctor and she mentioned it was her sister.

'Please thank her. I'm so grateful.'

'I can do, Harriet, but the thing is... she is actually outside. She slept in the relatives' room. She asked if she could stay, because she wanted to speak to you and... well, it's completely against policy, but her sister, Dr McTeer, cleared it with the night manager and since it was only a few hours...'

Harriet felt her heart begin to thud so hard it felt like horses galloping on her chest. 'Can I see her? Can I see her right now?'

'Of course you can.' Yvie stretched back, signalled to someone on the other side of the ward window. Harriet couldn't see who it was, her eyes not great at long distances without her glasses.

'Good morning, Mrs Bassett.'

'Maisie.' The name came back to her, as if it had been there all along, as if this beautiful woman had been there all along too.

'You remember my name.'

Such a wonderful smile. Just like... Harriet stopped herself from saying anything. She had already tried that last night and surely they'd think she'd lost her marbles if she started going on about it again today. 'I do, dear,' Harriet beamed. 'Please come, sit. Is that okay, Yvie?'

'Of course it is. Sit yourself down right there,' she said, pointing to the blue chair on the other side of the bed.

Maisie came round and slipped into it, so now she was right by Harriet's side, only a few inches from her, and Harriet remembered the other thought she'd had yesterday at the garden party. Harriet conjured up a memory of herself, on her wedding day, and... Maisie could have been that young woman's sister.

Harriet tried desperately not to stare, suddenly at a loss for words. Thankfully, Maisie spoke first.

'Mrs Bassett, last night, when we met in A&E, you asked me to look at the photograph and you said you wondered if I might be related to the person in it... It says on the back of the photo that his name is Leo Bassett. Can I ask who he is?'

'He's my son,' Harriet replied, hoping the tremor she felt in her chest wasn't obvious in her voice.

When Maisie spoke again, Harriet could hear a tremor in there too. 'Do you think it would be possible to meet Leo?'

Every time she had to say it, it twisted the knife in her heart. 'I'm afraid not, my dear. You see, Leo passed away. Not long after that photograph was taken.'

Maisie's reaction was instant. Her eyes filled with tears, but, so brave, Harriet watched her try desperately not to shed them. 'Can I ask when Leo died, Mrs Bassett? If it's upsetting, you don't have to...'

'December. 1995.'

Maisie sucked in a sharp intake of breath. 'Did he have any children?'

Harriet could see where she was going with this. 'He did not, dear. The similarity in your photographs, I wondered myself if we might be related. Can I ask where your parents are from?'

Maisie leaned forward a little, and Harriet saw that her hands were shaking.

'Mrs Bassett, I was adopted. I have no knowledge of who my biological parents are. All I know is that I had a different name when I was born... I was called Leona.'

'Oh my goodness,' Yvie gasped.

Harriet had quite forgotten that she was there. She'd forgotten that anyone else was there.

'I was born on the twenty-ninth of June, 1996.'

Harriet closed her eyes, but that didn't stop the tears from falling.

Behind her lids, she watched as images flickered. Leo on his fourth birthday. Leo on his twelfth birthday. Leo on his eighteenth birthday. Leo on his twenty-first birthday. Leo on his twenty-fifth birthday.

Twenty-five pictures in all.

And every one of those photographs were taken on the twenty-ninth of June. They had the same birthday.

When Maisie next spoke, her words echoed Harriet's thoughts, bringing the kind of joy she'd thought she would never feel again.

'Mrs Bassett, I think your son may have been my father.'

As the sun glinted on the waters of the loch that ran beside the gardens of Lomond House, the violin quartet began to play. Maisie cast an anxious glance at the Pavilion, where Janice and Jane were behind the serving area, putting the final touches to the buffet. Janice gave her a thumbs up, and then raised a glass in a silent toast. Maisie got the message and blew them a kiss. It was going to be fine. The food was ready. The bar was stocked. The waiting staff had been circulating with champagne since the guests arrived. And there wasn't a penis cake in sight.

She smoothed out her dress, cream silk, off the shoulder, and flicked back her cascading curls, hoping that she didn't dislodge the simple chain of daisies on the crown of her head. Hope had helped her put them there. Now she could see her sister, sitting up in the front row of seats, blowing her kisses. They would never be blood-related, and that would never matter one iota to either of them.

Next to Hope, Sissy and Cole were preoccupied as always – Cole was playing with the gorgeous little Freya, and Sissy was rubbing her own back, trying to relieve some of the pressure from the bump that, once again, was the size of a space hopper. Their next baby was due any day now. She'd just about recovered from the shock of being pregnant again, but she said that this time she was definitely calling it Marzipan. Or Orla Storm, after Maisie's character in her new Netflix show. They'd wrapped filming a few months ago, and the first episode was due to air next month. Maisie was somewhere between excited and terrified, but the early reviews from critics who'd had a sneak preview were terrific, so she hoped that was a good sign. And if it wasn't?

Well, she always had her theatre stints and a career in adverts for pharmaceutical creams to fall back on.

The music changed to the instrumental version of 'Landslide' by Fleetwood Mac. The lyrics weren't an obvious choice for a wedding, but the song had such significance that it was the only choice for this moment.

She glanced to the man by her side and took a step forward. It was time.

* * *

In the back row of white seats, set out in front of a flower-decked gazebo in the glorious garden of the Lomond House Estate, with the waters of the loch glistening behind it, Kelly watched the bridal party move slowly up the aisle. On her knee, little Garth gurgled quite happily. Scott had chosen the name as a tribute to his spiritual home in Nashville, where, he told her, he would sit on any open mic sessions he could find and play Garth Brooks songs until last orders were called at the bar. He'd tried to persuade Sabrina and Rick to call their new daughter Dolly, so they could have the perfect duet, but Sabrina had resisted and gone for Sienna instead. Garth and Sienna had been born only fifteen days apart and it had been wonderful to share the pregnancy and births of their children with her sister. And Rick too. All the secrets from last year had been put in a box and locked away, and they'd gone back to being best friends who loved each other in a purely platonic way.

It helped that at the end of last year, another box had opened.

Beside her, Carson was in his full RAF dress uniform, and he'd been getting admiring glances from several of the single guests and a few that weren't. Kelly understood. He had the same effect on her, which had been a bit of a surprise. Turns out they'd both missed some pretty significant details. After Scott had jetted off to Nashville, Carson had begun visiting her whenever he was on leave, and after a few months, she'd discovered that the attraction she'd felt for him that night she'd kissed him wasn't just the result of loneliness and alcohol. In fact, it was the effect he'd had on her every time he'd walked through the door since then.

When she'd plucked up the courage to tell him, he'd revealed that when he'd said, 'What if all the good ones are taken?' he'd been talking about her. He'd never acknowledged his own feelings because she was married to his best friend, but with Scott out of the picture, and with his blessing, they were seeing where it would go. And so far, it was going to a level of happiness that she'd only ever heard described by Rick. She loved Carson with everything she had.

* * *

As Scott took another step forward on the red carpet in the centre of the aisle, he caught his son's eye and stuck his tongue out, making Garth giggle. He wasn't even six months old yet, but already he was sitting up on Kelly's knee enjoying the music. Scott was going to buy him a drum set for his first birthday. He couldn't wait to see Kelly and Carson's faces when they unwrapped it.

Another step forward. His steps were in perfect timing with the woman standing next to him. It was Carny who had persuaded him to go along to one of Maisie's shows when he'd come back from Nashville in time for the birth of his son. It was a three night run of Blood Brothers at the Kings Theatre, where she was standing in for the leading lady after both the star and her understudy had gone down with laryngitis. He found out later that it was a show she'd performed in on a previous run so the director had called her in as a favour. After the curtain came down, they had gone back to her flat for a coffee, and that had led to so much more. To everything. His heart, his soul, his dreams, all of them were Maisie's now. Sometimes, he worried about the thirteen year age difference, but when he mentioned it, Maisie would just reply that Catherine Zeta Jones was married to a man twenty-five years older than her, and they'd worked out fine, so Scott should just shut up and kiss her. Besides, now he was teaching guitar full time, with a side gig playing in a local pub twice a week, nothing about his life was conventional. All that mattered was that he adored her, he'd never been happier, and he told her every day that Stevie Nicks would approve.

Carny did too. In fact, she was walking behind Maisie now, absolutely gorgeous in her pale pink bridesmaid dress. Scott and Kelly had flown to London just a week after Carny had gone there and told her everything. It had been a huge relief when she'd been absolutely cool and pragmatic about it all. She just wanted them to be happy, she'd told them, even if they were a bit of a beamer and far more irresponsible and chaotic than she would ever be. She'd come back up to Scotland for the birth of her little brother, bringing her new girlfriend, Elisa, with her. Elisa was a singer in the rock show Carny was working on and Scott approved of her as soon as she'd walked into Kelly's house and named every one of the guitars that still hung on the walls there.

* * *

As the bridal party reached the front of the aisle, Scott's mum, Sonya, opened her iPad to read her prepared speech about the imminent union of the happy couple. Unfortunately, she hadn't quite got the hang of the technology and the sound of a particularly raunchy scene from the *Fifty Shades of Grey* movie entertained the audience for a few moments, before she managed to switch it off. Her red-faced mortification was probably an indication that although she'd got ordained specifically to officiate this union, she probably wasn't going to take it up as a full-time role. George, her new gentleman friend, who was sitting in the front row, looked suitably mortified too.

Giggling, Maisie thought about how much Harriet would be loving this. She zoned out for a few moments as she thought of how far they'd come in the last year. Their DNA test had proven that they were indeed related, a grandmother/granddaughter match. They'd managed to piece together that Leo's girlfriend, Mandy, must have been pregnant when he died, and perhaps heartbroken and unable to see a way forward, she'd given Maisie up for adoption. Maisie still hoped she would find her one day, but in the meantime, her relationship with her grandmother, and Yvie, Verity, and all her grandmother's friends, had become one of the very best things about her life.

As her eyes locked with the man standing next to her, she knew that he was another one. Scott nodded to her, and mouthed 'I love you', as Maisie zoned back into one of the most important moments of the ceremony.

* * *

Sonya looked from the bride to the groom and back again, eyes big pools of water, and in a voice that was thick with emotion, she began to speak.

'Do you, Harriet Bassett, take John Bassett to be your lawfully wedded husband?'

Out of the corner of her eye, Harriet saw that Maisie was crying so much her tears were dropping into her bridesmaid's bouquet. It was wonderful to have her granddaughter by her side, and she knew that John was thrilled to have his grandson, Scott, as his best man. She was pretty sure when the young ones got together, they never expected that they'd one day be standing here watching their gran and grandad take their vows.

Harriet could barely believe it herself.

The last year had been both wonderfully unexpected and blissfully happy. After their first dinner, they'd talked long into the night and Harriet wasn't sure they'd stopped talking since. Within a few weeks, they were meeting every day for lunch, or a walk, or a lovely meal. 'At our age, we need to make all the days count,' John had told her one afternoon, early in their courtship, right before he'd turned up 'At Last', by Etta James, on the record player and they'd had a sway in her kitchen.

He'd asked her to marry him at Christmas, in front of all their families. Yes, she had a family now too. Her granddaughter, Maisie, her sister, Hope, their mum, and all their relatives had welcomed her into their clan with open arms. Then there was Yvie, who had truly become the daughter she'd never had. In fact, Yvie and some of the others at her weekly bereavement group, all of whom were now beloved friends, had helped her track down Jonathan, Anthea, and her niece, Meredith. Jonathan and Anthea were in their late seventies now, and Jonathan had the stooped shoulders of a man who had lived his life carrying a heavy burden, but all that mattered was that they'd had a chance to reconcile before it was too late. Their reunion had been emotional and heartbreaking, but it had also helped heal a wound in her soul that had been bleeding for far too long.

Today, her friends and family were all here, sitting in the front row and she had no doubt that Leo was here too. Over the last year, she'd felt his presence as she built a relationship with his beautiful daughter. Her darling boy. He was with her, right by her side and she would see him, would hold him again one day, but she had some more living to do first.

Strangely, she had a strong feeling that Dennis was looking down on her and he was happy that her life, once empty and lonely, was now brimming with joy. He had never been the most effusive or romantic of men, but she knew that he'd loved her, just as she'd loved him.

She was sure he'd be pleased that she'd found someone else who adored her, albeit in a very different way. John was romantic. He was fun. He made her laugh until her sides hurt and he treated her like she was the most precious thing in his world. His enthusiasm for life had, quite literally, restored her will to live, and she was grateful for it every single day.

That's why she felt so utterly blessed to be able to look into his twinkly blue eyes as she answered the question Sonya had just asked her.

"Do you, Harriet Bassett, take John Bassett to be your lawfully wedded husband?'

There wasn't a dry eye in the garden when Harriet gave her answer.

'I do.'

ACKNOWLEDGMENT

Big overflowing buckets of thanks to Amanda, Nia and Caroline, founders of Boldwood Books, Thanks too, to Ellie, Megan, to all the others in the Boldwood team and to their authors, who make it their priority to support and encourage each other. I'm very grateful too for Jane Craddock and Rose Fox, who, with Caroline, shape my books into the finished product.

To my family and my pals, thank you for celebrating the highs, making me laugh during the lows, and not disowning me when I don't return texts because I'm on a deadline.

As always, heartfelt thanks to all the booksellers and bloggers who spread the word.

Most of all, thank you to every reader who picks up one of my books.

I heart you all. I do.

Love,

Sx

MORE FROM SHARI LOW

We hope you enjoyed reading *One Summer Sunrise*. If you did, please leave a review.

If you'd like to gift a copy, this book is also available as an ebook, digital audio download and audiobook CD.

Sign up to Shari Low's mailing list for news, competitions and updates on future books.

http://bit.ly/ShariLowNewsletter

Explore more from Shari Low.

ABOUT THE AUTHOR

Shari Low is the #1 bestselling author of over 20 novels, including *My One Month Marriage* and *One Day In Summer,* and a collection of parenthood memories called *Because Mummy Said So*. She lives near Glasgow.

Visit Shari's website: www.sharilow.com

Follow Shari on social media:

facebook.com/sharilowbooks

twitter.com/sharilow

instagram.com/sharilowbooks

bookbub.com/authors/shari-low

ABOUT BOLDWOOD BOOKS

Boldwood Books is a fiction publishing company seeking out the best stories from around the world.

Find out more at www.boldwoodbooks.com

Sign up to the Book and Tonic newsletter for news, offers and competitions from Boldwood Books!

http://www.bit.ly/bookandtonic

We'd love to hear from you, follow us on social media:

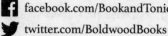
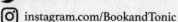

facebook.com/BookandTonic
twitter.com/BoldwoodBooks
instagram.com/BookandTonic